THE LIFEBOATMAN'S DAUGHTER

The Lifeboatman's Daughter

Elisabeth Clare

Foreword

LIKE MANY PEOPLE I HAVE long been fascinated by the lifeboat world and its mostly volunteer crews. I am in awe of their bravery and altruism; and interested in what motivates people to dedicate so much of their time to training weekly, in all weathers, in order to maintain their skills and be ready to head out on shouts at a moment's notice. When I moved to North Norfolk in the early 1990's I remember that every trip to Cromer with my young sons from our home in Aylsham seemed to involve hearing the eerie sound of the maroons heralding a shout with the people involved no doubt facing sometimes extreme danger from an always threatening, always powerful, sea, rescued and rescuers alike. This was in striking contrast to our visits there which invariably revolved around playful fun, freedom and summer sun only metres away from the lifeboat station at the end of the pier.

I often wondered how it would be to be a family member of these brave lifeboat crew. And so it was that this story evolved. In addition to the background reading undertaken before writing the novel (see bibliography) I am indebted to Paul Pretty, a volunteer lifeboat crewman based at Sheringham, who provided an invaluable source of facts and reality checking, always ready to answer any questions I put to him.

Long before I had even thought of writing this story, I found my visits to the lifeboat museums in Sheringham and Cromer over the years very enjoyable and very instructive. Additionally, the TV series *Saving Lives at Sea* is not only incredibly interesting, nail-biting viewing but, of course, very helpful to me in this endeavour. The series depicts so vividly, and yet so unsentimentally, the terrifying reality of the rescues as well as some background to the crew, their families, and to the rescued and their families. Other particularly useful sources of information and ideas are the many newspaper reports and video recordings of the numerous lifeboat rescues taking place around our treacherous coastline almost daily.

Discussing this idea for my second novel with a family member who reads mostly non-fiction, he said: 'Ah, you'll need to know about Grace Darling.' I do know a little about Grace Darling but she does not feature here despite her heroism when, aged only 23, she rowed out to rescue stranded passengers and crew from the wrecked steamship *Forfarshire* after it crashed into the Longstone Rock lighthouse off the coast of Northumberland on the wild and windy night – or, more accurately, the early hours of the morning, of 6th September 1838. Grace was in the habit of helping her lighthouse-keeper father, William Darling, keep watch over this perilous part of the English coast. On this occasion Grace, woken by the lashing rain and wind, spotted the wreck from her cottage bedroom window just before 5am. She ran to the telescope, but it was not until 7am that it was light enough to see that there were people on the rock. In appalling weather Grace and her father decided to row out to rescue the survivors, nine in total, needing to make two trips in ferocious weather. A further nine survivors were rescued by a lifeboat which was swept away by the current with all on board. They were picked up later by a sloop. Grace died from tuberculosis in her father's arms only four years later having won the hearts of the nation for her bravery.

The fictionalised account here of the child refugees from Hungary did, of course, really happen and the woman who escorts them in this novel, Rosemary, is, in fact, a fictionalised version of one of my aunts, Rosemary Hitchcock. I only discovered the part she played in escorting these children when listening to one of her children, my cousin, read the tribute to her at her funeral in October 2018. I discussed with Rosemary's three children, my cousins, my idea of incorporating their mother's role in this into this novel and they were very pleased that I planned to do so.

Further thanks are due to: Cora Mullenger and Kate Norris, both artists, for their advice regarding life drawing; Ginnie Stephens, a native French speaker, for her advice on the use of idiomatic, regional and nuanced French; Tim Strudwick for his expert knowledge of pink-footed geese and his reassurance that the idea of the last few leaving our shores as late as the end of March, is, at the least, plausible; Nick Webber for his knowledge of wind speeds and sea conditions; Andrew Webber and Hayley Meyer for their advice on autumn gardens; Chris Hewetson for his knowledge of emergency response times to coastal incidents, vehicles used, and routes in Norfolk; various paramedic teaching colleagues at the University of East Anglia (they know who they are); Rosie Doy, Reader in Health Sciences, also a colleague at the University of East Anglia, for her encyclopaedic knowledge of courses run by the School of Health Sciences and some other schools of the university, past, current and those just-in-the-planning-stage. These first-hand reality checks have been invaluable.

A glossary of the German words used in Chapter 33 is to be found after the bibliography at the end of the book.

This is, of course, a work of fiction and any errors are entirely my own.

A B i r t h d a y

My heart is like a singing bird
Whose nest is in a water'd shoot;
My heart is like an apple-tree
Whose boughs are bent with thick-set fruit;
My heart is like a rainbow shell
That paddles in a halcyon sea;
My heart is gladder than all these,
Because my love is come to me.
Raise me a daïs of silk and down;
Hang it with vair and purple dyes;
Carve it in doves and pomegranates,
And peacocks with a hundred eyes;
Work it in gold and silver grapes,
In leaves and silver fleurs-de-lys;
Because the birthday of my life
Is come, my love is come to me.

Christina Rossetti (1830-1894)

Chapter 1

MY FATHER DISAPPEARED THE DAY after he rescued the young girl which was on the day after my 9th birthday. It was in all the papers. She was 15 when he rescued her, he was 32, nearly 33. Some parts of that story and some parts of this story unfold in letters, which I now, aged 20, treasure, especially since nobody actually writes letters anymore. For this reason, I have learnt, in adult life, to print important emails but they don't quite have the same feel as those letters. And as for all those social media and text messages, where will they all go, where actually are they? So, yes, I treasure my letters.

Looking back at the events of that day from a distance of eleven years as I write now, aged 20, they seem to me to be part cataclysmic, part simply a catalyst for the subsequent upheavals in my life and in the lives of all those most closely involved. I say only part cataclysmic simply because the word implies that the changes were disastrous. This is not the case even though at the time there were elements of disaster, even apocalypse to my 9-year-old self; Dad was, after all, my world, my security. When I learnt later about the so-called "butterfly effect" being part of chaos theory I was able to superimpose the image of a butterfly flapping its wings over the image I held in mind of Carrie, aged 15, sitting on the cliff that day. It's as if the pack of cards which represented my life at that time, was suddenly taken, shaken and thrown into the air, the scattered cards ripe for reform into a different order, a different way.

My father, Doug Appleton, a volunteer lifeboatman, always wrote to me about the rescues. It was his way of getting the scary bits out of his system, he explained, getting it down on paper. He made it all so vivid; some bits were terrifying, but, as I read them, I always knew he was safe. It was exciting and I felt so, so proud of him. My mother was angry that he did this. I once thought it was because she didn't want him frightening me, but I came to understand that it was actually because she was jealous; weird, but it was so. My father told me that writing these letters was his way of teaching me about the sea, how it was no plaything, never to be toyed with, but to be known, understood, as far as that was ever possible, and, of course, respected, always respected.

The letters started in earnest when I was about 8, I think. I put them in the Da and Ma suitcases for safekeeping with the others which I found much later on. Those did not tell of rescues but of the love affair between my parents before they married and had me; odd to put it like that but that's how it seemed to me. My arrival put paid to the love between them; I could see that. I should just explain the Da and Ma suitcases. These were two very smart, leather suitcases given to my parents as a wedding present by a cousin of my father whom he had not known well. This cousin had had them embossed DA and MA for Doug Appleton and Margaret Appleton but on the rare occasions I caught sight of them in the loft I always thought of them as Da and Ma which is what I called my parents for a while.

From Doug Appleton (aged 30, just) to Amy Appleton (aged 8).

Wednesday 12th June 1999.

Darling Amy,

We got them all in safely last night but gosh it was cold suddenly after the rain. They were idiots being out like that, with no means of contacting anyone, all pretty much amateurs, taken in by the bright sun, light evening and sparkling sea. Just finished their exams. They should've taken notice of the forecast of course. The dinghy ran aground on the sand bank just off Wells. It was spring tide. We were called out at 10.30pm. I was tired. Been a busy week at work. I could feel every muscle aching as we hauled the last one in. Four of them, all about 18 years old, on the brink of manhood, may never have happened for them. I have a feeling the weekend will be a busy one for us. Keep your mum sweet for me.

Never underestimate the sea, sweetheart, Your ever-loving Da.

I had to ask him what "amateur" and "underestimate" meant of course. I knew about spring tides, that perfect storm of natural events. I understood the concept of a perfect storm, I liked that. Keeping Mum sweet was hard though. I felt it was my job. She hated Da going out on rescues. She hated him being a volunteer lifeboatman to be honest, hated it, and was actually angry and bitter about it. Again, I came to understand it was more a type of jealousy, a kind of burning resentment to do with something other than *her* needs taking his interest and time rather than actual fear for his safety or even concern for his well-being. That worried me and turned me against my Ma; I am sorry to admit this now, but I was just a child then.

Was he cold, hungry, tired out there? I worried about that all the time. He loved the whole thing though, being a lifeboatman. He loved both his "day jobs" too. These were a part-time job as an IT technician at Sheringham High School, which had a sixth form, unlike my school, Cromer High, which he had taken on in order to supplement his income as a full-time, self-employed electrician. He was much in demand in this role, but my mum even mocked him for this somehow; it's hard to explain but she did. I hated that. He was a highly qualified electrical engineer – they met at university in Bristol – but jobs were hard to come by and being self-employed was hard – when he wasn't working, he wasn't paid, simple as that. And sometimes his "loyal" customers who employed him as an electrician didn't pay up on time, or even at all, or quibbled over the invoices he sent out. He was never one for a fight. My mother mocked him for that too, called him lily-livered, but she never offered to help. The technician job really helped because he was paid what was called then "unsocial hours".

So, what with these jobs and being a lifeboatman my da was always busy. He just loved the whole lifeboatman thing: the teamwork, the daring, the need to be needed, the direct rewards, the drama, the accolades, the appreciation, the camaraderie, the physicality of it, being outside, getting to grips with the boats, facing the seas, facing his and others' fears, the winds, the storms, the rain, the mists, the fog, the cold, the dark, even the scorching sun sometimes, all of these in their elemental force. I loved to hear about it.

I relished spending Saturdays and most Sundays, if I could, with the men – they were all men there then as it happened – in the lifeboat station, or the

"Shed" as it was called among themselves, or sometimes "Boatshed". My mother hated this too, for similar reasons probably. She pretended she worried for my safety but in truth I was more protected there than I ever was at home. I'm sorry to say this, I mean really sorry in the sense of being sorrowful, sad and feeling disloyal to Ma. That whole chunk of missing childhood eats into me at times to be honest, such a precious, fleeting time but one that is mostly lost to me.

Weekends and evenings after school when I could get down to the lifeboat station were great. I loved the walk along the pier right to the end, the feeling of being out in the North Sea, poised, ready to help at a moment's notice, the station itself standing sentinel, proud, invincible. I helped wash the boats, took out wet towels and blankets and delivered them to the local launderette – where they washed and dried them for free – made cups of tea, coffee, hot chocolate – that sort of thing. I can remember the warmth, the steamy, detergenty smell of the launderette even now, twelve years later, the tiny grey haired old lady, Mrs Mack, and her grown-up daughter, Lynette, lifting piles of washing, writing out receipts, emptying and loading the washing machines and dryers all day and the whirr and click of them, incessant, comforting.

My best friend at that time was Rachel Willis from school. She was tall and had wavy, longish hair, strawberry blonde – apparently that was the technical term. I saw it as deep, sort of burnished, auburn. I loved it and wanted it. My hair was dark, curly, thick and untidy, or unruly, as my grandfather, Granda, used to say, ruffling it lovingly. Rachel was able to scrape her hair back into a beautiful ponytail and she had some lovely hair clips; my hair just would not stay pinned back in any way, curls escaped from any hair slides, hair slides slipped out.

We used to talk about swapping places on the register and how different it would be for her to be called first and me to be called last. It reminded us of that bit in the Bible, can't remember where exactly – the Sermon on the Mount, the last shall be first, the first shall be last. We tried it once with a stand-in French teacher, but Joanne Langston gave the game away straightaway. After school detention then it was for us, that was no big deal, I found it fun to be in school later in the day but Rachel's parents demanded to know the whole story and said we should not take advantage of stand-in teachers, it was close to bullying, how would we feel, that sort of thing. I felt really bad then, ashamed, sorrowful – again.

School was good, home was bad when Dad wasn't there and changed forever when he disappeared. I always worried about Mum, but from the day after my ninth birthday, I felt responsible for her; totally responsible – until things changed for her too. I used to shop on the way home from school, just the necessities. If she was well enough, I would make pasta dishes using bacon and tomatoes or vegetables and I could do a good, plain old spaghetti Bolognese. If she was not well, I used to be able to get her to eat scrambled egg or some soup, cheese on toast perhaps.

'You're a good girl, Amy, such a good girl. What would I do without you? If I didn't have to work so hard at these silly times, I could be a better mum to you. If he helped at all, things could be different.' I hated all that maudlin, blame stuff.

Mum had a job as an office cleaner working for an agency which, she said, ripped off its clients and its staff alike. She was on something called a zero hours contract, a phrase which made no sense to me. I just knew that she only got paid when she worked, that made sense, and often she would be too unwell, fearful of going out, believing that people were out to get her, including me. That was frightening. The best thing to do was to leave her to it and go to Rachel's or to my Granda's house, my da's dad, or, later, to Angela's house which I'll explain soon.

The community mental health nurses would visit, and Ma would be very calm and placid while they were there but just rage and rage and literally pull her hair out once they'd left. Terrifying. And on those occasions, I knew I couldn't leave her though I longed for the sanctuary of Rachel's or Granda's house. When she was a bit less crazy but still unwell I knew I could escape either to Rachel's or to Granda's house, though sometimes he would ask too many questions and want to go back with me until I was able to explain to him how she really was better left alone at these times. Rachel's mum, Jenny, understood this and I loved feeling safe in her house with her caring "grown-up" parents, at ease with each other and with us. Rachel has two brothers, Iain and Finlay – Finn. Finn is two years older than us, Iain just eighteen months younger, but I'll come to all that later. Rachel's dad, Paul, was a lawyer of some sort and worked ordinary office hours.

I can remember walking home to her house in the summer and feeling a sense of instant relaxation as we kicked off our school shoes, peeled off our socks and usually changed into jeans and T-shirts. Rachel had an endless supply it seemed, enough to lend me, sometimes passed down from Finn. Then, we would run downstairs, liberated from the cares of the day, into their sun-filled garden where home-made lemonade, cakes or biscuits (usually home-made too) awaited us on rugs on the expansive lawn. These were to keep us going, Rachel explained, until what the family called supper time, usually at about 7 o'clock once Paul was home.

From Rachel's house we could walk to a tiny, hidden shingle beach at West Runton, a cove really. We left through the furthest of the three garden gates, having cut through what they called the shrubbery which was full of delicious blackberries in September and October, dotted with dandelions and daisies in spring and summer as well as nettles, thistles, and tough little hillocks of moss and grasses all year long. From there we would make our way through a gap in the hedge, made wider by the family's frequent use, but remote from access by walkers, and down a not too treacherous sandy slope, again with tussocks of grass, clinging onto their sandy bed, toughened by their exposure to unrelenting salt, wind, and sun. The dangers of such coves had been drummed into us since toddlerhood, it seemed, and we respected the sea and its surroundings unreservedly.

Tales of rescues, triumphs and tragedies were frequently shared and of course, as I've mentioned, my da would write accounts of those he was involved with in the form of letters to me which I still prize greatly.

17ᵗʰ April 1999.

Darling Amy,

12 midday when I heard the maroon sound, I thought of you hearing it at school, lunch time for you. Bright, spring sunshine, the sea sparkling, brisk wind, 2 tiny ones on a lilo with their dad. The wind just took them, Amy, you could hear their toddler cries, the dad shouting but those noises didn't last. We searched for hours but their bodies were not found for three days, two washed up on rocks, spotted by cliff walkers, the third, the dad, later the same day but miles further round the coast. The helicopter was needed to winch the bodies up safely, tenderly secured by our brave crew.

We didn't talk much back at the Shed about that one, just had some hot soup, but we felt we had failed completely... it happens, of course, and you can't beat yourselves up, but we did a bit. Calling off a rescue feels terrible, a defeat, but you have to follow orders and the call off always comes after quite a discussion amongst the supervisors.

Oh, Amy love, perhaps I shouldn't be writing in this way to you, but it helps to "talk" like this on paper to you. Don't dwell on the failures, love, it doesn't do to do that. Just respect the sea, Amy, always respect the sea.

I'll come in and see you if you're still awake.

Your ever-loving Da.

And later that summer:

24th July 1999

Darling Amy,

One of those perfect days, first day of the summer holidays. The beach, the one Granda looks out on from the windows in the dining room, 2pm we get the call. The beach is crowded, the tide's going out, there's an offshore, brisk wind. Families are gathered in their encampments on the beach, windbreaks in evidence, a day at the beach paraphernalia everywhere, fun to be had. But then apparently a dad in his fifties decides it would be fun to tow the children out on the rubber dinghy he's just bought. He can fit the 3 smallest ones in it, the older two, who are 8 and 10, a girl and a boy, are on the plastic dragon inflatable he bought too. They're using their hands to paddle.

There are white horses further out, the wind's gusty and brisk and suddenly they're way, way out and the plastic dragon's blown far ahead of the dinghy. People on the beach hear shouts, they call the coastguard, many people congregate at the edge of the water, looking on.

We were quickly scrambled, used the new boat, Lady May, and got the children back just in time, cold, terrified, crying but the dad had jumped in to try to reach the dragon, madness, complete madness. He was lost.

Oh, Amy, how I love you.

Da xxx

Chapter 2

ONCE HE GAVE UP TRYING to persuade me to go back to Ma's with him, Granda's house became a different kind of sanctuary. Sometimes Rachel would come as well, she loved it, she said she found it so calm and peaceful. He told such interesting stories too, often about his own childhood, the time he spent helping the fishermen off the coast of Cromer, working on the pier during the school holidays in the café at the end, not the Pavilion Theatre one, but the one selling fish and chips, burgers and simple meals. He would often break off and fill in a bit more backstory.

I loved that, those digressions of his:

'But I digress,' he used to say. 'They're the best part, Granda,' I would reply, it became a refrain, a kind of mantra between us, a responsorial psalm almost. I knew about responsorial psalms from going to church with Gramsda before she became too ill to go. I liked it. The calm and the quiet and everybody pleased to see her and me, biscuits and orange squash after the service. I called her Gramsda, she suggested it, to match Granda and to help me enunciate my words clearly; she chuckled when she said this. She chose the name because she liked the "sda" at the end which were her initials, she explained to me: Susan Diana Appleton. Sometimes I shortened it to "Grams" or "Gramsy".

Granda told us too about being apprenticed, aged 16, to a silversmith, Karl, a Hungarian refugee who escaped with great courage and difficulty with many of his compatriots, arriving in England, Kent, in 1915. It always seemed so strange to me that all this happened less than a hundred years ago. Karl's experiences were so similar to Granda's; it was almost spooky and certainly sad. Karl had lost his parents and brother and sister in the First World War and Granda had lost both sets of grandparents in the war that followed on so soon after the so-called "war to end all wars", he would say to us sadly. His mother's parents had died on Boxing Day 1944, the first day of the fifty-day Siege of Budapest. This was when the Red Army and the Romanian Army terrifyingly encircled Budapest, Granda explained. Thirty-eight thousand civilians died during the siege, he told me, either through starvation or military action. His grandfather had been given his first two weeks of leave for years and he and his wife, Granda's grandmother, were returning from delivering Christmas presents to Granda's parents nearby when they were caught in crossfire and died instantly. Granda's father's parents died towards the end of the siege, basically from starvation, he said, they were much older and frailer than his maternal grandparents, he'd been told.

I remember coming to understand then that those two terrible wars followed each other in quick succession, only 21 years apart, 1918 and 1939. It was strange to me to think that Granda had never even known his grandparents having been born in 1946, his parents having married in 1945. Then, almost unbelievably, he explained to me how his country, the beautiful, beloved country of his birth had erupted into a Revolution in 1956, out of seemingly nothing he said despairingly, 'Pwoooof, like a volcano.' It lasted less than a month and was utterly pointless, he told me, but it changed his life forever. His voice became kind of small when he said that.

He remembered his journey to England, aged 9, nearly10, very well and he told me about it only once. Sometimes I wanted to ask him more about it, but I sensed it really upset him, well, of course it would. He was smuggled in the back of an open-backed lorry together with other children, who were mostly a bit older than him, to a remote railway station somewhere outside Eger, which he explained was a city about two hours from Budapest, and manhandled, pretty roughly, he remembered, up some high steps into a filthy carriage full to the brim with people fleeing the country. He knew, though, that they had to work quickly to get everyone on, he understood that. He could still remember the train snorting and harrumphing, he said, as it got up steam.

He was taken under the wing of a beautiful English woman who told him her name was Rosemary. She was an English nurse who spoke fluent German and Danish and had been asked to escort this train because she was known to be resourceful and persuasive under the guise of her gentle, femininity.

Rosemary took him and some of the other younger children under her wing, making sure they had a safe place to lie down to sleep and found them some blankets. He remembered her tucking him in tightly and telling him he was safe. She travelled with them all the way to Harwich, England, ensuring their safety and some sort of comfort, food and drink through what must have been a very long and very tedious journey. Of course, he wanted his parents, but he was never to see them again as they were both killed in early November 1956, he never knew the exact date.

He had worked out the route they probably took only after the event, much later in fact, when isolated memories of the journey emerged from time to time, such as the time American soldiers boarded and gave them chewing gum. I remember him showing Rachel and me the probable route using his big atlas, which I loved and could spend hours reading. Granda thought they must have travelled from Hungary through Austria and Germany then up to the Hook of Holland and across to Harwich by ferry.

The children had been accommodated in a big hut, like an army hut, with a huge kitchen and a block of toilets and washing facilities, big, old-fashioned baths, he remembers, housed in two separate outbuildings. Granda thinks they were there for about a week, during which people arrived from time to time as foster parents to take the children away with them. The children who remained were looked after by a team of women who served them hot, delicious food, and showed them places to sleep on mattresses with plenty of blankets. His foster parents, Jim and Jane Appleton, from Cromer, arrived towards the end of the week, he thinks, to collect him. They had come forward to offer their home.

'I was truly blessed,' he would say to me softly, 'truly blessed. I grew to love them like parents.'

It was just after his tenth birthday, close to the same age as I am at the start of the major event of my story, that they explained to him that a large Soviet force had invaded Budapest and other regions of Hungary on the 4th November that year, 1956, just after an agreement had been reached for the Soviet authorities to negotiate a withdrawal of its troops. However, Granda explained to me, the Politburo, which he said, was what the main policy-making committee was called in communist countries, changed its mind and the invasion was bloody…

'Sorry, Amy,' Granda had interrupted himself, 'I'm not swearing but it literally was bloody. The Hungarian Resistance put up a fierce fight but over two thousand Hungarian and seven hundred Soviet troops were killed. My parents were caught in the crossfire, similar to their parents ironically, tragically, by chance as they ran for cover during fierce fighting. They had been shopping for supplies for my aunt, my mother's sister, who was ill at that time, she had 'flu, but they never reached her house.'

I remember him looking into the distance, out to sea from his Sheringham flat as he said this. I'll explain about his move to the flat shortly. When he explained to me what communism was, I remember thinking and saying that it sounded like a good idea and I recall him looking at me with great wisdom and also weariness saying:

'In theory, Amy, only in theory.'

Granda remembers being treated with compassion and kindness in his foster home, at school and in the local community. As he grew up, he was keen to learn a trade and his foster parents were keen for him to do just that. He later set himself up as a silversmith in Garden Street in Cromer, just a step away from the seafront, having learnt all his skills, including those involved in running a business, from Karl. He had also spent some time studying design in London, based partly in the Chancery Lane Silver Vaults and partly at the Royal College of Art.

Karl was initially taken to be German and held as a German prisoner of war in Kent before being moved to help with farm work in Norfolk once his refugee status as a Hungarian was discovered by the "authorities". He had married a land girl, called Jennifer, and had become a British citizen. Together they went on to have four children. Granda became friends at school with Karl's son, Bob, and became friendly with his two sisters, Helen and Jackie and Fred his brother. He told me that he used to love going round to their noisy, action-packed household. It sounded a bit like my friendship with Rachel and her family, I thought.

Granda's name was Sebastyen, but it was changed to Sebastian with his willing agreement as he just wanted to fit in, feel at home. He was always known as Seb. Granda's birth surname had been "Apa" meaning father or dad in Hungarian and, by a happy coincidence, as he put it, his foster parents' surname was Appleton so, in order to fit in, he changed his surname by deed poll to Appleton. This was not to deny his origins, he explained, but to extend them. He told me the Hungarian word for "grandfather" is "nagyapa". How I laughed; I loved it! "Naggyappa", I called him, when he wanted me to change into warm, dry clothes after running in all weathers to his house from the bus, or to do my homework before chilling out in front of television or talking to friends, usually Rachel, on the phone.

Granda met the woman who was to become his wife, Sue, when she was 16 and he was 22. Sue was working in the sandwich shop during her school holidays and summer, peak season, weekends and would later return to work there in her vacations as a student, home in Norfolk from university in Kent. The sandwich shop was also in Garden Street, handily, as Granda said, next to Karl's shop in Cromer where he was apprenticed to learn the retail trade in silver. Pure serendipity, as Granda said. I can remember his beam as he said those two words to this day and I've always loved the ring of that phrase. This shop would later be called, Appleton's Silver Ltd and, in fact, still is, as the new owner wanted to keep the well-respected name.

Granda went to the sandwich shop every day for his lunch as he had soon realised, he was falling in love with Sue, he told me. She also made good, over-filled, sandwiches freshly especially for him when the owner was not too much in evidence. I loved to think of Granda being a young man in love. Actually, Granda gave me a small suitcase of their letters one day when he had been reminiscing. He said he wanted me to have them to read when I wanted to but also to know that they would always be safe with me. He knew where they were that way, he explained, if he ever wanted to re-read some of them – but that is for later in the story.

I can't now remember what Dad was like with Mum before she became ill so when I found *their* letters it was like reading a story really except there were not many, about ten in total.

27th December 1989

Hiya Mags,

Loved the ahead of time New Year message, found it on the answerphone, getting in early with that, love it. Wished I'd been there to pick up though.

Hope Christmas was alright for you, Magsy, alone in snowy Bristol.

Were you mostly working? Lots of tips in the Pizza Parlour, I hope. Chris' *Christmas was rubbish; did he tell you?* (Chris was my mum's twin brother.) *Felt he had to go home to your dad and Marie as you know, but he said it would be the last time, hated it, said he felt lonely, not wanted. Marie's kids were horrible, he said, 15 and 17, revolting ages, I suppose, been there done that. I know you warned him, told him he should've stayed in Bristol.*

Christmas here was fine, fun, did the Boxing Day swim off Cromer yesterday – brrrr – must be mad. Have managed to earn quite a bit working at the Black Horse, wrote up my coursework, started revising, got quite bored at times and I kept thinking of you, Mags, in the flat, moving in, working. Strange to think I've only met you twice, that time pretty late in the evening when you came to see the flat, then when you moved in on the day I went home for Christmas but I keep thinking about you, sorry.

See you in a couple of weeks, don't work too hard. I keep listening to Simply Red, but I liked you singing it best... I certainly don't know you by now, but I like what I see and hear!

Doug.

1st Jan 1990

Hi Mags,

Happy New Year! New decade, whatever! Who cares? It's gonna be a good one. I feel it in my water, haha. Out with friends from school last night just to the pub, Ben and Alex, I've probably mentioned them. They stayed over and we did the New Year dip off Sheringham this morning, must be mad, brr, brr, brrrrr, felt pretty yuck afterwards, not a good idea after a night out. It was ok but wished you were there!

Can't wait til Saturday,

Doug.

I often asked my da how he and my Ma met, mainly because they just didn't seem suited, so different. He explained to me that his best friend at university, Chris, the year below him but in the same hill-walking club, had a twin sister, Mags, my mum. Mags dropped out of uni halfway into her first term of Sociology and into his life halfway into the first term of his second year of Electronic Engineering. She had those three freckles on her nose and laughing eyes then:

'Those laughing eyes,' I remember so well him saying this, so sadly, 'it would be difficult for you to imagine them now, Amy love. She came to live with us,' he explained, 'me and my new housemates. She was earning money from three different jobs, always busy, always looking to the future, no regrets, out in the world, confident, couldn't care less about any long-term plans.'

13th April 1990 – Good Friday
Darling Magamuffin,

But it's not good coz I miss you, Mags. Friday 13th, oh no! Needed to come home though to revise and save money and check on the parents. They're fine, happy, feel I'm just a burden to them now, bit paranoid I know! Actually they're always so pleased to see me, it's still home in so many ways. I love it, miss it when I'm at uni too.

Have you heard when our new housemate will be moving in... Sarah? I was really surprised when Jane left, thought she was doing ok, hope I wasn't too rude to her face about her name. Have you heard from her?

Write if you have time.
Loveyoumissyoulots,
Doug.

And then I found just a few from my Ma.

4th Jan 1990, Thurs.
Hiya Doug housemate,

Happy new decade! New Year is so last year, won't even bother saying it!

Thanks for the letters. Glad Christmas has been ok for you. It's hard for me to imagine because I'm so pleased to be free of my lot, apart from Chris of course, my lovely matching brother. Do you think we look alike? Sometimes people ask if we're identical twins... erm, der!

Makes me sound horrible, I know, to be pleased to be free of my parents, I probably am... you'll discover that, horrible, I mean.

Anyway, I've been so busy, the PP was mad... who knew that so many people would want to eat pizza on Christmas Eve and Boxing Day? I got given pizza to take away for my Christmas lunch... had it cold – delish, I tell you. I envied no-one, poor sad soul that I am. Fixed the TV aerial too.

Not sad actually at all. I like it here, feels like home already. I've bought a couple of bright red and yellow cushions, a bean bag, and a black rug, all from the Oxfam shop – £6 in total! They look good, I think. Lots of cleaning stuff too. I've scrubbed the kitchen and bathroom until my hands got red raw. And cleaned all the windows, when the sun shone yesterday, they looked really grimy. I've turned into Magsy the Mop. Back at work tonight doing 12md til 11pm.

See you when you're "home" in sunny Bristol!
Mags.

15th April 1990, Easter Day!
Hiya Dougy,
Feels like summer! We were given a packet of mini eggs each by Carlo – PP manager – so being the child that I am I hid them all in our huge (not) garden, mainly amongst the rubble and the long grass. I'm going to look for them tomorrow before I go in for my 12 til 12 shift, doing the same today! Feet sore.

Happy, happy Easter Day – new life, new hope, more chocolate – that kinda thing. When are you "home" by the way?
Magamuffin xxxx
Ps am gonna buy a second-hand lawn mower – seen one in the junk shop in Carter Road.

23rd April 1990
Hiya Housemateplus,
Meant to say that it's good that your parents seem ok and you feel you've done your filial duty. I'll be out – PP of course – when you get back, note the sparkling windows. I might take up window-cleaning professionally to make some more dough in all my vast hours of time off.

See you Friday then. Come eat pizza if you want.
Magsy the homemaker.

Chapter 3

THE LETTERS WERE LOVELY AND relaxed-sounding and normal, how could it all have so changed? Da explained some bits to me and so did Granda. I loved Granda. He loved me, I knew that, and I worried that he worried when things started going wrong.

He had welcomed Ma 'like a daughter'. He told me this when I was about 11 or 12, I think. She seemed to fill a void in his life as well as Doug's, he explained. She was bright, vivacious, interesting, interested in everyone and everything. He could see Doug literally blooming in her presence but in a very natural, relaxed way, not forced. Doug, my lovely dad, being the precious, only child had often felt responsible for ensuring his parents were alright, especially when his mother became so ill, Granda explained haltingly. He was a surprise to his parents, they were young, and he was an accident but certainly not a mistake, as they had repeatedly told him, Granda had said to me, with a smile. And the baby boomers were seen as an affirmation of hope after the dark days of the war when so many lives were lost or damaged beyond repair, he explained. Technically the baby boomer years were 1946 to 1964, Granda had told me, but he said that he had felt so alone because of the war, that meeting Sue and having my dad, felt to him like his own delayed renewal after the war. He and Sue always considered Dad to be a late baby boomer. The nations were still licking their wounds, he had sighed as he said this, I remember, and renewal was the order of the day for quite some time, he explained.

Da's mother, Sue, same name as Ma's mother, thought she had sorted out the safe period of family planning as it was called then, a very haphazard form of contraception, Granda said, and then did a bit of a double-take, I noticed, as he realised he might need to explain contraception to me.

'It's alright, Granda we learnt all about that in PSHE,' I remember reassuring him quickly whilst managing not to make eye contact during this part of the conversation.

I had only the most fleeting of memories of my grandmother, as someone funny and lively, before she became frail and unwell, diagnosed with cancer of the ovary in 1996 aged only 45 when I was 5 and Da was only 27. I have vague memories of a deep sadness pervading the house, a bedroom full of medical paraphernalia, a frame for walking, medicines, strange liquids in bottles, calorie-boosting drinks in vivid colours, only half-drunk, smells of wound cleansing lotions and potions, community nurses visiting. I remembered, too, the all-pervading sense of a vital presence slowly withdrawing with utter reluctance from the family and home she loved and helped create; the inevitability of this was understood by all of us, even me, aged only 6.

'So, what happened, Granda, how, when did Ma become so sad? I think she didn't want a baby… not like you and my Gramsda.'

'Oh no, Amy, she loved you just like your Da, she still loves you, but she became gradually less able to cope and then became really paranoid, have you heard of that? It's a serious and recognised form of mental illness when people believe others are out to harm them or those closest to them. She and your daddy became almost unnaturally close following the horrific tragedy, you know, Chris' death, her twin brother, the uncle you never knew? It was the horror and shock of it that drew your dad into lifeboating actually. He felt he had to give something back. At that stage he felt himself becoming fearful of the sea, so he decided to conquer that by facing his fears, you know all this don't you?'

I did know this, the bit about the tragedy that is, not the bit about this tragedy motivating him to become a volunteer lifeboatman though. It made me wonder again why Ma hated him doing it so much, or even hated *him* for doing it. I didn't like that thought. Da had told me about the tragedy itself, the shock of it, but he had not really talked about Ma's reaction to her twin brother's death, lost at sea – horrible.

It happened at the beginning of the summer term of their third year, just in the run up to finals. The three housemates were close, Da explained to me, it was fun; they knew each other well as people who live together do. He and Ma had been an "item" as he put it for just over a year then. Chris loved all sorts of active, scary, outdoors adventure type activities: hill-walking, climbing, windsurfing, surfing, kiteboarding. He had taken himself off to Cornwall with some friends doing the same course for a last weekend of freedom in April at the beginning of the summer term before serious revision took over, he explained. It would be beneficial for all of them, he felt. The weather was tempting; bright, sparkling, warm in the sun but with a brisk, offshore wind and the sea still very cold. Capricious weather, capricious sea, Da had said without explaining the word to me, as he usually did, so I had had to look it up.

I listened without interrupting as Granda described how all this escalated, how Ma had been silent at Chris' funeral, had turned away deliberately from her mother, also called Sue, who I never knew as a grandmother. She died six months after Chris in a road accident, whilst being driven by a friend. Ma's dad had died when she was only 2 from an accident at his work involving heavy-lifting gear.

'She seemed to turn in on herself after her brother's death; that's the only way I can describe it really, Amy, it was distressing to see it. Your dad tried so hard to help,' he explained, 'but he seemed only to make things worse.' He explained to me how I was becoming damaged by Ma's rages, the unpredictability, the shouting, screaming, crying, how he, Granda, would arrive to take me out, away, take me to the beach, the soothing sounds of the sea calming me as we walked along the beach, skimming stones, picking up driftwood for Granda's wood burner, winter and summer.

He explained to me how Ma and Da had been taken by surprise when Ma discovered she was pregnant.

'They were both pretty young, she 20, he 21, but not as young as your Gramsda was, Amy when she had your da.' Granda smiled gently. I knew Gramsda had fallen pregnant with my dad towards the end of her first year at uni, when she was still only 18, nearly 19. And that she had carried on with her degree, after having my dad the day after her end of first year exams finished. She returned in October at the start of her second year with Granda, his foster parents, and Gramsda's parents, my great grandparents who I don't remember at all, all helping look after Dad between them whilst Gramsda was at uni. I don't remember my great foster parents either but Granda tells me that they were definitely great! So like me Dad was not planned, as Granda explained. 'But rest assured, Amy, that we, like your parents, were excited, full of trepidation for sure but so, so excited,' he told me, 'and we made the mistake of never relying on the safe method again.' He shook his head looking sad as he spoke and I know now that they regretted not having managed to produce a sibling for Dad.

Back to my parents though, Ma had been feeling restless apparently and was making no secret of the fact that she regretted throwing away her chance of a good degree.

'It would have been a good one, Amy, she's a bright cookie, your mum. She also felt that she had missed out on the whole university experience too, slaving away at poorly paid, long hours jobs. She wanted to turn the clock back a bit then. Poor Magsy didn't have the family support that we had when your dad was born. So, well, I don't know really, Amy love, but it seems surprising to me, an old fogey I know, that people get pregnant by accident these days; you're probably a bit young to understand that, just your old Granda's musings really, love, take no notice.'

But, of course, I did take notice. I remember thinking about the idea of getting pregnant by accident, couldn't work it out at all. I knew how babies were made of course, after all I was 11, nearly 12, when he was telling me all this, so it was weird to think of this happening *by accident.* I shared this information with Rachel, we shared everything then. We pored over information leaflets about contraception, even found a chapter in a book in the library – the YA section – but we still didn't understand it so gave up on it as one of life's mysteries... just my Granda's ramblings, as he said. But later I wondered about this observation and agreed with him. How could it have been an *accident*?

I loved being at my Granda's especially after he moved. Two years after Gramsda died, when I was 8, he decided to move to a newly built, ground floor flat in Sheringham which had stunning views of the sea from nearly every window as it was set up high above the town. You couldn't imagine anything more different from the much-loved, but very crowded, five-bedroomed, former farmhouse which the family had lived in at West Runton when my da was growing up. Da told me it had been built in 1860 and added onto. It had been left to Granda by his foster parents, who both died in their early 70's, his foster dad from a stroke and his foster mum from a heart attack misdiagnosed as indigestion. They had looked after a series of foster children but all of them on a much shorter-term basis than my orphaned Granda, hence the need for plenty of bedrooms.

I remember loving the house but feeling scared of all the dark places, the attics and cellars especially, but also the huge mirror at the top of the first flight of stairs. I always expected to see some fierce man creeping up behind me. Granda told me he was finding it difficult to cope in the house with the ordinary upkeep and maintenance of the house and garden and, as the sea was in his blood, he used to say this, he felt he wanted to be nearer to it in what he called his dotage; in fact he had only just turned 52 when he moved.

He had, though, recently been diagnosed with rheumatoid arthritis, aged just 51, shortly after Gramsda died having initially delayed seeking advice about his symptoms during her last illness illogically putting some of his aches and pains, and even swollen joints, down to his overwhelming sadness. He also felt he simply didn't have time to think about these things whilst Gramsda was so ill. This devastating diagnosis had caused him to give up the silversmith work he loved. I was only 7 when he was diagnosed but I could vividly remember his once brisk walks down to the beach for his daily swim; he used to take me with him in the summer.

Granda still used to swim nearly every day, usually early in the morning and just before dusk, weather permitting, making sure he had taken his medication first and sometimes resorting to his rarely-used mobility scooter to get down to the beach. I still walked beside him in his mobility scooter when I could and nearly always swam too. He did it for enjoyment; it felt beneficent, he said, and he believed it alleviated some of the pain of his arthritis, mostly in his knees, elbows and finger joints. Sometimes I could see red, swollen, sore-looking nodules on already red, swollen joints. He would often be feverish during a flare up too and feel "all-overish", as he called it, with aching muscles and tired to his very bones, he would say. Granda used to call this his "arthuritis"; some of the friends and neighbours he met in the pub called arthritis "arthuritis"; it amused him. He said it was apt as he had known (and hated) a boy at his school called Arthur who was a real pain and a big bully, 'just like my arthuritis, Amy love.'

Granda certainly respected the sea's changing moods though and would not swim in treacherous conditions. He knew enough about all the lifeboat rescues of foolhardy people, putting their own children in danger at times too, and the risks the crews took, to vow never to be one of those idiots, as he put it. He loved to watch the changing moods of the sea; he always had a set of large, old-fashioned binoculars ready. These had belonged to his foster dad, and he would – *too often* – he said, see the lifeboat ploughing its brave way across to individuals in distress in all weathers. He would usually watch until it returned.

Many of the rescues were necessary as a result of people's stupidity and arrogance he explained, especially in the summer months, the world coming out to play.

'But never forget, little Amy, the sea is no plaything, respect it well always, its moods, its deceits, its tricks, its treachery.' He told me about the Happisburgh lifeboat being called out recently to rescue two 20-year-old men, 'Just boys really,' he said, who had tried to launch their boat off Cart Gap in a strong south-easterly wind. He showed me the exact spot on the map he kept close by, showing navigation channels. They were not wearing life jackets and although they had taken a VHF radio neither of them knew how to use it. The tide and waves were building up and the boat couldn't be seen. The crew found them off Waxham beach and shepherded them back to Sea Palling telling them not to attempt to get back to Cart Gap until low tide at 4pm. But they returned at 2pm when the tide was still high, tried to get the boat onto a carrier but it capsized only just avoiding falling onto them.

I shuddered to think of my da being involved in such rescues but could also feel the thrill of it, the adrenaline rush, as I later understood it. In fact, the Happisburgh Lifeboat Station was smaller than Cromer's and the two often helped each other out. For some reason there was less rivalry between the Cromer and Happisburgh Stations than there was between the Cromer and Sheringham Stations, friendly, but rivalry nonetheless, as my dad explained.

From his flat in Sheringham Granda could walk into town for shopping and he soon got to know most of the local shopkeepers. He was not too far from us either as we lived in Cromer. I could cycle or get the train or the bus to his new flat but I was only allowed to do that because it was so close to us and as long as I went via East and West Runton and not along the main road. My schoolfriends were amazed I was allowed to do this, but I had passed my cycling proficiency tests aged 8. To be honest, Mum was often not well enough to say yes or no, she just wanted to be left alone. I always made sure I left her a note so she knew where I was going. Rachel's mum worried about it too and would offer to give me a lift or see if Finn or his friend, Harry, both two years older than me, would cycle with me. They often did.

Granda's flat and Rachel's house were my main places of refuge then really, I felt lucky to have them. I used to go with Rachel to hers straight from school most days. Rachel loved coming to Granda's too; she loved the peace and quiet, she told me, and listening to the stories of his younger days. She loved sitting in the window with him, drinking tea, eating custard creams or shop-bought ginger cake or chocolate mini rolls, things like that. We could go down to the beach very easily from there too, and, in good weather, buy ice creams or hot, salty chips when it was chilly, and eat them on the prom or on the groynes just like the visitors did.

I told myself that going to Rachel's or Granda's after school gave Ma more peace and quiet to do her Open University work on the days she was home, other days she would be working at her new part-time job on the checkout in the big, anonymous supermarket which had recently opened in Cromer. She'd lost her office cleaning job because, she was told, she was too unreliable; as I've explained, there were days when she was simply too unwell to go in. It didn't occur to me then, that on the days she was home she might have wanted me to come straight home after school. Perhaps she felt lonely, unloved, or perhaps it increased her paranoid fears that she was a rubbish mother.

Rachel's mum, Jenny, often used to give me what she said were leftovers from the homely, delicious casseroles and one-pot dishes she would make in bulk and freeze. This meant that there was always something to be heated through, she explained to me, for her ever-hungry family without entailing hours of shopping, preparation and cooking when they came in from school. In reality she had obviously made "extra" on purpose (I only came to understand this later) and put it into smaller dishes for Ma and me, and Da when he was home; they were lovely.

When we first got home to Rachel's Jenny was always ready to chat if we wanted to or tell us something of her day. She worked from home as a freelance translator for various clients so could be her own boss timewise as long as she met the deadlines. She always seemed full of energy and liveliness despite often working late into the night. Again it was only later that I came to understand that one of the things I loved about Jenny and being at Rachel's was that the whole family seemed to be able to live in the moment, enjoy it for what it was, or hate it for what it was, or live it for what it was; it's difficult to explain exactly but it was just so different from my home where my Ma was in a permanent state of worry it seemed, or tense, brooding, coiled liked a spring, consumed by anxious, even morbid, reflection, somehow inward-looking, whereas at Rachel's it was all outward, open, simple.

That ability to live in the moment reminded me of Da when he was in his lifeboatman role, concentrating on the job in hand, focused, committed, clever, brave, not worrying about Ma then because he simply could not have that distraction. I imagined him living in the moment during the rescue the night he disappeared. I need to get back to that really having tantalisingly started this story with it; people often say to me now: 'we don't need all the backstory, Amy, get to the point.' But you do need it, I'd say to myself, you need the context, the nuances in order to understand how it could have happened in the way it did.

I still believe that if Rachel had better understood some of the background and nuances, she would not have so completely condemned Da for how it happened and condemned me, her oldest friend, for my understanding of it all. She dropped me like a stone; that really hurt. Seeing her laughing and whispering with Lauren Peters cut me to the quick, I mean, Lauren Peters of all people! We used to hate her. This ostracising of me by Rachel lasted the entire Easter holidays after Da's disappearance and the whole of the summer term, and, though that bit was more my fault than hers to be fair, it was torture all the same. I felt cast out, adrift, friendless, unloved, unlovable, unlikeable even.

Just before school started for the summer term a letter arrived for me from Rachel. I'm pleased that it was drummed into us that letters should always be dated because it helps me unravel the sequence of events after Da's disappearance.

Sheercliff House,
West Runton,
Norfolk.
NR27 7AA
11thApril, 2001
Hi Amy,

I'm the worst friend in the world, I'm sorry. Can we be friends again?
Pleeeeeasssse. I've missed you. I shouldn't have been so rude about your dad,
I don't understand it but it's not your fault and I'm sorry, sorry, sorry.
Luvyouuuu, please take me back,
Rachel.

This letter made me feel bruised, kind of exposed and needy. I wondered whether just to ignore it, sit next to Harry's sister, Hannah, hang out with her at lunch next term. I liked Harry better than Hannah to be honest; he was two years older than us, already in Year 7 with Finn, having survived that scary and apparently all-important leap to high school, *transition* as they called it. To us that seemed far, far away. Year 6 seemed scary enough.

Harry, which was short for Harrison, had recently joined the Junior Sea Cadets with Rachel's brother, Finn and they loved to come to the lifeboat station to learn about that aspect of seamanship. I longed to be able to join too but my Ma just wouldn't let me. In the lifeboat station setting though I had the superior knowledge and could help them but it's true that, as they gained more and more skills, and grew taller and stronger, they soon overtook me in skills and experience and I looked up to them both, literally; I liked that. They were always interested in the rescues and would come back to the boatshed after training and help clear up, listening with me to the gossip and sometimes to the more formal "debriefs", as they were called.

By hanging out with Hannah I hoped to be invited back to hers and if I went back with Rachel that wouldn't happen, I thought, as she couldn't stand her. And I wasn't just going to drop Hannah, I decided, I knew how that felt. I thought we could form a bit of a threesome but didn't factor in Finn and Harry's good friendship. I didn't stop to think much further than that threesome idea but kind of fanned my hurt, my rejection from Rachel, nursing it unhealthily so that it became embedded in an invasive, sickly way. It was horrible. I didn't reply to that letter, I was in a state of shock and grief having lost my da of course so I need to write about that now. I was also very busy coping with Ma. It was a difficult time.

Chapter 4

THE NIGHT OF THE RESCUE, 31st March 2001, a Saturday, was wild. I will tell this part of the story now as it unfolded, with no digressions, no twists and turns. In this way it will be a kind of reflection of those tumultuous years of my life between the ages of 9 years and 1 day and 19 years and 364 days, the day before my 20th birthday when this part of my story ends. The facts themselves are tortuous enough to be honest and it's difficult now to recall the exact sequence of events that day. Some of them seem to have been eclipsed by the darkness, distress and confusion of the days immediately following the rescue.

We had had several days of very bright March sunlight which actually felt warm on your face for the first time for months. But that Saturday, the first day of the Easter holidays, dawned cloudy and wet with ever-strengthening winds, exactly as forecast. It felt as if winter had returned with a vengeance for a last fight, or a last hurrah, as Granda said. March storms were not unusual, and this was long before they started naming storms in the UK, but the crew certainly had a name for this one alright. I heard my da call it a bitch of a storm when the first boat returned from the shout at about 7pm with two injured crew, the other was still out searching. It was the first time I had heard anyone in the lifeboat station refer to the conditions like that; it really frightened me I can tell you. I only happened to be in the lifeboat station then because I hadn't wanted to be in the house with such a raging storm rattling the windows and causing the lights to flicker; Dad's pager had gone off about half an hour before Mum was due home from work.

A man out on his evening walk with his dog near the cliff had reported seeing a young girl, a teenager he thought, sitting on the cliff apparently reading, holding onto the book with some difficulty, then being nowhere to be seen on his return trip though her backpack, with a book and sketchpad inside, was still there, a sketch half-finished. The walker thought he had heard a scream. It was about 7pm and would be dark in just under half an hour. The clocks had only recently been put forward for summertime. The mayday call was received in the station at 7.10pm, I remember that bit so well. Ma had called to collect me, but I had insisted on staying.

The inshore lifeboat (ILB) had already set out from Cromer by the time Dad and I arrived but after what seemed like a very short time returned with three injured crewman who had attempted to reach the rocks where another member of the public thought he'd seen a red object – like a jacket, he thought. Dad set out with three others in the other Cromer boat, the ALB (All Weather Lifeboat), to continue the search. This took only a matter of five minutes or so whilst the ambulance ferried the injured men to hospital for treatment of their multiple cuts and abrasions, one had three fractured ribs and a broken ankle too. This second boat, my dad's, returned after only about half an hour, the crew having radioed and asked for the coastguard helicopter to be scrambled as their boat, which they'd managed to right after it was upended, had been badly damaged on the rocks. They had been unable to locate the casualty after the first sighting and a crew member was missing too. The inshore lifeboat from Sheringham was also still searching, having joined the search after hearing the second Cromer boat, the ALB (All Weather Lifeboat) was out of action and a crew member missing.

I should explain here that the Cromer station had two lifeboats then: one ALB and one ILB, the D-class, and Sheringham had one ILB – the B-class Atlantic 75 rib. ALB's can operate at high speeds and in all weather conditions. They'll right themselves after a capsize and carry a lot of specialised equipment. My dad sometimes commented darkly: "More to go wrong." He certainly admired their capability, though, and called them "a good piece of kit." This meant that Cromer were responsible for shouts as far away as a hundred miles at times. The ILB's operate closer to shore and in shallower waters. They can rescue people stranded on rocks, or from boats stranded on rocks. They can even rescue people from inside caves. The type of lifeboat at any given lifeboat station depends on its geographical location, coastal features and the cover provided by nearby stations. Dad, my lovely dad, had taught me all this.

I didn't know then that the crew member they were searching for was my da, as well as searching for the person sighted briefly in the rough sea, near the cliffs. There had been a spring tide, nothing to do with the rapidly approaching spring equinox, I knew that. I knew only too well that spring tides occurred twice a month all year long when the Earth, the Sun and the Moon are in alignment: the tide literally springs up high, my da had explained this to me. That night the hours of darkness were only fractionally longer than the daylight hours, yet those dark hours of waiting were terribly, terrifyingly long.

I was keeping out of sight as much as possible in the boatshed, my fear evident in my churning stomach as I realised, whilst scanning the crew disembarking from the second boat, that it was my da who was the missing crew member. I listened to the men talking. I heard snatches of the conversations: 'it's wicked', 'a real demon from hell, this one', 'they've opened the gates of hell out there for sure'. Then Doug, Scots Doug, not Dougy as my English dad was known, suddenly became aware that I was there:

'Mind your gassing, the bairn's here.'

I can still recall the stinging wind and rain whipping my face as I slipped out of the Shed the back way and walked back along the pier wanting to be even closer to the churning sea, wanting to see my da as he staggered ashore. The tide was on the way out but the surf was still high as the waves crashed against the pier, and then when I reached the shoreline, the waves were still strong enough to be tossing stones and shingle onto the beach with each surge of water, and dragging even more shingle back into the depths with a satiated suck and roar as they receded. The noise was deafening, brutal, relentless. It seemed to me then that the slanting rain, blown sideways by forty mile an hour onshore winds, was as nothing compared to the seething ocean. I scanned the horizon, my eyes half-blinded by the stinging rain, just willing the second lifeboat to return with good news, and my da recounting the details of another heroic rescue to me.

Scots Doug came after me and said quietly:

'We need to keep ourselves safe and warm and ready for what's to come, lass. Come on in, we're having a brew and Mary Jane's is bringing fish and chips.' I always liked Scots Doug, he taught me a lot and never talked down to me. I remember feeling really hungry suddenly. By this time the rescue had been going for about three hours, Ma would be at work, knowing nothing of this anxious wait. Granda would probably have seen the boat go out from Sheringham; as I mentioned, it had joined the Cromer team on this tricky shout. At this stage there were no reports of any missing girls.

I remember Mrs Mack bringing round a load of clean, dry towels with the help of Dan, the owner of the hire van and car business next door to the launderette. I remember hearing the crew break into song: *Eternal father, strong to save...* I shuddered and became angry when I heard the melancholy melody and concentrated on distributing the packets of fish and chips, passing salt and vinegar as required. I added neither to mine; I didn't like vinegar and loved the taste of the fish and chips just as it came. I remember feeling it to be wrong that I actually enjoyed the fish and chips, but it was a combination of real hunger and the delicious taste. It was after 10pm and I had last eaten a sandwich at about 1. I felt better after I'd eaten, and the fizzy orange helped. I remember collecting all the rubbish in a big bin bag and taking it to the wheelie bin out at the back. I needed to be busy and useful. The darkness felt total.

Granda appeared at the boatshed at about 10.30 to take me home. He had telephoned Ma and she was on her way to his house. He looked stricken, buttoned up in his grief and anxiety but he took me in his arms and whispered,

'We know he knows what he's doing, Amy love, we know that.'

There were still no reports of any missing girls. The plan was to spend the night there though we knew we would watch and wait at his window, not sleep. Ma was remote, I'm sorry to say, but that was to be expected. What was not quite expected was the tirade of vitriol – I'd only learnt that phrase recently from reading *Harry Potter and the Goblet of Fire* – she poured out about Da: selfish, thoughtless, after the glory, stupid, reckless, feckless – it was the first time I'd heard the word "feckless". Granda quietly warmed up milk for hot chocolate for us all and found some biscuits. This was comforting. He then suggested I get comfy on the sofa under the duvet that I always used when I was there, while he and Ma stayed up a bit. I watched them sitting at the table in the window, not speaking, but at least Ma had calmed down a bit.

To my surprise I slept, comforted by their presence. I don't know whether he slept but I woke the next morning to the reassuring smell of bacon and eggs being cooked by Granda. He looked much older that morning. Ma was asleep upstairs, she had gone up at about 2am, Granda said.

'Come and have your breakfast, Amy,' he said, softly and so, so gently, 'they went out again at first light, just after 6, no sign yet. We need to keep our strength up, love.' The food, cooked to perfection as always, literally tasted like dust in my mouth. I now understood that expression. Usually I loved bacon and eggs at Granda's, Ma never cooked it.

'The helicopter's out too,' he told me, 'weather's in our favour, at least.'

The mad March winds had died down and the brilliant sunshine returned, heralding the arrival of April, of spring, revealing a calm sea, with just the occasional white horse on the horizon, stirred by the gentle breeze. *Butter wouldn't melt,* but, as Dad always said, 'Never be fooled, Amy love, never be fooled.' Capricious weather, I said to myself then, I liked that, *capricious,* another recently learnt word. I walked out onto the short, damp grass in Granda's small garden, feeling the sun warm on my face.

That morning the birds in Granda's garden were busy, daffodils and primroses basked in the warmth, unfazed by yesterday's battering. Cobwebs glistened with early morning dewdrops, suspended, ephemeral, clinging but poised for destruction, it seemed. Da always called daffodils and other early spring flowers "Nature's brave advance party". I looked down to the beach. The tide was out, and the beach was host to several walkers and swimmers on that benign morning, the swimmers fully kitted out in wet suits. I remember whispering to myself,

'Please, Da, be safe, please, please, please, come back.'

After breakfast, which Ma and I cleared away and washed up almost in silence, we all headed out to the lifeboat station. Two lifeboats were already out continuing the search. There was little useful to be done and it was clear we were not helping by being there as we only increased the tension in that fraught atmosphere of waiting and watching. We did hear a bit more though about the build up to the rescue. Apparently, a walker had first raised the alarm when he spotted a young girl, about 14 or 15 he thought, sitting on a rocky promontory which jutted out beneath the sandy cliffs. This was surprising in itself as by then the weather had been rapidly deteriorating, with dusk not far off, and he wondered if somebody should go and warn her, check she was alright. He didn't want to frighten her by approaching with his very nervous, unpredictable German shepherd dog only recently acquired from a dog rescue centre. The wind was already vicious at that stage with occasional bursts of harsh, stinging rain, the rain that was soon to set in in earnest. The walker reported that the girl looked to be engrossed in a book holding onto it with some difficulty, but well wrapped up against the weather at least. It seemed she had abandoned her sketch as the weather worsened. Just as he approached the spot on his return about forty minutes later, the tide was in, he heard a splash, a sharp cry, then nothing. Her rucksack and sketch pad were still there, higher up on the clifftop, well anchored down by rocks.

This promontory was bordered on both sides by two quite deep channels of water which did not fully empty during spring tides but usually provided a safe, natural playground for children to jump and splash in and smaller children to try out their first, tentative swimming strokes, to sail toy boats, and small inflatable toys and, when dry, build sandcastles in the sure and certain knowledge of destruction as the tide came in. The walker had phoned the Coastguard using the 999 service and the Marine and Coastguard Agency (MCA) immediately decided to send the lifeboat out from Cromer, the *Lady May*. I knew this was normal procedure as my da had explained it to me many times.

The crew told us that the young girl had been spotted in the water, clearly unable to make any headway in the strong current and hampered by her cumbersome clothes it seemed. She raised an arm from time to time, obviously in distress, and close to a range of jagged rocks just beneath the surface. Da was selected to go to try to reach her and pull her to safety, fully kitted out in wet suit and carrying a spare lifejacket, roped onto his kit. The sea was high with an enormous swell and the rain, by now unremitting and blown almost horizontal by the ever-strengthening wind, almost completely obliterated any sightings of the girl, only an occasional shout was heard as Da swam towards her. Then, seemingly out of the blue, an enormous wave engulfed the waiting *Lady May* upending her and tipping crew and equipment into the broiling surf. The men battled for more than twenty minutes to right her and once all aboard, shaken, bruised, wet and very cold, there was no sign of either my da or the girl. A mayday call was made back to base and another vessel, the *Lady Bella*, ploughed across the tossing waves, and the two lifeboats searched and waited far into the night along with the inshore lifeboat from the Sheringham station. Both Cromer vessels, fully crewed, set off again at first light, helped by the helicopter search and rescue team.

And so, the waiting and watching continued. Ma, who had remained calm and remote, set off, surprisingly, to buy food for a good, hot meal that evening.

'I'll do a roast,' she declared, 'we need something settling. We'll eat at 6.30.' This was completely out of character but my Granda readily agreed that it was a good idea:

'Keeps her occupied, Amy love, and we need to eat, we need our strength.'

I texted Rachel and she came to keep me company at the boatshed, I refused to be anywhere else. Rachel knew it was pointless to express any false hope, but she somehow kept my spirits up and we played endless games of cards: Rummy, Cheat, even Snap. She came with sandwiches made by her mum and I asked her to come back to Granda's for the roast too and to stay over; there was of course no school the next day. I checked with Mum first of course and she was relaxed about it; that was unusual and a welcome change. I remember it being around this time that I had stopped referring to Mum and Dad as Ma and Da even at home; at school I had stopped the habit previously as it sounded silly and different and I just wanted to be like everyone else. Dad told me he felt sad when this happened although he could understand it, he just liked the association of Da with Doug Appleton and Ma with Mags Appleton.

So it was that our first long day of waiting began and ended with no news. The helicopter had been stood down as darkness fell. And strangely, there was still no report of a girl having gone missing. Her rucksack, which was being held at the local police station, contained nothing that could help identify her, only an empty lunchbox with an apple core and a chocolate bar wrapper, a sketch pad, a pencil case with no name but quite a collection of pastels and a range of pencils for drawing, a good quality rubber, and a copy of *Of Mice and Men* with pencilled notes in the margins, obviously a school set text. This information was broadcast on all news channels in the hope of finding somebody who may know this girl, but no information was forthcoming.

Next morning, Monday, the first proper day of the Easter holidays, Mum went to work in the supermarket, Rachel had stayed over and the three of us, me, Rachel and Granda, went over to the lifeboat station. Granda only stayed for about half an hour then went into town to do some shopping, go to the post office, just the ordinary rituals of life carrying on normally, though we all felt life to be far from normal then.

I felt closer to Dad in the lifeboat station; I remember though that the atmosphere was subdued and tense. The weather was sunny, bright and calm, but being only early April, it was mainly dog walkers about rather than families with children on the beach for the day. Dogs were allowed on that part of the beach from 15th September until 15th April and there were plenty having the time of their life, it seemed, making the most of every last day of beach-going freedom for them. There were some windsurfers about but not actually much surf.

None of Dad's volunteer crew friends were about; they were out looking having again set out at first light. It was just the regular, paid lifeboat station staff, two of them. I knew them well but on that day they appeared uneasy, avoided eye contact and got on with their jobs. Rachel and I asked if there was anything we could do to help. I noticed that the bright sun showed up mud and rain streaks on the large windows, so we decided to clean those, each taking turns to go up the ladder to reach the highest bits. It was satisfying and looked good; Dad would have loved to see it. Cleaning the windows was nobody's allocated task, they were just done when the dirt was noticed and when there was time.

When we'd finished that we walked into town to meet Granda who had gone to do the necessary shopping, he suggested lunch in a café, and we opted for all-day breakfast. Returning despondently and aimlessly to the boatshed to pick up the car about three hours later, it was easier to park there, I remember feeling overwhelmed by a sense of sadness and loss. I found myself sobbing uncontrollably in the safety of the car as we headed back to Granda's. Rachel put her arm round me, we were in the back seat together, and again, she did not give me any false reassurance. She spoke quietly:

'Just cry all you want, Amy, I'm here for you and so is my family. We all love you. Do you want to come back to mine for the afternoon/evening? Your mum's working this evening, isn't she?' Mum was going to her new "moonlighting" job as an usher at Cromer cinema that evening, it was a regular evening slot from 6pm until 10pm. I relished the idea of being at Rachel's, and thought about the warm welcome there, the busyness, liveliness, the hug Jenny would give me, and said that I would like that if it was alright with Granda. I remember Rachel and I both thinking simultaneously that Granda should not be on his own, and Rachel immediately said,

'Please come too, Mr Appleton, Mum and Dad would want that, I know.'

Granda knew the Willises well through my friendship with Rachel and readily agreed but he asked Rachel to text her mum to make sure it was alright. It was. We spent the evening playing Monopoly in a distracted but concentrated way, all of us. It was sort of fun, but my heart wasn't in it, as the expression goes. I tried to hide that; it was difficult though.

It was about 9.30pm when there was a knock at the Willis' front door. Everyone looked up, there was trepidation in the air; I remember it so well. Jenny went to answer it and squeezed my shoulder as she passed. It was my mum.

'He's been found, the idiot's been found, he'd been hiding up. Can you believe it? The girl's been found. They're both in hospital, he's under police guard.' And then Mum started crying loudly and unrestrainedly. Jenny took her off upstairs; I held Rachel's hand tightly, feeling a sense of utter confusion but also relief. Dad, my dad was safe, alive.

'He's alive,' I shouted, 'and the police are looking after him.'

But, of course the next part of the story is my dad's to tell, only my dad can tell it as it was and he wrote it down for me as he remembered it; but I'll get to that account later.

Chapter 5

I VIVIDLY REMEMBER THAT THE others' looks of confusion made an unwelcome intrusion into the pure elation and relief that I felt. Granda followed Jenny and Mum upstairs. I will never know how that conversation went but he came down quite soon asking if I wanted to go to the hospital with him. Of course I did! I jumped up eagerly and he took my hand saying,

'We have to be prepared for whatever we find, Amy love, but the main thing is that he's alive. Your mum's not coming with us this time, she's going home shortly, though Jenny has asked her if she wants to stay here.' He paused briefly. 'It may be best if you come home with me tonight or stay here, your mum's fine with that.'

'I'll come home with you tonight, Granda; I'll just tell Rachel so she can tell her mum.'

I ran off to find Rachel who was sitting in a kind of huddle with her brothers; again, I remember that so well now.

'He's safe, he's alive!' I remember almost shouting it. 'He's in hospital so's the missing girl he rescued, I'm going there with Granda now and I'll go to his tonight.' They looked round at me almost warily, it was weird; Rachel didn't catch my eye. That really hurt and confused me, but I needed to get going to see Dad.

'Can you tell your mum thanks for tea and everything?' I finished uncertainly. Why wasn't she jumping up to hug me and ask me about it? I didn't understand.

But I was busy then going off to the hospital which was about twenty-five miles away and it would take nearly an hour to get there. We decided not to delay by going home first and picking up things Dad might need as it was already late; we could take them in tomorrow once we had discovered how long he might be in. I think I must have kind of blocked out the "police guard" bit at that stage – perhaps in my excitement and relief in knowing he was alive.

So we headed off to the Accident and Emergency Department, A&E as it was known. On arrival the receptionist seemed not to be completely friendly somehow and asked us to wait whilst she called somebody to speak to us.

'Can you tell us how he is, at least?' my Granda asked. 'He's been missing since Friday; we've been out of our minds with worry and fear.'

She seemed to thaw a little then, remarking,

'I know he was conscious and talking when he came in... but I'll get somebody now. Please – just take a seat.'

The waiting room was crowded with people clutching bandages, holding arms in slings, a few had their shoes off revealing temporary, makeshift strapping on ankles, and there was a girl about my age holding a bloodied pile of tissues to her nose, she was soon called through. After about forty minutes Granda's name was called and we both moved towards the area we were directed to. I was told, kindly, I remember, to wait in the waiting room a little longer whilst they talked to Granda then we could both go and see Dad who was being transferred to MAU which stood for Medical Admissions Unit, I was told. When Granda appeared to fetch me he looked older, tired out and troubled.

'I'll explain everything as best I can soon, Amy love, let's go and see him.'

Dad was sitting up against a large pile of pillows, obviously in pain. He had a bandage all the way round his head and was covered in cuts and ever-darkening bruises. He had three broken ribs, so it hurt him to breathe. A bag of blood dripped its contents slowly, rhythmically into a vein in his arm. As we approached, we could see his eyes were closed but he was grimacing in pain. Granda spoke quietly:

'Doug, Dougy, here we are, I'm here with Amy to see you,' and he took hold of his son's hand clutching it gently.

There was just one police officer sitting close by reading a newspaper and drinking tea or coffee from a polystyrene cup from the vending machine. Dad opened his eyes and looked first at Granda then at me. His face was wreathed in smiles but almost immediately, something I'd never seen before, he started crying quietly. This was so frightening, I felt myself grow up about ten years then. He pulled me as close as his injuries allowed, wincing in pain, stroked my hair, kissed my face, my forehead, my hair, softly and almost wonderingly.

'Oh, Amy, here you are, just as ever, thanks, Dad, thanks. I guess Mags isn't coming? Probably best at the moment to be honest.'

Granda spoke calmly and in a measured way.

'That's right, she's alright, she's been at the Willis', we all have, but she'll be at home now. She's okay though. No need to worry.'

I remember wondering why all this emphasis on Mum when it was Dad who was lying injured in a hospital bed, bandaged, bruised, cut and in pain. But of course, I said nothing.

'Rachel's a good friend to you, isn't she, Amy love?' he said in a very emotional way.

'Yes, she is, Dad. But you, we were so worried. Are you hurting now? What happened?'

Dad looked intensely weary and somehow stricken, I remember using that word to describe it to myself afterwards and even noting that it was the first time I had ever used it.

'I'll explain it all, love, when I can but at least she's rescued. Her name's Carrie, she's 15 and she's here too.'

'Not too many questions for your dad just now, Amy love,' cautioned Granda gently, 'he's in pain, exhausted, he lost a lot of blood from quite a deep scalp wound, probably hit his head on a rock, they think, needs his rest. It's probably best to leave him to rest now we know he's safe, go home, get some sleep and come back in the morning.'

Dad nodded wearily.

'Best thing, darling girl, come back tomorrow, can't wait to see you and I'll be much more chipper soon. I just want to know how Carrie is though, whether she's still in A&E, she had a shoulder injury and was cut and bruised like me. We looked after each other.'

'I'll see if I can find out before we go,' Granda said and walked over to ask the policeman.

'She's been admitted to the children's surgical ward for tonight but can probably go home tomorrow, I've heard,' he closed the newspaper. 'Oh, whoops, that might have been confidential, anyway a WPC is with her, I do know that.'

It was cold and windy as we left the hospital, I remember, the wind seeming to howl round all the concrete nooks and crannies and alleyways which formed our route to the car park. I clutched Granda's hand tightly. He'd forgotten exactly where he'd left the car, all the car park blocks looked similar, but we found it eventually. He turned up the heater, put on some music which I didn't recognise but it was nice, folk music, Joan Baez and Bob Dylan singing together. I remember *Forever Young* best. I fell asleep quite soon and only woke up as we pulled into Granda's drive. Granda asked me if I'd like a hot drink and some toast or something but I was too tired for anything and wanted the morning to come quickly so I just speed-cleaned my teeth (I always had my own washing things at Granda's) and tumbled into the familiar, comforting bed feeling so relieved that Dad was in a clean, warm, safe hospital bed with people looking after him.

Next morning we had a lovely breakfast of cereal and boiled eggs and toast, nice and sustaining, Granda said, and I phoned home to tell Mum we were going to call in to collect some things to take in for Dad. She sounded remote, not well, I knew, but she just said,

'Fine, see you shortly.'

When we arrived, she was still in bed but got up to find Dad's washing things and shaving kit. I decided he'd need some clothes to come home in so I looked for those, the comfiest I could find thinking of his sore ribs and cuts and bruises. Granda asked Mum if she wanted to come with us but she said quietly and calmly that he was better off without her right now, she used exactly those words: "right now" and I took it to mean that while he recovered he didn't need to have to cope with her stress, anxiety and anger. I wondered where her relief that he was safe was, her care and worry about his injuries, but again, it seemed that all her feelings were turned in on herself or turned off perhaps. I didn't like that and felt the distance between us growing.

I left our house with the usual sense of relief and freedom flooding over me, so happy too that we were off to see Dad, my lovely, brave, heroic dad. Granda stopped on the way to fill the car up with petrol and bought a local newspaper, the *Eastern Daily Press*, always known as the EDP. This carried front page pictures of Dad and the girl he rescued, not in their hospital beds but pictures given to the paper by the police perhaps. The headline shouted out at me:

Missing lifeboatman under arrest in hospital

then, in smaller letters underneath:

Rescued girl, 15, safe

The article went on to explain:

Missing lifeboatman, Douglas Appleton, 32, was found injured but safe yesterday evening sheltering with rescued 15-year-old, Carrie Longford, in her grandmother's house at West Runton. It is not yet known why he did not inform the authorities that they were safe, both having sustained injuries which required hospitalisation. He has been arrested on suspicion of child abduction and remains in hospital under police guard. Carrie has been discharged to her grandmother's care today as her mother is currently visiting relatives in New Zealand. The Norfolk and Norwich University Hospital has declined to comment.

Granda read the article out to me before leaving the forecourt of the petrol station. I was pleased he did because some things started to make a bit of sense, but he looked strained and deeply sad as he read it out.

'I know your dad was unhappy, Amy love, but I also know he wouldn't hurt a fly, never mind a child.'

What didn't make sense to me was why people thought Dad had done something wrong. He had, after all, rescued this girl, Carrie, endangering his own life; it just didn't make sense. I didn't get it. I felt crushed, uneasy, all my happiness and relief washed away, it seemed, by these mysterious events. I desperately wanted to see Dad though.

'Is this why Mum's being so weird, even more weird than usual?' I asked Granda hearing my own words sound harsh, unkind.

'Oh, Amy, you mustn't talk about your mother like that, you know that. She's upset, yes, confused, hurt maybe, I don't know, but you know that things weren't good between them even before this don't you?'

'Oh yes, I know *that;* I have to live with them remember?' Again, I heard my harsh, sarcastic words and I hated myself even more. The traffic was slow that morning and it took us over an hour to get to the hospital, with another fifteen minutes circling round the car park looking for a parking space but eventually we were on our way to MAU; Dad was still there.

A tall, elegant woman, about 70 years old or so I thought, stepped forward as we approached and held out her long, slim hand in greeting. I noticed she wore a beautiful engagement ring, a cluster of diamonds, obviously old and well-worn, sitting snugly on her slim finger, but no wedding ring. Her soft, silvery grey hair was drawn back into a perfect French pleat emphasizing her strong jawline, fine bone structure and long neck, scarcely lined. The pleat was secured with a large silver clasp studded with pearls.

'You must be Doug's father,' and she held out her hand to Granda. 'My name's Angela Longwater, I'm Carrie's grandmother, similar surnames by pure coincidence, her mother only had to change half her surname when she married,' she smiled gently. 'And it's Carrie by the way, not short for Caroline or Carol, just plain Carrie, the apple of my eye.' This was the first of Angela's many expressions I heard and came to love.

Granda shook her hand and replied, 'Yes, that's me, Seb Appleton, and this is Amy Appleton, Doug's daughter.'

'Hallo,' I smiled shyly up at this beautiful woman whose eyes were deep green. I thought she looked like a ballerina or an opera singer to be honest.

'I haven't seen Doug yet, but I understand he's on the mend now. Carrie will be coming home with me later today once the doctors have seen her, I hope. Her mother is in New Zealand where her brother-in-law, Carrie's uncle, is very ill with a brain tumour. Oh dear, it's been a chapter of disasters... a simple misunderstanding. Let me explain. I thought Marianne, my daughter, Carrie's mother, was leaving *next* weekend, and I was away in Yorkshire visiting a friend who has just lost her husband. I was planning to get back in time for Carrie's arrival, oh dear, what an idiotic thing to get muddled up about.' Angela shook her head before continuing rather sadly, 'So, no one knew Carrie had arrived at my house, she has her own key, has had for a while now as her mother thought it a good idea if they both had one in case I fell over or anything...' Her voice tailed off a bit, then resumed with a kind of proud strength: 'I hate being worried about, comes with the territory, old age that is,' she looked rueful. 'Carrie sensibly decided not to tell her mother that I wasn't around, just made herself at home, she's always been sensible and mature for her age. I think she quite liked the idea actually; she's self-sufficient, and can always keep herself busy, likes her own company. She brought all her GCSE exams revision, poor girl; they seem to be under so much pressure these days.' Again, she tailed off. 'Anyway, I'm talking too much. I'm going to go home and bring Carrie's clothes back, so I hope to see you later and I'd love to pop in and see Doug and thank him, seems an understatement. What an incredibly brave thing to do, what a hero, you must be very proud of him, both of you?' At this she turned to look down at me, and I felt myself beaming, actually beaming, partly pride, yes, but partly pure relief that somebody seemed at last to be recognising my dad for the hero he was. She continued, 'Carrie tells me he's told her all about you, Amy, and how proud he is of you; she's looking forward to meeting you too.'

Meanwhile Granda too was looking relieved, less strained I noticed, that pleased me. Things seemed to be getting better. I was impatient to see Dad now and Carrie's grandmother, Mrs Longwater (as I thought of her then) seemed to sense this.

'Well, I'll be off now, I expect I'll see you later. We must arrange a proper get-together, a celebration. Perhaps I could have your phone number, Mr Appleton?'

'Oh, please call me Seb. Of course.' He jotted it down for her on the back of a till receipt he had in his wallet and handed it to her.

'Please call me Angela, you too, Amy dear.' She jotted his number down in a tiny, sparkly, silver-coloured notebook with an equally tiny, silver-coloured pencil slotted into it; that fascinated me, I loved it. She then turned and tapped off in her high heels, so elegant.

Dad did seem to be quite a bit better; the police officer was still there though. *Why?* I thought, *why?* He was going off for a different type of scan later that day, he told us, as the doctors were fascinated by, and worried about, his transient amnesia and his persistent headache which could, of course, have been caused by the bang on his head. I remember Granda explaining both "transient" and "amnesia" to me. We told Dad we'd met Carrie's grandmother and how lovely she seemed. We also told him that she wanted to meet him, and that Carrie was expected to go home with her grandmother later in the day. We mentioned the planned celebration too, and I saw the police officer glance over towards us quickly.

'Ah, I'll look forward to that,' Dad sounded weary now. 'I'd love to see Carrie but they're not letting me.' He seemed to change the subject then quite abruptly. 'How are things with you, love?' he asked me, sounding more like the old Dad. 'Easter holidays soon?' I explained that they'd just started.

Chapter 6

I REMEMBER THOSE EASTER HOLIDAYS of my year 5 at school as life-changing in so many ways. For a start, Rachel just cut me out of her life completely, I couldn't understand that, and it hurt me very much. Granda was a great comfort and his house was, as usual, a place of refuge, but he shook his head sadly when I told him how Rachel had cut me out.

He muttered,

'Mud sticks, Amy, my love, and girls can be very cruel.' I didn't understand what he meant by "mud sticks" but I certainly knew how cruel girls could be, that's for sure.

This was the holiday though when Carrie Longford and her mother, Marianne, and grandmother, Angela, came into my life. I loved them all. Carrie is six years older than me and she became like a sister to me then as well as a best friend. It was Carrie who explained many things I didn't at first understand. I could have spent all day and every day in her grandmother's house with her but of course I couldn't; Dad was at home and I wanted to be with him, and besides poor Carrie was very busy revising for her GCSE exams at that time.

Dad was discharged from hospital on Good Friday which came at the end of the Easter holidays and I tried my best to make home as welcoming for him as possible but that was hard too. I bought him an Easter egg made from his favourite dark chocolate. That felt strange, as if I was the parent and he the child. I got an Easter egg from Granda and from Angela and Carrie but not from Mum or Dad. I didn't mind that exactly, I just felt sad. Mum was distracted, remote from Dad and me. She was working extra hours and completing the final two assignments for her Open University degree in Sociology. She went off to a residential revision course for four days the Tuesday after Dad's return, after quite a strained and tense Bank Holiday weekend. I'd never known her attend this type of course and I didn't even know that the OU ran these, but it suddenly seemed to be happening out of the blue.

Dad seemed different, often deep in thought, sad, defeated-seeming, and he missed his lifeboat volunteering. He had been ordered to take six months off from doing that because of his head injury which still gave him bad headaches and sometimes short-term memory loss, but this, at least, was intermittent and improving daily it seemed. The headaches continued for a long while. He had been interviewed at length by the police, as had Carrie apparently, and he was considered to be clear of all suspicion. At that stage I still didn't fully understand what he had been suspected of.

Carrie's grandmother, Angela, felt a party was in order as we had much to celebrate: Carrie's and Dad's rescue, the fact they were both out of hospital and on the mend and that Dad's name had been cleared plus Marianne's return from New Zealand despite the sad circumstances. Angela had explained to me that Carrie's mum, Marianne, was due to return on Friday that week, Good Friday, the very day of Dad's discharge from hospital. She invited Granda, Dad, Mum and me for the planned celebration on Bank Holiday Monday. Mum wasn't able to come as she was too busy getting ready for her residential course, she said. Angela also decided to invite Jason who was the architect designing the studio. He had his two little boys, Jo and Ben, aged 6 and 4 and his daughter, Tiffany, Tiff, aged 3, with him for the long weekend as their mum needed a rest, I was told.

'We'll have a proper tea party,' Angela declared with an excited chuckle, 'sandwiches, cake, scones, buns, that sort of thing, and jelly and ice cream,' she added, looking at me. 'Would you like to come over in the morning, Amy, and help prepare? We'll call it tunch and have it about 3 o'clock, mixture of lunch and afternoon tea. We can just leave Carrie to work in peace, she's already had enough disruption from her adventure at sea, poor child.'

The short drive, or slightly longer walk, to Angela's house in West Runton always felt to me like a liberation, an escape from the tense, unhappy, always fraught, atmosphere at home, another place of refuge for me, I hoped, like Granda's. The house was set quite far back from the road with the front garden made into a really beautiful rose garden with intersecting, red brick paths. From the back you could clearly see the sea, which was no more than five minutes' walk away. I loved it from the moment I saw it. There were only about five other houses within walking distance, all newer than Angela's, but all built in very individual styles. Some of the houses, even the newer ones, were built of brick and flint in the local style and were very pretty in that way.

Angela told me that her house reminded her of a house that a child would draw because it stood four square with five small-paned windows evenly spaced across the top storey and four similarly placed across the bottom storey with the front door in the middle. She'd fallen in love with it as soon as she saw it, though technically it was bigger than she needed then. She told me she had had a vague plan of doing bed and breakfast when she retired but had never quite got round to it. This was partly because, she explained, her heart wasn't really into changing beds and cleaning loos and bathrooms endlessly, but mainly because she liked to have room for Carrie and Marianne to stay whenever they wanted to, they both had permanent bedrooms there. This reminded me of my bedroom at Granda's always being there for me, I liked that thought.

She explained that the house was in fact two farm cottages, built in 1890, knocked through later, in 1910 apparently, to make one house. She said it had all the advantages of a big, grand house without being particularly grand. The garage was completely separate and reached by driving towards the sea at the back of the house, set sideways on and not in any way visible from the front of the house. There was quite an impressive sweep of a drive up to the front door with the rose garden spread out before it.

The back garden comprised mostly an extensive lawn with deep, colourful borders, flower and shrub-filled, with lots of ground cover, for low maintenance but also perennial colour and prettiness, in other words all-year-round prettiness, she told me. The studio only took up one far corner, nearest the sea, and it was interesting to see it taking shape during those Easter holidays when I visited often. The diagonally opposite corner, close to the house, contained a greenhouse, where Angela grew mostly tomatoes and some herbs, anything easy and low maintenance she said. She explained to me that if she thought she were ever going to become a proper gardener it would have happened by now, she was, after all, in her dotage, she chuckled as she said it, aged 77. The way she had planted the garden to be pretty and colourful all year long had more to do with Marianne's advice and help when she could, she explained, as well as the skill of her gardener, Pete, who had come to work for Angela when he retired, about ten years previously, from being head gardener at Felbrigg Hall, a nearby National Trust property.

'Dear Pete, absolute salt of the earth, he's now in *his* dotage of course, but you'd never know it. Must've been all those years of hard graft in all weathers, could be barely 50 though I know he's about the same age as me,' she looked thoughtful.

Angela told me that she gave up the bed and breakfast idea after approximately ten seconds' thought about the reality and the disruption. She realised she preferred to make money now by running art workshops and fulfilling commissions working as a freelance artist, sometimes landscapes, seascapes and such but also portraits of animals and people. She had retired from teaching A-level Art and Design at the local sixth form college in nearby North Walsham just over ten years previously. She also enjoyed having various cousins and friends to come and stay from time to time and sharing, or showing off, as she put it, her beautiful corner of England. One of the inside rooms was a permanent art studio but the reason she was in the process of having an outdoor studio built in the garden was in order to maximise the light by having floor to ceiling windows, she explained to me. So the house was well-used and very lived-in, as she said, and I loved it.

And it was whilst Angela and I were companionably making the sandwiches and jellies that I felt able to ask her what Granda had meant by "mud sticks". As she explained it carefully to me a lot of what had happened after the rescue suddenly fell into place; it really felt like that, falling into place like missing jigsaw pieces. To this day, eleven years on and counting, I expect, the wholesome smell of freshly hard-boiled eggs, crumbed ham slices and smoked salmon reminds me of these revelations unfolding. I can still taste the dissolving, delicious sweetness of the raw jelly cube Angela gave me to suck as we worked and chatted, telling me it would make my nails nice and strong. I can remember being shown how to slice the eggs; I loved that egg-slicer and being able to choose the way in which to cut the oval shape, lengthwise or across the middle. It was so precise. I still love egg-slicers.

As I laid out the slices of bread on wooden boards and buttered them and

Angela filled the sandwiches she explained that Dad and Carrie had managed to make their way back to her house that night, probably about 1 o'clock in the morning, it was thought, struggling because of their injuries, but helping each other up the cliff path and in through the back garden gate. Once there, they managed to clean up as best they could, Carrie made warm drinks and toast and they collapsed into bed. She knew her mum's room was already made up, because it always was, and it was all ready for her return from New Zealand at Easter.

'So your dad slept in Marianne's room, Amy, Carrie in her room, she has always had her own room here, and your daddy behaved with absolute propriety towards my beautiful granddaughter, Amy, absolute propriety,' she repeated clearly, 'understand that, my love, because it is the simple truth.'

At this point I remember the jigsaw picture going out of focus a bit because I didn't know what 'propriety' meant but I felt I could ask Angela and she wouldn't think I was stupid.

'Oh, how silly of me,' was her response, I remember it clearly. 'I forget you're only just 9 years old, you seem so sensible and wise. Well, Amy, your father is both a hero and a saint in my eyes and in Carrie's,' she had her back to me as she reached into cupboards and drawers for scone-making equipment. 'It's hard to explain the word, Amy,' she continued, 'but people thought your dad had deliberately hidden away with Carrie and taken advantage of her... erm, he could have behaved inappropriately towards her... Oh, this is difficult, I mean he might have wanted to kiss and cuddle her, that sort of thing, in a man to a woman sort of way. So, propriety means behaving properly or fittingly, doing the right thing in the way you behave.'

I understood at once and nodded to show that I did as I knew I was blushing deep red and felt embarrassed. Angela continued to explain, not looking at me, as she showed me how to weigh the flour accurately and how to sieve it into the mixing bowl lifting it high to incorporate as much air as possible in order to make the scones light without losing any of the flour:

'That's why the police were with him in hospital, Amy, he'd been arrested on suspicion of abduction of a minor, that's a child in normal speak by the way, and possible abuse of his power over her. Abduction means taking or stealing when it involves a person, a bit like kidnapping but that includes asking for a ransom, money. Your daddy was in a befuddled state, Amy, and

Carrie was subjected to horrible questioning despite protesting his innocence.' She paused briefly, sucking in her breath: 'It seems that they even examined her physically,' she spoke as someone does who's in pain.

'She hated that of course,' Angela continued. 'She simply explained he was her rescuer, her hero, that she wouldn't be alive today if it hadn't been for him, but the louder she protested his innocence the more suspicious they became, suspecting her of collusion in the abduction at one point... collusion, that means agreeing to it, going along with the idea. The press didn't help either and not just the tabloids. Grrrr.' Again, she helpfully explained to me what tabloids were.

'It's been terrible for her and very bad just before GCSE's, let alone her injuries and near drowning. She'll take a while to get over it, not just the accident but the horrible aftermath too. She simply lost her footing on the cliff; she knows she was too near the edge, silly girl, but she was enjoying the wildness of the weather; lesson learnt for her that's for sure.'

Angela was chopping the butter into small chunks as she spoke, almost viciously it seemed:

'People threw mud and it stuck, Amy, it'll take a long time to unstick it, that's why your dad needs all our support and love. It's a difficult time for him,' she said quietly as she showed me how to rub together the flour and butter, lifting it high, using light fingers, something I'd never done. She told me then of a similar expression: *no smoke without fire* as she poured boiling water onto the cubes of jelly, stirring them slowly. I cannot see or smell jelly now without remembering that. I liked the expression; it was so vivid, but I didn't like it being applied to this rescue and to my dad's part in it. It felt wrong, so wrong.

It was as I was arranging chocolate biscuits on a pretty plate that I learnt another new phrase: "transient amnesia". Dad had suffered from temporary memory loss lasting from about an hour before the call out to this rescue until about twelve hours after it. Apparently, it can happen after a bang on the head and even after being submerged in very cold water. He simply could not remember who he was, his name, his family, where he lived, or what he was doing there; he explained all this to me in a letter later that summer.

As Angela and I laid the celebratory tea out on her dark mahogany dining table covered with a beautiful, old-fashioned, cream coloured lace tablecloth brought out specially for the occasion, I also discovered why Carrie had been on her own at her grandmother's, why nobody reported her missing and learnt another new word, "mundane". I kept using that too. Angela explained that it was all just a mundane misunderstanding for which she took the blame entirely.

Angela told me again that Carrie's mum, Marianne, was due to return on Friday that week, the last week of the holidays. She had been away in New Zealand visiting her terminally ill, brother-in-law, Jasper, to whom she was very close, especially since Carrie's dad, Julian, had died, aged 28, in a motor bike accident when Carrie was only 2. He was 20 years younger than Marianne, Angela explained. It seemed terrible that Carrie's uncle, Jasper, her father's only brother was now dying of a fast-growing, malignant brain tumour. His wife, Sue, a New Zealander, was also close to Marianne and their three children were only 2, 4, and 7 so Marianne had gone out to help as much as possible for about three weeks and planned to return on Friday, the last day of the holidays having arranged for Carrie to stay with her mother, Angela, Carrie's grandmother.

'All very normal, so far so good,' Angela said wryly.

But Angela had muddled up the weekend of Carrie's arrival and had simply been visiting a friend in Yorkshire who had just lost her husband. Carrie knew where the spare house key was always kept, underneath a certain loose plank in the greenhouse and had not wanted to bother her mum by telling her that her grandmother was not at home. I remembered then that Angela had mentioned this the first time I met her at the hospital visiting Dad. It all made a kind of mundane sense, a simple misunderstanding, as the papers explained in a tiny paragraph towards the end of the local news section, buried really. The truth, hidden in plain sight, like Dad and Carrie.

The tea party was a very jolly occasion. Dad was in good spirits, so was Carrie, relieved for a while to be away from her revision books. She told me she was looking forward to her A-levels because she could drop all the compulsory subjects and concentrate on lovely Art, Psychology, Biology and English. She explained that she would be taking these at the sixth form attached to her school in Sheringham and was pleased to be staying on as she loved the school. She wanted to go on to university she explained, in another part of the country, but she wasn't sure exactly what she wanted to study yet.

She was interested in rocks, their different textures and how they formed but she thought it was more of an artistic interest than a scientific one. Dad, Angela and Granda all reassured her that it was completely normal not to know yet what she wanted to do after school. It felt so good to have Angela and Carrie, and, to some extent, Marianne, in my life now that Rachel and her mum, Jenny, and all her family really seemed to be out of it. That still hurt a lot to be honest.

Granda decided that Dad and I could do with a holiday treat and thought a day trip to London would be just the thing to lift our spirits. Mum was remote at that point, seeming distracted and permanently tense. Granda and Dad thought that a day left to her own devices might help her though in truth I spent most days at Angela's or Granda's then. Granda decided we would do it on the Tuesday after Easter, an INSET day so I had the day off school, the last day of the holidays.

This would give Dad a bit longer to recover his strength and Granda planned it carefully so as not to tire him out too much. Mum was going off to her workshop. We planned to leave early enough to make the most of the day, taking in the Science Museum in the morning followed by a trip to the London Silver Vaults in Chancery Lane in the afternoon, the route there would include looking at St Paul's Cathedral from the outside at least. This would be my first trip to London, and I was very excited. It was my choice to visit the Silver Vaults; they sounded to me to be mysterious, magical places, Granda had often told me about them.

Chapter 7

AS WE PLANNED THE TRIP, he told me the history of the Silver Vaults. They had started off in 1876 as the Chancery Lane Safe Deposits where people could safely store their valuable household silver, jewellery and important or precious documents. People rented strongrooms to do this. Gradually businesses started to use the rented strongrooms too and when the building was seriously bomb damaged during the Second World War it was rebuilt as retail units by popular demand of many of the silver dealers who rented space there. It reopened in its present format in 1953, he told me.

I loved the journey. It was my first experience of travelling by Tube and I was impressed that Granda and Dad knew their way round it so well. I felt quite overwhelmed by the number of people walking very fast, dead set on reaching their destinations, and I did feel a bit scared by the noise and rush of the underground trains as they roared into the tunnels breathing warmth and purpose. I had occasionally been on an escalator in some of the bigger shops in Norwich, not often though, and these were much faster, steeper, more crowded and, again, pretty scary. By the end of our day trip though I felt quite used to all the noise and people and rush and tear and actually kind of liked the buzz.

It felt so relaxing being with Dad and Granda, and knowing Mum was leaving for her workshop, not feeling resentful at home, unhappy, or going off to her unfulfilling job, or even not managing to get to work at all because of a bad day mentally. I found myself thinking about Mum a bit on the train journey from Norwich to Liverpool Street. My feelings towards her were always such a jumble of emotions. I worried all the time about her, kind of acutely during the really bad times but always chronically, like an ache. Part of the ache was a simple wish for her to be normal and loving and happy. Added to this was the overwhelming need to keep all the turmoil at home away from my teachers and my schoolfriends, even Rachel. I felt a sort of shame about Mum; it's hard to explain why – even to myself. I always felt her unhappiness was because of me and her changing moods simply terrified me. Even when she was almost manically happy, dancing round the kitchen, talking very fast, full of ideas, I was frightened this would change any moment into a mindless, uncontrollable fury, though I never feared she would hit out at me or hurt me physically.

Strange to think that Rachel had only come to my house once – when we were about 6, I think. It ended badly as Mum was so tense and tearful and over-the-top when either Rachel or me, can't remember now, spilt a drink of orange squash. It was terrible. Rachel was quiet, subdued and frightened when Jenny arrived to collect her, and Mum didn't even come to the front door, a haunting, horrible memory.

From a practical point of view, I felt I had to help and always try to solve whatever it was that was getting to her. I loved her and hated her all at once, but the hating was always transient whereas the love was deep inside me. I knew she loved me too in her complicated way. I remember almost consciously shaking myself out of thinking about her too much during this buzzy, exciting day trip to London.

Aspects of the day stay clearly in my memory. I remember the Science Museum was great especially the bits where you could join in with the experiments. I loved seeing the film of *Earth, Our Beautiful Planet* in the Imax Cinema but it gave Dad a headache after about five minutes so he said he'd go to the café to get us a table for lunch nice and early before the crowds. That was good, I was hungry.

We planned to take a taxi from the Science Museum to the Silver Vaults so that I could see some of the famous sights of London en route, Granda said. I knew it was easier for him too with his "arthuritis" though he never complained. He took a lot of painkillers which he hated having to do, and I sometimes saw him looking actually grey with pain. I stroked his hands gently as we navigated our way along the wide pavements to hail a taxi and I could see his finger joints were red, swollen, and hot to the touch. He felt "bone tired" on some days he would say to me, not on this London day luckily, and he often told me that I lifted his spirits, did him no end of good, said that I had healing hands. I felt so sorry for him and I really wondered how he manged to keep his spirits up.

He loved pointing out the iconic sights to me and Dad. It was the first time I'd heard the word *iconic*; I liked it and began using it a lot which must have been annoying for people. The taxi driver was very friendly, and he liked the fact that it was my first trip to London. He loved Norfolk too, he told us, and came to Cromer on holiday each year, small world, he said. He pointed out all the sights: I was amazed at the number of lanes at the roundabouts and how fast people zoomed round them. I loved the names of the streets: Exhibition Road, Park Lane, Piccadilly, Constitution Hill, Pall Mall, Strand, Chancery Lane – just like the Monopoly Board. I could feel a buzz in my blood, I told Dad and Granda; they laughed.

The Silver Vaults reminded me of stepping into Diagon Alley. I absolutely loved them, dark, mysterious, busy and full of such beautiful, sparkling things to treasure. I expected to see Hagrid at any moment. It seemed to me to be utter magic that we could just step in off a normal, busy London street into this dungeon-like, but magical, underground maze of rooms leading off a dull coloured, nondescript corridor, lit with harsh, unforgiving, overhead fluorescent lights and lined with heavy iron doors. It seemed to me to be a kind of tantalising trickery the way these doors opened up into a whole variety of glittering, shiny, light-filled shops each with their own specialist wares. And, to my amazement, there was a shop called "Olliver Vanders" selling very precious silver but not wands! We talked to the owners of "Olliver Vanders", a father and son, and asked if JK Rowling had sought their permission to use the name. They chuckled and explained that it was the other way round. The whole family were huge fans of *Harry Potter,* they told us, and loved hearing people wondering just the same thing as they came across their shop. They usually just listened to the exclamations of surprise and wonder, they said, and grinned quietly to themselves.

Granda was in his element and knew several of the people who owned the shops and their fathers and grandfathers before them. The people I had thought were silversmiths, were, with very few exceptions, mostly just retailers now and doing only some minor repairs; all those we saw that day were men. One of them, the biggest *Harry Potter* fan, recounted how he liked a good bash at silver on bad days! Dad asked me if I wanted to buy a little souvenir of the visit and a present for Mum. He said he was going to buy something for Carrie and Angela as they were being so kind to him. What I didn't know then, but I soon discovered, was that Angela had offered Dad a room to stay in her house, to lodge with her, as she called it. This was because Mum was being weirder than ever – but I'll come back to that.

He chose an elegant silver teapot for Angela, because she had told him all her china teapots dribbled when pouring tea. Actually, we had noticed this at the tea party and had carefully put the teapot on a separate mat, so the tablecloth didn't get stained. She was reverting to using loose tea, she'd said, because of the shocking discovery about the plastic used to make tea bags. For Carrie, he chose a skein of silver thread and three thimbles of different sizes packed into a tiny silver case, a sliver of silver, as Granda noted.

These were perfect presents, I thought. Carrie had shown me her sewing, which was linked to her talent as an artist. She liked using water colours for painting best she told me, but her love of sewing related too to her increasing interest in mermaiding culture. She said she'd introduce me to this properly when she had more time once her exams were finished. Granda had mentioned this to me, I know he and Dad were worried about the swimming safety aspects and actually Dad had already told me about this mermaiding trend and explained that it was more and more becoming associated with trans culture, which he carefully explained too. In fact, it was the sea-based mythology surrounding mermaids and her love for their fey, mysterious, evanescent qualities that attracted Carrie's interest. It continued to worry Dad greatly from the safety point of view but he said he could understand its attraction for people – but I'll come back to all that. It was at this stage that Carrie was beginning to feel like a cross between a big sister and a real friend to me.

I was fascinated by the idea of silver thread. It made me think of fairies flitting about in gossamer thin, silky dresses, the silver thread catching the shafts of dappled sunlight in wooded glades. Granda, and Mr Fitzgibbon, who owned this beautiful shop, explained between them that silver thread these days was usually made of a synthetic material that is most often a special type of plastic coated with metallic finish but further back in time metallic thread was made out of very thin strips of metal, usually silver, wrapped around a silk or linen fibre. This was the type still made by the silversmith who supplied this shop. It was beautiful, really beautiful, and not very expensive as the amount of silver used was very small. They started talking about the ever-changing value and price of silver then, but this sounded so complicated. I remember they talked about "volatility" and knew that that meant "rapidly changing" as people often talked about Mum's volatile moods.

Thinking about her moods made me sad then so I wandered off explaining that I was going to buy a little slide viewer of the Silver Vaults as my souvenir. This way, I knew I would be able to keep looking at it, taking myself through them in a magical way. I didn't know then that Dad had bought me a book about the vaults which had been made using paper engineering, so it contained very accurate, three-dimensional cut-outs of the shops and passageways. You "entered" the book through a picture of the exact, nondescript doorway through which we'd entered this other-worldly place and then whoosh, you were transported again and again to this magical, sparkling emporium. The words told the history of the Silver Vaults, I love that book. I love my slide viewer too which is always there to look at and, when I do, it never fails to bring back these precious memories of my very first trip to London.

I decided to buy a few postcards too, one for Rachel's family – just because she was cutting me out didn't mean I would cut all ties with her family – one for Harry and Hannah, one for Mrs Mack and her daughter, Lynette, and one for Mum. I still love sending postcards actually. It's something I plan to keep doing and hope I sometimes receive them, lovely, special mementoes. People hardly ever send them now that it's so easy and quick to take photos on phones and send them instantly but that just makes them even more special, I think.

As I wandered round that magical place I decided that I would do my Easter Broad Topic Project on hallmarking in silver and on the Silver Vaults themselves. It was all so interesting and different. I found some leaflets to get me started. The project was called "broad topic" because it could encompass any of the subjects we were taught. It would always be mainly English of course, but this topic would include a bit of history, a bit of art, science because of the metals, even geography a little; a trip to London was geographical really after all.

I wrote the postcards there and then asking if I could use one of the low glass-topped counters as I wanted to post them in London. It turned out that the owner of this shop, Mr Whitehead, Alan Whitehead, he told me, knew Granda too. He found me a stool so that I could reach the counter-top for writing and asked me if I'd like a hot chocolate as he was just making one, he always had one at this time of day. It sounded lovely and he gave it to me in a beautiful silver goblet; it felt like a non-scary version of *Harry Potter* and that's how Dad and Granda found me: contentedly sitting on a stool chatting to Mr Whitehead, drinking hot chocolate. He offered to make some for Dad and Granda too, finding similar goblets in which to serve theirs, and this seemed to be a good start for our journey home and a perfect end to our visit. I remember thinking this as I put the postcards into the large red post box outside, about four times the size of the post box closest to us at home. Dad showed me that it said "George V" on it, the Queen's grandfather, which seemed wonderful to me.

The final treat of the day was to be a meal in a Hungarian Restaurant in nearby Greek Street in Soho, called the Gay Hussar. Granda knew the place well from his student days and he had booked us in for the early evening sitting, useful for those going to the theatre, or heading home to North Norfolk, he said to me with a gentle smile ruffling my hair in the way I liked, then smoothing it into place again. Dad had been looking tired but had perked up considerably since the hot chocolate and he was all for getting a bus and seeing some of the delights of London's Theatreland on the way to the restaurant. I was so excited to be taking a ride on a real, red, double-decker, London bus, something else to tell Harry and Hannah about. Granda, to my amazement, even remembered the bus stop and the number of the bus which zoomed to a stop just as we reached it, shortly after 5pm, causing Granda to murmur:

'Will wonders will never cease on this magical trip?'

London looked beautiful in the mid-April, still bright, late afternoon sunlight, busy and bustling, with even some early blossom on the trees lining the wide pavements in places. I felt the buzz of it all keenly and loved the fact that we had managed to get seats on the top at the front of the bus. Granda gamely climbed up, with Dad supporting him from behind, and making maximum use of the handrail to help haul himself up the steps.

'I used to run up these steps, Amy, not so very long ago, it seems,' he said wistfully. 'Your Gramsda and I, we always made for the front seats at the top and felt cheated if they were occupied.' He smiled quietly to himself.

It certainly felt like being on top of the heart of the world. And the Hungarian meal was delicious though I cannot now remember the details apart from the ice cream and gateaux we had for pudding. I remember the sun was setting in a fiery red bowl of light as we left the restaurant and some of the shop windows looked actually to *be* on fire. By the time we got back to Cromer it was 11.30pm, the latest I had ever been out. I looked forward to telling Angela and Carrie, and Harry and Hannah, all about it but, once again, I felt keenly the absence of Rachel's friendship.

Looking back now as I write this many years later, occasionally checking my treasured five-year diary, it seems to me that that memorable visit was the last day before everything changed, with all the certainties in my life shifting and new realities forming. I had been given this diary, pale blue with a little gold-coloured lock and key, for my 8th birthday by Jenny, Rachel's mum. I kept it sporadically from the age of about 8 to 14 or 15, I think.

Chapter 8

THAT EASTER HOLIDAY FELT LIKE a turning point in my life in so many ways. I was aware that at the same time next year I would be 10, double figures – that felt old to me, so old! But more important, this turning point, as it seemed to me then, was a time during which the people around me all changed too. It was good that I had my Broad Topic Project to concentrate on because I didn't want to go to the lifeboat station without Dad being there, that would have felt weird and a bit lonely. Harry and Hannah had gone on holiday to Wales with their parents and Rachel and I were still not on speaking terms, mainly my fault, I know, as I had ignored her letter. And Mum, well Mum, she really changed, but I'll come to that.

The first odd thing was that Dad told me, as we drove into Norwich to get new school shoes for me on the first Saturday after we'd gone back for the summer term, that Angela had offered him a place to stay in her house for as long as he wanted to, as a lodger. That meant paying her a bit, he explained. He said he and Mum were not going to make any earth-shattering decisions just yet; *earth-shattering* was the phrase that lingered in my mind. I had never heard the expression before, but it certainly didn't need explaining. He asked me if I'd noticed any change in Mum recently, and actually I had. She was certainly calmer; I thought it was because Dad wasn't going to the lifeboat station anymore and possibly because he was safe, though I was not so sure about that and didn't want to think about it. I knew too that she had only one more assignment to complete for her degree; this was her dissertation which she seemed to enjoy writing and she talked about it a lot. It was something to do with social mobility or social identity or both. I didn't really understand it then to be honest, but I liked hearing her talk about it in an upbeat and interested way.

'She seems to be calmer,' I said to Dad quietly, at the same time as thinking to myself that she also seemed happier, but I didn't say that because I thought it might be hurtful to Dad as they had obviously discussed his moving to Angela's house.

But he said it himself:

'You're right, Amy, she *is* calmer because she's happier. You've always been a perspective little thing. I guess you've needed to be though...' his voice tailed off then, seemingly lost for words to explain the difficulties between him and Mum, or it could have been that he was negotiating the trickiest roundabout ever, as he described it, made trickier then by lines of cones marking major roadworks. He went on to explain using words I will never forget and for which I admire him to this day:

'Thing is, my love, Mum wanted me to explain this to you – the thing is,' he said again and paused for a moment as if collecting his thoughts or feelings or something before continuing, 'she's fallen in love with someone else.'

The words hung in the air as he pulled over carefully to let an ambulance zoom past, sirens going, lights flashing.

Somebody else's life's changing, I thought to myself. I remained silent wanting more.

'His name's Robert, Rob, and she met him at one of those OU tutorials she attends,' Dad continued, determined, it seemed, to get facts out there in as straightforward a way as possible. 'He's a widower and has three young sons. It's tragic actually as his wife died in a car accident; apparently she was driving on her own to visit her mum who was in hospital and it seems she fell asleep and drifted into the fast lane of the M11. It doesn't bear thinking about, the youngest boy was only 3 months old. Anyway, Mum and Rob plan to get married and she wants a divorce from me. She'll take the blame, but she wants it to happen as soon as possible. He lives in Cambridge, the older boys are already settled in school there, it's close to his parents and they plan to live there.'

Again, I remained silent waiting for more. Dad continued:

'We thought you were old enough now to decide which of us you want to live with mainly, but of course, whatever you decide Mum and I will want you to be with us both a lot. So, we're talking to our solicitor early next week; it'll be straightforward because it's the best thing actually.' We were close to the car park now and I knew that meant the protective shell of the moving car and the low, soothing hum of the engine would soon go and we would have to concentrate on the very boring job of buying school shoes.

After he'd parked Dad turned to me and said quietly:

'You *do* understand don't you, Amy, that none of this is your fault?' I nodded because I did understand that; it was about them and their mess of a marriage, not about me. *Mess of a marriage*, though I did not say it aloud, sounded harsh as it echoed in my mind but even at that age, I can remember feeling the sadness of waste, of failure. It was only later as that miserable summer term drew on that I started to wonder if it *was* actually my fault, my fault for being born when they were both too young.

'Let's get this shoe job out of the way anyway,' Dad said now, 'then go and find some lunch, shall we? There's a lot to take in, a lot to think about for you and, as I said, apart from the fact that we know we need to divorce, sad though that makes me, we're not going to make any other earth-shattering decisions just yet about who lives where, what to do with the house, that kind of thing.'

Again, that phrase echoing and re-echoing in my mind as I went through the task of trying on shoes. I remember looking at other children and parents doing the same thing and wondering if any of them had just received *earth-shattering* news. Some thoughts felt certain and settled in my mind straightaway though, I remember them clearly:

1. Mum was happier because she was leaving Dad and me. I simply blanked out the thought of her being in love with this unknown, sad, widowed Robert surrounded by little boys.

2. Dad seemed resigned, sad, but not crushed or devastated or even shocked or surprised.

3. I felt a sense of freedom and excitement; this was so odd that I sort of suppressed it.

4. I wanted to live with Dad. No question about it. No contest. Easy-peasy.

5. I felt sad and worried about number 4 so not really so easy-peasy in some ways.

6.   I felt cross with Mum because I'd be missing the best parts of her.

7.   I didn't want to meet Robert and his sons, ever!

8.   I wanted to talk to Rachel and her mum.

So that was the first shift, and it was a harbinger of many more shifts to come though I didn't at that stage know that. And then not seeing Rachel; that was different; strange and hurtful too. Going back to school for what should have been the best term of the year with lots of outside PE, warm break times and long, light evenings after school, was difficult. Rachel and Lauren Peters were always together, laughing and giggling. I made myself become friends with Hannah but actually I found her quite annoying and quite boring. She was never interested in doing anything fun like Rachel and I used to and she lived miles away – in Bessingham – so I lost that sense of freedom I used to feel with Rachel as we hopped on and off buses, or walked, or cycled between our houses and the beach or town. I really missed that. If we went anywhere now Hannah's mum or dad would drive us. Things always felt sort of tense in their house, bottled up, constrained. Harry was so much more relaxed when he was with Finn and Rachel's family, and I was usually there too. He was already counting the days before he could learn to drive; there were a lot of those still as he was only just 13.

The best thing that term was that my class teacher, Mr Stebbings, really liked my project and put three gold stars on it. I was the only one in the class to be awarded three gold stars and that meant points for my house too, Hickling. There were four houses in our school named after the Broads: Hickling, Ranworth, Wroxham and Barton. My project was on display for Parents' Evening too and, wonder of all wonders, Mum came and looked through it closely. She told me she was proud of me for putting so much work into and producing a really interesting project. She would read it from cover to cover, she said, when I took it home at the end of term and would learn a lot, she felt sure. She grinned light-heartedly and in a relaxed way as she moved on to talk to Mr Stebbings.

The next major change was that Dad was asked to leave Sheringham High School and not return after his remaining three weeks' sick leave which he needed following his head injury. Angela explained this to me. She said that at least the head teacher had had the grace to come round to the house to talk to him in person.

'Remember, mud sticks, Amy. No smoke without fire.' I remember I looked at her in surprise and quizzically. She went on: 'But to be honest, Amy, it may be sort of the best thing as Carrie will still be there for another three years, including when she's in the sixth form, and they've got to know each other in a different way now.' She broke off abruptly then and looked at me, a little flustered, I thought: 'What I mean is that they have become real friends and that might be tricky as he works a lot with the GCSE and sixth form Art students because of the technology and equipment they use. Carrie loves that school, Amy; she went there after just one term at Cromer High where she was badly bullied by a group of girls.'

I tried to imagine being friends with a sort of teacher at school. Dad wasn't actually a teacher of course, but I just couldn't imagine it, it would be weird, I thought. It was true that Carrie and Dad had a good, natural friendship developing with many shared interests. He talked to her a lot about mermaiding culture, the dangers associated with it, of course, and the sea generally but he was also very admiring of her artistic skills and her experiments with different techniques and materials. I sometimes noticed that he would sit and watch her, especially when she was unaware that he was doing that.

It was a happy and relaxing set up at Angela's to be honest. This meant that this particular change made me think of earth-*shifting* events rather than earth-*shattering* ones. That felt better, reassuring; *after all, life does change, nothing's going to stay the same for evermore,* I told myself repeatedly, *this was no big deal.* I spent most of my time at Angela's because Dad was living there. Angela made me my special bedroom in the smaller room in the dormer space, next to Carrie's when she stayed, which she often did, and Angela let her use some of the half-finished studio space both for revision and for her art work as it was more spacious than her bedroom and warmer when the sun shone on the specialised glass. Dad explained that it deflected heat in summer and attracted it in the winter. The studio was lovely, even half-finished, but Angela planned to take it over properly once it was completed and weatherproof. She would move all her equipment in there, she explained, and was looking forward to having more space, such a beautiful space too, as she said.

I liked Marianne too. She was beautiful in a similar way to Angela and to

Carrie which was not surprising of course. She had the same long-necked elegance and dignified bearing. Her hair was a darker blonde than Carrie's with silver streaks, which she sometimes coloured in bright highlights, and she wore it just to her shoulders often using colourful clips to pin it back from her face. I was surprised to learn from Carrie that she was 61.

'Nearly 62,' whispered Carrie looking worried as we chatted in her bedroom one day. 'She had me when she was 46, on her birthday actually.' It seemed so strange to think that she was so much older than my mum and dad. We talked about it, Carrie and I, working out incredulously that Carrie's mum was 10 years older than my grandfather and 30, nearly 31, years older than my dad and mum, *nearly a third of a century,* we breathed incredulously but then Carrie quickly changed the subject.

Marianne was a graphic designer and it was she who had recommended Jason, the architect, to her mother. She had worked with Jason on many projects; he was likeable, reliable, creative and easy on the eye, she had said laughing, another new expression for me. She had known him for a long time having worked with him in the same firm of architects for many years before they both left separately to go freelance each wanting to be able to be more imaginative and creative and both seeking a better work/life balance. He had recently left his wife, Julia, of ten years after he discovered she had been having a series of affairs. They had two little boys, aged 6 and 4 and a little girl, aged 3. It sounded sad. Jason was 49, Carrie told me, about the same age as your Granda and she wondered if her mum liked Jason in *that way*, you know what I mean? We both giggled. I loved being at Angela's even more when Carrie was there. Marianne often travelled quite far afield if she had a particularly lucrative commission, so it was great that Carrie had her grandmother's as a home from home.

She and Marianne lived in Overstrand just down the coast from Cromer. Theirs was a brick and flint cottage, built in 1840, Marianne told me. She and Carrie's dad had bought it as a wreck when they had been married a year and had just finished doing it up together when he had his fatal accident. It was the first time I had heard the phrase: *fatal accident.* It sounded so horribly final and stayed in my mind with all the other things I seemed to be learning in rapid succession. The cottage was built with its back to the sea, like Angela's house, in a little street full of similarly pretty houses but theirs had an enormous picture window extending on both floors at the back of the cottage overlooking the green sward and the cliffs above the sea with the view stretching for miles on a clear day. This was one of the things that Carrie's parents had planned for, saved up for, and they had just finished hanging the blind for the new window on the day he died. He had nipped out to get a particular type of wall bracket to hang some pictures. It made me shiver a bit when Marianne told me that detail, but it was fun sometimes being able to visit Carrie there too, of course.

Marianne was good to have around but she was always busy and, at that time, preoccupied by the family tragedy taking place 12,000 miles away in New Zealand. She would often use Granda's QuickCam device to call Sue, or vice versa, and talk for a long time. This was a brand-new means of communicating then and predated Skype by about two or three years. In fact, Granda had one of the first commercially available QuickCam set ups as he loved that kind of technology, so did Dad. Marianne explained that the internet connection was quicker at Granda's too. It was all dial up modems then and I remember Granda being one of the first to get Broadband WiFi in his flat sometime in the early 2000's; he called himself 21st century man when it arrived.

I can vaguely remember there was a lot of talk about the millennium bug at the time which I conflated in my mind with the arrival of Granda's Broadband; I saw it as a kind of actual bug then, like a beetle, green – in my mind – though really I knew it was something inside computers. It was only recently that I discovered that the millennium bug was actually something to be feared, not a green beetle of course, but simply something to do with having to reset computer calendars to four figure dates to save everything disappearing into cyberspace when 1999, set as 99, turned into 2000, set as 00, with computers thinking it was 1900 and resetting themselves. It was almost banal really, once averted, but devastating if not.

As Marianne's webcam conversations with Sue in New Zealand were so long, she would often stay on for a meal with Granda. He was teaching her to cook some Hungarian dishes. They were happy times at Granda's despite the sadnesses in Marianne's family both here, having lost her husband, and overseas. I was at Granda's too, quite often as I was alternating between my two safe havens, as I thought of them, my homes from home.

My actual home was a bit empty and miserable at that time. Mum and Dad had decided to let it through an agent until they decided exactly what to do with it. The debate was whether to refurbish and redecorate a bit before selling it, or just put it on the market as it was. The former was impractical at that time, not least for financial reasons, as well as lack of time and inclination to do it. It was Granda who explained all this to me. Luckily, as it was right in the middle of Cromer it would be suitable either for a holiday let or for young people, or a young family even, working locally, he told me. This all sounded reasonable. The rent would pay the mortgage each month, Dad explained to me about mortgages. I was really learning a lot, fast. He told me that both of them needed to split the money from the sale of the house as soon as possible though.

I had summoned up the courage to tell Mum and Dad that I wanted to live with Dad. I explained that it was because I didn't want to move schools, move away from my friends, that kind of thing. Neither of them seemed surprised.

'You must come and meet Rob and the little boys when you're ready to, Amy,' Mum said this in a very calm and reasonable way, not putting any pressure on me. 'We can use Granda's gadget to talk when you want to, or ring each other whenever you like and Cambridge is not far away on the train so I can come up here and see you, or we can have days in Norwich or Cambridge, just us, you know, get to know the cities, have some fun times.' That sounded okay, I liked the thought of having Mum to myself and fun days out.

This meant I spent a lot of time at Angela's, I loved it there in the same way that I loved being at Granda's. It felt safe, settled. Just as Granda was teaching Marianne Hungarian cookery Angela was teaching me plain English cookery, giving me some good tips about basic skills like making pastry, bread, cakes, stews, fish pie, the best way to make omelettes, scrambled eggs, that kind of thing. I loved being busy with her in her warm kitchen, with delicious cooking smells pervading the whole house. Angela promised to show me how to make marmalade when the Seville oranges arrived in February; this gave me a nice feeling of permanence and continuity amidst all the so-called earth-shattering or earth-shifting changes around me. It sometimes felt as if handfuls of bricks and earth and stones were being hurled up in the air and landing randomly, I think it's because the phrase "earth-shattering" made me think of earthquakes. And there were certainly plenty of heaves and rumbles then not to mention the upcoming aftershocks.

It was during one of these "cook-ins", as Angela called them, that I learnt another interesting phrase: *extending the olive branch.* Gosh, that was vivid, I could just see the dove flying out of the Ark, zooming back with the olive branch and placing it carefully – like a gang plank – I imagined, when the flood waters subsided and the animals could safely leave the sanctuary of Noah's Ark. I remembered this from RE lessons at school and hearing the story of Noah's Ark. Angela chuckled when I told her that.

'Yes, indeed,' she said, '*Genesis*, that comes in, and in Ancient Greek mythology and Roman times too. I mention it because I was wondering how that nice child, Rachel, is. Your daddy told me you were really good friends but that you fell out after he was found. That sounds troubling.' I felt myself withdraw a bit from Angela's warm solicitude but truth to tell I missed Rachel so much; she was always on my mind and I hated myself for not having replied to her letter, her own "olive branch" really.

'Well,' I muttered, 'she's friends with Lauren Peters now. She was one of those "mud sticks" types anyway,' I said sulkily, knowing that I was leaving out the bit about her letter, and not liking myself at all.

Angela was listening carefully. 'It's just that I quite often see her nice mum, Jenny, in town, and she always asks after you and your dad in such a caring way.' She paused, almost expectantly, it felt. I carried on rolling out pastry for the apple pie we were making and said nothing.

'Well friendships do change, I know,' she went on, 'and you have Hannah as a friend now, don't you?' Again, there was a kind of expectant pause.

'I do, yes,' I muttered. I could hear my sulky tone and hated it.

Angela showed me how to lift the light as air pastry over the dish of prepared cooking apples and make an air hole where she had placed the pie funnel. She showed me how to brush the top with beaten egg to make a rich glaze, and slipped it into the oven, setting the timer:

'Let's use the rest of the pastry to make some little treacle tarts, your daddy loves them.'

As she bent down to get the baking tray out, she said, without looking at me:

'Jenny told me that Rachel really misses you, Amy, she said you were the best friend she would ever have and that the whole family misses you.' I stayed quiet, I had not known that Jenny and Angela knew each other, apparently their friendship stemmed back to school gate pick-ups from Cromer Primary. Carrie was in Year 4 at Cromer Primary when Finn started in Reception and took him under her wing a bit, Angela explained. She had often done the pick-up and drop-off because of Marianne being a single parent and having to fit in with her work, she told me, and she and Jenny would chat at the school gate.

'She also said that Rachel had written you a letter of apology and that you hadn't responded.' She paused again as she searched through the oddment drawer, as she called it, for the pastry cutters. I remained quiet.

'Jenny said that she had explained to Rachel that there was a lot going on with your dad being in hospital and things and that you might write soon. Do you think about Rachel too, Amy?' she asked me directly, looking me straight in the eye.

'Yes, I do,' I replied in less of a mutter, and found myself struggling, really struggling, to hold back tears, sobs really, great gulping, embarrassing sobs to do with the loss of Rachel's friendship. I knew that Carrie was working upstairs and might come in at any moment. Dad was out at an interview. He had decided to do the electrical repairs as a sideline when he could and had applied for various IT technician type jobs. The interview today was at the University of East Anglia in Norwich and was due to last most of the day.

Angela put the kettle on and suggested we have a break and a hot drink: coffee for her, hot chocolate for me. She found a tin of ginger biscuits and we sat at the table, surrounded by the cooking paraphernalia. She made the drinks, checked the pie and sat down, pushing away a stray, silky, silver hair with a slightly floury hand. She got straight to the point which I liked actually.

'So, you didn't answer Rachel's letter, her *olive branch,*' she chuckled softly, 'and you went on not answering it and ignored her when you went back to school. How did that make you feel, Amy, how do you feel about that now?' I was still crying, more quietly now, but managed to splutter out:

'I hate myself; I feel as if I have something twisted up inside me. I miss her, she's funny and fun. There's nothing to do at Hannah's house, she doesn't have anything interesting to talk about and she's always saying things aren't fair.'

'Yes, I can imagine that twisted old thing inside you, Amy, I can almost see it.' She reached over to the drawer and pulled out a corkscrew. 'It's probably a bit rustier than this one by now, so bits of that rust are flaking off and poisoning you. Oh, dear, that was a bit too vivid really, sorry, love.' I started crying with renewed strength then and felt Angela push my hair behind my ear off my face just as I was really trying hard to use it as a curtain to shield me from her steady gaze. 'So how *are* you going to get rid of the nasty old thing then, Amy, my love? It seems as if the ball's in your court.' I liked these expressions of Angela's but not the image of the flaking off rust from the old corkscrew poisoning me from the inside out.

'I need to talk to Rachel,' I said quietly, 'write to her, like she did to me.' As I said it, I could feel the corkscrew kind of beginning to untwist inside me. 'Can I do it after we've filled the tarts?'

The image of the olive branch is one I've often thought about since then, and in fact olive branches and groves were to form another lasting memory much later on, but I'll come to that. The seeds of that memory though, yet to be formed, were sown during that earth-shifting summer term.

Chapter 9

I CANNOT NOW REMEMBER MUCH of that summer term apart from the glory surrounding my project on hallmarking; it was even shown to Mr Stevens, the head teacher. I stayed friends with Hannah and often went back to her house for tea. We were collected by her mum. The best thing about those visits was sometimes seeing Harry though he always seemed to be busy and didn't take much notice of me since I was no longer going to the lifeboat station and was friends with his baby sister. I longed to get back to the lifeboat world and I do remember being worried about Dad. He often got bad headaches and seemed tense and somehow troubled. I felt that he was feeling a failure where Mum was concerned, and I worried a lot about that.

I asked him on the first day of the summer holidays if he was thinking of going back for a visit to the boatshed soon as it was just over four months since the accident. I knew he was not due back volunteering until mid-September and that he needed a medical check-up before that. He seemed to answer me from somewhere far away; we were at Angela's house but were the only ones in. It was a beautiful day, cloudless blue sky, smell of new mown grass; Dad had just mown Angela's lawn making beautiful stripes up and down. I loved those. As our own house was now let for the whole of the holiday season, I spent all my time in-between Angela's house and Granda's house.

'That sounds a great idea, Amy, shall we go after lunch?' Dad seemed genuinely pleased.

When we got to the lifeboat station it felt strange at first, but Dad soon got chatting to his fellow crew members as if nothing had happened. I had wandered down to the beach in front of the boatshed and started skimming stones when a voice said,

'It's Amy isn't it?' It was Finn, Rachel's older brother, who was standing on board the *Lady Mary,* busy varnishing.

'Oh, hi, I didn't know you came down here.'

'Yeah, I'm a cadet with Harry, he told me all about it. He's here too, somewhere.' He shaded his eyes against the sun as he looked up and down the beach, then:

'There he is.' He pointed down the beach towards Overstrand. 'We shadow the lifeguards when they let us and learn masses. We're both planning to do beach lifeguarding training when we're old enough. Apparently we can do the basic lifeguarding training during sixth form enrichment sessions on Wednesday afternoons so we plan to do those, then we're going to book onto a beach lifeguarding course in the summer holidays after Year 12, maybe down in Cornwall.' I looked towards where he was pointing and, sure enough, I saw Harry loping along with his long-legged stride carrying a bucket in each hand both seemingly full of ropes.

It felt really good to see them both again. Being with the boys made me feel older, whereas with Hannah I always felt much younger. I suddenly felt sorry that she was missing this and wondered what she was doing. I saw the long summer holiday stretching ahead and asked Harry if Hannah ever came down to the beach with him.

'No, Mum doesn't let her, I feel sorry for her actually, Mum kind of babies her a bit, I think. She's always thinking about that tragedy at Metton, you know when that girl went missing and has never been found, though her bike was. Way back, 1969, it was, she was 13, I think. Mum often mentions it and there are anniversaries of the day she went missing with the police trying to jog people's memories. Her dad died a couple of years ago or so without ever discovering what happened, it's hard to imagine their sadness.' Harry had stopped to talk but now he picked up the buckets and started walking on.

'Oh, yes,' I replied, 'I knew there'd been an anniversary, Mum talked about it. I don't know the details though. I don't think I want to really. It's so sad. What are you doing with those ropes?'

'I was cleaning them,' he responded, 'boring but necessary,' he added, 'so that they feed through the cleats quickly when necessary. They're all done now.' Harry admired his handiwork and handed the buckets up to Finn.

'Do you want a game of Frisbee, Amy? There's a clear space over there.' Harry pointed a little way ahead and we set off but first I ran back to the Shed to tell Dad where I was. He was engrossed in looking at some new navigation equipment. It was good to see him like that: absorbed, interested.

We played Frisbee until about 6 o'clock when Harry and Finn said they were going for fish and chips from *Mary Jane's*, and did we want them to get some for Dad and me. Again, I ran back to the boatshed to ask Dad.

'That's a good idea, Amy, we'll have them here. Angela and Carrie are both at Granda's this evening because she wants to finish that painting from his garden in this glorious light. He and Marianne are cooking them all a Hungarian meal. Cod and chips for me please, same for you I expect?' He handed me a £10 note and I went back to the boys to give it to them.

'I'll make a cup of tea; it'll be ready when you get back. Don't forget ketchup for me, tartare for Dad please, no salt or vinegar. Thanks.' It felt just like old times. Next time Dad and I came down I planned to ask Hannah, we could go and collect her and her mum would be fine with that as Dad would be with us. Harry and Finn usually cycled down.

That evening I wrote to Rachel. It suddenly felt easy, handing out this olive branch.

28th July 2001

Dear Rachel,

I'm sorry I've been ignoring you. Things have been difficult but they're better now. I hope you're okay? Lots to tell you. Please can we be friends again? I've missed you. I saw Finn and Harry at the boatshed today, it felt like old times. Sorry again, I really am.

Love Amy xx

Ps Our old house is let out for the summer, I'm staying with Dad at Angela's house, I'll tell you about her. The telephone number is: 01263 566432.

I told Dad and Angela that I had written to Rachel, they both looked pleased. I felt as if a burden had lifted, whatever the outcome of sending the letter would be, and the corkscrew inside me, so vividly described by Angela, had not only untwisted itself but miraculously disappeared.

Four days later I found a letter from Dad tucked under my pillow where I could easily see it.

Doug Appleton to Amy Appleton, an account written in a letter between 30th July 2001 and 1st August 2001

Darling Amy,

These are the events of 31st March 2001 to 2nd April 2001 as I now, only now, remember them. I need to tell you about it, need to write it down, let it out – kind of thing. It feels so strange these memories returning, cannot describe how weird that is to be honest. Perhaps writing down the way I remember will somehow seal them in my brain, I just don't know. I know I can't not write them down, weird as that might seem too.

I woke stiff, thirsty, mouth cracking, taste of salt, head aching, shoulder stinging where the worst of the gashes were, left ankle throbbing, and saw the full moon through a gap no wider than a metre. I could hear faint, reassuring sounds of a gently running sea. I raised my head gingerly, felt bile rise in my throat and I was sick, mostly water, lots of it it seemed, mixed with yellow bile, it was horrible and stung my throat as it came up.

Next thing was that I became aware, I can only describe it that way, of a low whimpering sound, low but in some ways quite high-pitched. Looking towards the sound I saw a young girl and called out to her: 'Hallo. What's your name? Are you hurt?'

'Carrie,' she whispered, 'Carrie Longford.'

'Are you in pain, Carrie?' I asked. She looked about 14 or 15 years old perhaps. I discovered later that she would be 16 in a few months' time, June, midsummer day actually.

'My shoulder,' she sobbed.

'I'm coming over,' I said softly, 'don't worry, stay still.'

When I saw her shoulder, I realised immediately that it was completely dislocated, and I knew that I needed to put it back as quickly as possible. I knew that I knew how to do this, but I didn't know why I knew. I know that sounds weird, Amy, but that's how it was. Trust me.

I knew this was the only way to stop the pain for her, but I also knew it would really hurt whilst I did it. So, I explained this to her, I remember saying something like:

'Carrie, I know you're in a lot of pain, and I know the only way to stop this is to relocate your shoulder to where it should be. This will hurt even more for that minute or two and I have nothing to give you to help this. You need to be very brave, scream as loud as you like if you want to and it'll be over really soon, I promise you that. Will you trust me to do that?'

'Yes, I will, please stop this agony.' She was sobbing uncontrollably now and shivering with cold; it was freezing, I remember, the wind biting, pummelling us mercilessly.

'Okay, I will. On the count of three you'll feel more sudden, sharp pain then it'll be over, promise. Ready?' Carrie nodded, looking frightened but resigned to more pain. I took hold of her upper arm; it was very slim; the skin felt cold and silky soft. I placed both my hands around the displaced joint. 'Okay, 1, 2, 3,' and it went back so easily. Brave Carrie, she was so brave, Amy, it reminded me of the time you cut your leg so badly on the rocks at Happisburgh when we went to see the lighthouse. You were only 4 so you probably don't remember, sweetheart.

Carrie seemed half child half woman to me, Amy, you won't understand that really, but think of it as seeing someone as a mermaid, half earth creature, half sea creature, mysterious, real, touchable, yet untouchable, that'll help you understand how it was then when I saw her, I think. She was beautiful, Amy, that's for sure, even with salt-tangled hair, scratches all over her, mud and seaweed still clinging to her, as it was to me too.

After I'd fixed her shoulder, she helped me clean up a bit by picking bits of seaweed out of my hair, I did the same for her, then we actually laughed. Hard to believe it but we did! I managed to hobble to the entrance to the kind of cave we were in and saw that the tide would come up high again, so we needed to move from there fast. I understood there had been an accident of some sort but nothing more at that time. She asked me my name and I didn't know it... that was frightening, weird. She asked me how old I was too, I just didn't know, she laughed and said she'd guess, she seemed light-hearted and carefree and I felt like that too, my mind felt clear, empty, untroubled, though my head throbbed. We made our way along the beach, the tide was miles out, and we saw that somebody had once roughly cut some steps that seemed to scramble up the cliff. Carrie managed to get her bearings somehow even in the pitchy dark and we made our way back here, which she told me was her grandmother's house. We were hidden in plain sight it seems.

I hope this helps you understand a bit, my darling girl. It's helped me to write it down actually.

Lots of love as ever,

Dad.

I fell asleep thinking about this strange and frightening time Dad had been through, Carrie too, of course, but it seemed terrifying to me to lose your memory, really terrifying.

Next morning, Rachel rang after breakfast.

'I'm glad you wrote, Amy, and erm, sorry again.'

'That's in the past and you held out the olive branch first, I didn't take it.'

'What are you on about, Amy?' Rachel was laughing.

'It's an expression, Angela, Carrie's gran told me about it, she's lovely, she's friends with your mum. Anyway, I'll tell you everything when I see you. When can you come over? Today?'

'Yep, sure, I'll cycle over now. See you soon.' I told her how to get to Angela's.

That was great, I was missing Carrie. She and Marianne had returned to New Zealand, staying for six weeks. This would be *that summer,* when the Year 11's finished school in June after their last exam, that glorious oasis of freedom in a desert of late childhood exams and futures to think about. It worked well; I could see what a good opportunity it was. Marianne wanted Carrie to get to know her father's side of the family a bit while she was still technically a child, she said, and while her uncle was still alive.

I wonder now sometimes, eleven years later, and thinking about the events of those tumultuous years, as I tell this story, whether I would have contacted Rachel at all if Carrie had still been around. I hope I would have. Since Carrie had been free of exam revision, she and I had become close, like sisters really. She was teaching me to sew and to paint, I preferred the painting, but I wasn't very good at either to be honest.

Dad and Granda had driven Marianne and Carrie to Heathrow, they'd decided to share the driving because Dad would still get blinding headaches at times and they had thought carefully about what a horrible journey it could be with heavy traffic, delays, airport stress, that kind of thing. Dad had asked if Angela could look after me for the day and I loved that she'd replied:

'We'll look after each other, Doug, don't worry, you two look after my girls for me.'

Rachel loved hearing all about Angela, Marianne and Carrie, I remember her saying excitedly, 'It's like you have a whole new family, Amy!' We sprawled on rugs in the garden and I can remember to this day the smell of the hot, slightly prickly, grass, the whirr of a mower in the distance and the warm, heady smell of freshly cut grass. Angela had made us a picnic lunch which of course I had helped her with. She told me that I was now an expert at egg sandwiches. She painted busily in the half-finished outside studio most of the time when the weather was good; it did not yet have windows, but she always liked to make the most of the light. Jason had rigged up temporary tarpaulin covers which were pulled down at night and if rain was forecast.

'I'm sorry your mum and dad split, though, Amy, that must be hard,' Rachel was lying on her back watching a couple of tiny white clouds scudding across the blue sky. I was making a daisy chain. It was so good talking to Rachel, I knew I could be completely myself, completely truthful.

'To be honest, Rach, it's better, Mum's much better, I haven't met wotshisname, don't want to. Dad seems a bit strange at times but then he's been through a lot really, and he still gets blinding headaches. He lost his job – did you know?'

'That sucks,' Rachel was making a daisy chain too now. I can see her now, her straight, auburn hair, framing and shading her face as she concentrated on the intricate task. And those smells of summer. I remember that part of Angela's garden so well; we were in the right angle of the L; the half-built studio was completely out of sight round the other side. Even now, eleven years later, I can easily bring to mind the huzzy-muzzy, almost murmuring, scents of those flowering shrubs, my senses melting and merging in the heat it seemed. Angela had told me the names of the shrubs: the deep pink buddleia, chockfull of butterflies, jasmine which always released its scent in the evenings and, nearer the ground so less need to weed, as Angela explained, the pretty ground covering of daphne and abelia, all pink and white, delicate, lacey, but also richly and subtly scented.

I could almost *hear* the smells then it seemed, hear the warmth even, then, and again now. And still, in summer gardens and in certain moods it's as if all my senses are assailed by the vibrant life around. I can feel the warm sun on my face, see the blue sky with the merest wisps of tiny white drifts of cloud far, far above me, hear the bird song, pigeons with their muffled, soft cooing, sparrows calling more urgently, not even drowned out by the distant whirr of grass-cutting and hedge-trimming machines. I can still taste the sharp tang of the fresh lemonade Angela made for us, sweetened with honey from her neighbour's bees. Seeing, touching, tasting, hearing and smelling merge into one all-pervading, amorphous memory of warmth and promise, hope and expectation: a feeling that is impossible to conjure at will in the depths of winter.

'Yep, mud sticks, no smoke without fire,' I shrugged and tried to pretend it was nothing. 'Angela's got loads of those expressions,' I told Rachel. 'He's going for interviews though. He's got a second, it's a follow-up to the one he's already had at UEA, with another test to do there, and one at the Art School in Norwich coming up but they're both a bit of a trek from the boatshed, and I know he'd hate not to be able to continue as a volunteer lifeboatman.'

We decided to include our two temporary friends, as we thought of them, Hannah and Lauren, in most of our plans for the summer holidays, mainly going down to the boatshed and seeing what was happening. The grown-ups decided that now Harry and Finn were there so much we didn't necessarily need Dad to be there. I knew it made him feel sad being a bit "out of things" as he put it. So that very next day during which Dad and Granda needed to recover from their trip to Heathrow we asked if we could all go together. The grown-ups were happy for us to do that because Finn and Harry would be responsible for "looking after" us.

'More like the other way round,' Rachel whispered to me with a grin.

Lauren's mum dropped her off at Rachel's for breakfast before she went to work, and Hannah's mum brought her to Angela's at 10 on her way to Norwich for a shopping trip. I felt quite angelic then that we had asked her as her relief at being spared a shopping trip to Norwich was lovely to see. Jenny brought Rachel and Lauren round (Finn and Harry had gone down earlier on their bikes) and stayed chatting to Angela whilst we headed off. They had given us money for food for the day as it seemed simpler this time than carting provisions in cool bags on such a hot day. Fun and freedom beckoned enticingly.

Chapter 10

THE FIRST SURPRISE OF THAT day was how different Hannah was. She was relaxed, ready to join in anything, not whiney or whingey as she often was at home and school. When we got to the lifeboat station Finn and Harry had just finished varnishing the bench seats in the *Patsy Rose 2*. This was a fast dinghy which the station had bought second-hand from Wells Lifeboat Station as it was better suited to the slipway in Cromer. They suggested a game of Frisbee and we found a pleasingly empty bit of beach a little way along from the boatshed.

The sun was hot, the sea sparkling with a gentle offshore wind, white horses visible only on the horizon.

'White ponies really,' remarked Harry, and they were indeed pretty small as I remember. I found myself contrasting this idyllic scene with how it must have been on the night of Carrie's rescue, just under four months ago. Dad's latest letter was very much in my mind. Of course, I knew enough about the sea to know how quickly conditions could change; well, we all knew that; we had been brought up on this coast.

The second surprise, shock really, was how close Harry and Rachel seemed to be. Obviously, Harry and Finn were friends, so she knew him well, but I had always thought of Harry as *my* friend to be honest. I didn't like to see him and Rachel being so friendly, and I couldn't work out why I minded so much. I knew I had to get over it. I thought about how if Rachel and I had not fallen out I would have known about this friendship. Lauren Peters was just slightly less annoying than she was at school, but only slightly. She wasn't very good at Frisbee either, she would stand and twiddle her hair and look around all the time rather than concentrating on the game.

The summer assault on the senses was so different at the beach. It was raw and ragged somehow, still all-engulfing, like summer in the garden, but not soft, not containable. There was the tangy, sea salt smell, clean, elemental, mixed with the iodine odour of the seaweed strung out in briny, raggedy heaps, along the water's edge like so much unravelled, mucky, salt-and-sand-encrusted lace. When the tide was out, I loved to pick pieces up and take them to deep rock pools to swirl them around and restore them to their floaty, delicate prettiness. This sharp, salty, iodiney tang was mixed with the fleeting, sweet, cloying whiff of sun cream, the differently sweet, delicious smell of ice cream and the occasional mouth-watering smell of fried oil surrounding chips or fish and whatever else.

We bought ice creams from the stall nearest the boatshed, then, as the tide was going out, we decided to walk along the beach towards Sheringham, aiming just to get as far as East Runton and climb the pill box. Families, mostly with groups of children younger than us girls, but also some we knew from school in the other Year 5 class, were arriving thick and fast on this beautiful summer's day early in the holidays. We felt smug and superior because we didn't have grown-ups with us and pretty much ignored the other Year 5 lot apart from throwing back a Frisbee which accidentally came our way. We were amazed at the amount of equipment the families brought to the beach. Rugs, beach chairs, windbreaks, inflatables, bags of clothes, picnic baskets, books, radios, buckets and spades, beach balls, the odd beach cricket set, Frisbees. I remember feeling as free as air as we sauntered along six abreast; we had left all our backpacks at the boatshed. Finn carried the money in his pocket.

Just as we reached the pill box and had climbed a little way up it Harry spotted a yacht with a man waving and we could hear a faint calling sound which seemed to disappear into the wind and be carried back out to sea. Beach lifeguards had just started patrolling this area for the summer season, so Harry ran across to one of them, a lad called Tim, who he vaguely knew from sea cadet training updates. Tim sprang into action, sprinted back to the shoreline to pick up his board, then paddled ferociously towards the yacht. It turned out that the yacht had ventured too close to the shoreline at low tide and got stuck in sand.

'A rookie mistake,' Finn said quietly to us. Tim alerted the Marine and

Coastguard Agency and within ten minutes we heard the familiar sound of the maroons, calling the crew (all of whom had pagers too) thereby also alerting the public to the fact that the lifeboat had been called.

This warned them to expect cars rushing along the promenade and it meant that many onlookers gathered to watch rescues, a fact which in turn provided much needed support for the lifeboat crews. Dad told me recently that everyone mourned the loss of the maroons when they were subsequently taken out of service, on health and safety grounds, he'd scoffed scornfully, the fear being that somebody would be injured in the firing of the maroon. Many petitions continue to be signed to this day to reinstate them.

It was exciting to be part of the group which had instigated the call out and fun to watch, knowing that the rescue would be fairly straightforward, or so we thought. But the reason the yachtsman, an experienced sailor – in fact he was a retired airline pilot in his late 60's – had not simply waited for the incoming tide was that he had recently been diagnosed with Type 2 diabetes and was unused to what was needed to keep his blood sugar stable. He had felt himself becoming weak and very unwell. Finn came to the rescue as he remembered he had some mints in his pack, so, checking with the crew, he asked if he should give him one or two. The sailor whose name was William, was becoming drowsy but was intermittently agitated. He looked pale and sweaty and was able to tell us that he believed he was having a hypo episode as he had been out for quite a while and had probably over-exerted himself without having eaten enough. Luckily, he was still able to understand the need to suck on the sweets and confirm that it was necessary. He perked up a little after having three and sucked on another three before the paramedics arrived.

The paramedics praised Finn and gave us a quick rundown on hypoglycaemic versus hyperglycaemic episodes, hypo being too little sugar and hyper being too much, and how easy it was to confuse the two. They were able to measure William's blood sugar then and there and found it to be less than 4 millimoles per litre despite the mints. They administered glucose intravenously, into his vein, they explained, and he quickly started looking better. They took him to hospital in Norwich for a check over and the lifeboat crew reassured him that they would keep his yacht safe and tow it back to the lifeboat station as soon as the tide was high enough. At this stage the tide was coming in rapidly. I found all this really interesting and started thinking what an exciting job being a paramedic might be.

The rest of the day was spent swimming back at Cromer, from the bit of beach in front of the lifeboat museum. The tide was coming in, lively and sparkly. We bought fish and chips for lunch at about 3 o'clock and ate it sitting on the slipway occasionally being splashed with sea spray blown our way. As the tide went out, we spent some of the early evening looking for amber on the beach, playing more Frisbee and generally relishing that glorious sense of freedom. I wished Carrie could be with us too; she would have fitted in well. I thought of her being so far away in New Zealand in the winter, meeting lots of family and experiencing the sadness surrounding her uncle's terminal illness.

I thought of Mum too, in her completely new life. I was surprised that I didn't really miss her; in fact knowing she was happier gave me a sense of liberation from all the responsibility and worrying. What was nice, and new, was that she wrote to me a lot, I loved that, it was like a new dimension to our relationship. I'll come to some of Mum's letters soon, I've kept them all. I felt so relieved not to have to worry about her and look after her, but I did worry about Dad a lot. He was preoccupied and distracted all the time.

'Oh, it's just this wretched head of mine, Amy love, you have no need to worry, it'll get better in time the docs tell me. It was quite a bump they say.'

Most of that summer holiday passed in a similar way, with trips to the lifeboat station or to Rachel's or Angela's house. By unspoken agreement, it seemed, we agreed those were the best places to go because we were not fussed over by the grown-ups and it was easier to get to the beach, go for walks or just chat in the garden. We made our own mini-picnics and snacks and would often go strawberry or raspberry picking, either at the farm barely a mile away from Rachel's house or just round the corner from Angela's.

Angela was very busy painting because the studio build was on hold for three weeks whilst Jason was on holiday with his parents and his children, first in Spain, then visiting his wife's family in Devon. Julia had said she needed space away from the children. This seemed to me so sad for the little children during their summer holiday. I thought they were probably having a good time with their dad and both sets of grandparents though. Jason being away meant that Angela was making the most of the hours of daylight and uncluttered space. She and Jenny would chat a lot when one or other of them dropped us off in our respective houses.

Dad had been offered the IT tech jobs at both the Art School, which had just become Norwich University of the Arts (NUA), and at UEA but he also had another interview with the Norfolk Tourist Board, who were upgrading their IT systems across the county. If he got that job he would be based in Cromer. He was successful with this application too. I felt so proud of him. In the event he decided to go for the Tourist Board job for several reasons which he talked over with me as if I was another adult. I loved that. The most important factor was that this was the only full-time position and we needed the money, he explained. A close second was that he would be based much nearer the lifeboat station for shouts. Additionally, neither the Art School nor UEA wanted him to start until September, and he really wanted to get back to work, earn money and feel more normal again he said.

He seemed to relax a bit when that was all sorted and his start date was set as the beginning of August. He didn't have to work his notice from Sheringham High School, he was informed, as he had been told to leave, effectively dismissed, sacked, as he explained to me. I hated that. But horrible though that was, Dad said it was probably for the best and that it felt like a clean break for him.

I only saw Mum once during that holiday. Dad had asked Mum to take me shopping for new jeans and some more summer tops as he said that I was growing like a beanstalk. So that worked well especially as the weather took a sudden, very temporary, turn for the worse that day with lashing wind and rain.

'Oh well, it keeps the country green and pleasant,' Dad and Granda said resignedly, more or less in unison, it being one of Granda's well-word sayings.

Mum asked if I wanted Rachel to come too and she said it would be good to catch up with Jenny. That sounded good and so "normal"; I remember thinking that with a sense of relief. It was all part of the relaxed feeling of that summer holiday. Jenny and Rachel were doing school shoes shopping and combining it with a trip to Strangers' Hall Museum; this was our favourite museum, apart from the lifeboat museum at Sheringham of course which we still like to visit in its new premises and now known as the Mo. Mo was the name of the house which is now the museum, the house itself named after a child called Morag, the daughter of the owner of the house, a prominent maritime lawyer in the town. Morag lived in the town during the late 19th and early 20th century. Some of exhibits there, which include the bones of an elephant found at the base of cliffs to the west of Sheringham beach, are believed to date back 1.5 million years when our part of the world enjoyed an almost tropical climate. All the exhibits used to be housed in several fishermen's cottages.

Rachel and I often used to go there and, when we were younger, we would pretend that we lived in the cottages and helped our imaginary fishermen fathers bring in the catch. Sometimes we pretended that we owned the museum exhibits, moving them around in our minds and playing with them. We talked about the museum a bit today, though not about our imaginary games as it seemed embarrassing to us then. Mainly we discussed the fact that Angela and Marianne, admittedly only a baby then, had both been alive during the Second World War when Sheringham and Cromer had been front line towns. We found this amazing as World War 2 to us was history lessons, another time, yet Angela and Marianne belonged so vividly in the here and now. It is well known that German aircraft used to drop their left-over bombs in the general direction of the two towns on their way home from bombing missions. We also liked the lifeboat museum in Cromer, the Henry Blogg museum, named after the town's most famous, and the country's most decorated, lifeboatman. Although we sometimes went there it didn't feel like such a special trip as it was just our "local", we saw it in passing nearly every day.

We met Mum at the station and decided to go to the top of Jarrolds for lunch before going on to the museum. Jenny had driven us in, and it felt good to have her and Rachel with us. Mum looked so well and so pretty, and it was lovely that she was the most relaxed I had ever known her. I remember feeling really pleased and relieved about that. She put no pressure on me at all to visit her in Cambridge, I liked that too. That was okay by me.

At Strangers' Hall I could feel myself going back in time as we entered the different rooms with their displays of ordinary lives lived in different periods of time. In my head I would become a child of the family who inhabited the house at that time. Rachel and I played this together on that visit, slipping backwards and forwards from Tudor to Georgian to Edwardian, like time travellers. It was fun. We would move from being "downstairs" children who helped peel vegetables to "upstairs" children who slept in big four-poster beds and had a nursery with a rocking horse and dolls' house. We pretended to sample the replica food, commenting on its deliciousness or disgustingness. Even though we had had a proper lunch that day we were allowed to go to the cafeteria and have tea and scones and cakes, it was all lovely. That gave us more energy to go exploring the museum again whilst Mum and Jenny stayed chatting.

During the time we were in Norwich there was a terribly sad incident pretty close to the lifeboat station in Cromer. Finn and Harry were both there on the beach. What happened was that two twelve-year-old boys, who we all knew a bit from our school before they went up to the high school, were fishing for crabs near the pier and decided to go for a deep paddle at about 8 . Josh was suddenly caught by a rip tide as he paddled, laughing and joking with Sam. At first Sam thought he *was* just joking but Josh felt himself quite suddenly to be out of his depth and being pulled by the current, he just couldn't get back. Sam tried to pull him out but didn't have the strength and there were very few people around because of the weather, only a couple of dog walkers who initially simply didn't realise that Sam was calling out to them for help and just carried on walking.

By the time Sam had run to the lifeboat station Josh was gone, pulled miles out by the strength of the current in no time at all. His body was found just before midnight, four miles down the coast, by two lifeboat crew members. This was in such stark contrast to our happy day, it haunted both me and Rachel for the rest of the holidays but would of course haunt Josh's family forever, and Sam too, they were really good friends.

And then a letter from Mum:

4th August 2001
Darling Amy,
It was so good to see you yesterday and lovely to see that you're back friends with Rachel. Jenny and I had a good old catch up too, as you saw. I hope you're pleased with your summer wardrobe; the tops might last a year or two, but your legs are getting so long I expect you'll soon grow out of the

jeans. Just let me know. Although neither of us are keen shoppers it was a fun way to do the necessaries and we can always do it that way again if you like.

The train to Cambridge was delayed by 20 minutes, signalling problem or something, but I met Julie on the station. Do you remember I used to be quite friendly with her when I worked at Delfin's? We went for a coffee in Pumpkin; that was another good catch up!

I'm looking forward to starting my new job in Cambridge in September but it's great to have the summer to get used to my new life and do some decorating. (Mum had got a job in student administration at Cambridge University, something to do with outreach and student recruitment, I think, though she had been told she may be asked to move between different departments at times as part of a training scheme the university ran and to help out when necessary.)

We're off to a family wedding next Saturday in Devon, Rob's niece, and we'll spend a week down there visiting other family members and generally exploring. We've rented a cottage by the beach. It will be lovely for the boys.

(I remember kind of blanking out those details when I read them, knowing that I was being sulky, childish; I would've loved holidays like that. I guess you're allowed to be childish aged 9, with no-one there to see it!)

We're thinking of getting a puppy when we get back from Devon.

(And that's when I felt real, nasty resentment, jealousy; it felt overwhelming, like a body blow. I'd always wanted a puppy, but I was told it would be too much to cope with. This wasn't fair. I felt all the positive thoughts about our day in Norwich vanishing just like that, and all the good feelings I had about Mum being happier, just went. I didn't like myself. I read on.)

We haven't completely decided yet, puppies do take a lot of looking after, I'm not sure quite how it would work but if I was at home more, well, we're thinking about it.

I hope your summer's going well, sweetheart. Are you looking forward to moving up to Year 6 in September? Top of the tree! Make the most of being a senior in junior school though. Haha, it'll be fun Is it 4th September that you go back? The dates in Cambridgeshire are slightly different sometimes.

I'll look forward to hearing all your news, my lovely girl. I've got a mobile

phone now, they're getting much better, cheaper too. When you go up to high
school, I'll get one for you if Dad's happy with that. My number is 0734
6712004.

   Take care of your darling self,
   Lots of love from Mum.

As I was still feeling really horrible, I hoped that Dad would think of getting me a mobile before Mum and just do it without telling her. I hated myself even more then. I dug my nails into my right hand at the crook of my thumb so much that it bled. That made me feel better though, strangely.

We did go back on the 4th September, a Tuesday, ready to be "top of the tree" as Mum put it, but we were all – Rachel, Lauren, Hannah and I – really worried about the reputation of the Year 6 class teacher, Mr Smithson. He was known to be very strict and could bellow across the playground and even the classroom like a clap of thunder. He was well known for it and I remember looking at the Year 6 children in my younger years to see if they were in constant fear; in fact, they never seemed to be, quite the opposite actually.

But before this scary event happened in our lives Angela decided to throw a party – 'Of course you "*throw*" a party, Amy, it's a good expression for throwing all the vital ingredients together,' she said, laughing. 'Food, drink, place or *venue*, as people say – I hate that word *venue*, it's so ugly – and people, well, they're obviously the most important thing.'

It was to be a wonderful late summer, evening party for Carrie's and Marianne's belated joint birthday celebration on their return from New Zealand and to celebrate Carrie's good GCSE results. Angela decided, after consulting her daughter and granddaughter, that it would be an early evening barbecue with Jason, who would be back by then, Dad and Granda doing the actual barbecuing.

'Keeps them out of the way, you see,' she whispered to me, 'and we'll make all the accompaniments, Amy, salads, etcetera. We'll buy the French sticks, there won't be enough time to make bread and still have it nice and fresh.'

Chapter 11

AND WHAT A PARTY IT was! Angela was right, you only needed the right mix of ingredients and it just happened. My whole "new family" was there and of course our group of four girls: me, Rachel, Lauren, Hannah, the two boys: Harry and Finn, and Iain, Rachel's younger brother, plus Carrie and eight of her close friends from school and some of their friends. This added another four boys and five girls from their year (Year 11) at school. Dad had invited two of his closest crew member friends and their wives and children, ranging in age from 6 to 11. He had also invited one of the teachers from Sheringham High who had been particularly supportive to him. Angela invited Jenny and Paul, Rachel's parents, and Jason and his children and her friend, Julianne, who lived in Norwich. Granda invited three of his neighbours who had become friends since he had moved, and Marianne invited about five or six friends from work who nearly all brought partners.

Angela was completely laid back about the whole enterprise. About a week beforehand when we were all sitting round the big table in the dining room Jason was there going through catalogues of the different types of glass that could be fitted in the studio. Whilst Angela fetched coffee and Carrie and I poured out cold drinks for ourselves and for Marianne, Jason suddenly asked:

'So, who's actually coming to this party?' Marianne, Carrie and I started listing the people. I remember Jason rolling his eyes and, as he went over to carry the coffee cups back to the table, he said to Angela very seriously,

'You do know that teenagers and parties can be quite a dodgy mix, don't you?'

'Oh, it'll be fine, don't worry, there'll be plenty of grown-ups around and they won't do anything too dreadful in front of the little ones surely? Besides, Finn and Harry seem to be sensible lads,' she replied blithely. Jason merely kind of grunted. Marianne and Carrie glanced at me quickly, I made a mock growling, cross face; they both grinned. I was unsure whether Rachel, Lauren, Hannah and I counted as little ones in Angela's eyes.

'Well,' Jason was guarded, cautious in his reply, 'there certainly needs to be rules and we need to police them a bit. What about alcohol?'

'I'll make a fruit punch, a mildly alcoholic one for the 15-and-over-year-olds, they're allowed to drink alcohol at home, even younger actually, but 15 and over is recommended. Then I'll make a non-alcoholic fruit punch for the younger ones and we'll have the usual range of lemonade, coke and all that.'

'Hmmm, yes, well,' Jason looked unconvinced. 'They'll bring some stronger stuff you mark my words, disguised in ordinary soft drinks bottles, you'll see.' He glanced across at us and winked. 'Obviously you realise that I remember all the tricks, and yes, I was a teenager once.'

'Well, we'll confiscate any suspicious looking bottles as they come in,' Marianne said brightly. This time Carrie rolled her eyes. 'You *can't* do that, Mum, you just *can't*. It would be *so* embarrassing. We just make a no spirits rule, that was what they did at Louise's 15th birthday party,' she said. 'The boys'll want to bring beer or cider and the girls'll bring those little bottles, you know…'

'Okay, good idea, love.' Marianne turned to Angela, 'we'll get Carrie to tell them, Mum, it'll be fine.' Jason still looked sceptical, I noticed, as he declared,

'I think the third rule, just one more rule, should be no going off piste. We'll have to set garden boundaries, it's just too dangerous having them wandering down to the beach, on the cliffs etcetera. So: no alcohol to under 15's, no spirits, no wandering out of the garden.'

'Fine, fine,' Angela replied, still blithe, and started poring over the catalogue again.

I noticed Jason catching Marianne's eye and shrugging helplessly but with a tolerant grin on his face. Angela remained blissfully happy about the whole thing. Of course, I told Rachel all about this discussion, we looked at each other excitedly; it felt fun to be part of a teenage and grown-up party. Upcoming Year 6 fears felt far away then. I still had not replied to Mum's letter, I thought I'd wait until after the party or even until I went back to school. I still felt sulky resentment at that stage.

That last week of August brought with it some reminders that autumn was not far off. The leaves on the trees were very dark green and looked tired, getting ready to drop, it seemed, in just a few months. There were some chilly gusts of wind and the nights were certainly drawing in. Meanwhile Dad had been asked if he could contribute to some of the safety talks and mock-up rescues which were to take place at Caister on the late August Bank Holiday Monday as part of the farewell celebrations and thanks for the decommissioning of the *Sheila Bray*.

The *Sheila Bray* was a Waveney-class lifeboat which had seen fifteen years' service and was held in great affection by all the lifeboat crews around the coast despite the well-known rivalry between them. She was credited with having saved thirty-two lives and was to become a floating museum maintained by volunteers. This rivalry was always put firmly on the back burner when they were involved in joint rescue missions, Dad had explained to me, adding:

'Obviously it would be, Amy, more important things at stake during a shout and the rivalry is just banter really.'

Dad was upbeat, busy, loving his new job. Angela and Marianne thought the traffic would be bad, but Dad wasn't worried. It was just going to be the four of us this time, parents and children, Dad and me, Marianne and Carrie, Dad driving, he was getting far fewer headaches now. Carrie was becoming a real friend to me, I remember, yet strangely, unlike Rachel, and even Hannah, I felt she was always holding a little bit of herself back. I decided it was because she was older. I detected the same trait in Marianne, not aloofness exactly, but a kind of wariness, as I thought of it, a holding back, a little watchful. But on this trip, they both seemed to let go a bit. It was fun, Carrie and I often talk of it even now.

Dad was at his absolute best, in control of things, knowledgeable in a good way, light-hearted. He explained to us that Caister Lifeboat Station was the first completely independent lifeboat station, a sign of true grit and determination, he said, because the RNLI decided to close the station in 1969 after 124 years of running it. There was a huge public outcry as the Caister station held the record for more lives saved at sea than at any other lifeboat station in the British Isles. Nothing daunted, he told us, the crew decided to launch an independent lifeboat station, which went into service on the very day the RNLI withdrew. This enterprise was led by the veteran mechanic, Jack Skipper Woodhouse, Dad said, and he became even more well-loved and respected in the town. They started with a small, fibreglass boat, followed by an inflatable, he explained and the Caister Volunteer Rescue Service was formed to maintain the long tradition of saving lives at Caister. Energetic fund-raising began and continues so it felt good still to be part of that today.

The first surprise for us that day was that we headed off towards the boatshed in Cromer, not towards the main A149. Dad was singing away to himself, specifically: *'Oh I do love to be beside the seaside...'*

'Dad,' I called from the back, 'what's going on?'

'Going on?' he called back. 'We're going on... here we are, we're going on a boat to Caister. Haha. Much less traffic: should take about three and a half hours. It's much longer than by car but much more fun. Anyway, this good old workhorse, the *Sallyann,* the ALB, is needed for one of the demonstrations so I've been asked to bring her along and some volunteer casualties. That's you lot, I'm hoping, by the way. We're going to pick up Tim, the mechanic, and Luke as navigator at the station.' This was going to be great; I wished then that Rachel and the others were with us. I glanced over at Carrie to see how she was taking it. She was smiling quietly, just loving it. I can see her now trailing her slim hand through the water as we chugged steadily along, sometimes gazing out to sea, seemingly lost in her own thoughts.

The day was really busy, really hot and really fun. It was packed out which was great because being a major fund-raiser, one of several, most taking place throughout the summer months, the more people attending the better. Marianne, Carrie and I were volunteer casualties of various types and we all put our acting skills to good use. We gave out stickers and bracelets and pens, handed out safety quizzes, and collected them in. This was for a competition and the first prize was a voucher for entry to Thrigby Hall Wildlife Park for a family of four, second prize was tickets for two people to the Hippodrome Circus in Great Yarmouth, third prize was one free entry for a child with one adult to Sea Life in Great Yarmouth.

St John Ambulance crews were also kept busy that day, mostly with people fainting in the heat, the odd bee sting, and children with minor cuts, a sprained ankle and one child with what was probably a broken wrist. His parents took him off to the James Paget Hospital A and E department. His dad said he hoped it was just a fracture. The volunteer first aider explained, very tactfully, that a break and a fracture were the same thing, I already knew this actually as Dad had told me, but this boy's dad looked unconvinced just like my classmates had when I had insisted, aged 7, that they were the same thing. No teacher backed me up, I remember, and I will never forget the loss of faith I experienced in teachers that day.

Carrie and I took the opportunity to enquire about volunteering for St John Ambulance. We planned to start together as cadets in September having discovered that you had to be aged 9 and a half to 17. It was good that we could do this together and we completed the forms there and then. Dad and Marianne were really pleased, always useful skills, they said, and good for CV's. Carrie explained to me about CV's, and I remember that Dad told me why it was St John Ambulance, not St John's as most people mistakenly referred to it; understandably, he said.

I loved it when Dad shared his knowledge of interesting facts in this way. He explained that it was an international organisation whose origins dated back to eleventh century Jerusalem when the first Knights of St John set up a hospital to care for sick pilgrims. The eight-pointed cross, which the volunteers still wear, was worn even then by those first carers of the sick. He told us that the brand name and the logo is owned by the Most Venerable Order of the Hospital of St John of Jerusalem and its international office is in London. We had noticed, and been fascinated by, the white, eight-pointed cross which comprised four V-shapes joined at their vertexes so that the other two tips spread outwards. The UK branch of St John Ambulance was founded in the late nineteenth century, he told us, and each branch obviously has to abide by that country's rules: medical and legal, and their cultural norms. Despite its Christian sounding title, it's non-denominational, and Dad helpfully explained to me what that meant without me having to ask, I loved him for that.

'The organisation provides non-judgemental care for all-comers,' he explained proudly, 'just like we lifeboat people do, even for the idiots.'

At about 4pm some real action took place. We heard the maroons sound and several pagers bleeping. Out to sea, quite far out it seemed, we could just see a windsurfer waving. The Caister lifeboat was ordered to get out to him by the Marine Coastguard Agency. They arrived to find that he had injured his shoulder badly and couldn't get back in. He had been getting very frightened of course, was in pain and close to panic. He was taken to hospital by land ambulance. It was, by chance, almost the very first call out of the recently launched air ambulance, which had already been alerted but was stood down in readiness for more urgent cases. St John Ambulance provided shelter and reassurance for the casualty whilst awaiting the land ambulance.

We left Caister shortly after 6 and were back in Cromer by just after 8 following a beautiful, peaceful, evening trip back on a flat calm sea which scarcely stirred as we powered steadily along at just 16 knots per hour. We chatted mostly about the success and fun of the day on the way home but also, as the party was now only three days away, we made some more plans. Finn and Harry were to be in charge of the playlist we decided and remembered to think about vegetarian barbecue options, planning to remind Angela about that. As it was well after 8pm, but still warm, we decided to have takeaway fish and chips from *Mary Jane's* so we could still look out over the sea in the dying light. Eating fish and chips is quite a feature of my childhood memories, I realise.

Marianne and Carrie chatted about their New Zealand trip that evening. In line with their personalities they had been fairly quiet about it on arrival home mainly of course because of Jasper's death midway through their trip. But that evening Carrie started talking about the mermaiding culture in New Zealand, which was pretty strong, with lots of mermaiding clubs springing up. I remember Marianne putting her hand on Dad's wrist and saying lightly,

'It's alright, Doug, they're really, really safety conscious, don't worry. Mermaid tails are banned in public swimming pools. But there's a huge mythology around this antipodean mermaid which is interesting. She's not thought to be golden-haired, like the German *Lorelei,* and like Carrie,' she smiled across at her daughter who I thought was looking especially stunning that night, 'nor does she alternate between seal and woman like the Scottish *skelpie.* Her hair is dark and thick, like kelp. The most amazing thing about her is her tail. Carrie and I visited the mermaiding centre in Auckland; do you remember the guy talking about her tail, Carrie?' Carrie nodded.

'He said it was both translucent and opalescent, a combination of indigo, violet and green,' she said softly. It seemed to me that she could feel and see the tail as she spoke.

Opalescent was a new word to me but I loved it and immediately somehow knew what it meant. It was such a vivid picture that Marianne painted that day that I could easily understand Carrie's fascination with this culture, especially as she was so mermaid-like herself, the golden-haired type, kind of calm, remote at times but, as I have said, never exactly aloof. And her love of silky fabrics and her various artistic skills all added to the image somehow. Dad was looking from mother to daughter with an amused smile as Marianne continued to talk about this visit.

She told us that some people thought the sighting of a mermaid was akin to a good luck charm bringing good fortune and others likened it to a visionary experience, a sense of being uplifted. There was also an association with being imbued with artistic and poetic gifts after such a sighting.

'Mermaids' voices,' Marianne told us, 'were compared to choirs of women singers, melodious, lullaby-like, intensely soothing yet seductive (another new word for me) sometimes drawing people into the sea.'

That seemed terrifying. *Perhaps Carrie had actually seen the mermaid she was painting on the clifftop on the night of her accident*, I thought to myself.

Carrie spoke up then:

'I was telling Mum that there's a club in Caister, I talked to some people from it today, and there's a club opening up in Cromer next April. To be honest I'm not really into the whole swimming bit,' she laughed, looking at Dad, 'you'll be relieved to hear that, but I thought I'd offer to do some painting commissions via the club, I'm looking into it. I could also make costumes and things. It's that side of it I love, all those shimmery, beautiful materials.'

Marianne chipped in, 'I think it's a great idea actually, she's so good at it, but better get in quick, love, before the pc brigade start accusing the mermaiders of cultural misappropriation! You know what they're like. It's such a niche market too. Doug might be able to help you set up a website, global appeal and all that.'

This was some years before the local university made international news headlines with this issue caused by the lovely *Pedro's* Mexican restaurant in Norwich handing out sombreros to students at UEA during Freshers' Fair. The restaurant staff argued that this *celebrated* Mexican culture and was not "racist", as the Students' Union accused of them of being, but they withdrew the promotion, nonetheless. The Union was criticised widely for its hypocrisy as one of its annual events called *Pimp my Barrow* included several challenges that could be deemed "racist". Several other events were similarly criticised all over the country.

But on that sultry evening I just remember Carrie replying thoughtfully,

'Yep, but I still want to study Art at uni and I'll need money while I do that.' She hugged her knees, 'It's exciting. Oh, Amy, you wait 'til you can just study the subjects you really like and ditch the rest, it's a good feeling, it really is. And I'm nearly there, at last.' She sighed in relief.

That felt an age away to me then, with scary Mr Smithson's Year 6 class and the whole of even scarier Year 7 and high school ahead of me, but it was lovely to hear Carrie talking about her ideas and seeing her excitement. Dad obviously thought so too, he was looking at her, sharing her excitement.

'Sure, I'll help with that. It'll be fun. I can help with promotion via the Tourist Board too of course. A good project for the deep, dark days of autumn and winter, I think.'

Marianne mentioned that she'd told Granda about the idea and he thought it was just great.

'His silversmith contacts could be useful too, he thought,' Marianne added. 'And Doug can give safety talks to the clubs, brilliant!' Marianne explained to us that as the mermaiding culture had taken off in New Zealand in such a big way people were making links with Maori tradition. 'Fodder for another interesting school project perhaps, Amy?' she grinned at me.

As we sat chatting and eating the best fish and chips ever the last of the daylight faded into the warm, silken, star-studded darkness, kindly, non-threatening, and I felt an all too rare deep sense of contentment which I told Carrie about as we waited for the bill to arrive. Later, aged about 13 or 14, I think, I called this rare feeling: *blissful wellbeing and contentment,* shortened to *bwc,* and it became a catchphrase which Carrie and I used and still do. She smiled at me then, catching her fine, silky hair up in one hand, making a ponytail, letting it out again and shaking it into its original position, one of the many mannerisms which I loved about her . Back then, that evening, it seemed that the world was everyone's oyster as we finished off with Norfolk ice creams and headed for home.

Chapter 12

IT HAS BECOME A FAMILY catchphrase now: *It was not without incident, I grant you,* usually intoned in a rather tight-lipped, raised-eyebrows, wry monotone. This was how Angela summed up the party when discussing it afterwards, but she certainly saw the funny side. Still does.

Looking back from this vast span of eleven years now as I tell this story I see myself as a child who seemed to be almost permanently worried then, looking for nuances and meanings in people's expressions, conversations – everywhere really, trying to make sense of it all. Eleven years is of course a lifetime in one sense in that I was 9 years old when this story really started with the rescue and I write eleven years later, aged 20.

The first thing is that the *bwc* feelings I experienced eating fish and chips on the prom at Cromer that evening were indeed fleeting. On arrival back at Angela's, Jason was just leaving, it was 10.45pm. Apparently there had been some hitch in the roof design causing the builders to ask him to have a look at it and he had been working on that in the only time available to him. I noticed Marianne was cool to the point of hostility towards him. This shocked me; Marianne had worked with him for years, Jason was great; my friends and I all liked him, Carrie was always more guarded, but that was just how she was, as we knew.

Carrie headed straight for bed when we got home but I wanted to tell Angela all about our exciting day. Dad said, kindly as ever, that we were all tired, the adults would be up early, and all the news could wait for tomorrow. Angela was lovely, gentle, smiling, unfazed by Marianne's behaviour towards Jason, it seemed, and the sudden tensions which had arisen out of nowhere.

'I'll look forward to hearing all about it tomorrow, Amy love, you go on up and sleep well.' She kissed the top of my head. As I left, Dad went out to the car to bring in his backpack and I heard him say lightly to Marianne,

'Well, that's his story and he's sticking to it, I suppose.'

'Oh, Doug, don't, just don't please.' This was said quite sharply. What could it all mean? I was worried. But, as I climbed into bed, I could feel my eyes closing almost before my head touched the pillow. *Sea air, Amy love, sea air, it gets you that way,* I could nearly hear Granda saying this as I drifted off into a sound sleep.

It was agreed by all generations present that the party itself was an all-round, cracking success, despite the *incidents.* Everyone felt it should be an annual event.

'Perish the thought,' muttered Dad jokingly and Jason nodded in ready agreement.

Everyone, all the younger guests that is, had stayed the night apart from Lauren who needed to be home early the next day as she and her family were going to her grandparents in Devon for the last weekend of the holidays, one of their own family traditions.

So, the *incidents:* first off, the saintly, reliable Finn got drunk, really drunk and was very sick about three times, but was also very funny. Jason talked to him, *man to man* about the dangers of mixing drinks:

'Just find something you like, lad, and stick to it. You don't want to mess with these silly, sparkly things the girls bring, they're lethal. My advice is to stick to beer, nice and wholesome, manly, cheaper, not so many calories either, though certainly you have no need to worry on that count.' Two of the girls in Carrie's year, mainly friends with Harry, got drunk too and were sick but they weren't funny like Finn.

Next, despite the rules, laid down in friendly but no uncertain terms, two of the girls, Laura and Sarah, Carrie's friends, whose younger brothers were on the periphery of Finn and Harry's friendship group, took off for a walk shortly before 8pm, wanting to watch the sunset over the sea. It was well known that despite these stretches of North Norfolk beaches being basically in the east of the country you could actually see the sun both rise and set over the sea from May onwards, most spectacularly from the end of Cromer pier, close to the lifeboat station. Dad had explained to me that this was because Cromer pier extends into the North Sea in the direction north by north-east. The girls knew they could see Cromer pier from Angela's nearest bit of beach at East Runton.

Harry and Carrie came shamefacedly to tell Dad and Marianne that the two girls had wandered off. Dad and Marianne were sitting chatting quietly having cleared away and cleaned up the barbecue together. Jason and Angela were nowhere to be seen at that moment. Dad went pale and swore; something I rarely heard him do.

'Jesus Christ! The idiots! I expect they went out just in their party dresses and party shoes too, little idiots!' Carrie said she could guess where they would have gone. Harry offered to gather about three of the boys and go and look for them.

'Good lad,' I remember Dad looking at him approvingly, 'do that but I'm coming with you. I know exactly where Carrie means. No, Carrie, you stay here. Have they replied to your texts? Signal's terrible here. Idiots!' he said again. 'I'll just tell Angela, where is she? And Jason? He could come along too.'

'I saw them heading out to the studio a little while ago, they're probably checking the rain isn't coming in,' I said and noticed Dad glance at Marianne, his look was unfathomable.

A gentle but persistent summer rain had just started usefully bringing everyone inside.

'Right, love, thanks, I'll nip out. Coats needed everyone and some spares for the girls, I'm sure they didn't bring any, it was still very warm when they arrived. Can you rustle up some coats, Amy? Angela's got a stack of likely looking jackets hanging outside the downstairs loo.' I went to get the coats but also decided to slip out to the studio quickly – I knew it would take me less than five minutes to run out there – to see if Jason would go with them. I wanted another grown-up man to be with Dad; it felt important and I still felt protective of my brave Dad at times.

And so it was that I saw them: Angela and Jason, standing close together, his left hand rhythmically stroking her left buttock. Rachel and I always found that word hilariously funny and sometimes repeated it multiple times to each other, faster and faster until we couldn't speak for laughing... well, you had to be there. I found myself thinking of that now with one part of my brain while with the other part I felt actual shock and also revulsion. It was obscene, a word I had learnt only recently but it felt right here. What was happening? Why was Angela not moving away? I needed to stop it happening, so I just retreated slightly then rushed in calling out before I had them in view:

'Angela, Jason, two of the girls have gone out, Dad's going to look for them with some of the boys, he wants you to go too, Jason, quick.'

Fair play to Jason, without hesitation he came with me to the waiting group having grabbed his coat on the way. I quickly gave the boys some coats. They had found enough torches (which Angela always kept handy in case of power cuts) and set off towards the beach and cliffs. Angela returned to the party and provided reassurance in her normal, carefree way:

'Silly girls, but at least it's a warm night, they'll be chilly though in their party dresses.' She behaved as if nothing had happened which I suppose for her nothing *had* happened in a way, after all she didn't know I had seen her and Jason in that compromising position; the strange phrase felt apt.

Marianne was much more worried and really cross with the two girls.

'They've been very silly but we're responsible for them, Mum. I'm just thinking how I would feel if I was one of their parents thinking they were safely here at a house party.' Carrie looked stricken; she too was cross with them:

'I should never have invited them; I knew they were idiots. Finn and Harry said they could be sort of okay out of school but now they've ruined the party.'

This wasn't really true to be honest as most people continued dancing to the playlist or talking in small groups, either just not worried or not understanding the potential dangers. This was before the days of everyone having mobile phones. Although mobile phones were just beginning to take off then teenagers didn't yet routinely have them; it seems hard to imagine those days now. I knew Dad had a pager when he was on lifeboat duty, but he wasn't on duty that night, he wasn't even allowed back to volunteer crew duties yet. That wasn't to be until the middle of September after another medical check-up.

It felt as if we waited for hours for news; in reality it was probably about fifty minutes, fifty long minutes. I asked Carrie how she'd known where they'd be.

'There's a kind of wooden shack,' she said, almost reluctantly it seemed, 'just about to fall into the sea now, it used to be used by fishermen to store bait and stuff, I think. Your dad knows it. Some people from school go there.' She hesitated then. 'Oh, Amy, you really don't want to know what they get up to, and I'm not going to tell you.'

The search party arrived back with the two girls, Laura and Sarah, at about 9.30; it was pitch dark and raining more heavily by then. The two looked sheepish and were very chilly, their shoes and legs mud-spattered and scratched to bits by brambles. Angela suggested they have a nice hot shower and a warm drink. She went to find them each some jogging bottoms, sweatshirts and a clean pair of fluffy socks to put on too. Marianne told them off in no uncertain terms, Carrie seemed to have made herself scarce, but I found her making Dad some hot chocolate in the kitchen while he had a quick shower in the other bathroom.

The next "incident" occurred at shortly after 10pm. One of Jason's sons, Jo, aged 6, running around, excited to be up way beyond his bedtime, was stung badly by a bee or a wasp, we were not sure which as it buzzed away so quickly, having been nestling inside a can of drink, as they say in Norfolk, a sugary, fizzy drink. Jo's lips and tongue became so swollen so quickly that Jason rushed him off to hospital believing it would be quicker than waiting for the ambulance. He was given antihistamine and gradually the swelling went down but he was admitted to the children's ward overnight for observation. Jason stayed with him knowing that his other children, Ben, 4, and Tiffany, Tiff, aged 3, would be safe in the care of Angela and Marianne and Dad. The two of them had been tucked up already on spare mattresses in Angela's room.

I felt pleased actually that Jason was out of the house; I'm ashamed to say this now but I remember it so well. It was if the party had been tainted by his presence, his actions. Angela was just her normal self, but I simply couldn't look her in the eye. I went off to find Rachel, but she and Harry were dancing wildly. I looked away, unable to watch, I wished Harry was dancing with me. I was confused by this feeling, the violence of it took me by surprise. Finn and I joined them, I got lost in the music, and the party suddenly felt fun again, but different, a more wild, reckless sort of fun.

The next "incident" was that one of the girls, Becca, a friend of the two who had wandered off, was sick, very sick, without managing to get to the bathroom. Angela and Marianne dealt with this between them and then set about finding blankets, sleeping bags, and some folding camp beds for people to sleep on. Lauren's dad came to collect her at about midnight as planned, then, unexpectedly, just after half past midnight, Laura's dad arrived to take her home as she had phoned him having changed her mind about staying the night. I wondered if it was because Marianne had told the girls off. Marianne told Laura's dad about the two of them wandering off with Laura standing at the front door looking ashamed. I felt embarrassed at first that she had "told" on them, but Angela said it was the right thing to do. Her dad told her off really soundly then and there and took her off home. Marianne explained to Sarah that she would have to tell whoever came to pick her up tomorrow too. Sarah looked a bit sulky but said nothing.

Rachel was sharing my bedroom, we had put a spare mattress on the floor, Carrie's two closest friends, Chloe and Emma, were sharing her bedroom, and Harry and Finn offered to keep an eye on the rest of Carrie's and their friends who were sleeping downstairs. They were instructed by Angela, Dad and Marianne to call one of them if there were any problems. Finn and Harry were a good team in that way. The rest of the adult guests who stayed slept either in Marianne's or Angela's room or in the Studio. Rachel's parents and Jason had brought four extra camp beds between them. Dad was busy all this time bagging up empty bottles and rubbish to take out to the respective wheelie bins. He had had a shower on return from his unexpected, late night walk to find the girls and seemed completely restored energy-wise following another hot drink and some toast made for him by Marianne.

Rachel, Harry, Hannah, Finn (who had just about sobered up but was still being very funny) and I started helping clear the rest of the worst of the party debris, especially bottle tops which somebody could have trodden on and hurt themselves. We either threw away or put away the leftover food, and it felt companionable, the five of us together, being sensible.

I still couldn't make eye contact with Angela though and I was conscious of being rudely offhand when she asked me very kindly if Rachel and I needed another spare duvet. She asked me if I was feeling alright, again very kindly, but luckily the shrill sound of the telephone interrupted what would have been my non-committal response. Angela went to answer it and I heard her saying how pleased she was that Jo was sleeping soundly, and that the swelling had gone down. She told Jason that the two little ones were fast asleep and that she hoped that he managed to sleep a bit himself. I didn't want to hear any more to be honest so I kind of slunk away not wanting to hear Angela speaking to Jason not only as if nothing had happened, nothing *obscene* that is, but also I just didn't want to hear her caring, soft, concerned tones as she spoke to him, almost tenderly, it seemed, about the sleeping arrangements for parents on the children's ward.

After this the party wound down naturally, the only other minor incident was finding one of the girls, I can't remember who it was now, one of Carrie's friends, asleep in the empty bath, she just wanted to lie down she said. Marianne miraculously found her another folding bed to sleep on, a spare sleeping bag and tucked her up on it. The rest of us went off to bed after raiding the freezer for some *Ben and Jerry's* ice cream which I suddenly remembered Angela buying specially for the party. Harry and Finn settled downstairs into their own sleeping bags, which they had brought with them, but they were ready to leap into action, they said, if required. They were both just a bit tipsy by now, as Dad called it, but they had stuck to beer so seemed to feel alright, just mellow, as they said to each other, laughing in a kind of languid way, mellow indeed.

The next morning Marianne and Dad offered to cook breakfast for everyone before parents arrived to take their children home but the five of us – Rachel, me, Harry, Hannah and Finn – and Jason's two were the only ones who wanted it. It was delicious. Marianne had put herself in charge of getting Jason's two little ones up and dressed. Angela had been up very early, painting in her half-finished studio, Marianne told us, while the light was just as she wanted it. I was pleased that she wasn't in the house. I busied myself pouring out orange juice for those who wanted it whilst Carrie made teas and coffees all round including for the cooks.

We then lounged about watching little children's cartoons on television, Tiffany and Ben were quite sweet but a bit annoying at times. I thought they must be missing their dad and felt a bit sorry for them and I quite liked it when Tiff snuggled up next to me to watch the cartoons with her thumb in her mouth. Dad and Marianne cleared up the breakfast, and people drifted off as their parents arrived. Marianne made a point of telling Sarah's mum about the two wanderers when she arrived to pick up her daughter and another friend. Marianne purposely told her with Sarah, one of the two miscreants, as Granda called them, chuckling a little as he said it, standing at the front door looking more shamefaced than ever as her mum told her off in no uncertain terms, just as Laura's dad had. At first again I thought she was being a bit of a snitch and Carrie was mortified, embarrassed by her mother, but Dad explained to both of us that their parents needed to know and that they would deal with it as they saw fit. Carrie looked mutinous, but, though I was much younger, I could see Dad's point especially as Angela had made the same point when Marianne had told Laura's dad. Dad looked at Carrie fondly and I remember him saying,

'If you ever become a mother, Carrie, you'll understand, you really will.'

After lunch Jason arrived home with Jo who seemed full of beans and excited, keen to tell us about his hospital stay and all the toys in the playroom attached to the ward. I hoped they would all go home but he, Marianne, Jenny, Paul and Angela decided to take the three little children off for a walk asking if we wanted to join them. We all felt really tired and decided to lounge around watching more television; it felt good to be the familiar foursome plus Hannah. It seemed a bit mean putting it like that to myself but that's how it felt. Rachel's parents said they would take all five – Harry, Hannah, and their three – home in two cars on return from the walk. And when they and Jason and his three eventually left after a snack lunch it felt as if the dreaded Year 6 loomed even closer. School started on Tuesday 4th September; it was now Sunday afternoon.

Chapter 13

YEAR 6 TURNED OUT TO one of my favourite school years of all time. We were indeed "top of the tree" as Mum had said, without the fear of the move to high school looming too close, and I really liked Mr Smithson. He was fun and, yes, he could be pretty terrifying at times but only with the kids who played up constantly and were rude and disruptive. The rest of us liked it when he bellowed at them and it worked. That was partly what made the year so good come to think of it. I also detected that he was a very kind man; later, when looking back at teachers I had known, I came to realise that he was one who truly had our best interests at heart, probably why he was so furious with kids who wasted their own and others' time. I realise how "grown-up" I sound now, writing this!

We had two Broad Topic Projects (BTP's) to do during this year, one to be completed by Christmas and one by Easter. I decided to look at mermaiding having discussed the idea with Dad and Carrie. Dad looked doubtful, he had a real "thing" about it he admitted, purely from the safety angle, but we had a good discussion about that aspect, and we felt I could include safety as part of the topic. The project would encompass some history, going back as far as ancient times, some geography, I would look at the Maori tradition of mermaiding too, some design and technology because of the costumes, and of course safety aspects as part of PSHE.

For the second 'BTP' I decided to look at the lifeboat service, past, present and future. Everyone knew my dad was a volunteer lifeboatman and found it exciting to hear about the shouts. We had to write down our ideas for our projects during an English lesson in the first week of term, giving our reasons for choosing the topic, what we planned to cover and how we planned to tackle it. We had to write this using the headings: Rationale, Method and Scope. We would get feedback and guidance from Mr Smithson and it all felt very grown-up. I couldn't wait to get started.

A week after this promising start to the term though the world appeared to tilt on its axis, metaphorically speaking. What was to become known simply as 9/11 shook the entire world to its very core it seemed. Like everyone I remember exactly how and where I heard the news. The head teacher, Mr Stevens, and deputy head teacher, Mrs Wood, decided to break it to all the classes individually having first called the two children whose fathers were working in the Twin Towers into his office where the news was broken to them on their own and separately from the rest of the school hearing it. One of the two children was in Year 5, Lucy Hanson, and the other in our year, Year 6, Simon Smith. The Head and Deputy Head had called each class teacher out to explain to them too first.

I learnt the word *cataclysmic* that day. This was later, on the tv news bulletins which ran the story of the unfolding disaster continuously. At school I remember mostly the shock and incomprehension on all the adults' faces as they seemed to struggle to explain these atrocious acts of terrorism to us and to tell us that two of our school community had fathers working in the Twin Towers. Both men died that day. The children were away from school for about two weeks and were treated somehow deferentially on their return.

I remember on hearing the news having an urge to go home right then and there and talk to both my parents about this, not Angela, not Marianne, not Carrie but my own two parents, together. Impossible of course but at home later in the day I told Dad I wanted to ring Mum and I wanted him with me while I did. There was an upstairs phone in Angela's bedroom, and she said we could of course use that for some privacy. This was at about 4pm. Unbelievable as it seems now Mum hadn't heard the news as she had been out all day at a remote beauty spot just outside Cambridge on her own, on impulse, she told us.

I remember Dad spoke to her first explaining that I was there and that I wanted to talk to her with him there too. I remember so clearly him saying,

'It's all pretty emotional here. Here's Amy for you now,' and her light-hearted, almost giggly response as he handed me the phone.

'It's pretty emotional here too, I can tell you,' she laughed excitedly. I wasn't sure if she still thought she was talking to Dad, but she went on immediately to say,

'Obviously it's early days but I discovered this morning that I'm pregnant, only Rob knows at the moment. I'm very happy and excited about it.' For the first time then I understood the expression *lost for words* and handed the phone back to Dad without saying anything.

Dad said, 'Magsy? Amy's just handed me back the phone. What's up?'

Still giggly and excited, I guessed, she said exactly the same to Dad. He looked worried, slightly puzzled but spoke to her tenderly.

'I'm very happy for you, Magsy, believe me, I really am. You must look after yourself and not work too hard. Things must be pretty busy for you with your new job and the children. I'm guessing if you've been out, away from civilisation all day, that you haven't heard the news?' He went on to explain what had happened in America. I slunk away.

I remember that clearly too, and even using that word, *slunk,* to myself as I did so, as if I was telling the story to someone else, living outside my own experience, looking on. I even remember thinking it would do as an example of onomatopoeia which I could use in my homework that very evening. We had to do an exercise for English homework where we wrote sentences showing examples of things like similes, metaphors, and onomatopoeia. I loved that word, which I had first learnt when Angela had told me about the slapping, boinging, glugging sound needed when beating batter for Yorkshire pudding with a wooden spoon.

'It's only when it makes those sounds, those *actual* sounds,' she informed me emphatically, 'that you're really getting air into the mixture to make it rise. Good words aren't they?' I remember her saying gleefully, onomatopoeic, each one!' Of course she then did one of her double takes: 'Sorry, Amy, maybe you haven't heard of the word yet?' We then went onto think of lots more examples.

It was fun as usual, cooking with Angela, but when we came to learn the word "onomatopoeia" in class I remember suddenly hating myself and feeling so, so embarrassed as I was the only one who put their hand up when the class was asked if we knew what it meant. I remember trying almost literally to shrink myself lower down in my chair and hide behind my desk. It was horrible. Up until then I had always loved English lessons and homework.

Why on earth I remembered all this trivial pain and hurt that I had once suffered in class so clearly and suddenly on this terrible day in world history when the Twin Towers were destroyed and so many lives lost, destroyed, families shattered, I have no idea. It was so strange to remember and dwell on this irrelevant detail at that moment. Perhaps it was a kind of self-protective turning away from the reality, the shock of the events, similar to Dad's post traumatic transient amnesia. I don't know. I do know that what I could not do then was analyse or interpret my own feelings. I just knew I didn't after all want to talk to Mum. I decided to shut myself in my bedroom and make a start on my homework. That felt like a bit of normality in a world literally tumbling all around me. I had control over that, and I wanted to produce good work for Mr Smithson.

I remember I had hardly spoken to Angela since the party other than being superficially polite. I had overheard her asking both Dad and Carrie if they knew whether I had started my periods as she felt I seemed to be moody and was wondering if it was hormones. For the record I hadn't, though I knew a couple of girls in my class had. The rest of us were a mixture of envious, awed, scared, and revolted by this.

After what seemed like ages but was probably only about fifteen minutes there was a tentative knock on the door.

'Who is it?' I replied in neutral tones though normally I would have just said: "Come in".

'It's me,' said Dad's voice. I walked over and opened the door, pulling him by the hand inside. He sat in the chair by the window and said: 'Obviously I told Mum about the attacks in the States, explained about the kids in your school, how emotional it all was and how you had wanted to talk to her.' I remained silent and he continued: 'Mum felt bad that she had just blurted out her news like that, but I must admit I feel genuinely happy for her. It feels good to have something positive, new life, and a half-brother or sister for you Amy. Life goes on – sort of thing.' That had not occurred to me actually and I felt sudden real excitement.

'I love you, Dad, you're the kindest, loveliest man in the whole world.' And I remember climbing on to his lap, big as I was, for a cuddle in that lovely, welcoming, old armchair.

He hugged me close and tightly and we remained in that comforting, warm embrace for a few minutes until he said, seemingly half reluctant to end it:

'I'm going to cook tea now, Amy, it's sausages, baked beans and baked potatoes. I'll do them the quick way, so it won't be long. How's homework going?' He glanced over to the desk.

'Nearly finished,' I replied, 'I'm starving. Mr Smithson says being hungry is good for the brain for a little while, something to do with blood carrying oxygen not having to worry about digesting food, just preserving vital organs or something.'

'Sounds plausible,' Dad replied with a grin.

Jason was there that evening, wanting to see how the studio was progressing. Marianne had suggested asking Granda for tea so that he wasn't on his own watching the terrible events still unfolding in America. Jason had wanted the television on whilst we were eating, something that never happened at Angela's, but we all overruled him.

'We need a break, Jason, we'll hear how it's all going on in later news bulletins,' said Angela firmly. Carrie was very quiet, almost withdrawn. Marianne and Granda both tried in their separate ways to draw her out a bit.

'How's Year 12 going, Carrie love?' asked Granda gently. 'I know that some people find the leap to A-level quite hard and pressurised. Can be grim, I've heard.'

'Not too bad so far,' Carrie replied reflectively. 'It just seems as if it's all the teachers talk about, exams, exams, exams. I try to spend as much time as possible in the Art Room, it's more peaceful there and I can just get on with my Art coursework. We have triple Art on a Tuesday, my favourite day. The other subjects are annoying but I'm loving Biology at least.' She paused a bit but then, 'I just can't get Lauren out of my mind tonight, sorry, people.' Lauren was Lauren Smith, not "our" Lauren. She was the eldest sister of Simon, in my year, whose Dad had been working in the Twin Towers. She was in Year 12 with Carrie and they had another sister in Year 8, called Lilly, she always had to tell people it had two l's in it, apparently.

Marianne, who was sitting next to Carrie, reached across and gave her a spontaneous hug.

'Yes love, it's terrible for them and all the others, just terrible,' she shook her head as she spoke as if still unable to comprehend what had taken place.

'It just seems so quick for so many lives to be changed,' murmured Carrie, 'let alone all those who actually died, but at least they're out of it now. It's the ones left behind. I mean one minute we were strolling back from break, the next she was summoned to the Head's office. She's never in trouble so we couldn't think why. Then we had the assembly where he told us what had happened. She'd been collected by her uncle.' She shook her head as if trying to shake the dispel the images from her mind.

Angela had made a blackberry and apple pie with the blackberries they'd picked the weekend before, the Sunday after the party during their afternoon walk in fact, which now seemed a lifetime away. When she came back with it and served us all, I saw her eye Jason, and a brief nod passed between them.

'I have some other news for you all. Jason will be staying here for a bit which is very handy as the studio is at quite a crucial phase, but sadly he and Julia have decided to part ways as they've not been happy recently. The children will stay with their mother most of the time but will spend the odd weekend here – this house just expands as necessary as we know. One of the many things I love about it.'

I noticed Marianne and Carrie exchanged glances and I saw that Dad and Granda noticed that too. I felt then once more to be on the outside looking in, trying to make sense of it all. Without looking at Dad, I suddenly blurted out,

'I have some news too; I'm going to have a half-brother or sister.' It was Carrie I noticed mainly this time. She glanced at Dad, looked astounded, there was no other word for it, and then back at me,

'What do you mean, Amy?' she asked, a strained note in her voice.

'I am, it's true,' I remember saying this almost defiantly, as if to say: *and you'd better believe it.* 'Mum's going to have a baby, she told me and Dad today.'

'Oh, oh, I see. That'll be lovely for you then.' Carrie glanced at Dad again. He just looked surprised I had shared this news but all he said was:

'Yes, Mags told us today, but she's only just found out so...' His voice tailed off.

Marianne helped him out, mainly for mine and Carrie's sake, I think.

'What Doug means,' she explained, 'is that often, well, usually actually, people don't tell many people until they're about twelve weeks pregnant as sometimes miscarriages – when the baby dies inside – can happen and these are actually quite frequent in the first three months of pregnancy. I lost two early on before Carrie, she knows this, and my friend, Louise, lost one too.'

She turned towards Angela who responded sadly,

'Yes, love, you did and so did I. I lost one before Marianne early on. It's not something that's talked about much but it's such a loss, all that expectation. I was very young of course and people may have thought it was the best thing, but I just remember sobbing and sobbing. I learnt then that sobbing is a form of crying that specifically reflects loss, interesting,' she mused quietly, 'who'd have thought you could have different sorts of crying? So don't worry about telling us, Amy love, we're all more or less family and let's pray that all goes well for her and rejoice for her. Angela looked at all of us sitting round her table. 'What a day of revelations all round it is. In the midst of life, we are in death – or something. But it's lovely to hear about new beginnings on this dark, dark day. I suggest once we've cleared up that we go for an evening walk down to the beach while we still have light evenings, all too soon they'll be gone.'

And so it was that at the end of that world-turned-on-its-axis day we found ourselves walking along a deserted beach, everyone glued to the news no doubt, and I for one derived unexpected comfort from the simple, timeless beauty of watching the incoming tide creep slowly up the beach on that golden September evening.

Chapter 14

THE IMMEDIATE EFFECT OF JASON spending so much more time at Angela's, well, moving in really, was that often Dad and I would choose to go to Granda's; Marianne and Carrie spent less time than usual at Angela's too. Marianne was enjoying her Hungarian cooking lessons from Granda, but Carrie missed her safe space at Angela's, I could see that, and she told me that she always felt she had a special bond with her grandmother. She said the house at Overstrand felt empty and quite lonely with just her and her mum there, and her mum often worked late. She missed me and Dad as well as Angela, she said sadly.

But Jason now seemed somehow to make us all feel uneasy; it was hard to pinpoint why exactly and it certainly bothered Angela. It was strange because we sort of liked him too. Marianne muttered something vague about the work on the studio being noisy at times when Carrie was working, and it was, after all, her first year of A-levels, quite a step up in workload compared to GCSE's. I was in the kitchen when this conversation took place and it was obvious to me that Marianne knew that Angela knew that Marianne knew that this was a kind of "cover" for other, unspoken reasons.

Angela asked me about it one sunny Saturday when she invited me to help her make sandwiches as we were planning an all-day beach outing to Cromer. I loved those and I loved it when it was just us, the ever-expanding household, even though I also liked just being with my friends there.

'You could do the egg,' she prompted, 'I know how you love that machine!' Her tone was light-hearted, she was referring to the egg-slicer and yes, there was something about it that still really appealed to me.

'Yes, I'll help,' I readily agreed partly because I genuinely enjoyed helping and partly because I couldn't think of any excuse not to. I loved making picnics anyway.

It felt companionable in the warm, sunny kitchen; it was the last weekend in September, I think. Angela asked me how school was, what it was like being at the top of the school, those sorts of questions. I was able to talk about my BTP, Broad Topic Project, I explained it again in case she'd forgotten. It was going really well especially with Carrie being so interested and helping, even producing some drawings of costumes and samples of materials for me to stick in. I told Angela about this, chatting away just like old times. She asked me if I'd talked to Mum since she'd broken the news of her pregnancy and I had to admit that I hadn't. To be honest I had got over that searing stab of jealousy I'd felt when she first told me, all excited. I had genuinely been too busy to write to her and didn't want to ring in case Rob answered, though I recognised that to be the poor excuse it was. But Angela asking me that made me feel silly and a bit guilty, so I resolved to write to Mum during the weekend. I told Angela this, she seemed pleased.

After a while of working companionably together, the picnic taking shape temptingly, Angela said to me,

'I've always thought of you as very perceptive for your tender years, Amy,' she said carving some ham off the bone, 'so I'm wondering if you feel able to explain why people seem to take against Jason so much. It's upsetting us both, I have to say, and it would be good to get to the bottom of it.'

Whether it was the mention of the word "bottom" or what, I had a sudden vision of the sight of the two of them standing so close on the night of the party, Jason's hand… well, I didn't want to remember it but I also felt an almost uncontrollable urge to laugh at the memory, a strange mixture of reactions to Angela's question. I wished I could share this moment with Rachel, then and there and feel that delicious explosion of laughter between friends, laughter which sometimes comes from a release of tension, even more delicious when you're supposed to be quiet at school or serious, as now. I struggled to find an answer and then decided honesty was the best policy.

'I don't really know, Angela, to be completely honest.'

'So, it's not just our imagination then? That makes me so sad, I wonder what it's all about. But I do appreciate your honesty, Amy. Try and think a bit, it may help to tease things out. Jason's here to stay; it's important people know that. His divorce will be finalised by the end of next month. I've talked to Marianne, so she knows that, but she wasn't very forthcoming on her feelings about Jason being here either.' Angela sighed heavily as she zipped up the cool bag, so unlike her usual untroubled self.

'I will try and think about it and talk to Carrie too if you like?' I said. 'We may be able to pinpoint things a bit. I'm sorry it upsets you.' I really was and I made proper eye contact with Angela then for what felt like the first time since the night of the party and was struck by the sadness tinged with anxiety clouding her normally optimistic, open, carefree expression.

We were interrupted then by Granda, Marianne and Carrie arriving; she and Carrie had spent Friday night there after her cookery class with them both realising it would be easier to bring him over reasonably early in the morning for the Cromer outing. I rushed over to Granda to give him a hug as I always did. He, for one, was an unchanging, reassuring presence in my life. Feeling his freshly shaved face against mine, just that nice, slightly rough, feel of men's skin, the smell of his familiar shaving cream or after-shave, I was never quite sure which it was, and loving his responsive hug back, I felt all was well with the world after all and was looking forward to the day.

Jason and Dad loaded up the two cars between them. Angela drove Jason, me and Granda, and Marianne went with Dad and Carrie. It was very warm and sunny, the sea was flat calm and Mediterranean blue, like the sky. We set up camp on our favourite part of the beach, almost in sight of the lifeboat museum, near the slipway. Dad would be backwards and forwards up and down the pier to the station to see any of the team who were there; he enjoyed that. Harry and Finn were both on Assistant Lifeguard duty as part of trying to build up work experience before undertaking their beach lifeguarding training in Cornwall in a few years' time. The courses were always oversubscribed and there was intense competition to get onto one. They waved when they saw us but needed to be doing their patrols so couldn't come and chat. That was fine. The beach was busy, and we spotted them giving several families advice and saw Harry towing in a body boarder who had drifted out dangerously beyond the safe swimming area probably not even realising that he had.

We all swam lazily, the sea was fairly warm, being the end of the summer, but still had that characteristic North Sea bracing shock of cold when first going in and strength of current when swimming out, even at low tide. I remember the familiar feeling of exhilarating exhaustion, strange as that might sound, that feeling of grappling with an elemental force which leaves you weakened and humbled having been swept along helpless in its treacherous embrace. The suck and drag and sting of the shingle against my calves as I came out each time combined with the rattle and roar of the swirling stones, and the froth and foam at the water's edge reminded me of the sea's relentless, controlling power – truly a force to be reckoned with, as Dad never tired of reminding anyone who would listen.

Carrie was in and out the quickest of us all. I remember her pulling her wet hair back into a high ponytail as she dried, eager to get to her sketch book. Everything felt relaxed and easy, even Jason's presence seemed to be causing less silent hostility than usual; that felt good. He and Dad chatted easily and played an evenly matched game of beach bat and ball. I heard Dad telling him about some aspects of lifeboat volunteering, the sometimes repetitive nature of the training, the need to summon all reserves of energy and commitment on cold, wet and windy days at the same time as battling partners', husbands', wives' resentment, almost jealousy, he said, because of the time taken away from "family time". I was pretending to be lost in my book when this conversation took place, but I could hear Dad putting "family time" in inverted commas as he spoke. I wondered why exactly but that overheard conversation helped me to understand Mum a bit more, I realised.

It was strange to think how Angela, Marianne and Carrie, and Jason by a kind of default, had become so much a part of our lives, and we, I mean me, Granda, and Dad, a part of theirs. We had somehow melded into one, pretty harmonious unit, I thought to myself, looking at Granda and Angela deep in conversation. I overheard her recommending various natural remedies to ease Granda's arthritis which recently had been "playing up badly", as he put it.

Marianne asked if anyone wanted an ice cream. She suggested just a couple of us went as we could easily carry seven between us. There was an ice cream kiosk not far along from our camp but as the sun was hot at that time of day, we decided to take the smallest of the cool bags and to go for tubs, rather than cornets, for ease of carrying. We took everyone's first and second choices and Marianne suggested I would remember four and she would remember three.

As we walked along companionably Marianne asked me how my school project was going. I told her I had discovered that the mermaiding movement took safety seriously, running proper classes and how pleased Dad had been when I told him that. I also told her that I had finished the historical bit and that I had been surprised to learn that the whole movement dated back as far as 1382, according to scholars of the subject and how much they can ascertain from the period. It has to be remembered that mermaiding only became associated with "gender fluidity" much later. I discovered barely two years ago now, in 2010, I think, that the organisation, "Mermaids" had been providing support to parents and children encountering transgender issues as far back as 1995. I didn't explore this aspect in my school project, undertaken in 2001/2002, because I didn't know about it. Perhaps I saw mention of these terms but blocked it as I didn't understand it, perhaps felt fearful of it even.

Certainly, Carrie's mermaiding interest was more to do with its associated shimmering, opalescent beauty and quintessential femininity than with any perceived hermaphroditic qualities of mermaids; this I know for certain because we've talked about it quite recently. The whole concept appealed to the rather fey, mystical side of her artistic nature. To be honest, I don't know for sure but I believe that this idea was below the radar then and has only emerged as something to be not just treated with respect, which is fair enough, but almost revered, it seems, as I write now, aged 20 in 2011.

I told Marianne the story of Melusina as we walked along the water's edge before climbing the slope up to the kiosk on the promenade. As the waves slapped against the shingle, I could almost see the mythical half woman, half fairy in my mind's eye, her fish tail, sometimes referred to as a serpent's tail, swishing through the water catching the light. I had discovered this story in my research into the history of mermaiding.

'Melusina was one of three triplets whose mother, the Fairy Queen, Pressyne, met the king of Albany/Elynas, thought to be the old name for Scotland, while she was walking in the woods and she later agreed to marry him,' I explained to Marianne. 'This was on one condition though: that he agree never to see her giving birth,' I avoided eye contact when mentioning this detail, 'or bathing their children. When he broke this promise she punished him by locking him up in a mountain dungeon with all his treasure and fled with her three daughters.'

'Bit harsh, bit OTT,' Marianne interjected light-heartedly.

'Gets worse, much worse,' I replied. The legend felt too remote to take it seriously for both of us and I had found it confusing that the tale was told in different ways. I explained this to Marianne, and she agreed that she had never really related to Greek and Roman mythology, could never remember the names and whether they were male or female, human or animal, spirit or mortal. It was lovely chatting to her like this and we continued pondering the story as we joined the long queue for ice creams.

'Some tales say that when Melusina locked him up her mother punished her for doing so, by banishing her to the forest and ordering that her lower half change into a serpent every Saturday. Bit harsh again as you would say,' I said wryly, looking at Marianne's reaction. She was chuckling as I continued: 'So, when she met and married a poor, but handsome, nobleman who she met while wandering in the forest, she was stunningly beautiful by the way...'

'Of course she was,' Marianne interrupted with a grin.

'... she ordered him never to see her on a Saturday. But he took a peek as he became suspicious about what she did when she hid away...'

'Reasonable,' mused Marianne, 'I think I quite like the King of Scotland! And I suppose you're going to tell me curiosity killed the cat, or she turned him into a cat or something?'

'Well, sort of but not quite. What happened was that he called her a serpent...'

'Hmmm, reasonable again,' muttered Marianne watching a toddler's loud distress as his ice cream slipped out of his small hands landing on the gravel path beside his buggy in a soggy, melted mess. The ice cream stallholder quickly saved the day and everybody's ear drums by appearing with another in a tub and a wafer biscuit too. The hot, red-faced little boy looked adoringly up at him through his grimy, tear-streaked face and peace reigned once more as the queue patiently shuffled forward.

'...and she was so cross she flew off, never to be seen again. They had ten sons by the way, and they had improved the value of the land by felling trees and growing crops,' I finished the tale.

'Well there's a story, Carrie loves all that sort of thing, loves painting mythological creatures. Here we are, it's us next.'

We got all the ice creams back to our little gang safely and once we'd finished them Jason suggested a walk along the beach towards Overstrand. I immediately offered to stay and keep Granda company. This meant we could both keep an eye on our things and Carrie wanted to finish her sketches so Marianne, Angela, Jason and Dad set off taking the rubbish across to the bin on the way.

I tidied up the rugs a bit and lay on my back feeling the warm sun on my face making muted red, dancing colours on my closed eyelids, giving me that muzzy, hazy feeling of well-being that you get on summer days.

'*Bwc,*' I called out to Carrie drowsily. She looked across at me and smiled and I drifted off to sleep.

When I woke up, feeling groggy and wondering for a moment where I was, the foursome had still not returned but I realised to my surprise that not that much time had actually passed. Granda was looking through his binoculars back towards the cliff.

'Look at this, Amy love,' he called out to me. 'It looks as if Harry and Finn are making themselves useful.' I went across and peered through them at the unfolding drama of a cliff rescue. I could see Harry and another lifeguard, not Finn, and a collection of bright colours seemingly entangled in the high branches of the only tree for miles. One of the colours translated itself into Harry's Assistant Lifeguard T-shirt, red and yellow. He was wearing a bright yellow hard hat too as he worked high up in the branches untangling ropes and twisted metal in the tree.

Apparently, according to the local newspaper and television reports we saw later, the hang-glider, who we had seen earlier, had become stuck eighty feet up. We then heard the whirr of the East Anglian Air Ambulance arriving and watched its descent on to a bit of the cliff where there was a large green sward, normally crowded with families and dogs enjoying the space. The police had quickly cleared the area prior to its arrival.

Finn came over as he spotted us watching through the binoculars.

'Wish I was up there,' he said with a sheepish grin. 'I know it's bad to want to see people get into trouble but it's what we're here for and it's exciting. Harry got there first,' Finn spoke almost enviously adding, 'I was bringing in yet another family on an inflatable who had drifted too far out. We think the guy up there on the cliff is not badly injured, just stuck, but it's a tricky rescue, for sure.' He stood watching for a few minutes then, 'I'd better carry on with my patrol now though, there'll still be idiots about,' and with a cheery wave he was off. The drama was over in about half an hour and I asked Granda if he'd like me to fetch him a cup of tea from the kiosk.

'That would be lovely, Amy, thanks. And something for you and Carrie, here's some cash.'

Carrie and I set off companionably. There was no queue this time and we were quickly back with polystyrene cups of steaming tea and three chocolate bars. As we tucked into the snack, I decided that now was the time to metaphorically test the water a bit regarding Jason, seizing the opportunity before the others returned.

'I love these beach days, but I love them better without Jason,' I said being deliberately provocative. I noticed Granda glance across at Carrie who was simply gazing out to sea shading her eyes against the bright glare with her hand.

'Why do you say that, Amy,' Granda enquired, 'he seems to fit in okay?'

'Too okay,' muttered Carrie, still gazing out to sea.

'What do you mean, Carrie?' Granda asked. 'He certainly makes your grandmother happy.'

'Exactly,' she responded, 'and he's young enough to be her son!'

'Oh dear,' murmured Granda sadly, 'I thought it was old people who could be a bit judgemental.'

'I'm not being judgemental,' Carrie protested, 'he just makes me feel uneasy, the whole thing…' She tailed off seemingly embarrassed both to be caught out being judgemental and the difficulty of discussing such things with Granda.

I decided to come to her rescue.

'I agree with Carrie, it's creepy, he's creepy…'

I heard myself faltering then in a similar way to Carrie and almost wished I hadn't spoken, feeling Granda looking at me reflectively.

'Well, this *is* interesting,' Granda mused, 'I always remember when I studied philosophy A-level in my last year of school purely because my foster parents thought I should get some academic subjects under my belt before I went off on my silversmith course – I loved it actually – my teacher told us we should learn to analyse what he called the "yuck factor". It's a fun thing to do, I can tell you. Carrie and I glanced at each other uneasily. Granda continued, apparently oblivious to our discomfort. 'So, given that we've established that we all know Angela and Jason have become an item,' he paused gauging our reaction it seemed, 'that's the unspoken bit between us all isn't it?'

Carrie and I remained silent.

'So, given that *fact*,' Granda continued doggedly, 'what makes you uneasy?'

I looked across at Carrie who was staring fixedly at her sketch book, I really had unleashed the monster, it seemed. I half wanted to run away from what I'd started, half wanted to feel the wound probed so speak. I remained silent, tense, while the sounds of the summery beach continued as a careless, unheeding backdrop.

'Let's try this,' Granda continued obviously enjoying the conversation even whilst walking on eggshells it seemed, 'what if Jason were the same age as Angela or a bit older even, what then?'

I suddenly found that I loved being part of this grown-up conversation and became fascinated by what Granda was saying. Both Carrie and I had the sensitivity not to say that being old was part of the "yuck factor" and anyway this was much less what disturbed us than the age *difference* between the two of them and, yes, the man/woman thing did make a difference. But *why* should it? I wondered to myself. I remember Carrie and I looked at each other and then across at Granda who was himself now gazing out to sea through his binoculars seemingly not that interested in our reply. I spoke first, knowing that Carrie wouldn't, and it was me after all who had unleashed the beast so to speak.

'It shouldn't make a difference, but it does, and I don't know why,' I murmured.

'Good, honest answer, Amy, well done,' said Granda warmly. I glowed inwardly at this praise as he continued musingly: 'the whole age difference thing is interesting actually. Clearly the age gap narrows as people get older. I remember your grandmother, Amy love, always saying that she was rapidly catching me up age-wise even though there were eight years between us, and of course that gap did narrow as we became older in some ways if you think that she was only 16 and I was 24 when we met.' He chuckled at first then his face clouded, 'of course, when she became ill she not only seemed to catch up but actually overtook me age-wise, poor darling.' He shook his head sadly then sort of rallied: 'So, where we have got to in this interesting discussion?'

Carrie and I were listening avidly to every word now.

He continued: 'If you think of, say, a 15-year-old boy being interested in an 8-year-old girl, that is deeply troubling and wrong of course, even though there are only seven years between them. But if a 27-year-old man and a 34-year-old woman got together, or a 32-year-old man and a 39-year-old woman for example, and onwards and upwards, the gap gets narrower and narrower. And if two people of maturity love each other and make each other happy who are we to judge and look at ages and genders? So,' he paused briefly, 'analysing the "yuck factor" is a fun and important exercise at times.' With some difficulty he got slowly to his feet and started gathering up our cups and chocolate bar wrappers to take to the bin.

'Ouf, this old man has stiffened up that's for sure, I need to stretch these creaky limbs,' he chuckled, 'and here come the others.'

Chapter 15

AFTER THAT THINGS BECAME NOTICEABLY easier around Jason. Carrie and I talked about this conversation quite a lot and tested age gaps to prove Granda's point. I began to look forward to talking about it with Rachel too. I think Carrie talked to her mother about it as well because even Marianne seemed to relax a bit. I overheard Granda and her talking about our beach conversation analysing the "yuck factor" about a week later and once again the earth seemed to tilt a little as I heard Marianne say:

'I trust Doug absolutely, Seb, but you must've noticed how they are together?' I couldn't quite hear Granda's reply as I quickly slipped further back into the house. They were sitting, drinking coffee, on the paved bit of the garden near the open French doors into the living room, one sunny, mid-October, Sunday morning. Somehow, I knew immediately that they were talking about Carrie and Dad; I had noticed their closeness certainly, but I hadn't wanted to think about it. I shut it out, turned away from it, sometimes physically, sometimes metaphorically. I knew their closeness made me feel jealous; I'm ashamed to own this feeling yet again. Yes, sometimes it seemed a little strange, their closeness, but I sensed no "yuck factor" to be honest, just an occasional pinprick of jealousy. This time though I really did *not* want to hear any more and I crept back upstairs to finish my homework for Monday, concentrating fiercely, drowning out what felt like a tumult of feelings. I dug my thumbnails into both my palms and focused on watching the skin break and blood ooze slowly out. It felt good but about twenty minutes later I wanted desperately never to do that to myself again.

The following weekend was the beginning of half term and Mum, and I were meeting in Cambridge this time. She had asked if I wanted to stay for a few days during the holiday and I had at first declined very quickly. I decided on impulse then, just as I finished my homework, to ring her. She now had a mobile phone, so I didn't need to worry about Rob answering. I planned to ask if I could come for the whole of half term. I felt like escaping from my adopted household for a bit and I realised that I didn't even want to tell Rachel about that overheard Dad and Carrie conversation remembering how she had shut me out so completely after the rescue. I had to use the landline and can almost recall even now my urgent, visceral need to talk to Mum as I went searching for the cordless phone to take back upstairs. Some people in my class already had mobile phones but they had to give them in to the class teacher at the beginning of the day. Dad had promised I could have a mobile when I went to high school next year.

Mum was so pleased and sounded so happy that I wanted to come, and I started to look forward to it like a holiday. Neither Mum nor Dad were willing to let me travel by train alone on a Friday evening; that made me cross but cared for at the same time, and kind, lovely Dad said he'd drive me to Mum's after work. They said it was because there was an awkward change at Ely with a long wait, not the best place to be hanging around at nearly dusk on a chilly October evening. It would have been fine, they said, if the train went straight to Cambridge. Mum and Rob would bring me home.

Marianne, Carrie and Granda were going off to Lanzarote for half term, Carrie told me she wanted to get away too, and Marianne felt some warmer sunshine, more or less guaranteed, would boost Granda's immune system for the winter to come and that the warmth would ease the pain of his arthritis a little. Dad was very busy at work at that time and he also wanted to do a bit of work on our old house, which was now let only at the weekends. He wanted to make the most of the last few light and warm days before the winter set in to make it ready for the next spring and summer holiday lets; he would move in there during the week whilst we were gone. This obviously left Angela and Jason on their own but I shut this thought out of my mind too.

The week at Mum's was really good, and it felt good to see Mum so happy. She was suffering from morning sickness at that time, but it wasn't too bad, she said dismissively and was helped by eating two rich tea biscuits before getting up. Rob always stocked up the tin beside their bed she told me and brought her a cup of green tea every morning, she was very lucky, she said. Unspoken was a kind of criticism of Dad, I felt, who would either have already gone to work by the time she woke up, or be recovering from, even still out on, a shout. I said nothing of course and I might have imagined this silent criticism. It wasn't my business I felt.

The three boys, Fred, 7, Aidan, 5, and Jack, 3, were fun to be with too. On rainy days we played long games of hide and seek indoors, grandmothers' footsteps in the hall, and we used cardboard boxes to make ships or dens and bedcovers to make wigwams on the landing. These were Mum's suggestions for games and she always managed to find us what we needed. She and Rob had made a dressing up box for the boys, that was great. It was full of slightly musty-smelling, old dressing gowns, shoes, some hats, scarves, shawls, even some cheap jewellery. I was amazed as I had never seen Mum so lively like this.

Once we were settled in any den we'd made the little boys loved to hear stories of some of the lifeboat rescues and were excited that my dad was a real, live lifeboatman, especially Fred who obviously understood better than the little ones what that meant. I only told them the stories with happy endings of course and I found myself repeating some of the safety warnings about the deceptive strength of the sea to these little boys, hoping I was spreading the word and that Dad would be proud of me.

Rob was fun, relaxed, and so welcoming to me. I liked him, I realised quickly. He had taken a few days' holiday during half term and during those precious, dwindling hours of daylight when the weather was kind he loved getting as much as possible done in the garden with the boys and me "helping". I loved those days. Mostly I played with the boys: raucous races with me pushing Jack in the wheelbarrow and the older two pedalling furiously on the paved paths in the garden on their little bikes. We played long games too of a different sort of "outside" hide and seek which Rob had been taught by his grandmother: it was called "Coventry Tree". The person who was "it" stood in the middle of the paved garden to the side of the house and the others had to sneak up on "it" without being seen, then touch "home" which was the tallest rose bush in that part of the garden. This meant that at least you had some chance of remaining hidden until that triumphant shout of 'home!'. If "it" spied you before you reached the bush he or she called out: 'X come to Coventry' and you were taken prisoner by "it" and had to stand still. The last one still to be hiding was the winner and the next "it". It was good to see Fred joining in as much as the other two and helping Jack especially who called the game 'Covtree'. So that's what we all called the game and that's what whoever was "it" called out.

We liked doing proper gardening jobs too, helping Rob "tame", as he called it, the very wild garden. He wanted certain bits of it to remain wild and he explained to Fred and me that it was easier said than done to get a proper wild garden going, surprising though that may seem. I loved the rich, fruity scent of the damp earth coupled with the paradoxically wholesome smell of decay as the plants started to bed down for the winter. It was good to spot the occasional vibrant, late blooming flowers and shrubs.

Rob told us their names: golden rod which seemed to capture all the light and reflect it back in a warm golden haze; gladioli: the hardy type with their pretty, lavender-coloured, white and apricot blooms which, he said, would last well into November; autumn crocuses too which always kept their rich colours until mid to late October, he explained, because they were nestled in amongst the protective shrubs. I loved the proud, beautiful irises, especially the ones with their deep burgundy hearts lying snugly at the bottom of their delicate, smoky-pink petals which seemed to caress the centre, like soft hands. Rob told me that he always thought of the gladioli and the irises as uninvited, but very welcome, guests as they had somehow just appeared one year and had at first seemed a bit out of place but his first wife, Cynthia, known as Cindy, had loved them. They had originally put some in the less wild part of the garden and he admired their cleverly inveigling of themselves into this rampant part of the garden going "wild" themselves: 'like a child playing truant from a too strict and regimented school,' he said to me one day.

We needed to lift the Michaelmas dahlias now though so that they could spend the winter in the greenhouse. Their golden centres reflected the light much as the golden rod did; at times they almost appeared to be in competition with each other to see which could achieve the most radiant depth of colour. I shared this thought with Rob, he agreed but commented later that perhaps in harmony with each other would be a better way of thinking about it.

I liked the way Rob always really listened to what I had to say, he was the same with Mum and the children too, I noticed. He told me he was planning to experiment by putting some of these, known as asters, in the greenhouse to over-winter there. We would wrap them in newspaper, he explained, and see if some in the more sheltered part of the garden would survive outside. He told us that they were in fact perennials and explained to Fred and me the difference between annuals and perennials. I loved the hydrangeas too, which Rob said would gradually fade and turn a kind of textured, sort of chunky, brown but that some would secretly reveal their original colour if you looked closely. I could see how gardens could absorb grown-ups in this way and also what hard, never-ending work they were. I wondered briefly if I would ever become a passionate gardener in my own home one day.

Marianne enjoyed gardening and helped Granda with the gardening jobs he could no longer manage in the small, but lovingly tended, shared garden surrounding his flat. He had confided to me recently that not being able to garden now was one of his biggest regrets about his arthritis. Dad did gardening jobs out of necessity more than pleasure but of course his lifeboat duties always came first. And Angela made no secret of the fact that she wanted her garden to look beautiful but was no gardener, and never would be, meaning she relied totally on Pete and, to some extent, Marianne to maintain its "life and loveliness", as she put it.

I remember now as clearly as if it were yesterday sweeping up dead leaves in the Cambridge garden, Jack and Aidan running through the piles, Fred calling them to order to help him put the leaves into black bin bags to make leaf mould, dispose of old tomato plants, fill up the compost bin, and even doing some weeding in short bursts. Sometimes we would come across some weird looking fungi which Rob made sure we understood never to touch. I can still recall the damp, earthy smell of the late autumn, somehow wholesome decay, harbinger as it was of renewed growth, even as the "life and loveliness" of this summer garden took itself into itself as it bedded down for the long dark of winter.

Ever since then I have felt acutely aware of the pulse and vigour of the turn of the year, the endless cycle of decay, renewal and rebirth. I can still bring to mind the sight of my breath in the cold air, the boys' breath too, trees becoming silhouettes in the fast-fading light, fingers and toes nipping with cold, nose running probably, the boys' noses certainly did. I half looked forward to Rob calling it a day but never wanted to be the first to make for indoors. And when he did call it a day I loved the cosy warmth and light that beckoned us in, the smell of cooking as we trooped inside to wash our freezing hands, enjoying the feeling of hunger knowing we would soon be eating, and the sudden, deep dark as we looked out from the lighted up house to the night time garden.

Mum loved watching the garden take shape and sometimes helping when she had time, though she was taking care during her pregnancy not to do the hard, physical work involved. She loved pottering about in the greenhouse, checking on the plants and seedlings, watering when necessary. Rob had cleaned out and renovated the greenhouse when he first bought the house. He told me much later, when I was about 15 or 16, I think, that he had found this chore a great source of comfort after Cindy died. It was hard, physical work, he said, but he liked to think of nurturing and preserving plant life for new life in the spring. He said it reassured him that life did go on. Fred and Aidan would often quietly help him, and Jack could sleep in his buggy in there as he had installed heating. It was snug and safe and somehow full of hope, during that dark, sad time, he explained.

We children also loved all the animal life, which we sometimes disturbed in our digging or when we moved big stones and rocks Rob was collecting to build a rockery. This was especially for Mum, he explained, as she had always wanted a rockery and thought it would look nice on the slope down to the garden from the house. We watched busy, scurrying ants, setting about repairing or relocating their disturbed nest with focus and renewed vigour it seemed; pinky-grey worms wriggling away; shiny, scuttling, black beetles looking cross, their antennae seemingly frowning or waving us away angrily; woodlice curling into tight balls as we approached.

These last fascinated Aidan and Jack so much that Rob had to tell them to stop dislodging the bricks from the rose garden paths and the rocks put in place for the beginning of the rockery. He explained it wasn't fair to tease and frighten them like that. I suggested I could show them how to build their own miniature gardens in old biscuit tins, just as Dad had once shown me. Rob was relieved to hear this suggested distraction, also really interested as it wasn't something he'd ever done. We managed to find a collection of old tins, sorted ready to be thrown out, retrieved just in time. I remember too that one day Rob and I went on our own, just the two of us he said, on a fun outing to a nearby garden centre to choose some plants for Mum's rockery; that made me feel special and even now I love seeing our creation, still flourishing, when I go to Cambridge to see them.

A hedgehog with a younger one in tow would often emerge at dusk and it was funny seeing their stately progress across the silent lawn in the moonlight. Rob would call us to watch if he noticed it when doing early evening jobs in the greenhouse or putting the wheelie bins out perhaps. He surmised that they were trying to build up their fat reserves before their long winter hibernation and we decided to help with this by putting out fresh water and food for them. He warned us not to give them cows' milk though as it could give them diarrhoea. I showed Fred and Aidan how to scramble eggs for them and we tried to save them some minced beef if Mum was making burgers or cottage pie or spaghetti Bolognese.

We all enjoyed playing football too; sometimes Fred and Aidan's schoolfriends would come and join in, and Rob would often referee always giving little Jack some tips and help. Best of all though were my times with Mum. We went shopping in Cambridge, took a picnic to eat by the river one day, just us, cooked together at home; it was lovely and calming as I remember it now. She seemed so different, affectionate, fun. Sometimes I sensed – rather than actually saw – her looking at me a little wistfully but perhaps that was my imagination.

One day, out of the blue, Mum commented that it was nice that I had adopted a new family, meaning Angela, Marianne and Carrie and sort of Jason as well and that I should consider *her* new family my very own, not even an adopted one. She said I must come whenever I liked and that if I ever wanted to move in with them permanently, I would be very welcome, but that there was no pressure for me to decide something so big. I liked that, it made me feel very secure and very loved. I felt Dad needed me though and I needed him for sure. Then she started talking about what a terrible time Jason had had, that Dad had told her about it, and how pleased he must be to have found a safe refuge with Angela.

We were making a blackberry and apple pie at the time, I remember, and I can still in my mind's eye see the deep, shiny purple of the blackberries as I rinsed them in the colander. My mouth waters even now at the memory and I can almost smell their sharp, tangy scent as I tipped them into the pie dish and stirred them round to jostle for place with the sliced apples. I quickly suppressed any expression then which would have betrayed my immediate thought which was: 'What *is* she on about?'

'Mmm, he must be,' I murmured noncommittally as I turned to select the cutlery to lay the table for tea.

'It's strange isn't it,' she continued almost to herself, 'that we tend to think of the victims of domestic abuse being women? I mean, I knew it happened to men too, but since I heard about Jason, I've read about it and it seems there are vast numbers of men who are victims and no-one knows the true figure because often they're even more reluctant than women are to report it due to embarrassment, protecting the woman, fear of being laughed at because of not being man enough to cope with it and stop it... that kind of thing.' She hesitated then. 'Gosh, Amy, sorry, this is a bit of a heavy subject, isn't it?' She carefully lifted the pastry on the rolling pin to place it over the pie. I never even knew she could make things like pies. Then she continued: 'Apparently, the abuse is often really subtle though and even the physical abuse is caused to places that no-one can see. Poor man.' She stopped suddenly and looked at me. 'Sorry, Amy, sometimes you seem so mature I forget you're only 10 going on 20. I hope I haven't upset you, love.'

'Oh no, you haven't, Mum, not at all, it is terrible for Jason, yes,' I said quickly as if I'd known all along, yet all the while I felt the world once more seeming to spin out of focus, shake a bit then settle into a new reality. I wondered briefly if she was about to share some new horror from her own life. I didn't want to hear it, whatever it was. I wanted to tell Rachel about this conversation, but that could wait. I enjoyed Mum chatting to me in this way, she was so relaxed and happy, and I felt relaxed and happy too. This was the pattern of our relationship it seemed: she treating me as older than my years maybe because I had looked after her when she was so unwell. I don't know. I liked it though. It was just the way it was.

Although this "new" Mum was happy I noticed that Fred sometimes gave her a bit of a hard time. He could be rude and sulky and would object to the simplest request just for the sake of it. I asked Mum about this and she reminded me that it was only just over two years ago that he had lost his mum and that he was really the only one of the three who could remember her, so he couldn't share his memories of her, or even his grief, with his brothers.

To both her and Rob's delight he had just started to call Mum Magsamum, his own name for her, and she loved it. She told me that she purposely made time to be with him on his own, read to him at bedtime, that kind of thing, and she felt he was thawing out and that they were becoming close. The two younger ones had also adopted that name for her, but they both usually called her Magsamummy. She wondered what would happen when Jack started school, and whether he would, as Fred and Aidan had, explain to their friends that Mum was not his real mum. She wondered aloud to me how much they really understood of the fact their "real" mum had died.

'Time enough for that to become his reality,' she said, and I sensed the weight of all their sadness then.

Sometimes I noticed Rob looking at Mum with the children and I was struck by the love and laughter in his eyes as he watched them together. He was quick to tell Fred off if he was rude or unhelpful. I tried to suppress some horrible feelings of bitterness and real jealousy that Mum had not been there for me in that way but I hated myself for feeling like that and believed if I had been a different daughter, not always wanting to be with Dad at the lifeboat station for example, that things would have been better between us. Towards the end of the week I really started to look forward to going home but also felt torn in two at having to leave this lively, happy set up.

As the days grew shorter, the nights longer and the year sped towards Christmas there was a lot of discussion about Carrie's next steps, both at her sixth form with her teachers and at home. It seemed an exciting time for her with choices spread out before her, horizons widening into an expansive and tantalising future. I felt a kind of envy that she could soon shake off the shackles of school and forge her own path. This envy felt okay though, not bitter and searing like the jealousy I sometimes felt round Mum and her new life; that was strange because I had always thought envy and jealousy meant the same thing and I now understood that they didn't.

The whole household took an interest in these discussions. Carrie had, in the end, chosen science courses for her AS and A-level subjects, dropping art after the first term of sixth form. This had surprised everybody, except Dad and Marianne, it seemed. They had discussed her choices with her a lot at different times. She had decided that it would be silly to waste her really good GCSE grades in subjects like Maths, Biology, Chemistry, Geography and Physics and just concentrate on Art and Design, despite her love of those creative subjects. Carrie had told Dad that she knew she had a natural talent for Art and Design which she believed she could hone by using it as an enjoyable hobby and that studying those subjects for exams might lessen the pleasure she took in them. Her science teachers at high school strongly agreed with her and she started to look into studying Marine Biology at university.

She and Dad pored over the university league tables together, sometimes Marianne joined in. Carrie became very strategic, looking at the overall reputation of the universities that offered the course and all the league table parameters carefully including entry requirements. She eventually settled for her five choices being: Durham, Newcastle, Liverpool, Southampton and Exeter as her safe option as it had lower entry requirements for her course. She knew she wanted to go to university in England, and that she didn't want London or Oxbridge. She then booked open days sorting out how to get there and who would be able to go with her. Dad was keen to drive her and had holiday owing so he could take days when she needed to go. Marianne seemed conflicted about this but was less able to take time off work, she also didn't like the thought of the long drives.

In the end it was decided that those where an overnight stay was preferable, which was all of them apart from Southampton, Dad and Angela would go. Angela seemed to have friends she could call on and stay overnight everywhere it seemed. I overheard she and Marianne discussing it while they cooked together in the kitchen one Saturday afternoon as the rain poured down and the murky November day gave up its feeble effort at daylight and sank resignedly into the long night.

'They can't just go off together, Mum, they just can't, you know they can't.' Marianne sounded both adamant and fretful about this. Angela was her usual calm, untroubled self.

'Well, darling, I know you're worried, but I really think there's no need to be. And I would love to go anyway, you know how much I enjoy jaunts and it'll be interesting seeing these different places and hearing about the courses, they call it Earth and Marine Sciences, don't they? Fascinating. It'll be good to catch up with friends too and it'll save on hotel bills. Happy with that?'

Marianne breathed a sigh of relief which I could almost hear, and I could definitely sense her hugging Angela.

'Mum, you're a star, a star grandmother. I'm very happy to think you'll get something out of it too apart from chaperoning my wayward daughter,' she said in a much lighter tone. Chaperoning was another new word to me.

'Oh of course I will, darling, and she's not wayward at all as you well know. Don't talk it up!' I had no idea what that phrase meant and decided I would look it up too. 'She's hard-working, focused and incredibly beautiful and I'm so proud of my only granddaughter. You must be very proud of her too and of course, it's natural to worry.' In the event they decided to stay overnight in Southampton too, Angela had a cousin there who she had not seen for ages.

So quite apart from all this mysterious talk, which I planned to unravel for myself later, the whole next steps thing for Carrie was all just so exciting to me then, and I felt impatient to be planning my own future one day. Of course, I had yet to get through the rest of Year 6 and the whole of high school, and sixth form awaited me, almost another lifetime really at that age.

Chapter 16

AFTER CHRISTMAS DAD RETURNED TO lifeboat volunteering at a similar full-on level as before, having gone back part-time in late September. It was a terrible time to return weather-wise, long hours of darkness too. There were fewer idiots about of course, as he explained to me, but some terrifying rescues in ferocious winter weather. I recently came across some of the letters he wrote to me then. He chose to handwrite them as he did it last thing before going to bed and he preferred just to grab some paper and a pen at that time of night rather than wind up his laptop, as he put it.

4th January, 2002

Darling Amy,

Here we go – your crazy dad at it again. I do get such a buzz from it though. Gosh, the cold was biting last night. I think the winds were in excess of 50mph, freeeeeezing, onshore, brutal. A fisherman reported seeing an empty fishing boat at about 7pm, pitchy black of course by then. We got to the search area off East Runton really quickly, and we found ourselves tossing about like a toy boat. Mike was at the helm, cool, calm, collected as usual. The sea was black and truly menacing as if somebody had upset it and it was after revenge, horrible. I even felt a bit seasick, couldn't believe it, talk about mind over matter. I think it was to do with looking so hard at the churning blackness, froth and spume flying into our faces, while the poor old Lady Prudence *– you know the one don't you? – just back in service after a repair, was chucked about like a piece of discarded rubbish.*

Anyway, we searched and searched and thankfully just after 9pm we heard that he'd been pulled safely ashore by some other fishermen who had joined the search. They were putting their own lives at risk to be honest and their livelihoods, those boats are not really made for seas like that but there's no stopping them when it's one of their own, as you know, so fair play to them.

We got back to the Shed at about 9.15 – it was a long couple of hours I can tell you. Wow, those new showers and the drying room are fabulous. Mrs Mack's Lynette still brings us piles of clean towels every day and extra on Saturdays to cover Sunday – absolute treasures, mother and daughter. Did you know Mrs Mack's husband, Lynette's dad, was a fisherman who lost his life at sea 10 years ago this January? Tragic. It was a foul night apparently, a bit like last night, I imagine.

We made a brew, had some of the fruit cake Mrs M had left for us, got everything clean and ready for next time and headed for home. The chap's fine so that's a good ending. Oh, it was lovely to get home here and see you sleeping snug, warm and safe, darling girl.

Love you lots, Da. Xxxx

I remember, as if it was yesterday, finding letters slipped underneath my door in the morning. Sometimes when Dad was out on a shout at night I was so worried I couldn't sleep for ages, then I would fall asleep very late even though I didn't want to, and wake up feeling groggy and tired but always just so relieved to know that Dad was safe and sound. Reading those accounts of the rescues in his letters now can still evoke the exact same feelings of relief that he was/is back safely even all these years down the line, eleven years to be precise. Strange to think that that is more than my whole lifetime had been when I read this one aged 10, soon to be 11, in March:

27th January 2002

Darling Amy,

Phew! Home safe and sound. Sadly, that's more than can be said for the young chap, only 21, who we pulled into shore successfully after a passer-by had spotted him falling off the end of Cromer pier. We got him back in, he was conscious and talking more or less coherently, shivering violently, the Air Ambulance was sent and got him to the N&N in about ten minutes. But once we'd showered, feeling pleased with ourselves, made a cuppa etc. we heard he'd died from secondary drowning.

I can't get him out of my mind, Amy. All alone in that wild, cold darkness, I doubt it was an accident, unless he'd had too much to drink and simply slipped. But all alone, it doesn't bear thinking about. Maybe he was with his family for Christmas, oh, it makes me shudder, who knows? Nothing can ever be that bad, surely?

Oh, Amy, promise me that if ever... no, I just can't think about that. Just know that I'm here for you and always will be, sweetheart. Mum is too you know and our adopted family here, honestly. You reach into people's hearts, you really do. I know things have been strange for you lately, well for most of your nearly 11 years if I think about it, but I think you have incredible courage and resilience without being as hard as nails, far from it. I'm wittering a bit now, tired out, deflated, sad. I'll go in for a debrief tomorrow, they're really helpful actually.

Sleep tight, my darling girl, love you xxxx

I had to look up what "debrief" meant. It seems to me now that the letters themselves were a kind of debrief for Dad too.

5ᵗʰ February 2002

Darling Amy,

Well, just when I was saying it wasn't the idiots in winter rescues... a gaggle of them, about eight, from a stag party, decide to take out two Wayfarer dinghies owned by two of their dads. They were being made ready for the summer season on the hard at Blakeney next to the dinghy park. It was 1 o'clock in the morning for goodness sake, vile weather, the rest of the party were watching and cheering them on, far too many for each boat, but at least they had the sense to raise the alarm about half an hour later when they had lost sight of them. I know we're not meant to judge, and we don't at the time to be honest, but ye gods, the idiots. Sheringham came to help too, Ron was with them, it was good to see him again.

Oooh, it's good to be home, tired to the gunwales! See you in the morning, my love, Dad.

Tired to the gunwales was one of my dad's pet phrases, always pronounced 'gun-wales'; it never failed to make me smile and I sometimes use it myself, Rachel's and Harry's families have adopted it too.

Only just over a year before this, shortly before Christmas 2001, on 5th December, a storm surge caused terrible damage to the pier though that was nothing compared to the damage caused in November 1993, eight years earlier. I was only about two and a half years old but Dad told me all about it on several occasions and how cross Mum had been when he was called out as apparently I was suffering from a feverish cold and chesty cough, crying and fretful, and she was finding it hard to cope. I always wished he would stick to the drama at sea when he recounted the story to be honest, not that bit about frantic Mum, frantic me.

It was a foul day apparently. Just as it was getting dark with children still on their way home from school, a member of the public noticed that the rig at East Runton seemed to be collapsing and called 999, Dad told me. Then just after 4pm more 999 calls came flooding in to say that the rig was adrift, people didn't know then that it had been evacuated the Saturday before because of the weather. By 4.30pm, the coastguard and lifeboat station, already alerted, saw that the rig seemed to be heading towards the shore, but it then started heading west towards the pier. This was before the new lifeboat station was built at the end of the pier between 1997 and 1999, but the smaller one there was certainly under threat.

The pier was evacuated and the sightseers on the promenade were moved along as the foul day was turning into an even fouler night. Shortly before 5pm the rig appeared to be beached and started crabbing towards the shore. Those monitoring the drama were informed that there was a 700-gallon fuel drum on board and a strong smell of diesel was noticed. A few minutes later the metal accommodation block was knocked into the shallow sea and sparks from power cables were seen as the structure smashed through the pier like an angry, giant robot wreaking havoc as if seeking some sort of revenge; this was the way Dad described it. It finally came to rest on a breakwater at Overstrand pretty much wrecking that too. 'Job done,' Dad always says when he tells the story.

Following this the lifeboatmen (it was all men there then apparently, same as when I was growing up though there were and still are plenty of women lifeboat crew in other parts of the country) had to use a rickety, temporary bridge to reach the lifeboat station at the end of the pier. But that night they just had to stand and watch helplessly as the rig sliced through the pier "like butter", the coxswain, Richard Davies, was quoted as saying in the EDP – *Eastern Daily Press*, the next day. Lots of tourists flocked to the town in the days and weeks following this, which was a good boost for the town just before Christmas. It was the worst storm surge since the 1953 floods. Dad always thinks that years ending in a 3, spell trouble; he has a point, to be fair.

I thought of that year-ending-in-a-3 omen the following year when I went on holiday with Mum and Rob and the little children plus 1 year old Joshua, known then as Joshy, who was a mid-summer baby, born on 22nd June 2002, two weeks after his due date – but I'll come back to that summer of 2003.

Cliff walkers and their dogs often caused problems during the winter, Dad told me. I remember him returning from one such rescue in particular, where a little poodle-cross dog had fallen off the cliffs near Overstrand on a late evening walk. This happened after dark, and you couldn't blame the owners for the time of day, he said, because it would already be dark when people took their dogs out after work. Or it might happen during early morning walks, in both cases the dogs would of course be very lively and raring to go. What he did blame the owners for though was letting their dogs off the lead near cliff edges, 'idiots,' he said.

This dog was called Percy, only about 6 months old. It was late February, about 6pm, high tide, high winds, big seas, freezing cold when the dog ran towards the edge of the cliff and either slipped or blew off onto the rocks below, somehow landing on a tiny patch of sand in a sort of alcove with waves lashing against the rocks all around it. The skill was partly in preventing one or more distressed owners going after the dog. Dad told us this story when he returned from the shout at about 9pm. He described vividly how difficult it was to get the lifeboat close enough to the sandy alcove to be able to get off and reach the dog.

The waves were so high that as the boat, the *Lady Prudence* again, was buffeted about in the furious surf, they repeatedly lost sight of the little dog which was crouched low, probably shivering, and silent with fear it seemed. Its owners were distraught but the woman in the couple was sensibly intent on trying to prevent her male partner from going in recklessly after the dog. The crew were speaking to them as best they could from a loud hailer, trying to reassure them it was all under control, though Dad told us it was far from certain that it was. The coastguard was contacting the crew to see if they could be of any assistance but it was hard to know how they could best help unless they might be needed for winching up rescuer and dog. They were on standby for this but were soon called away to help the Caister lifeboat rescue a lone cliff walker with a broken leg. This obviously took priority.

When Dad was eventually able to reach Percy, the dog barked uncontrollably and snapped at Dad, just frightened out of his mind, Dad said, and probably even more so because of the big, yellow hi-vis kit and helmet Dad was wearing. The owners had told the crew that he was a friendly little dog; as the crew relayed this to Dad, he looked back and gave them a rude sign, knowing that the owners couldn't see this, he confessed, not looking at me, but muttering, 'Sorry, Amy, terrible example, and Carrie of course.' We both laughed and wanted to hear what happened next.

'Anyway,' Dad continued, 'we have these big, strong bags for rescuing animals, pull-string tops, you've seen them, Amy. Luckily little Percy had a harness on, so I was able to grab that like a handle and bundle him into the bag, talking soothingly all the time, poor little thing. I pulled the drawstring tight making sure he couldn't leap out. As soon as I'd lifted him up in his harness, I think he sensed he was going to be safe and quietened down; whether he's learnt his lesson is another question. I'm sure his owners have though.' Angela asked him if he wanted anything to eat or drink and went to get him and Jason a beer from the fridge. He opted for a cheese and chutney sandwich and continued:

'We kept opening up the string on the trip back to shore to check he was OK. It was still very bumpety, but we were feeling elated actually and he looked really cute with his little black button eyes looking up at us. When we handed him to his owners it was really sweet to see him excitedly licking their faces all over. They were almost speechless with gratitude. They said they would send in a large donation. Good outcome but it was hairy at times, I can tell you.' He looked tired out suddenly and asked how our evening had been; that was funny. The Caister rescue turned out to be really tricky, he told us the next morning, but the rescued man was now recovering in hospital.

Another of the winter rescues was one he never forgot because it involved a fishing vessel belonging to one of the volunteer crewmen, Jack. He'd known and liked Jack for years and Jack had been one of the few people who had openly stood by him following the rumours, and no-smoke-without-a-fire shenanigans following his rescue of Carrie. After Dad was asked to leave Sheringham High he and Jack would meet down the pub when they could, he was just quietly supportive apparently. I remembered overhearing him telling Angela about Jack's support one day. Dad described this rescue in a letter to me.

15th March 2002

Darling Amy,

Terrible night. We got the call out to a fishing boat taking on water at about 5pm. It was the Juliana, *Jack's boat, eleven men on board. It was his night off and he responded to the call out not knowing until we were racing towards the stricken vessel that it was his boat. He knew literally everyone onboard. He went very pale and silent and just concentrated hundred percent on getting there. We knew time was of the essence. It took us about an hour to get out to her and at first all seemed reasonably calm, the boat had somehow been holed, they couldn't quite work out where, never mind why. They were baling out with the pumps quite effectively it seemed and everyone, including their skipper, thought they could get back to shore in time. The seas were high but far from the worst I've seen.*

The coastguard helicopter was scrambled to see what help was needed. It was decided they would winch down an auxiliary pump and that Jack was the best person to put aboard as he knew the boat and the men. Getting alongside for him to board was really tricky because of the enormous swell. I had this sudden urge for my own feet to be on dry land, I suddenly hated the chopping, churning relentless, bloody sea. I wanted to shout out: 'give us a break, we're trying to help for God's sake!'

If our boat had been holed too that would have been it. Eventually Jack managed to get aboard, by which time the vessel was stern down, taking on water, it was rushing everywhere, Jack's boat was going down fast. It was now impossible to remain alongside to get them all off effectively, we managed to pull some across like sacks of potatoes, but many were in the water having simply jumped off the boat in response to our shouted advice to do that. The danger then was that the boat and the men in the water were at risk of being crashed into by the heaving, rampaging skipperless boat, lumbering around totally out of control of course. Jack said afterwards that the harder he swam the more he felt himself being pulled towards and under it. It was the most terrified he's ever been, he told me, and that's after a long life at sea.

It was terrible for him. We got all the men off safely – which was fantastic – but of course the boat was their livelihood. Jack's 58 now and he thinks he'll give it up, not try to buy another boat.

Pleased to be home, though, so, so pleased and seeing you asleep safe and warm, darling Amy. I've made myself some hot chocolate and toast and marmalade, so I'll have that and head to bed.

See you in the morning sweetheart. Dream sweetly.

xxxxxxx

(Dad had scrawled through "bloody", but I could still make out the word, I smiled to myself and didn't blame at all him for using it!)

It was only much later that I discovered he also wrote to Carrie about the rescues. He didn't use terms of endearment, as he did with me, but he often said things like he thought of Carrie during the rescue. I hated finding these, hated reading them, hated myself for feeling this way. I found them when Carrie was away on holiday with her mum, later that year in the summer, after looking in her top drawer at Angela's for a hair slide to borrow one day.

They were in a little box with a clasp, tucked away right at the back. I am ashamed of myself and have never told her I found them. I don't think I ever will. While reading the one describing this rescue, I must've been digging my nails into my palm again, the palm on my left hand, I must've been holding the letter in my right hand to read it, I guess. Luckily, I noticed the blood, only a little, before I folded the letter and returned it to the box, first just tearing off the tiny, stained area on the edge of the paper. I wouldn't want her to find blood stains on the letters, she would guess I had invaded her space. I vowed to return and read the rest while she was away. I found I did this when I wanted to physically hurt myself, it became a sort of linked activity: read letters, draw blood, the one enhancing the pain of the other. I was always careful not to stain the letters. I knew it was weird and I wanted to stop but I couldn't.

15th March 2002

Carrie,

I have to write this down for you, I do this for Amy too, don't worry. Terrible shout last night...it was to a fishing boat which had been holed pretty far out off Cromer. We got the call at about 5pm. It was the fishing boat which belongs to one of our own, Jack, you don't know him, but he's a real friend.

I hated the sea that night, found myself cursing it under my breath. It was brutal even without the worse sea ever. It was similar to the conditions when I rescued you, I think, from what I've been told. As you know I can't remember much about that night. Actually, it's nearly the anniversary of that rescue come to think of it. I've only just thought of that.

It was difficult to get alongside, Jack was trying to get aboard, the men onboard were baling furiously. It seemed okay at first, as if they would get back to shore in time. We gave them another pump and the coastguard helicopter was about to winch down another type of pump when the boat started going into the water, sinking, stern down, pretty fast. It was bad enough for us to see, must've been truly terrible for Jack, his livelihood of course. He too was baling furiously, he said afterwards that he hadn't even noticed his boots were full of water. We gave the order for the men to jump into the water. The boat's engines had cut off, it was lumbering around out of control. There was a real danger of it bashing into the swimmers, sort of lumbering over the top of them. Jack said as fast as he swam the faster he could feel himself being pulled towards the boat, he said it's the most terrified he's ever been, he's 58, spent all his adult life at sea really.

Anyway, we got all the men onboard eventually, some we literally dragged over the edge like sacks of potatoes, they were cut and bruised, some of them, but that was a small price to pay for being alive.

I don't want another shout like that for a while, that's for sure. Just going to have some hot chocolate and toast and marmalade then head for my warm bed. I might take some of the mac cheese you had for tea for my lunch tomorrow, it looks lovely, but I don't fancy it this late.

Goodnight, Carrie, sleep tight.

Chapter 17

THE 21-YEAR-OLD ALONE ON the pier on that cold, dark, January night was brought vividly and unwelcomely to my mind during an amazing event in Cromer during the first week of the summer holidays, late July 2003, my first summer holidays of being a high school girl, having survived Year 7. This event was held to commemorate the centenary of the founding of the Women's Social and Political Union (WSPU) by Emmeline Pankhurst in Manchester in 1903. The organisers decided to re-enact some aspects of the extended visit to Cromer by the Empress Elisabeth of Austria in 1897, known to her friends and family as Sisi. Sisi, like Emmeline Pankhurst, was also an independent-spirited woman in times of total dependence on, and subordination to, men.

Granda told us all the background to Sisi's visit to Cromer. He reminded us that Cromer's very own Henry Blogg, the most decorated lifeboatman in the country, would have been an 11-year-old boy during the year of Sisi's visit to Cromer. He no doubt would have spent as much time as possible in and around the pier and lifeboat launch area, helping his father, also a lifeboatman, 'a bit like you do, Amy,' Granda said. He would most probably have seen Sisi and been struck by her elegance and beauty. Granda had been fascinated and saddened by Sisi's story for years and loved the Hungarian background to it, also the fact that, because she was brought up in Hungary, Sisi loved that country and missed it terribly, often fleeing there for comfort, solace, familiarity and safety after her lonely marriage.

Sisi sounded to me to be an incredible person. Carrie and I talked about her a lot. We already knew about Emmeline Pankhurst from History lessons. I told Rachel and her mum the story of Sisi too. They came with us to the commemorative event. Paul was working, they always had to box and cox childcare during the school holidays and Rachel often came to Angela's, just slotting in, she loved it there. I relished being able to ask her back to my adopted home having never been able to invite her to mine when Mum had been around. Harry and Finn were on duty as usual and very busy all day with minor incidents including, bizarrely, helping to free a dog who had run under the wheels of the lifeboat launcher which was going out to rescue a yachtsman aground on a sandbank at low tide.

Luckily the dog only sustained minor injuries, but the newspapers had a field day reporting the story with its spooky echoes of Emily Wilding Davison's sad death. Emily was a fellow suffragette and contemporary of Emmeline Pankhurst. She died tragically two days after being hit by King George V's horse, Anmer, when she walked out onto the race track at the 1913 Derby, on 4th June, carrying two flags in the colours of the Suffragette Movement, purple, white and green, which she had taken from the WSPU office. The horse apparently rolled over his jockey, Herbert Jones. Emily died two days later in Epsom Hospital from a fractured base of skull, Herbert Jones suffered concussion but was able to race at Ascot two weeks later. He remembered very little of the incident. That reminded me of my Dad's transient amnesia after he'd rescued Carrie.

Back to another strong-minded woman. Sisi was married to Franz Joseph, aged only 16, barely older than Carrie was when I first knew her, it was hard to imagine. This meant that Sisi acquired the title of Queen of Hungary but when her husband became Emperor of Austria and Hungary, she became the Empress Elisabeth of Austria too. Her full list of titles was impressive to say the least:

Elisabeth of Wittelsbach, Duchess in Bavaria, Empress of Austria, Queen of Hungary and Bohemia, Dalmatia, Croatia, Slavonica, Galicia, Lodomeria and Illyria; Queen of Jerusalem; Archduchess of Austria, Grand-duchess of Tuscany and Cracovia; Duchess of Lorraine, Salzburg, Würzburg, Franconia, Styria, Carinthia, Carniola and Bukovine; Grand Princess of Transylvania; Margravin of Moravia; Duchess of Upper and Lower Silesia, of Modena, Parma, Piacenza and Guastalla, of Auschwitz and Zator, Teschen, Friul, Ragusa and Zara; Countess-Princess of Habsbourg and Tyrol, Kybourg, Gorizia, and Gradisca; Princess of Trenta and Brixen, Berchtesgaden and

Mergentheim; Margravin of Upper and Lower Lusatia, Margravin in Istria; Countess of Hohenhems, Feldkirch, Bregenz, and Sonneberg; Dame of Trieste, Kotor and Windischgraetz; Grand Voivoda of Voivodina of Serbia.

I remember Granda telling us this story at Angela's when everyone was there for dinner and how we were all stunned into silence as he reeled off these titles verbatim and very fast. Carrie and I just exploded into laughter at the last one and the way Granda said it, so triumphantly; he was obviously only just holding back his own laughter to get the list out. When we had recovered sufficiently, he told us that *voi* came from the word to do with wars in Old Slavic and that *voda* denoted "leader" in a war or battle situation. Jason said it sounded like something you cleaned rusty metal with – that made us all collapse into helpless laughter again. Dad then devised a quick advertising jingle for such a product which went something like:

All you need is vim, vigour and voivode for very very sparkling metal, somehow making it fit to the tune of *The Beatles' All You Need is Love.* Jason added "viagra" somewhere but got a sharp look from Angela. We were laughing so much we hardly noticed it but I kind of subconsciously clocked Angela's reaction and looked up "viagra" later. Marianne felt that Countess-Princess as a title was just plain greedy, for some reason we thought that hilariously funny too, and Angela thought she'd prefer to be a grand duchess to a plain, bog-standard, boring old duchess. More uncontrollable laughter, I remember.

Granda also explained that *mark* came from the German for border and that *graaf* meant "count" so the word *Margravin* that we all found nearly as hilarious as *voivode* meant a kind of ruler of borders and boundaries. This made sense given all the countries Sisi was landed with having some sort of role in governing or regulating. He said that when we were next at his flat, he'd show us some of the old maps from his collection of antique maps and point out the old names and borders of the countries. I'd always loved looking at these with him even before I knew about Sisi. I vowed to call any daughter I had "Sisi" as I liked the name and I liked her spirit.

Another vivid memory of that time was that the next day it was pouring with rain all day and this was an excuse for getting out my Sylvanian families sets, one of my favourite toys. It seems childish now, looking back. I was only 12 and not quite a half of course, but even then, I remember thinking this is childish and I love it. Carrie entered completely into the spirit of the game even though she had recently turned 18. I think she loved the childishness of it and the inventiveness. We thought Sylvania sounded like a country Sisi might have governed.

I don't think I could have played it with Rachel then, she would have thought it was silly and babyish. Carrie and I set it up in the conservatory and gave all the families different titles and roles taken directly from Sisi's story. We made them go on a visit to Cromer too taking their cows and horses with them as Sisi did. It lasted all summer, on and off, that game. Angela let us leave it up in that corner of the conservatory; it was lovely that the pretend families were always there. Only recently I found some sketches of Carrie and me playing with the families in one of Angela's many sketch pads. They were beautiful and took me straight back to that time, even evoking the sense of contentment, the freedom to play childish games and the knowledge of the long summer holiday stretching ahead.

Returning to the real, live tragedy of Sisi though, she apparently hated the constraints of the Habsburg court life and wanted to travel, to be free and alone sometimes. She had at least enjoyed, lucky for her, a free and happy childhood but now she hated her mother-in-law, the Archduchess Sophie. Sophie took over the upbringing of her two little daughters, one of whom died as a baby. Sisi had a son, the heir-apparent, Crown Prince Rudolf, and that slightly helped her standing in court but was a strain on her health. That was the main reason for her trip to Cromer. She was very keen on trying to maintain her health and beauty. She stayed in Lower Tuckers Hotel on the Promenade. Sisi was exceptionally beautiful and life felt both precious and precarious to her; she constantly feared for her own life. Every morning her cow was milked, and the milk brought straight up for her to drink for fear it would otherwise be contaminated. She believed this milk helped her skin too. I can imagine her feeling afraid, but not lonely, as she gazed out at the wild North Sea and took walks alone on the beach, far from home. She wanted solitude. I wondered if she had any close friends, perhaps her maid was her confidante; I don't know.

She had such a sad life though: her daughters, Sophie and Marie Valerie, taken from her by her mother-in-law; then baby Sophie dying; I don't think she loved her husband, and vice versa, and, later, her only son was killed in what was thought to be a terrible murder-suicide pact. This took place with his teenaged lover, Baroness Mary Vetsera, who was only 16, in his hunting lodge at Mayerling, near Vienna but hidden deep in the Vienna Woods, on the Schwechat River at the end of January 1889. He was aged 31, another cold, dark January, I imagined, and it was this which brought the 21-year-old on Cromer pier to mind, I think. I remember, too, that the bizarre thought came to my mind that Crown Prince Rudolf was about the same age when he died as my dad was when he rescued Carrie, who was very nearly the same age then as Mary Vestera when she died. I just don't know what made me make that sinister comparison, but I know it made me shudder and push it out of my mind quickly.

Sisi's fears for her life were justified as only a year later she was stabbed to death by an anarchist, 25-year-old Luigi Lucheni, whilst waiting with her maid to board a steamer to cross Lake Geneva. Granda explained that there were many anti-establishment anarchists roaming about at the time and Sisi was an easy target. Stangely, we even incorporated this fatal stabbing into one of our games I remember. Her death was so sad, and this discovery made me change my mind about naming a daughter Sisi.

It was well-known that Sisi loved to look out at the pier in Cromer and apparently found the whole concept of piers fascinating though she would never walk out along it as this would make her feel exposed and vulnerable. This was despite the fact that Cromer pier, just a wooden jetty in those days, two hundred and forty feet long and built for "promenading", had a "keeper" employed to maintain order and safety. In Cromer ladies were required to leave the pier by 9pm. I remember Granda commenting that it was ironic that she was subsequently killed in broad daylight amongst crowds waiting to board a ferry to cross Lake Geneva with her maid beside her.

The information about Sisi's life on display in Cromer museum told us that she was only vaguely aware of the existence and uses of piers mainly from her travels outside mainland Europe but that she particularly liked the jetty in Cromer reaching out bravely into the North Sea. This jetty was destroyed in 1897 when it was smashed into by a boat carrying coal in stormy seas and gale force winds. Sisi was killed only a year later. Strange to think that the current pier was built only five years later.

And here Sisi's story insistently intrudes again. Despite her sad and lonely life, I remember feeling a strong urge to forge forward myself, sort of fast-forward, to being grown-up, to experiencing everything: love, sadness, happiness, sorrow, adventure, passion, everything. I had an urge to embrace it all, good and bad; again, I recall that feeling even now. I told Carrie that I wanted to feel everything as if *everything* was a tangible thing. She gave me one of her enigmatic, or *Mona Lisa* smiles, as Granda called them, I remember, and told me it would come in due course. She sounded like Angela then, older and wiser than her years. I still have that feeling about fast-forwarding at times, aged 20, although I am not untouched by "experiences" for sure, neither is Carrie; it's a kind of excited anticipation of all that life will still hold for me. Carrie told me recently that she still had that feeling quite often too.

The commemorative event itself was brilliant. Again we went as a whole household group including Jason's children who were staying with us for the first two weeks of the summer holidays while their mum went on holiday with a new friend, a man; I overheard Jason and Angela talking about that. I couldn't call our party a family group, of course, but it was fun with lots of us including Rachel and her mum. It took place on the Friday of the last week of July. It was felt important that it didn't clash with Sheringham or Cromer carnivals, nor with any weekend sport, but it needed to be in the school summer holidays. With all the summer events and busyness, it was hard to fit it in. I knew this because one of the organisers was a good friend of Angela's and I heard her chuckling with Angela about all the summer jollifications one day, leaving no time to draw breath, she said.

There was a fancy-dress parade along the pier. The idea was to dress up in late nineteenth century clothing, so there were women and girls in long, cumbersome, crinoline dresses, with big, puffed sleeves and tight waists. I don't think anyone would have been wearing corsets though luckily it was not a roasting hot day, just normal English summer weather really, as far as I remember, probably quite breezy near the coast. Men and boys were wearing long jackets, breeches, boots, some were in military style uniform – all sorts. Carrie and I decided to go as nineteenth century horse riders. She had mostly made our costumes from various scraps of strong material she had. We wore skirts which buttoned through, jerkin style tops, hats like small top hats with black net veils over the top and riding boots which pulled closed over our legs and laces all the way up. We actually hired these from a costume hire shop in Norwich.

As Sisi was known for wanting to maintain her health and youth and beauty there were lots of stalls selling herbal remedies, not only for maintaining youthful skin but for actual skin problems too, and aches and pains, again, all sorts. There were some lovely shower and bath lotions as well. I bought some to take as a present for Mum next time I went to Cambridge. I remember Marianne, Jenny and Angela chuckling together sceptically about these stalls but spending a long time looking at the products and buying quite a few!

There were fast food stalls placed strategically throughout the town and in North Lodge Park. These were organised by the café there which is run to this day by a team of volunteers. I recall there were massive queues at all these stalls, especially those selling nineteenth century street food such as strips of fried fish in batter, miniature Cromer crab cakes, hot eels, gingerbread, hot meat puddings, spice cakes and muffins. There were also brightly coloured cold drinks made with sherbet. Jason's children loved those, and, of course, ginger beer and tea and coffee.

The café in North Lodge Park sold little sailing boats which you could race across the boating lake, also known as the Duck Pond as a joke because there were never any ducks on this small bit of shallow water, just a man-made construction. Jason, and his children and my dad just loved this, and became competitive. I loved it too, but I noticed Dad was helping little Tiff a lot and I'm ashamed to say I felt intense, burning jealousy again. I hated myself for that.

Real tennis games were being played on part of the bowling green. It was a proper tournament which teams had signed up to, and practised for, before the event. It followed real tennis rules as they would have played them in Sisi's day, Granda explained, though that version was starting to give way to the modern, apparently easier, version of lawn tennis even then, he told us. I felt that if she played tennis at all she would have gone for the modern version probably. I hoped she had had someone to play with. There were also bowling matches going on, but we all decided that they were not as interesting or as exciting to watch as the tennis.

Coinciding with this commemorative festival a funfair paid its annual visit to the town, staying for a week as it was travelling round the country visiting seaside towns. We decided that rather than leaving all the main festival events in order to go to the fair we would visit it later in the week. I find it hard to remember now exactly where it was set up. It seemed vast and magical and I have the impression it was somewhere between Cromer and East Runton, though closer to Cromer than East Runton, easily walkable from town, overlooking the sea, near a very large, static caravan park. The feeling of galloping along on the merry-go-round, catching glimpses of the sea as we rode high, wind in our faces, is one I'll never forget. The fact that it was not fast and terrifying like the rollercoaster rides meant that you could really concentrate on the feeling of gentle ecstasy rather than just holding on for dear life. Fabulous fun. Not *bwc* exactly but different, more ecstasy and excitement, *e and e,* as we called it that day. *E and e* has never quite caught on as a phrase that Carrie, Rachel and I use in the same way as *bwc* has.

I asked Carrie the other day if she could remember exactly where the fair was, but she couldn't, even more surprisingly neither could Dad. This made the whole experience seem even more dream-like and magical to me. As it was only in Cromer for a week before it travelled off to another seaside resort we must have gone quite soon after the commemorative event, but again I cannot quite remember when.

During this Sisi commemorative year the funfair incorporated some Victorian rides and attractions in keeping with the festival. This meant that, as well as the usual sideshows and games and modern rides, they had some wonderful wooden carousels with brightly painted wooden horses which "galloped" to the music, each one different and somehow characterful. There was also fun game called *Racing Waiters.* This consisted of wooden waiter figures, looking French, with moustaches and bow ties, carrying replica glasses of wine on trays. You chose a waiter and made him move by rolling a ball into a numbered hole, then, when it dropped down, the waiter was propelled forward and the trick was to try to roll the ball gently but firmly enough so that the wine wasn't spilt. I can't remember now how you "won" but it was really good fun, kind of addictive; we played it for ages.

A group of puppeteers was running hour-long daytime shows in the Pavilion Theatre at the end of the pier portraying the happier parts of Sisi's life and especially her visit to Cromer. They showed her cow being milked against the backdrop of Lower Tuckers Hotel and her maid bringing the fresh milk to her. It was so clever and the scenery, just painted backdrops, was brilliant. The shows somehow managed to convey the kindness and generosity she showed towards the people of Cromer too. That was my second favourite part of the whole day. Watching the puppets transported me right into Sisi's Cromer experience.

The highlight for me though was the show in the Pavilion Theatre in the evening. This was a compilation of some of the best-known songs from the German musical of her life interspersed with a narrator recounting Sisi's story. Jason's children went home with him earlier, after we'd had fish and chips in *Mary Jane's*, as they were too young to appreciate this. I loved that I was included automatically with the grown-up trip to see this, no questions asked. Granda had told me about the German musical and that he and Gramsda had seen it on their last holiday together to Hungary in September 1996 when I was only 5. It had been showing throughout the summer at The Open-Air Theatre of Szeged. They saw it on a beautiful, golden evening, he told me, and even then, they'd thought it would be their last holiday together because of her illness, and so, sadly, it turned out to be.

Although Sisi's story was so tragic, I found the show surprisingly uplifting and inspiring. I so wanted to be like Sisi and experience all those emotions. Granda gave me a CD of the songs from a live recording of the musical as a souvenir of the day. It's one of my real treasures and I often listen to it. When I do it brings back memories of that happy, buzzing, magical day but also some of the most tortured moments of my teenage years, because I listened to it throughout that time. Strange to think that these had not yet happened when I first heard the music, yet it was just such experiences that I craved.

Before all that though there are some golden, usually summer, memories of my own to relate before things once more tipped and tilted in my life. Interspersed with these golden memories though is a horrible awareness that I was becoming a child, then teenager, who listened behind closed doors without really wanting to. I certainly didn't like or understand most of what I saw or heard then though I was not exactly unhappy, just a bewildered onlooker most of the time, or so it felt to me. I sought ways to maintain my own equilibrium as my world shifted and shook. I talked to Rachel about most things, not all, sometimes Carrie, but she became even more remote and enigmatic at times.

Chapter 18

THE YEAR BEFORE THE SISI event, 2002, everyone seemed to be planning their holidays. This was the summer between the end of primary school and the beginning of high school. By everyone, I mean everyone except Dad who was not able to take holiday during August that year, as it was the busiest time of year in the Tourist Office and the staff had to take it in turns to take annual leave during August. Most of them had school-aged children it seemed.

Marianne and Carrie were going up to Scotland to visit a cousin of Marianne's; I only discovered just before they went that Granda was going with them. Angela was too busy to go away that summer. There were various art exhibitions, plus the final stages of the studio renovations and she had taken on some pupils to teach too. She was considering running week-long art course holidays and was busy planning the promotion of these with Dad's help. Jason was actively involved in this venture it seemed and was busy designing some holiday accommodation which would make use of a really ancient, huge and rickety old barn in the field near Angela's. It was a bit creepy with hidden, dark corners in the rafters and odd scuffling noises of nameless wildlife as you entered. I hated it. Angela had bought the barn and the field from the farmer who owned the land next to her house and garden.

Angela always loved being in Norfolk during the summer anyway, she told me. I agreed with her even then and still do: the wide skies, long days of unbroken sunshine, or so it seems looking back on those long summers of childhood. Lingering twilights and early dawns (Angela often saw those dawns, I didn't – then) are a lasting memory of childhood and even now Norfolk's my favourite place to be during the summer.

Mum and Robert and the little kids including baby Joshy, were going to France, camping, not in a tent but in a static caravan in deference to having a 1-year old baby in tow. Thinking back, they did ask me if I would like to go with them but when I said no I hadn't realised that everyone at Angela's was making their own plans. So then I felt pretty sad; abandoned and left out of everything. Dad picked this up and I heard him discussing it with Angela.

'I don't think it's fair for her to be here when I'm working all the time and you're so busy with Jason. I don't think it's fair on you two either. It'll be nice for you to have some time alone, won't it?'

'Well, yes, it will, Doug, to be honest, you're the only one who understands and doesn't condemn us, it seems.' Angela sounded sad.

'I would never condemn you. Why would I? What for? Cradle-snatching? It's great that you've both found such happiness and why shouldn't you?'

'I hate to say this, Doug, but it feels good to have Carrie and Marianne away for a bit, much as I love them. It's mainly Marianne who gives us the evil eye but that probably rubs off on Carrie, it's bound to really. Darling Carrie, she's probably pretty confused about things herself and she's got a lot on her plate generally what with waiting for AS results, then the whole university thing if she's successful. There's also that lad that keeps calling and texting her. Did you know? I'll have another coffee if you're pouring, there's enough hot in the pot.'

'No, what lad?' Dad's voice sounded sharp with something odd – anxiety, anger, I couldn't tell. There was a brief pause as he poured the coffee.

'Thanks. You know the one who was quite helpful at the party, can't remember his name – Josh? Joel? – something like that, I think. I don't think she's interested, to be honest, but she certainly plays her cards close to her chest. Oh, we need a bit more milk, it's in the little fridge.' I heard Dad opening the fridge door to get the milk and suddenly had a vivid picture of a Mona Lisa type Carrie holding a fan of cards up close to her chest. I liked the expression, but I didn't like what I was hearing.

'Just a drop, thanks, Doug. Anything *you* want to tell me while we're talking like this?' Angela spoke lightly, almost laughingly, I detected from my hidden spot, then more seriously: 'Don't worry, Doug, I don't condemn, I might advise but I won't condemn.'

There was a brief pause. 'There's nothing, Angela,' Dad seemed almost abrupt, 'back to Amy, I think I'll talk to her and explain what everyone's doing and suggest she goes on holiday with her mum after all. I know they've asked her, and I know they'd love to have her. It'd be helpful for Mags too to be honest. She'd love that. It would be a good break for Amy and good for her to have some normal family life for a change.' He laughed hollowly and I suddenly realised what that phrase: "hollow laughter" actually meant.

'Strange to be saying that where Mags is concerned,' Dad continued, 'never thought I would, but I'm really happy for her, truly I am.'

That sounded more like nice, normal, generous-spirited Dad; I liked it and decided then and there that I would change my mind. Normal family life, having fun being helpful with the little ones, time with Mum, was what I suddenly really wanted, and I knew I wasn't wanted at Angela's that summer, that's for sure, perhaps never again. This thought filled me with such sadness and worry that I just couldn't linger on it. I felt like kicking off the dust of my complicated, adopted household, at least for a bit, washing my hands of them, no more listening behind closed doors and not liking or even understanding what I heard. What did it all mean? What on earth did *cradle-snatching* mean? It sounded horrible and frightening. I asked Carrie later and almost wished I hadn't. She asked why I wanted to know. I said I'd read it somewhere; I knew she didn't believe me and, to be honest, it sounded unconvincing even to me.

'Don't give me that, Amy,' she laughed – but not joyously, 'I reckon you've heard people talking about Jason and my grandmother. Well, don't think about it, don't talk about it at school for goodness sake, they'd never understand.'

I remember the holiday in France mostly being really fun. Even the long drive was relaxing. Mum and Rob had selected a series of audio books for us all to listen to in the car; they were absorbing, good stories and the miles flew by. This did feel like normal family life just as Dad had predicted. On one occasion though, I overheard Rob and Mum talking when they thought we had all fallen asleep in the car; in fact, I had just shut my eyes as the sun was so bright. Mum was explaining how it all seemed so easy with Joshy compared to me, first time round. I hated that.

'I don't know why it's okay this time, obviously I'm older and maybe wiser, ha ha, but I think it's because I know you're there for us and won't suddenly go rushing off, like Doug always did. I guess too because Josh was totally planned there's none of the shock/horror there was when I discovered I was expecting Amy. Of course, I loved her, of course I did, I think, I'm sure, but it was all so difficult…'

I remembered my earlier confusion then when Granda had talked about planned babies. Mum's voice trailed off and I felt my nails digging into both palms as I heard Rob mutter: 'I love you, Magsy and just remember you weren't well then. You're better now. Everything's fine… we're on holiday, it's lovely and great that Amy's with us. She's a great kid, you did good despite everything, she's a credit to you.'

Then I remember Rob asking Mum to put the *Frankie Goes to Hollywood* CD in while we were all asleep. I've always loved the *Power of Love* song since hearing it that first time, full of intense, mixed emotions as I was having heard that conversation, the music belting out as we drove along the empty roads in France. I recall vividly the sight of repeated mirages appearing, one after the other, tantalising, mesmeric, the illusion caused by the bright sun beating down on the long, straight roads, shimmering in the heat haze like so much shiny material undulating, unfolding before us as we approached, intangible, evanescent, magical. That song still evokes for me those hot, dusty, roads, often tree-lined, and summer freedom stretching ahead just as my future lay before me, unfolding gradually, as yet out of reach but leading me onward and onward enticingly, always feeling that need to fast-forward a bit, to grow up, to experience *everything,* without understanding then what *everything* was.

Staying in the caravan was fun. It was situated on a Eurocamp site in Arcachon in south western France, close to many lovely beaches, several within walking distance of the campsite. These beaches were pounded by Atlantic rollers with more significant tide changes and less gentle seas than those that rolled in lazily onto the Mediterranean beaches in the south of France.

I remember it being surprisingly cold at night in the caravan and Mum putting a little warm jacket on Jack, over his pyjama top, to sleep in. Rob called this his smoking jacket for some strange reason that I never quite discovered. I also remember that all the children on the campsite liked to congregate in our caravan. I think it was because Mum and Rob had brought plenty for Fred, Aidan, Jack and me to do: colouring books, sticker books, puzzles, board games, playing cards, Lego construction kits, that kind of thing. I think it was also a relief for the children staying in tents to be inside properly, out of the relentlessly hot, bright sun. I certainly found it a relief to be inside at times.

The "tent parents", as we called them, didn't seem to have brought things for their children to do, maybe because of having less room in the tents, and were only too happy to be sunbathing and relaxing knowing their children were fully occupied in our caravan being looked after by us, especially by Mum and Rob. I felt indignant about this on Mum and Rob's behalf, but they seemed relaxed about it and found it quite funny.

I remember one day a couple of the smaller ones, aged about 2 and a half and 3, I think, went rushing back to their tent to get something and nearly tripped over a huge carving knife just carelessly left lying out on the ground. I got to it quickly enough and placed it somewhere up higher in the tent, but I clearly remember thinking that the parents were stupid. We became quite friendly with some of the families though and on some evenings, we would organise an impromptu barbecue with people contributing meat, fish, salads and bread from their own supplies. That was good. Every morning, Fred, Aidan, Jack and I used to go with Rob to buy a fresh baguette and pains au chocolat for breakfast, fresh fruit too. It was a good routine, and the campsite shop owner used to give us little sweet treats, energy for the journey back to the caravan, he said, laughingly, in good, heavily French-accented English.

Another vivid memory is of the doughnut sellers on the beach which was just a short walk away. There were several of these but one in particular comes vividly to mind with his high-pitched, insistent shouts of: 'Beignets, beignets!'. He wore a frilly pink sunhat, flowery swimming shorts, and was bare-chested and bare-footed as he leapt about the beach like a mountain goat, sometimes jumping up on the black, volcanic, rocky outcrops to reach parties of people encamped, very comfortably, in the crevices between the rocks, away from the itch-making sand. Jack found him terrifying though and would go bright scarlet in the face as he cried and pulled away, saying loudly:

'I don't *like* him; I don't *like* him.'

As we all wanted his delicious doughnuts Fred and I would be asked to go and get them to try to stop him coming any closer to our encampment. This we did willingly, clutching the warm doughnuts in their paper wrappers, savouring the thought of biting into them. Fred thought Jack was just being a stupid baby, embarrassing with it, but I could see why the doughnut-seller frightened Jack so much; it was his otherness, I think, combined with his loud, coercive calls. I believe Jack could not quite place him within his 3-year-old's knowledge and understanding of how men and women behaved. Jack told me recently that this memory still sends shivers down his spine, despite his greater life experience now, aged 14.

Out of a clear blue sky was how Mum described what happened on the last beach trip of our holiday, about three days before we were due to leave to return home. It was the first time I'd heard that expression, "out of a clear, blue sky", I remember, as she sobbed and gulped while pouring it all out to Rob afterwards. The expression was apt. Fred was in a bolshy mood that day. This still sometimes happens. He was certainly not in the mood for being told what to do or what not to do. The barbecue the night before in the campsite had gone on really late and Fred never did well on too little sleep, I already knew that. He also, like me, found the relentlessly bright sun and piercing blue, cloudless skies quite wearing and boring at times. I longed sometimes for the subtle nuances and shifts of weather and mood in our North Norfolk/ East Anglian climate enabling different activities, different states of being, not this everlasting jollity and need to be permanently outside.

We missed 'proper' weather as we called it then, and still do when greeted by a brisk east wind, fine drizzle and overcast skies in our summer months. This is not to say that we don't also relish those perfect English summer days too: gentler, more nuanced, more fleeting therefore precious, compared to the months of blistering, unchanging heat in the south of France, only briefly broken up by ferocious thunderstorms which scarcely refresh the parched ground.

Fred was not in the mood to follow instructions from anyone that day, least of all Mum or me. On this particular day Rob had been invited to make up the numbers in a friendly golfing competition taking place near the campsite as one of the golfers had been struck down by food poisoning. It was something called a foursome golf competition which, as Rob explained to us, is a side or team made up of two players taking alternate shots using one ball. The team who completes the hole in the fewest shots wins that hole. In fact, he explained, the competition was sometimes called "alternate shot". The players take it in turns to tee off, then they carry on, alternating shots, until the ball is holed.

Rob was at first hesitant and reluctant to leave Mum to cope with all of us, a new baby, and four children. But Mum, the new, confident Mum, was insistent that he go off and enjoy a game of golf; it was his sport and the others had seen that he was a strong player, they needed and wanted him. This was why he was torn. I remember so clearly the sense of pride I felt when I heard Mum say to Rob (she didn't know I could hear which made it even better):

'It'll be fine, darling, I've got Amy to help, she's so competent and willing and loves to help. She and Fred get along well and she's great with the little ones, they love her. She even changed Josh's pooey nappy the other day... she's a natural.'

'Well, if you're sure, sweetheart, it sounds to be a fun competition to be fair. I'll text you when I can to report on progress and see how things are with you.'

The day on the beach was going well, despite Fred's mood. We set up camp fairly close to the water's edge as the tide was going out. We had raffia beach mats, a cool bag, buckets and spades, and Jack's beach ball which had been a birthday present for him. His birthday is 31st July, so he had asked for this specially to take on holiday and guarded it fiercely, even being known to take it with him to bed at night.

Fred, Aidan and I swam and paddled with Jack, Fred and I taking it in turns to whoosh him through the warm, shallow water as he shrieked with joy and fear while Mum looked on smiling, holding Josh and paddling through the lacey foam at the water's edge. Aidan swam quite well considering he had only just turned 6, and he was fearless. We all stood holding hands at the water's edge, I remember, and, as the sea drew back with that familiar squelch and suck, it was if the very earth was shifting around us, causing us to hold onto each other even more tightly to combat the strange dizziness we felt as the sand beneath our feet slipped and slid.

When we tired of this, we dug a channel down towards the sea. At this point the tide was coming in quite fast so it was satisfying to see the water swirl into the channel and find its way through it. There were not the vast differences between high and low tide that I was used to at home. I remember so clearly that we made a fantastic sandcastle while baby Josh slept on a mat in the shade of a big parasol and Mum was able to help with the this incredible construction; we all believed it might last longer than it would have at home. We explored some close by rock pools full of tiny, darting, luminescent fish making Aidan and Jack laugh as they felt them slip through their fingers.

Mum, Aidan and I unpacked the picnic from the cool bag on to a big plastic tablecloth in the shade of the parasol while Fred kept Jack amused by playing football and baby Josh slept on. The goal was a small crevice in the rocks. Luckily there was no wind so that the ball usually went more or less where it was kicked. We had transported this cool bag down to the beach quite precariously on the bottom of Josh's buggy bought specially for its beach-worthiness for this holiday. Mum was keen to lighten the load so she urged us to finish every scrap of food reminding us we could always top up with doughnuts or ice creams when the sellers appeared. Everything felt good and relaxed.

Aidan and I cleared up lunch, there wasn't much to clear as we had eaten just about everything, apart from some apples which we could eat later. Fred and Jack carried on with their game at Jack's insistence. Fred was great at this point because it was difficult playing with a just 4-year-old when you're 8, going on 9. Mum was feeding Josh contentedly and told me she felt really sleepy; this often happened when she fed Josh, I'd noticed.

'Make sure I don't nod off, Amy, won't you because I need to keep an eye on everything.'

'Don't worry, Mum, everything's fine,' I assured her.

I remember squinting up at the sky and noticing a kind of haze around the sun whilst simultaneously some scudding white clouds appeared from nowhere. We had literally seen no clouds the entire time in France up to then, thirteen solid days of piercing blue skies. I knew enough about sea and weather conditions to realise that an offshore wind had sprung up, again seemingly from nowhere. I had noticed some lifeguards patrolling the beach earlier, but they were nowhere to be seen just then. As we had made our way down to the beach earlier the flags had been green indicating safe swimming conditions. I had explained to Fred and Aidan what the different colours meant – the notice was in French, English, German, Spanish and Italian and I enjoyed noting the different words for danger as we lingered beside it waiting for Mum, slowed down a little by pushing the buggy, loaded up with our beach paraphernalia.

Almost imperceptibly at this stage of the day, about three hours after we'd arrived, the colour of the sea changed from sparkling blue to a kind of dark green, becoming a menacing black in some areas where the cloud cover above had increased and cast shade. While I was gazing at the clouds and realising that France did have different weather after all, I heard Jack running up behind me, his little face the picture of distress.

'My football's blowed away, it's blowed away into the sea.' He blurted this out between sobs bravely suppressed so as not to wake Mum or Josh. Aidan and I looked out to where he was pointing and saw that Fred had set out after it wading fast through the shallow waters of the ebbing tide as the brightly coloured ball bobbed teasingly ahead of him. I told Aidan to watch Jack and not let him out of his sight and to sit close to Mum while I went to help Fred. I spoke quite fiercely to them both as I knew they had to obey me.

'If you don't sit still here, we won't be able to get your football because we'll have to look after you so just be sensible and good and don't move.' I glanced at Mum and Josh sleeping soundly, remembering how important sleep had been to Mum when she wasn't well and also sometimes what a relief from tension it had been for me at home when, unwell, she'd fallen deeply asleep. These thoughts whizzed through my mind and I didn't stop to weigh things up, I knew I had to get after Fred quickly; perhaps I thought waking Mum would delay things and only panic her, this would just waste time. This is what I think I thought; I don't know for sure, I just knew that there was no time to lose, I *had* to get after Fred fast. Every second counted; I knew that.

Chapter 19

AS I RAN DOWN TOWARDS him Fred was already making rapid progress following the bobbing football, swimming not wading now. I noticed out of the corner of my eye that the green flags had been changed to orange and one was now flying red; it seemed that this is what the lifeguards had been busy doing when Fred and then I had set out after the ball. I knew I was a strong swimmer, but Fred was already so far out I wasn't sure I could catch him. I could feel my shoulders out of the water were quite cold as the sun seemed to have disappeared into a thick haze of cloud and the wind was brisk. I called out loudly to Fred, but the wind took my words just as it was taking the ball, and seemingly Fred, further and further out.

Now well out of my depth too, I summoned all my strength to increase my pace, but I realised, terrifyingly, that I was making no progress. I understood too late that the sudden offshore wind which had sprung up out of nowhere, something that Dad had warned me about countless times, was blowing the ball, Fred and me way, way out to sea. I felt like a complete idiot, but I couldn't worry about that then. I knew I was still a stronger swimmer than Fred because I was older and swam quite a bit both in the sea and in swimming pools at home, but the feeling of powerlessness threatened to overwhelm me.

I became aware then that there was suddenly literally nobody else in the water where previously there had been swimmers, body boarders, family groups playing around together, also that the wind had whipped up the waves so much that, as they rose and fell, they would hide Fred and me from anyone looking out to sea. I wondered briefly whether Mum had woken up. I yelled out to Fred again to swim back towards me, to forget the football which was by now only just in sight bobbing brightly, mockingly, on the horizon, way out of reach. It was obvious to me even at some distance, that, though he was trying his hardest to get back, the wind was pushing him further and further out.

He shouted my name. 'Amy, come and get me, I can't swim strongly enough, my legs...' The wind took the rest of his words. I concentrated on keeping calm, telling myself that the sea was fairly warm, not really rough, it was just windy. It occurred to me then, almost subconsciously, that the sea wasn't actually that warm out here as we were swept further and further out, *against our will*, I kept saying to myself. I remember that clearly, and thinking that the sea is a beast, it doesn't care. The wind was blowing stinging salt spray into my mouth and eyes, temporarily blinding me, hurting me, hindering my progress. I reached down to feel one of my thighs, it felt cold to the touch, this frightened me. I racked my brains to think what Dad would tell me to do and felt myself start to cry as I realised he would've somehow got to me and Fred but that he simply wasn't here. I shook my head to free myself of this pointless, despairing thought.

I looked around and noticed a buoy bobbing close to where Fred was obviously really struggling.

'Fred,' I yelled, 'keep calm and just try to get close enough to that buoy to hold onto it, don't worry the wind is taking you towards it so you *will* get there, just use your energy to help yourself towards it too.' He clearly understood and I could see he was making gargantuan efforts to try to swim towards it; he was losing strength though, so I needed to help him and keep his willpower going. 'We'll be alright, Fred, I'm coming to get you, then we'll be rescued if we just hold on tightly, remember my dad's a lifeboatman, this is what he would tell us to do, everything'll be fine, we'll get back safely.' I could feel my own strength ebbing away and I felt cold all over now. I concentrated on not talking or shouting, that in itself suddenly felt such an effort, but trying to steer myself in the direction of the buoy which was large and a little reassuring.

I saw Fred reach it and grasp it with both his arms which looked very small and white. I was nearly there, we would comfort each other, perhaps sing songs together, familiar, comforting ones. As I reached the buoy, it felt like a long time after Fred had got there, I saw that his face was white, his lips blue, and he whispered,

'We're going to die, Amy.' He was crying openly now.

'No, Fred, we're not going to die.' I summoned all my reserves of strength to speak firmly, almost crossly. 'We're both safely anchored on this buoy, we'll be rescued soon, don't worry. Try to get your legs up onto the buoy if you can because you'll be warmer that way.'

He managed to do that but it caused him to have to lie back on the water and move his arms to keep his upper body afloat so I told him to forget that and hold on with his arms as he had been doing. We were both holding on tightly now and our hands, all four of them, looked small, white and our fingernails were blue. I started singing, *Ten Green Bottles* urging Fred to join in. It was difficult summoning the strength to sing, I could manage a kind of low chant but each time we got to "accidentally fall" we chipped in as loudly as we could, just speaking the words: "we're not going to". It was good because we called this out fiercely, extending the "to"; it was certainly better than calling "Help, help!" into the wind.

Fat raindrops plopped onto the churning sea and we heard a rumble of thunder in the distance. It felt as if the temperature had dropped by about ten degrees. We progressed from *Ten Green Bottles* to *One Man went to Mow* but it wasn't quite as good as *Ten Green Bottles* because we couldn't do the chipping in "we're not going to" bit so we decided to do *Ten Green Bottles* backwards, then *Twenty Green Bottles* backwards and forwards.

I wondered what was happening in our beach camp, whether Mum had woken up and whether Aidan would be able to explain what had happened. I wondered if the anxiety would tip her over the edge into panic or whether she would contact the lifeguards somehow, gathering up baby Josh, Jack and Aidan to her safely. I wondered if the boys would be crying uncontrollably contributing to the pressure on Mum. I wondered how angry she would be with me; I was supposed to be the competent one. I couldn't think like that though, instead I thought of Dad saying: "That's my brave, Amy, you did just the right thing, telling Fred to hold onto the buoy, clever, sensible girl. Lesson learned for you both." This comforting thought gave me renewed strength to try to keep Fred's spirits up.

I had no idea how much time had passed since we had set out after the ball but singing started to make us more tired. I suggested playing *I Spy*. Fred was becoming quieter and quieter and was getting sleepy. I knew enough to know that I *had* to keep him awake so I tickled him vigorously under his arm with one hand then switched to the other arm. He didn't laugh as I had seen him do previously when safely on dry land, but he stirred enough to play the game. I started: 'I spy with my little eye something beginning with F.'

'Fish,' responded Fred in a dull voice.

'Wrong, I can't see any fish.'

'Fingers,' he said looking at our pathetic, white fingers with blue tips as well as blue nails now.

'Wrong but good try.'

'Feet.' He seemed to be perking up a bit and wanted to get the word.

'Wrong again but good try.' He was starting to look cross, but I instinctively felt that this game was keeping him going. I planned to tell Dad about this strategy; it briefly occurred to me that I might never see Dad again and I wondered how my death would affect him and his lifeboating in particular. I felt strangely calm about this thought, detached from it. I didn't care, it wasn't my problem, I just remember a sense of very low-key, almost subliminal, sadness.

'Foam.'

'Wrong, I do see some foam on the waves over there but it's not my word.'

'Froth.'

'Wrong but good idea, Fred. Do you want a clue?'

'No!' he insisted angrily; this was good I felt. But I felt myself beginning to feel sleepy now and shook my head from side to side.

It was just as I did this that I suddenly noticed a small yacht, its sails furled, making its way steadily towards what I assumed would be the nearest harbour. I remembered then Mum and Rob mentioning that there was a little fishing village close by and that some of our barbecue companions had bought some delicious fish there to cook on the barbecue. I heard the gentle throb of its engines and simultaneously clocked the fact that the wind had dropped completely and that the boat was heading straight for us.

'Fred, look, look, look, a boat, a sailing boat, we're going to be rescued, we are, we are!' Fred turned to see where I was pointing and then became fearful.

'We'll be run over, Amy, we will.'

'No, we *won't* be, Fred. Listen to me, let's shout, scream, yell together, now, we'll yell "help" together on my count of 3… 1, 2, 3…'

'Help, help, help!' we yelled together deciding spontaneously to yell it three times. The small yacht continued its steady progress.

'Again, Fred, *now,* 1, 2, 3…'

'Help, help, help!' we yelled at the top of our voices. I heard the engine noise lessen as it was cut back a bit and the boat's progress slowed. I noticed some figures looking towards us.

'Shout again, Fred, come on, 1, 2, 3,'

'Help, help, help!' we yelled again. It was obvious now that the boat was slowing and steering away from us but still getting closer. The relief was immense, I felt my strength ebb further and I noticed Fred's sleepiness again.

'Fred, stay awake, we're going to be rescued, come on you've *got* to stay awake. Don't give up now.' I tickled him again, roughly.

One of the people on deck shouted out to us, it sounded like "Oy!" but I couldn't be sure. Then they were there.

'Des gosses, deux petits. Est-ce qu'il y en a d'autres?' one of them shouted this out to us, angrily it seemed.

'Non, nous sommes tous seuls.' I remembered some French, enough to tell him that there were just the two of us, we were alone. I liked French and was good at it. We had studied it throughout Year 6, which was unusual.

'Français?'

He could obviously tell that I was not a native French speaker, probably because of the understandable but incorrect and non-idiomatic phrase I had just used. Later, I was able to repeat the point in better French.

'Non, Anglais.'

'Ne vous inquiétez pas. Nous arrivons toute de suite.' I translated these reassuring words for Fred's sake: 'He's told us not to worry, Fred, and he said they'll be with us in no time. It'll be fine.'

Just as I finished explaining to Fred what was happening, I noticed a different but similarly insistent, throbbing sound and looked up to see a khaki-coloured helicopter overhead, making its way towards us. The yacht was almost alongside the buoy now, trying to get close enough to grab us and pull us into the boat. I wondered if they had summoned the helicopter or whether the coastguard had. The helmsman was skilfully keeping the boat close alongside the buoy by reversing and then going forwards. At exactly the right moment the largest of the men, with a long, black beard, indicated wordlessly that he would grab Fred first. The noise of the helicopter was deafening and precluded any further speaking. He managed to grab Fred and hand him over to another crew member. I felt a simultaneous sense of relief and intense loneliness. I could feel myself giving up my strength and allowing whatever was to happen just to happen. I didn't care. It felt strangely relaxing.

Next though, he managed to lift me too and as I clung onto him tightly, I was ashamed to feel tears coursing down my cheeks, unstoppable. The large man lay me down surprisingly gently and leant down to say right into my ear:

'Ne bouge pas, petite,' using his hands to indicate that I must remain lying down. Somebody else brought some towels and a couple of blankets, indicating I should dry myself. He also handed me a dry T-shirt and some jogging bottoms, both obviously much too big but dry of course. I wondered where Fred was and then I noticed him beside me, also covered in blankets. There were three crewmen, I remember that clearly. One of them asked me again, very gently, if there had been anyone else swimming with us. I found my better French returned suddenly :

'Non, c'est juste nous deux.'

Talking to Dad about the sequence of events afterwards when he arrived much later that evening, he told me he had discovered that the yacht's crew had alerted the coastguard very shortly after Mum had managed to contact them by telling a lifeguard patrolling the beach that Fred and I were in the sea. Dad later had gone to talk to them, and the helicopter crew, to thank them and discover more details about what happened.

They had decided to winch me and Fred into the helicopter using the double strop method because it was obvious that we were both suffering from hypothermia and it was not clear whether we had swallowed sea water. This meant that it was important we were lifted horizontally, not vertically, to prevent what is known as "post-rescue collapse". I had heard about this before but by the time Fred and I were lying in the boat covered in blankets I was beyond coherent thought. We were considered to be at significant risk of this post-rescue collapse, it seems. Dad told me that the yacht's crewmen had been brilliant at following the helicopter crew's instructions. Apparently, the helicopter crew always takes charge in these situations, but the noise of the helicopter makes it very difficult of course.

Fred and I were taken to hospital, which was about fifteen minutes away by helicopter, and both kept in overnight. Mum and the little kids were not allowed to visit as they had an outbreak of norovirus in the hospital, but Dad and Rob arrived separately. Fred and I were in a four-bedded bay in the children's ward and the nurses treated us so kindly and gently and babied us a bit; for once in my life I liked that. I felt young and as if I had coped with a lot, but also very doubtful that I had done the right thing. Dad was full of praise for what I'd done, specially telling Fred to cling onto the buoy. He reassured me that he could completely understand my decision-making about going after Fred, even the bit about not waking Mum.

'You had seconds to make the decision, Amy, seconds, you did good, kiddo, really good and I'm so proud of you, so, so proud of you, darling girl.'

Dad and Rob had talked about the sequence of events in detail. Rob had, of course, come rushing from his golf competition as soon as he got Mum's text. I was pleased to see Dad and Rob being so natural and easy with each other. We were all of course forbidden ever to take any kind of inflatable beach ball to any beach ever again. Of course, we needed no persuading, lesson learnt good and proper.

Rob gave me a letter from Mum.

17ᵗʰ August 2002

My darling lovely brave Amy,

I am so, so proud of you, my love. You did absolutely right, Dad says so, so does the helicopter crew. If anyone's at fault it's Rob and me for allowing the inflatable ball to come to the beach with us, we were idiots, never again.

I'm so sorry I fell asleep, darling, but an inner, honest, insightful part of me, believes that if I'd been awake, I might have tried to stop you going after Fred... I dread to think of the outcome then. Suddenly all the lifeguards had disappeared so you couldn't even have run to find them. Some were changing the flags it seems, which obviously needed to be done, and two were bringing in a man who had floated out too far on a lilo having been drinking at lunchtime and fallen asleep, idiot. His stupidity could have cost you two innocent children your lives, but I mustn't dwell on that.

I only woke up when it started to rain and saw Aidan and Jack sitting as still as statues next to me, guarding me and Josh. They said afterwards that they'd been told to by you, bless their hearts, bless your heart.

Oh, Amy, how stupid I was to let Aidan and Fred play with that ball on the beach... Dad hasn't said so, but I know he's thinking it. He and Rob seem to get on well, that's good, kinda funny too, if you think about it!

I wish I could visit you, darling, but rules are rules and in place for a good reason. It would be terrible if we all went down with norovirus, especially little Josh, very dangerous for babies. I'm looking forward to getting home now, I expect you are too. Can't wait for you to get out of hospital. Dad has suggested you fly back with him. You may like to – we thought you should decide, of course.

It's so lovely having you with us, darling, remember if ever you want to come and live with us permanently you only have to say the word. Rob and the kids love you almost as much as I do, sweetheart but there's no pressure I promise you that.

I hope you're recovering well, brave girl, and not dwelling on what happened too much.

All my love to you as ever,
Mum xxxx

I loved this letter and found it the other day when I was looking for a suitcase; it was tucked into a side pocket. In hospital Fred and I played some good games of *I Spy,* and he asked me what my F word had been. I remember inviting him to guess again but he wanted a clue, he was playful now.

'I can still see this F,' I said laughing.

The penny dropped; he knew he'd got it:

'It's me, Fred,' he declared triumphantly. I laughed in agreement.

I decided after some thought to fly home with Dad, I suddenly wanted "proper weather". It seemed fair, too, when he had come all this way. I felt torn though as I found it fun being with my half siblings and Rob and Mum but we arranged that I would visit them again in Cambridge for the last long weekend of the summer holidays, the late August bank holiday before the leap into high school. That felt good and soon and as if it would somehow lay to rest the terrifying near drowning experienced by Fred and me.

Chapter 20

HOW BEST THEN TO DOCUMENT those high school years? Angela chuckled when I told her I was starting this chapter with that sentence.

'Oh, Amy, that vast distance of time, what is it now? You finished high school, hmm, when? All of three years ago? Oh, the wisdom of youth! Love it.'

I laughed with her; she meant no harm for sure but truthfully it's difficult to recall it all as honestly as I want to as so much seems to cloud my memories of that time now, good and bad.

Contrary to expectations I quite enjoyed being at the "bottom of the tree" in Year 7, perhaps as a reaction to the burdens of responsibility I had felt during most of primary school and, of course, during the rescue in France. I felt a sense of freedom and loved it when some of the Year 11 girls mothered us a bit. It was funny and fun. Rachel found it all a bit weird but then I guess her childhood had not been as weird as mine when all's said and done.

It was odd, and tiring at first, to have to go from classroom to classroom in between lessons; some of the classrooms were miles from each other, it seemed, and you couldn't be late for the start of a lesson. There was a strict rule about which side of the corridors you could walk on to save kids bashing into each other both accidentally and on purpose. There were teachers, teaching assistants (TA's) and prefects on kind of police patrol at this stage and numerous detentions were issued for pushing, tripping people up, swearing, that kind of thing. It felt different, too, not having your own desk in your own classroom with a class teacher who knew you and the others well, but it was pretty easy to adapt to all those aspects of high school to be honest.

Lunch times were manic and horrible and so, so noisy: loud voices, chairs scraping across the linoleum-covered floor, cutlery clanking, plates crashing, so many kids, queueing to buy hot food, or scrambling for somewhere to sit and eat a packed lunch away from trouble. I hated that. I couldn't understand why they didn't stagger lunchtimes from year group to year group, say between 12 and 2 – there were at least four half hour slots there. I felt sure it could be done. This issue was brought up by Student Council repeatedly, but it didn't change for the entire five years I was there.

There were some kids who had eating disorders, they were allowed to eat in a quiet area with a teacher or TA in attendance. Nobody else was allowed anywhere near. I didn't even know where they went or how it all worked if somebody just wouldn't eat. I felt so sorry for them.

I decided, without telling anyone at home, to audition for a part in the summer play which was being put on as a combined effort between the English and Drama departments. I loved my English teacher, Mrs Hebden, and she loved my work. The Drama teacher, Mrs Gordon, was great too in a different way. She had incredible energy even though she was pretty old, I think. She was down to earth and would take no nonsense. Everyone knew she preferred teaching the older age groups, she made no secret of that, but for some reason she took a liking to me from Year 7 onwards.

The auditions were tough, she would have no "pussy-footing nonsense" she declared openly; that was her well-worn phrase. If you passed the audition and there was a part suitable for your age, gender, height then you would get a part, if not you wouldn't, simple. It was well known that the parents were more upset by this approach than the students; we understood competition, we recognised talent and we wanted the play to be good.

In my case there was no parental involvement whatsoever, so I certainly didn't have to worry about any embarrassing parental interference. When I told Dad I had got the part of the youngest child, Phyllis, in *The Railway Children* he merely remarked rather vaguely that he had a crazy godmother called Phyllis. Of course, he had no idea that about fifty girls in Year 7 had gone for that part and about seventy in Year 8. Carrie was really busy in the sixth form at Sheringham, her last year, with A-levels looming, painting commissions to fulfil for the mermaiding group and some weekend work experience at nearby Pensthorpe with the recently formed Pensthorpe Conservation Trust. Angela was pleased for me but, like Dad, she had no real idea of the stiff competition for the part. To be fair she was genuinely busy with her many projects at that time.

Marianne seemed to be spending most of her time at Granda's these days. Granda was the person who congratulated me the most, understanding it all a bit more it seemed, and he was the only one who asked when the play was on and for me to be sure to get him a ticket. I told Mum in a letter about it but when she wrote back, she forgot to mention it; I remember how much that hurt. I felt as if I was a nothing to her, of no importance whatsoever. She talked a lot about baby Josh and what he was up to, crawling everywhere, taking a few steps, that sort of thing, and told me that Fred had won a prize at school for submitting a local news story to a local newspaper as part of a schools' competition. His prize was £50 and to shadow a reporter for a day. He also had an open invitation to continue to submit local news stories; her letter was full of pride about this, I remember it so well.

This lack of interest gave me a strange sense of freedom though and I remember it made me want to please the two teachers, Mrs Gordon for Drama and Mrs Hebden for English, as best I could. I drank in their praise and attention. It was similar with some of the older girls, specially, a girl called Holly who played Roberta, my older sister, who mothered me on and off stage and pretended to adopt me. I lapped it up, it was funny too.

The rehearsals were tiring but fun. I would sometimes go home first, eat quickly and try to get a lift back to school in time, it was usually Dad who did that, sometimes Angela, or I would cycle. Last resort would be Jason when he was there. Other times I would just stick around school like some of the others did, and the older ones took charge of us younger ones when we went into town to get snacks for tea. Rachel had got a role as a scene shifter; she was very happy with that and was just pleased to be involved.

Harry and Finn had undertaken to help with some of the technical, audio-visual stuff by videoing the steam trains arriving at Sheringham and recording train noises and some other sound effects; it seemed clever, skilled stuff to me. Rachel and I used to go and talk to them in the recording room when I wasn't needed on stage for a bit. There were only two other Year 7's who had got parts, more minor parts, so I felt proud of my part and proud of the fact that I could just go and talk to Finn and Harry as I knew them both out of school.

When the show started there was a real buzz of excitement backstage. Those of us in the cast felt like celebrities in school. It all felt just a bit different. Classrooms had been given over for use as dressing rooms in the evenings of the performances. These took place on five evenings in a row including the dress rehearsal on Tuesday. There were five performances open to the public: Wednesday, Thursday, Friday, Saturday evening and a Saturday matinée and we did two performances during the weekdays: one for Year 7's, 8's, 9's, one for Years 10 and 11. So it was all-consuming, tiring and really fun. Ordinary school seemed intrusive at this time. I was surprised that I had no difficulty at all in learning my words, I think this was because we had lots of rehearsals and because I felt myself to be right in character.

Looking out at the darkened school hall, packed with expectant faces, and hearing the professional-sounding announcements about turning off mobile phones and directions to the fire escapes produced enjoyable, stomach-churning feelings of excitement and anticipation amongst the cast. But this was nothing compared to the sense of proud achievement when taking our bows, hearing the applause and getting a standing ovation each time; this was music to our ears, we loved it. This experience caused many of the cast to aspire to go into drama as a career but I always knew that for me it was just an enjoyable hobby and a way to get lots of kudos and fun at school making me very relaxed about the whole thing.

Those school plays are definitely one of my best memories of school days. In the time I was there I auditioned and got a good part each time. In Years 7, 8 and 9 we did two shows, one in March and one in July, only one in Years 10 and Year 11, sadly there was just not enough time because of exams. Rachel and I were chatting about them the other day and trying to remember the order we did them in. We got our list right in the end with Harry and Finn's help: *The Railway Children*, I played Phyllis, *Tom's Midnight Garden*, I played Hatty, *The Secret Garden*, I played Mary Lennox, *David Copperfield*, I played Dora Penlow, *The Lion, the Witch and the Wardrobe*, I played Susan, *A Midsummer Night's Dream*, I played Helena, and *Goodnight Mister Tom*, I played Mrs Hartridge. I remember it feeling very strange to be playing a teacher in front of my teachers and to have to wear a cushion when I became pregnant in that play.

And in Year 11 the one production was *The Tempest.* I played Miranda, it felt like the pinnacle of my school career. One of my newer friends, Jordy, who I'll explain more about later, played Caliban, brilliantly. He became part of our close-knit group, at that stage: me, Rachel, Hannah and Jordy (somewhere along the line we had lost Lauren Peters to another friendship group with no regrets on anyone's part) and Harry and Finn in their last year at Sixth Form College but both came back to help with the technical aspects of the show, lighting and audio.

I remember that when I played Helena, Mrs Gordon had the idea of making a recording of me giving out the mobile phone announcement in Shakespearian language although she decided to give out the fire alarm message straightforwardly. She asked me to think something up if I could and she would think about it too. Between us we came up with:

Forsooth the hour is come,
Wherein our play begins,
So lend your ears to us, dear friends,
Not to your beloved phones.
Pray switch them off right now we beg,
And hear our play unfold
As with the Bard we take you forth
Into midsummer magic and mayhem,
Into worlds both new and old.

The audience loved it. This was the fun part of high school. The bit that was strange was how Harry changed so much. It started mainly at the beginning of year 9 for me when he was in Year 11. At first, I wondered if it was the stress of his exams, but he just started avoiding me, never making eye contact. It seemed such a contrast with the summer holidays after Year 8 when I went on holiday with Rachel's family, just a couple of weeks earlier at the end of August.

When Harry started to become so strange, I thought a lot about that holiday. Rachel's parents had suggested each of their three children ask a friend to come with them but I'm pleased to say they had invited me first before they had decided that it was only fair that if Rachel had a special friend with her on holiday then the other two should, two more children would make no difference at all, they felt. So Iain had chosen his friend, Sam, and Finn had chosen Harry. It then seemed mean to leave Hannah out as she was friendly with Rachel and me even though she had become really annoying again in high school, tagging along with us whether we wanted her to or not. And with her being Harry's sister, it just seemed kinder and the obvious thing to do .

It was to be an end of summer holidays getaway to Pembrokeshire where Rachel's parents had owned a holiday home for years in a little village called Abercastle, near St David's. I think the other parents contributed to the cost of food and travel, I don't think Dad or Mum were asked, but I don't know. Rachel's parents took both their cars with Jenny driving Rachel, Hannah, Harry, and me and Paul driving Iain, Sam, and Finn. Anyway, it was great, even Hannah was better here, less whingey and whiney, more willing to enter into the spirit of things and outdoor life. There was one shop and just a few houses in the village. I loved Abercastle. It had a working harbour formed of a narrow inlet making it special and secretive as well as providing protection from the prevailing winds.

I remember a great sense of freedom and relaxation towards the end of what had been quite a boring summer holiday with lots of strange undercurrents of tension at Angela's. Rachel's parents were happy for the seven of us to go off on our own as long as Finn and Harry understood that they were responsible for our safety and we understood that we all had to be sensible. We had all, including Jenny and Paul, hired bikes from a place in nearby Trefin and we all knew enough about life by the sea to be aware of the dangers; the main thing at Abercastle was always to know what the tide was doing otherwise you could easily be cut off by the incoming tide. We knew this which was why when it happened, *out of a clear blue sky*, that phrase again, we were all taken by surprise.

Most days we cycled down to the beach taking a picnic which we put together in the morning. Sometimes Jenny and Paul came but they often left us to our own devices whilst they did all the necessary jobs: shopping, cooking, some minor repairs and decorating in the house which they let through an agent for the rest of the year. They had some good friends in Trefin, and the two families always arranged to come down at the same time at the end of August if they possibly could. The other family, the Hudsons, had two children, a boy, Alex, who was the same age as Harry and Finn and a girl, Jo, who was the same age as Rachel, Hannah and me. We all thought it funny that their names could either be boys' names or girls' names. We liked that.

Most of the time we just wanted to laze about, swimming, snorkelling, talking about everything under the sun it seemed. The older ones compared notes on exams, future plans, sixth form choices, that kind of thing, and we all talked about annoying school rules and the weird ways of teachers and schools generally. Alex and Jo couldn't get their heads around the "vertical forms" system. In our school forms comprised pupils from all year groups from Year 11 down to Year 7 with a form teacher who, in theory, got to know you well throughout your time at the school. We had "Form Time" each morning and after lunch for registration. There were form activities too such as weekly quizzes which were very competitive and devised by the pupils. They were fun. The idea was that the older kids helped the younger ones to settle and were there to help sort out any issues such as bullying. It did actually seem to work most of the time, though I often saw some vicious ankle kicking in-between classes, and some ostracising of kids and disturbances amongst friendship groups. Alex and Jo thought this system sounded to be a good idea, but both felt that if it were suggested by Student Council at their school the idea would just be dismissed.

It was quite irritating at times to have Iain and Sam with us because they seemed so much younger but we included them as best we could, often setting them competitive missions to keep them occupied and out of the way for a bit. This wasn't really being unkind, they loved it. The missions were things like collecting the most razor shells in half an hour, or stone skimming competitions, or running from one side of the beach, shaped like a cove, to the other, as a race. We set them to digging channels, making as many bucket sandcastles as they could in a given time, in competition with each other, after which they could throw stones, carefully, to destroy them all.

The abiding feeling for me then was a sense of being completely relaxed, free and off guard. There was no listening at doors, no bewilderment about things going on around me. I loved being with Rachel's parents; they were so kind and caring and somehow safe and reassuring without ever treating us as younger than we were, which was what Hannah's mum always did. This was as well as her being always tense and somehow constrained by something unknowable at that time.

Perhaps it was the feeling of being off guard that led to the terrifying events unfolding in front of our eyes. I blamed myself entirely as I had invented the game to keep Sam and Iain occupied. Ironically, I was pleased with myself when I thought of the *idea*; it was called a scavenger hunt and I remembered taking part in one of these many years earlier as part of a church fête fund-raiser when I was staying with Granda aged about 7. The idea was to give a long list of items to be found and brought back as evidence of success and the first one home was the winner. When the game was used as a fund-raiser, I think participants bought tickets to join the hunt, I remember it being really fun.

We older ones all got together to compile the list. I cannot now remember all the items but some stay in my mind: starfish – there were loads of those on the beach; flat stone; cuttlefish – again there were lots lying about; anything plastic; a razor shell; a dead crab and of course the item I could never forget – green seaweed. Iain and Sam loved the idea of this game and set off speedily taking their buckets to carry their trophies back to us.

Sam arrived back first, triumphantly bearing his bucket held high above his head in both hands. 'I'm the first, I'm the winner!' he declared. We had to think of a prize quickly, deciding against an ice cream as we all enjoyed those every day and it would be unkind to Iain to exclude him from that treat. So we decided to make him a certificate when we got home and also clubbed together to give him a two pound coin. Luckily Harry had one and we all paid him the necessary pence. Sam was delighted and planned to save it.

We waited for Iain to return, chatting in our usual way, aiming stones at nearby targets, making a game of it. I think it was either Finn or I who, after about half an hour had passed, asked Sam where he had last seen Iain and whether he knew how he was getting on with finding the items. Sam remembered seeing him running over towards the next bay, he thought he had got many of the items already. Sam said the thing that was most difficult to find was green seaweed and he had found just one tiny piece deep in the crevice of a rock, the rest of the seaweed had been brown, he explained, and quite smelly.

Another half hour passed quickly whilst we were trying not to feel too worried but at the same time scanning the beach and looking out to sea for a sight of Iain. Then, abruptly, Harry and Finn thought we should divide into two search parties with Harry leading one, Finn the other, and search in opposite directions. It was decided that Hannah and Sam should stay in our camp in case Iain returned there. I was in Harry's team: he chose me and Alex, I remember, Rachel and Finn were together with Jo. Harry, Alex and I went off in the direction that Sam had last seen Iain heading, Rachel, Jo and Finn set off in the opposite direction. We planned to search for no more than half an hour and if we had not located him, we would have to alert Rachel's parents and the coastguard, Harry explained quietly looking tense and strained.

As we walked along towards the next bay, we called Iain's name repeatedly; the tide was coming in fast by now. We decided to run up the slope from our beach and carry on along the coast path so we could look down on the bay without being cut off by the incoming tide. Although this route was longer, we were all fast runners and it seemed sensible as it would give us a good vantage point too. Harry was wondering if we should alert Rachel's parents at that stage, but I suggested we at least get to our vantage point. It was a hot day and we were soon puffed out from running. We met a few walkers and asked if they had seen a young boy on their route. One of the groups asked if we had any adults with us and said we should contact our parents. We told them we were just going to get past the headland so we could see the bay and then we would. They were reassured by this adding that if we didn't see him, we should contact the coastguard, checking we had a phone between us. Harry did and knew the number for the coastguard; this satisfied them.

At first, I thought the cry was a seagull calling but then I urged Harry and Alex to stop and listen with me, and we all realised simultaneously that it was a cry for help. Quickening our pace, we rounded the headland and climbed up the steep cliff path, just a few minutes' fast trot, I remember, and looked down on the picturesque scene below. The bay formed a gentle cove, protected in some ways from the open sea but framed for the most part by sheer rock face with the odd, narrow inlet and the whole area crisscrossed with tiny sheep tracks forming sandy, hillocky, uneven pathways, frequently blocked by fallen boulders. The sea was sparkling blue, with white horses catching the sun far out to sea, whilst closer in it was obvious that the tide had nearly reached its height as there was just a narrow strip of beach soon to be covered completely, effectively blocking off any return by that route to our beach.

We decided to call out Iain's name telling him to call out again.

'Iain, we're coming, where are you?' I yelled. His answering cry told us to head on a little further up the cliff and then we saw him, trapped in a crevice between two rocks. We ran towards the edge of the cliff to see if there was a way he could climb up but as we got nearer we saw that his right leg was twisted at a horrible angle and he was bleeding from a cut on his shin.

'Shit, Amy, this is serious, he needs urgent help,' Harry was dialling the coastguard as he spoke.

'Don't worry, Iain, help's coming, be brave,' I called out. Alex texted his parents.

Harry then rang Jenny who said she and Paul would be there in about fifteen minutes, Harry was able to describe exactly where we were. Almost instinctively I whipped off my T-shirt whilst Harry was telephoning (I had my swimsuit on underneath) and threw it accurately down to Iain telling him to use it as a tight bandage over the cut. By now Iain was sobbing piteously, saying his leg hurt.

'The bandage will make it better,' I assured him, 'the coastguard are on their way and so are your mum and dad. Tie it tightly, really tightly, round the cut so the bleeding stops.'

'Amy, that's brilliant,' Harry commented, still looking stricken by the turn of events though, 'brilliant throw too, kiddo.' Despite the traumatic, scary situation I felt proud then.

After what seemed like ages but in reality was about seven minutes, Harry told me afterwards, we found ourselves deafened by the roar of the red and green Wales Air Ambulance and saw the lifeboat from Fishguard and Goodwick round the corner of the bay. Jenny and Paul arrived shortly afterwards looking shocked but calm. Jenny called out to Iain:

'Don't worry, love, your rescuers are here. It looks like you'll get a ride in a helicopter.'

We watched as two members of the helicopter crew were winched down towards Iain trapped on the rocks, it was obviously impossible for the helicopter to land safely anywhere close enough. Harry had told them that it looked as though Iain had broken his leg and that he had a bleeding wound.

We saw them insert a tube into a vein in his hand. This would be to give him some pain-relieving drug, Jenny told us, while they tried to immobilise his leg before moving him and checking the wound, apply another dressing, that sort of thing. She sounded tearful and looked very anxious.

'Poor little chap. I want to be down there with him,' she said shakily, holding on tightly to Paul's hand.

Skilfully the doctor and paramedic managed to move him carefully once they had given him some pain-killing medication and redressed his wound so that he could be lifted bodily out of the crevice. At this point one of the two crew members, the paramedic, was winched back up, then a stretcher was lowered. Once Iain was safely strapped onto that he was winched upwards with the other crew member, the doctor, and the lifeboat chugged back to base.

Chapter 21

HARRY HAD PHONED FINN TO update him whilst we were waiting for what we thought would be the coastguard helicopter and for Jenny and Paul to arrive and told him and Rachel to go back to our camp on the beach and wait there for news. He now phoned Finn again to say that we would meet them all back at the house, Jenny and Paul would drop us off there and head straight to the hospital, they had phoned the Hudsons to come and collect Jo and Alex and the rest of the bikes as they couldn't fit us all into the car. I noticed Harry was by now chalk white, his mouth set in a tight line, and, whilst on the phone, he kept obsessively rubbing his free hand backwards and forwards over his hair. I had to stop myself from putting a hand out to stop the incessant movement.

On the way back Jenny asked us why Iain had been alone on the rocks. She didn't sound accusing or cross, she just wanted to know what happened. I explained haltingly about the scavenger hunt and that only Sam and Iain had been taking part and then I found myself crying uncontrollably as I explained that it was all my fault for adding green seaweed to the list to make it harder. Harry was staring, unseeing, out of the window as the beautiful Pembrokeshire countryside sped past, distracted with anxiety it seemed.

I was conscious of not wanting to take attention away from Iain who obviously needed his parents to get to the hospital as quickly as possible, but I simply couldn't stop crying. I remember clearly feeling that I would never get over the guilt I felt at my part in what happened. Harry immediately came to my defence.

'No, no, we all made the list, Amy, we're all to blame, all of us but specially me as I'm the oldest. I'm an idiot, an idiot!' He sort of quietly shouted the word.

Jenny and Paul could not have been kinder. Jenny held me close once we reached the house and told me to look her in the eye and understand that I was not to blame. She turned to Harry who was sitting with his head in his hands.

'And, Harry, Iain is old enough to know the dangers, you mustn't take the blame on yourself like this, it does nobody any good. Hush now,' she said as she stroked the hair off my burning, tear-streaked face. 'Now, I'm going to collect some things for Iain, you find yourself another T-shirt, lovey and I suggest you eat your picnic here, Paul will make us all a nice cuppa, won't you, darling?'

Within barely ten minutes she and Paul had headed off to the hospital. Iain had been taken to Withybush Hospital, which was about half an hour's drive away, but only a few minutes by helicopter. We all felt very subdued and worried about him. Harry still looked pale, shut in somehow, as if waging a private battle with himself. He seemed to me to be unreachable then.

Just as we had cleared the picnic away, there was a knock at the door, which turned out to be Alex's dad who had brought our bikes round and come to see if we wanted to go round to theirs for the evening. Jenny, meanwhile, had rung Finn and told him that Iain had a compound fracture to his tibia and told him to tell me that the surgeon who spoke to him had said that whoever had had the idea of throwing a T-shirt down to Iain had possibly saved his life. The nurses had returned my blood-soaked T-shirt to her in a grey bag marked "Patient's Property", she told him, laughing a bit. She also explained that she and Paul would wait at the hospital until Iain came out of surgery and that she would stay the night there, Paul would come home. It was a severe fracture and Iain needed wires to keep the broken ends of bones in place.

I remember rerunning those words of praise from the surgeon through my mind repeatedly. I felt a glow of pride which went some way to assuaging my feelings of guilt, only some way though. I had phoned Dad that evening and told him the whole story. He listened carefully and then heaped praise on my action in tossing the T-shirt down:

'Genius, Amy, genius. I'm very, very proud of you.'

Iain stayed in hospital the next day and night and was discharged on the last day of our holiday. He travelled home with Jenny, Rachel, Sam and me and Paul took the others. So that event overshadowed my memories of that holiday although Iain made a quick recovery and certainly enjoyed the kudos of returning to school with a cast to be signed. I still think back to the sun-drenched days of that holiday before the accident happened and those relaxing days of easy friendships amongst our little group because I remember that it was on returning to school for Year 9 that everything changed.

Harry and Finn were in their GCSE year and wore different uniforms, no longer having to wear ties, instead just a jumper. They were both prefects and Harry was a House Captain. Harry, especially, seemed to be aloof, not making eye contact, even in drama rehearsals. I wondered if I brought back memories of Iain's accident and our part in it; it seemed so unlike Harry to take things to heart in this way. I was sometimes aware that he was looking at me, but he would quickly look away if I tried to make eye contact; it was odd and upsetting, and that all-too-familiar sense of bewilderment returned.

If I felt this bewilderment around Harry at school it was as nothing compared to the utter shock of stumbling on Angela in her studio one dark, rainy afternoon at the beginning of the Christmas holidays. I had gone to find her as she was wanted on the phone, so it was not even a listening-at-doors occasion, it was a completely legitimate search for her. The studio was beautifully lit, I remember, on that dark, gloomy afternoon, with the pale grey blind, which I had helped Angela choose, closed against the gathering darkness. I noticed the bright spotlight before I even saw Jason lying stretched out on the sofa stark naked. It was the first time I had seen a naked man, and I was taken aback by his beauty and strength and the amount of hair evident, especially the line from his belly button down towards his genital area or "you know, that bit" as I stumblingly described it to Rachel later.

Angela was at her easel painting him; the painting seemed to stare out at me as if to emphasize that yes, you are looking at a real naked man and I am here again in this painting for eternity. Neither Angela nor Jason turned a hair as I delivered the message, handed Angela the phone, and virtually ran up to my bedroom hoping not to meet anyone on the way. Dad called out to me:

'Amy? You OK?'

'Fine,' I mumbled, 'just getting a sweater.' I lay on my bed, stretched out, flat on my back, staring at the plain white ceiling, watching a tiny spider clinging to its cobweb. I remember really focusing on that tiny creature and wondering if it ever felt the same sense of being a part of this topsy turvy world whereby hanging on by thread to a wavering, uncertain fixed point was the only reality.

What was it all about? The atmosphere in the studio had been electric, charged with something unnameable and unknown to me. I knew that Angela had been giving life drawing classes, we all knew that; she had talked about it a lot. She had in fact been approached, she told us, by several sets of new parents wanting her to paint them naked with their new babies. She had declined because, as she explained, the world is a strange place and people have some strange ideas. She told me later that people had started using Artificial Intelligence, AI, to make avatars of dead people so that people could communicate with these avatars to help them grieve. I worried about this and it brought to mind Angela's refusal to paint people with their babies which seemed to me to be sensible.

It was becoming increasingly, insistently, evident to all of us, that Angela and Jason had become an "item", that they were in a relationship. We just had to get over the fact that she was 81 and he was 52, but it was hard, it just was. They both seemed very happy and Angela certainly had never behaved like an old woman, she could easily have been taken for early to mid-sixties, Dad said. I found it harder to tell, I'm afraid anyone over about 40 seemed old to me in those days. They still do actually.

Having lain there for a while I decided to text Rachel, we texted each other a lot then – we both had mobiles, as did Angela and Jason. I just said I had something to tell her, she knew me well enough to know that it really would be something. She suggested meeting up in Cromer that afternoon, we both had Christmas shopping to do, and had planned to see the just released latest *Lord of the Rings* film, *The Return of the King*. Harry and Finn wanted to see it too so we asked them if they wanted to meet us in Cromer, do Christmas shopping, see the film, which was showing at 5pm, fish and chips afterwards, *Mary Jane's* takeaway was open until 10pm on winter Fridays, home on the bus. Granda and Dad had both given me Christmas shopping money, and I had saved pocket money, so I felt I could afford this treat. Harry and Finn, who had turned 16 in September and October respectively, were working as pool lifeguards at weekends at the newly built Victory swimming pool in nearby North Walsham and Rachel had birthday money from her November birthday. It felt good to be planning an outing with my friends, to get away from Angela's for a bit.

And so it turned out that I told our close-knit group of four the latest saga in my adopted family's lives. I'm sorry to say that it was one of those occasions when, once again, we just could not stop laughing, it was like a kind of shock reaction. It didn't feel as if we were being unkind or mocking their age, it really didn't, we just found ourselves giggling and spluttering hysterically and had to stifle it as we had gone into the church for some warmth. There was a welcoming Christmas market set up, with the smell of freshly made holly wreaths bringing the sense of the crisp, frosty air outside into the cavernous church where it intermingled with the enticing, spicy aroma of mulled wine, warming, inviting. We sat down in an empty pew quite near the altar and choir stalls so I could tell my news out of the freezing cold wind which was still brutal near the open door of the church, the crowds of people, in their scarves, woolly hats, big coats scarcely troubled by it as they wandered round the bright, Christmassy stalls. I remember Rachel saying:

'Wow, Amy, your family's so exciting, ours are just plain boring.'

And me replying unnecessarily sharply.

'Well, for a start Angela and. Jason are *not* my family, as you well know, and I'll have you know that I'd give anything to have proper, boring parents who are together and just plain, boring old normal any day.'

I remember trying to hold back tears then, and my outburst certainly stopped us laughing, I hated myself for changing the mood though and felt the familiar digging of my nails into my hands, something I was determined to stop doing. Rachel looked uncomfortable, I felt sorry about that, I remember Harry kind of taking charge.

'It's OK, Amy, we understand, we really do, Rachel meant no harm. Come on, let's get this shopping finished, I want to smash it today, hate shopping.'

We got up to carry on and I tried to make eye contact with Rachel, but it felt awkward suddenly. I felt I had wrecked a potentially fun outing and was desperate to restore the fun because actually the hysterical laughter had really helped. I spoke without looking at Rachel:

'I'm sorry I reacted that way, Rachel, I know you meant no harm. I really like your parents and they make me feel safe, I think mine usually don't.' This had only just occurred to me; I remember that clearly now.

'It's OK, Amy, it really is. What I said was stupid. My parents really like you by the way. Let's nail this shopping and get to the film in time for the trailers and the ads.'

The afternoon was restored, and it was a really fun outing. We loved the film, all of us having read every one of the books in the entire *Lord of The Rings* series. We ate our fish and chips walking down to look at the sea as it was over an hour to wait for the bus, our breath making fleeting funnels of misty steam in the cold night air, tips of our fingers nipping with cold as we reached into our packages to pierce the battered, salty, greasy delight of our supper with plastic forks not quite up to the task.

The full moon, suspended like a benign, all-seeing potentate, above the endless black expanse of sea dispelled the inky darkness sufficiently to make us feel awed, safe and protected all at once. It did nothing though to dispel the strange sense of foreboding we all felt as we walked towards the pier. Perhaps it was the sense that the moon was indeed all powerful where the sea's concerned, perhaps it was the subtle tricks of dancing light it played on our vision. But it was a very high tide that evening and exhilarating nonetheless to see the waves thrashing against the pier and the groynes further along.

As we gathered up the rubbish and Finn sprinted over to the nearest litter bin he noticed a person at the end at the end of the pier standing perilously close to the edge, near the lifeboat station but beyond the Pavilion Theatre, which was open and brightly lit as the Christmas Show was on. I remember Finn beckoning us to join him and see what we thought was going on. It was too dark to see whether it was a man or woman, young or old, but we thought we would walk over and check it out. I remember Finn commenting gloomily that it was the time of year people often chose to do themselves in through loneliness, cold and despair and bloody freezing wind; I remember him saying that now as if it was yesterday, crossly, breathing on his fingers "to try to restore circulation", he'd commented sardonically.

As we approached, walking on past the brightly lit theatre, we realised the person was a woman, maybe in her fifties; it was hard to tell as she was bundled up against the cold, staring down at the broiling sea. Without turning her head, she said, slurring her words a little:

'Whoever you are, fuck the hell off, I'm going in.' Bizarrely, given the circumstances, I remember feeling very shocked that a respectable-looking, middle-aged woman should be slurring her words and using language that I associated with my age group and older, especially the rebels at school.

Finn indicated to Harry, in sign language known to them both from lifeguarding, to phone the police and coastguard, and to us to step back a bit. He told us in gestures that he was going to go nearer to talk to her. We watched him approach but kept out of sight. As he got nearer, she clambered up on to the railings, I felt my legs turn to jelly. We knew he was speaking to her but the wind and crashing surf drowned out his words.

After what felt like hours but was, in reality, about twenty minutes, we became aware that two police officers were approaching, a man and a woman. The woman asked us to explain what was happening, Harry summarised as quietly as he could. They seemed keen to ascertain that we didn't know the woman. We all watched quietly, the two police officers ready to rush forward if necessary, and noted the lifeboat chugging along a little way out; we understood that their plan was simply to be prepared.

Finn had been talking, seemingly at her rather than with her, as she continued to stare down into the sea, for about fifteen minutes, when she suddenly swivelled round and jumped down onto the pier our side of the barrier, conversing fairly animatedly with Finn, it seemed. They'd stood there for a few minutes, talking in the biting wind, when he unwound his scarf and offered it to her inviting her to start walking towards where we were waiting, more or less hidden from view by common, but unspoken, consensus. It had briefly occurred to me to ring or text Dad but I decided against it as I didn't want any noise disturbance from my phone, I thought even if I texted him he would probably ring back; in any case it seemed to be under control thanks to Finn. This made me feel nicely grown-up and independent and very close to my friends.

Finn and the woman, whose name was Susan, Finn told us, were now close to us chatting normally, it seemed. It turned out that Susan had recently had to retire through ill health from her teaching job at a high school in Essex. She had been diagnosed with multiple sclerosis and had a good idea of what her future would hold. Her husband had died from lung cancer three years previously and they had no children. Her parents had both died the previous year and she was an only child. She had loved her job as an English teacher and had hated her inability to be able to do it due to her rapidly worsening MS, especially her difficulties with speaking clearly sometimes. She had therefore made the decision to travel to Cromer, where she had many happy memories of childhood holidays, in order to take her own life by jumping from the pier whilst she was still physically able to do this. She had checked tide times and her mind had been made up but she had bought a bottle of red wine which she had been drinking steadily with the idea of numbing any pain, mental or physical, as she approached her death. Almost unbelievably what actually changed her mind about her planned course of action was Finn talking to her about the film we had just seen.

She always enjoyed the company of high school age children, she told us as we strolled back down the pier chatting easily, her speech still slurred at times, and to hear Finn talking so insightfully about a work of literature which she loved and always believed should be on the GCSE syllabus, possibly at A-level, had restored her faith in life. It was that very evening, she told me later, after meeting us, that she decided to sell her bungalow in Essex whilst she was still able to cope with all that entailed and move to Cromer in order to live out her remaining life there, whatever its quality, simply because she had always loved the town and resort and surrounding countryside.

At this stage we all realised we had missed the last bus home, even though it was only 9.15pm, so Finn decided the best thing was to phone his parents. I looked forward then to seeing either comforting Jenny or Paul and, sure enough, they both arrived, obviously needing to bring both their cars, having had the situation quickly explained to them by Finn. This was so that they could accommodate all of us. Iain came along too as he felt worried and wanted to be with his parents.

The two police officers talked to Jenny and Paul and, when satisfied that they were happy to take care of Susan, they talked to Susan herself, and were clearly reassured that she was no longer at immediate risk of taking her own life. Before leaving they gave Jenny, Paul and Susan some details of further contacts if needed, including the Samaritans. I had never heard of this organisation and made a mental note to look it up when I got home as it sounded interesting. When I did I understood that we had been Samaritans that evening, on the ground, as it were, in Susan's time of greatest need.

Once in the car Jenny immediately offered Susan what she called a billet with them for as long as she liked. This was really quite a start to the Christmas holidays and in fact this episode had put the life drawing episode completely out of my mind in a good way. Jenny dropped me off first; she had, me, Rachel and Finn in the back and Susan in the passenger seat. They chatted easily mostly about the delights of Cromer. Paul took Harry, Iain and Finn after first grasping Finn by the hand then giving him a real man hug, patting him on the back and saying quite simply:

'I'm so very proud of you, Finn, just so proud, well done, old man.' I noticed Jenny smiling at them both. I loved that. I had texted Dad to say that Rachel's parents were bringing us all home as we had missed the last bus, and that I would explain why when I got home.

Chapter 22

WHEN I WALKED INTO THE lovely warm house Angela was the first to say hello and ask if we'd enjoyed the film. Dad was helping Carrie move a new computer desk into her bedroom; she had arrived home for the Christmas holidays late the previous evening and I hadn't even seen her that morning as she had slept in. She had come home earlier in the term, for a weekend in November, quiet and looking a bit strained, we all thought. I'd heard Marianne and Dad talking about her after she had gone to bed very early on the Saturday.

'How was she on your walk, Doug? I mean, really how do you think she is?' I heard the worry in Marianne's voice.

Dad was reassuring: 'Well, she kept saying how lovely it was to be home, it's such a big thing going all that way isn't it really? New life, new ways of studying, fending for herself, sharing halls of residence with strangers, pressures of coursework. She is homesick for sure but she loves the course. She's made some friends; I think it's just natural.' Dad paused briefly and I waited to see if I should scuttle away. Then he continued: 'Maybe try to spend some time with her on your own if you can, nothing special, just here, chatting if poss. She's leaving tomorrow afternoon, I said I'd take her to the station, unless you'd prefer to, or you could come too? She's getting a train at 5.50 so it'll be dark unfortunately.'

It was well known that Marianne hated driving after dark, it had become quite a fear of hers.

'Yes, I'll make time, Doug, I will, and I would like to come to the station to see her off, gives us a bit longer together. I do miss her. Your dad'll understand. We'd planned to cook together again at his, he loves teaching me Hungarian dishes and I know it helps him as his arthritis is playing up quite badly. He's a brave, uncomplaining man. I know he won't mind though, obviously we didn't realise Carrie would be home when we planned it.'

I think she did make time; Carrie had certainly been quiet. She had said to me that uni was fine, very different, the course was good, there were some idiots in her shared flat in halls and stupid arguments over cleaning up the communal areas, like the kitchen. She told me that sometimes she just couldn't bear to go in there, and that she actually got on better with people in the adjoining flat on the same corridor. It sounded fun and adventurous and independent to me then, and again, I felt I wanted to fast-forward life a bit and leave all these home dramas behind, leave the adults to their own devices. She had then gone on to say:

'What do you reckon to Mum and your Granda spending so much time together then?'

I remember replying:

'Well, I know she helps him a lot and they like cooking together, he's teaching her Hungarian cooking. I used to love his one-pot Hungarian meals when I was there a lot.'

She had looked at me then, I remember, straight in the eyes.

'Ah, Amy, you're such an innocent, I love it, you're still young though.' I didn't like that. Carrie went on relentlessly, it seemed: 'I think there's something going on between them, old people do do it you know, you little innocent. Have you noticed they can hardly take their eyes off each other, let alone their hands?' she laughed. 'Well, fair play to them, I suppose, but well, erm… I just can't get over the fact that my mum is older than your grandad.'

I had felt hurt by Carrie mocking me for being young, and overwhelmed by what she was telling me though I tried to shrug it off in what I thought was a sophisticated way:

'Yeah, well, maybe, good luck to them.' I had left then to go and think.

Now I felt myself looking at Angela guardedly, told her the film had been great. Then she asked me to sit down as she wanted to talk to me about what I had seen that morning; only that morning, it seemed a lifetime ago in some ways. She offered me a hot chocolate and made it while I hid my Christmas shopping away upstairs, calling "Hi" to Dad and Carrie as I passed her open bedroom door and admired the new desk; neither asked me about my day, though, to be fair, Dad was crouched under the desk at that moment installing the computer and asked:

'You okay, love? Bad luck about missing the bus, ridiculous time for the last bus. Ouch! Dratted thing!' He peered at his thumb which he'd accidentally hammered instead of the thing he was supposed to be hammering. The news about our eventful evening could wait, I felt, though I couldn't help briefly imagining the scene at Rachel's house then; everyone chatting to Susan, making her feel welcome, showing her the spare room, Jenny, probably, making up the bed, planning the next day with Susan, perhaps even planning the next few weeks with her, Susan who had believed she would be dead by now.

Just as I was secreting away the last package Angela knocked on my bedroom door explaining that she'd brought the hot chocolate upstairs so we could talk in private. She closed my bedroom door quietly; I felt a bit crowded out in that small space; she obviously sensed this and decided we should go to the studio – of all places. Jason had his children staying with him and his parents at their house for the weekend before Christmas so I knew he wasn't about; I also knew he would be back with us on Christmas Eve having taken them back to their mum.

Walking into the studio, seeing the covered easel, the sofa, the drawn blinds, brought the morning's events vividly back to me. Angela did not beat about the bush, I liked her for that.

'You've probably heard of "life drawing" I should think, haven't you, Amy?' Well, I had actually because of Angela's teaching and I think she knew that but I shook my head without making eye contact.

'Look at me, love,' she said gently. And I did, I made eye contact for what felt like the first time in a while as Angela continued

'In that case you must be very surprised by what you saw this morning. I learnt life drawing at college years ago and we all enjoyed that aspect of the course for obvious and less obvious reasons. We were beyond being giggly teenagers by then, I'm not saying that's what you are, sweetheart,' she added hastily, 'but we considered ourselves to be "very serious artists,"' she laughed wryly, as she framed the quote marks with her fingers, 'oh the arrogance of youth.' She shook her head as she spoke.

Of course, I couldn't help remembering then our unstoppable laughing fit in the church earlier, but I quickly suppressed that memory and concentrated on Angela's kind face.

'I always wanted to get back to it,' she continued, 'and in fact I'll be offering life drawing classes in the New Year as well as my other classes. There are plenty of people around offering to be models: young, old, men, women, fat, thin, all sorts. I remember it was the same in my college days, all sorts,' she paused briefly as if seeing it all again. 'Some liked to chat, some got back into their clothes when we broke for coffee, some just put on kind of dressing gown type robes, some didn't put anything on,' she grinned at me. 'I love teaching, Amy, as you know, and it pays quite well, which helps of course. It's been tricky actually because I've been approached by some new parents via my website, you know – your dad set it up for me, it's brilliant. These new parents are wanting me to "life draw" them, that is, naked, with their new babies, all naked. I do remember that you kind of lose all inhibition for a bit when you have a baby, must be hormones running riot I should think,' she grinned again, briefly. 'Talking of which, I was reading the other day about a couple, new parents making a life-size model of their baby, fully clothed, so they could remember his features as a new baby before they changed. They were offering to do this for others and selling their replica baby as a doll via their website, some people thought that was weird,' she shrugged. 'Anyway, back to life drawing and naked babies, apparently some photographers offer a "boudoir" service of photographing parents with their newborns, all naked, but I've had to refuse that particular request as far as drawing them is concerned,' she paused looking thoughtful and rather pained, and continued, 'mainly because of the outsiders looking in, their take on it, I mean. If people think there's any weirdness about, they'll conjure it whatever, fan the smoke into flames, talk it up – sort of thing, just like when your dad found Carrie and saved her life.' She looked very sad about this briefly, not Carrie's life being saved by Dad obviously, but by memories of all the people believing the worst, Dad losing his job at Sheringham High, all that.

Then she went on:

'It's worth thinking about those naked cherubs painted by the oh-so-revered Old Masters,' she chuckled. 'I mean, there's a Watteau, for instance, called *A Lady at her Toilet*, well, it's positively salacious, it really is. And some of the Rubens, gosh, *The Judgment of Paris*. It seems he just wanted to paint naked ladies; they're really beautiful. It represents the story of Paris judging a beauty competition between three nude goddesses – very rash!' she smiled gently. 'You know about Paris, do you, Amy?' I shook my head, enthralled by this conversation, planning to look up *salacious* later. 'Well, he was the son of King Priam and Queen Hecuba of Troy, famously eloped with Helen, Queen of Sparta and caused the Trojan War. Exciting times they were, actions have consequences. There are lots of examples from the Old Masters,' she thought for a moment, 'some are beautifully erotic, I mean Turner's *A Nymph and Satyr,* phew!' She wiped her brow, theatrically. 'And, Rembrandt's *A Woman Bathing in a Stream,* less "phew!" but still. And again, Rubens' S*amson and Delilah,* it's only too obvious in that painting what they've been up to. Velaquez's *The Toilet of Venus,* her naked bottom features, beautifully painted. And then there are the much more modern famous paintings: Renate Bertlmann's *Exhibitionism.* She's an Austrian artist making a serious point using comic irony, I'll have to show you to explain, in fact I really must show you some of these pictures one day if you're interested or you can look online of course. Sarah Lucas' *Pauline Bunny* is another modern one. Be careful of your search terms though,' she was suddenly more serious, 'oh dear, it's a strange and dangerous world out there, Amy, it really is, I mean the online world, cyberspace, whatever it is. We should look together one day,' she paused briefly before seeming to gather courage from somewhere within to continue. 'Anyway, to return to this morning, you've probably realised by now that Jason and I love each other deeply, we have in fact fallen in love. I asked him if he would pose naked for me. I love his body, Amy, and I love painting him like that. That may well seem weird or even yuck to you because not only am I an old, old woman but old enough to be his mother – eeeeyuk, you and others must think. But, honestly, Amy, we just don't care, we love each other and make each other happy. And there it is.'

She said this softly with a smile, not defiantly or aggressively; it was obvious she just could not care less, what others thought, she was happy and looked it. She told me that they hadn't decided quite where to hang the painting yet, but probably they'd keep it in the studio behind a curtained area. This curtain was a very pale grey and didn't cover a window but was designed to soften a large expanse of brick wall and made a good background for certain paintings. I remembered using it for hide and seek with Jason's children, well, that would have to change I thought to myself, suppressing a wry smile. Perhaps I ought to warn Angela that it was a good place for hide and seek.

Surprisingly, I maintained eye contact throughout this conversation, feeling no need to look away embarrassed, because I wasn't. I realised how much I loved Angela and I had to hand it to her for taking the trouble to explain life drawing to me. I wanted to tell my close group of friends all this and I knew I would when we next saw each other.

'Drink up, love, it's getting late. But you enjoyed your day anyway? Doug said you told him you'd missed the bus. You had time to eat, I hope? I didn't even check, sorry.'

Dad appeared at the door just then.

'Hallo, Amy love, what happened?' This meant I was able to tell Angela and Dad together about our dramatic encounter at the end of the pier, Finn's brilliance, and sad Susan, who was now staying at Rachel's.

'Wow, Amy,' Dad spoke quietly, 'what an encounter. I'm so proud of you kids, well done to Finn and to all of you for keeping calm, just the right thing. How are you feeling now, love?' I glanced at Angela before replying:

'Well, it's been a strange start to the Christmas holidays that's for sure, but at least I've finished my Christmas shopping now, yay, no more shopping, I'll wrap tomorrow. And I feel so happy to think of Susan staying safely at Rachel's house, warm, dry and being looked after.'

'Doug, you must be so proud of your daughter and, Amy, gosh, here I've been rabbiting on to you about life drawing when this momentous event happened to you this very evening.' She turned to Dad and explained how I had happened on Jason posing nude for her that morning and that I had rushed out before she could explain especially as she was wanted on the phone then. 'Another commission, actually,' she said, looking pleased. I was pleased too and relieved that the morning's episode was all out in the open and that it all suddenly seemed just innocent and beautiful, pure art. I briefly wondered what Marianne and Carrie would make of it and felt ashamed again of laughing with my friends about it.

There were more revelations that Christmas holiday, I remember. Jason had had a little too much wine on Christmas Day, not so that he was blind drunk, just relaxed and very open with us. He kept commenting that he felt safe at last being with us; he and Angela were sitting close together on the sofa. We were just having a cup of tea and some Christmas cake, Marianne was picking up the Christmas paper that couldn't be reused and putting it into a large bin bag and Dad was helping by scrunching up pieces of paper and lobbing them into the open bag with impressive accuracy; I remember all those details very clearly. Granda was absorbed in a book about the Hungarian Cold War given to him by Angela, a huge, unreadable-looking tome; I can see it now.

Angela turned to Jason and said that she felt it was a good time to explain to us all whilst we were together why he felt like that. She said that I was old enough to be told and understand. I felt on edge then, but he turned to Angela and said,

'Yes, you're right, they should know, you explain, love.' He leant his head on her shoulder and closed his eyes while she spoke.

'It's important that you know that Julia, Jason's ex-wife and the mother of his three lovely children, they'll be with us tomorrow of course, is what used to be called a "husband-beater", that means she's a domestic abuser. She physically hurts Jason by hitting and punching and scratching him producing wounds and bruising in places that are not seen. We hear a lot about men abusing women in these ways, and in other ways of course, but it happens the other way round too and is often even more hidden, because men are even more scared to admit this is happening to them and seek help because they want to be seen as strong enough – mentally and physically – to cope with it or even, not to let it happen in the first place, they don't want to be seen as wimps.' Jason nodded slowly in assent, his head still on Angela's shoulder.

'She never hurt the kids,' he murmured, 'if she had I would have had to say something, but they're now reaching the age when they're more aware that things are far from okay between us. It was definitely time to leave. I believed it might help the situation actually,' he paused, 'it was horrible though, never knowing what mood she'd be in, I felt I could never do anything right, she mocked and despised me the whole time, blamed me for the slightest thing. Any feelings we'd had for each other were long gone.'

This sounded so sad to me and it changed my attitude towards Jason to be honest. Carrie was listening intently and kind of brushing her long, shiny hair with her fingers, I can see her now. I remember Granda shaking his head despairingly and rubbing his hands across his eyes, he looked very tired. Marianne got up to gather up the teacups and plates, I got up to help her. Dad was the first to speak:

'Thanks for telling us, Jason, old chap, that was brave. We're here for you and you're right, you're safe here, make no mistake.'

Again, I found myself suddenly imagining the scene at Rachel's house. Her family always played at least one board game on Christmas Day, Susan was staying with them over Christmas and planned to start house-hunting in Cromer in the New Year. She told me later that it was in the car on the way to Rachel's the evening Finn rescued her, the evening she decided to live, as she put it, that she also decided to move to Cromer. I wasn't sure how Harry's family spent Christmas Day, but I felt pretty certain that there wouldn't be all this emotional outpouring. Angela's house suddenly felt claustrophobic and I spent some time in the kitchen washing up the cups and plates, drying and putting away, thinking about Mum's Christmas and fun with the little kids.

I remember I rang her on Boxing Day and arranged to go to Cambridge to stay down there until after New Year, we were due back at school on Wednesday 5th January. As it happened I didn't go to Cambridge after all as they all came down with some kind of flu-like bug on Boxing Day starting with Fred and spreading rapidly. At first I thought I could be helpful to Mum but it just seemed better to stay put as they were all laid low by the bug and I would have just been an extra hassle for them.

Telling Rachel, Harry, Hannah and Finn all this adopted family news could wait, I felt, until we returned to school in January, that is if Harry ever came anywhere near me again. School was weird enough for me in that year with Harry in Year 11 being sort of remote, while we in Year 9 were starting grim, serious GCSE work in some subjects, teachers talking endlessly about those exams, our year being the first year to take some GCSE exams at the end of Year 9. I felt we needed some light relief, my revelations about life drawing might liven things up a bit, I hoped.

But in the event, on the first day of the new year, 2005, a Saturday, something happened which put all such petty thoughts of livening things up with my family news not only out of mind, but the news itself became almost irrelevant.

Chapter 23

THE CORONER TOLD US LATER that death would have been instantaneous which was a comfort at least. But it left so many devastated lives. Poor Carrie, poor Angela, poor Granda all struggled in their different ways. It was a ridiculous accident in some ways. The second day of the New Year, bright, sunny, absolutely no visibility issues, no slippery roads, literally out of a clear blue sky. Marianne and Granda were shopping in Sheringham at about midday. Granda had just had his hair cut and Marianne went to collect him; they planned to have lunch together in town, walk down to the promenade, have a New Year look at the sea then come back to Angela's for the evening. Marianne was going to practise one of the new Hungarian recipes taught to her by Granda. It was two days before school started again, Carrie wasn't due back at university until about the 14th January as I remember. Dad was going to drive her as she was taking a printer back with her and quite a bit of luggage, bulky winter clothes, walking boots – that sort of thing.

There were numerous shocked witnesses it seemed, plenty of people enjoying being out and about after the Christmas and New Year break. The schools were still out so there were lots of children too. Local newspapers reported the accident vividly using many photos of the scene with police cars and an ambulance in attendance. It seemed that Granda took Marianne's arm as they crossed the high street at the main zebra crossing, in fact he usually took her arm for support. The white lines of the zebra were a bit faded, due for repainting apparently, but it was a well-known, central crossing place. A driver, aged 87, was driving a little too fast down the main street, close to 30mph in a 20mph limit. He didn't spot the crossing, didn't see Marianne and

Granda stepping onto the zebra, and, when he tried to brake, too late, he accidentally put his foot down on the accelerator pedal, hitting Marianne at considerable speed, she just had time to push Granda clear, it seemed.

Marianne was first tossed up onto the bonnet, then she slid onto the road, and was run over by the car as it continued, still at speed, until a central bollard stopped its progress. The elderly driver was of course distraught but unharmed apart from a small cut on his forehead, caused apparently when he slammed his own head down onto the steering wheel in shock and horror at what he'd done. His was another devastated life.

There was a lot of discussion in the newspapers and on the television news about whether the driver should have had his licence confiscated after an earlier incident in a car park when a pedestrian sustained a minor injury. The police were facing much criticism about this. Police, in those days, were not able to confiscate licences on the spot when drivers refused to surrender them. They had to wait for the DVLA to withdraw it, a process that could take up to four days.

Two police officers, a man and a woman, arrived at Angela's house to break the news and offer to take anyone who wanted to go, to the hospital to see Granda who was in A&E and look after him. They also explained quietly that somebody had to identify Marianne's body. Angela and Dad decided quickly that we all needed to go to the hospital and that identification of the body could be discussed. Angela, Carrie, a very silent Carrie, and I went with Dad and Jason followed as we needed enough car spaces to bring Granda home.

When we got to A&E, we were asked by the receptionist to wait until the doctor came to explain what was happening. She offered us tea or coffee and went off to make it. The doctor arrived quite soon and explained that Marianne had been taken to the hospital mortuary and her body would need to be identified. She spoke tentatively but very clearly and straightforwardly I remember. She asked us who was who so Angela explained that we all lived in the same house but that she and Carrie were Marianne's mother and only daughter, Jason was a close friend, as were Dad and I, and that we were father and daughter. She explained to the doctor that Granda and Marianne were very close friends. I noticed she made eye contact with the doctor before she reiterated: '*very* close friends.' It was obvious that the doctor understood, and she then started talking most directly to Angela, glancing from time to time at Carrie's white, strained, face. Carrie was clutching Dad's hand tightly, and sitting close to Angela who was in turn clutching Jason's hand. I was next to Jason taking it all in, watching people's faces.

The doctor explained too that Granda was shaken up and feeling very bruised from having been pushed out of the way of the car, but that, thankfully, he had no serious injuries and we could take him home when we were ready, he was just having a cup of tea. She went on to explain more about Marianne's injuries and the formalities that would follow, having first checked with Dad and Angela that they were happy for me to be there while she did so, asking me too, very gently. I appreciated that, feeling myself slipping into my familiar, bewildered observer role, a bit of an outsider looking in, although the reality of what had happened was all too plain. The kind doctor told us that the death had to be reported to the coroner by law and that we would be notified when the body could be released for burial. This could be in two or even three weeks' time, she explained, and said she was sorry to have to explain that on top of everything else.

Dad went down to identify Marianne's body with Angela and they both came back looking even more white and strained, Carrie chose not to go with them. We gathered our thoughts and feelings and went in to see Granda. The expression "a broken man" was all too accurate. He sat with his head bowed not immediately making any eye contact but clutching both of our hands, Dad's and mine, tightly, one in each of his.

He started talking in a whisper then:

'We were just so happy, Doug, we'd found each other before it was too late. Our futures, even mine with this wretched arthritis,' he looked disgustedly at his bent fingers with their swollen joints, 'our futures seemed to stretch ahead of us like a sunlit upland or some such rubbish. We weren't looking for it, we weren't expecting it, it just happened. Neither of us cared about the age difference, she was older than me, so what? I mean what's a few years between friends, lovers, sorry, Amy? This is all a lot for you, I know.'

I found myself wondering whether any of us would ever laugh or even smile again. What had happened to Marianne felt like a physical assault on us too, I felt as if I had been punched in the chest, I remember it was a physical pain, and wondered how on earth Angela, Carrie and Granda must be suffering if I felt like that, not even family. We drove home pretty much in silence but when we got to Angela's she busied about, preparing the spare room for Granda, making tea and coffee for everyone, putting biscuits and cake out to offer round. Carrie, still chalk white and strained looking, sat close to Dad. She told me afterwards, long afterwards, that she remembered feeling winded and that the feeling lasted for days. She spoke only once, I recall, then and that was to state matter of factly that she was now an orphan. Granda sat on the other side of Dad on the large sofa. He kept rubbing his hands over his eyes and saying things like: '...in broad daylight...'; '...lovely weather...'; '...lovely day...'; 'Why her? Why not me?'

Dad rubbed his back trying to give comfort. I went to help Angela. I remember thinking about the two police officers who had arrived to break the news, all in a day's work for them I thought. But perhaps it wasn't. Perhaps in the car on the way to Angela's they had driven slowly, subconsciously, or even consciously maybe, driving slowly as if to delay the changing of several people's lives forever. Forever. I remember this thought going through my mind repeatedly. Marianne would not be returning, ever. Her life, her hopes and fears, her plans, her love for Carrie and Angela, and now for Granda, snapped off. That made me think of Angela dead-heading roses and occasionally accidentally snapping off a rose in full bloom. That always upset her, but she would put the beautiful bloom into a little vase in pride of place for its last blaze of glory, she would say, all the while knowing she had effectively killed it, cut it off in its prime. Marianne had been allowed no such last glory.

All these thoughts were running through my mind as I quietly poured and distributed tea and coffee for people. I thought of Marianne a lot. I thought about her having fun at the Empress Elisabeth of Austria's commemoration event in Cromer, laughing with Angela and Carrie as they chose skin products, fun at the Caister Lifeboat Station event. She had often seemed a little wary, a little withdrawn. I knew she'd been through a lot with losing Carrie's dad so young, supporting her sister-in-law through similar, never knowing her own dad.

She had always been so understanding about my problems though, quietly noticing my nails digging into my palms, saying little but closing her own hand over mine. She had certainly not used me in any way to get close to

Granda I realised. That had happened independently of Dad and me. If anything, she had withdrawn a little from us it seemed as her feelings for Granda developed. I wondered how much this had to do with her lingering mistrust of Dad's motives regarding Carrie, despite Angela's reassurances. Perhaps she felt her own mother was not to be trusted in that respect given her relationship with Jason. It was all so complicated, it seemed. I wanted to ring Mum to tell her what had happened, I wanted to talk to Rachel, and Harry, too. I heard Carrie speaking in a small voice then:

'Do you think the funeral will be before I go back to uni?' she asked the room in general. That was in a fortnight's time.

Dad spoke first:

'We'll just have to wait and see, I'm afraid. That's all we can do. I can't think there'll be too much delay. I mean, it's obvious what happened.' He broke off. 'There'll have to be an inquest though. You may want to take some time off, Carrie, delay going back.'

Carrie replied quickly and firmly:

'No, I'd prefer to get back and keep up with the others, it'll be good to...' she broke off and hesitated momentarily. I felt she was going to say *get away* but thought better of it, '...see some of the others,' she finished vaguely.

Granda rubbed his hands wearily over his eyes.

'I cannot bear to think of beautiful Marianne...' he glanced at Carrie then and stopped. Angela was just shaking her head. It was already dark outside even though it was only about 4.30 in the afternoon. Dark, the new year stretching ahead without Marianne. Marianne would not see the first signs of spring ever again. I told myself to stop it. I had to stop these thoughts running through my mind. I said I just wanted to go and phone Mum, Angela suggested I take the phone upstairs or into the studio. I went into the studio and turned on all the lights. The darkness outside was intense.

I thought of Marianne in the dark and cold, alone. It was good to hear Rob's cheery voice as he picked up the phone.

'Hallo, Amy love, most of us are on the mend a bit now. Do you want to come for the last few days of the holiday? How was Christmas? New Year?'

'Erm, Christmas was all fine but...' I stumbled over how to tell this terrible thing. I could feel my voice breaking up. 'Something terrible happened today,' my voice seized up, I just couldn't speak because I knew if I tried to, I would simply cry and cry and that I wouldn't be able to untell this terrible news, that somehow just telling it would make it even more real.

'Oh, Amy, you sound upset, here's your mum now, love.'

'What's up, darling?' I was silent at my end as the tears were by now flowing freely. She waited a moment then:

'Do you want to come here now, love? Rob can come and get you this evening, no problem.' Mum was expecting another baby and suffering from bad, all day long sickness then, even though she was now about seventeen weeks pregnant and she had thought it would have been getting better by then. The baby was due on 12th June, another June baby, like Joshy.

'We can get you back tomorrow or Tuesday in time for school on Wednesday...'

I broke in: 'No. No it's alright. I need to be here.' I rushed into explaining what had happened probably clumsily: 'Marianne and Granda were in an accident this morning, knocked over by a driver on the main zebra crossing in Sheringham, you know the one? Marianne died, Mum, Granda just has some scratches and bruises. Oh, Mum, we've been at the hospital.' I was sobbing freely by then.

'Oh, my good God, what a terrible thing to happen. What a shock for everyone. I expect you want to be there for Carrie... oh gosh, Amy love.'

We carried on expressing our shock and sadness, talked about the driver a bit, that kind of thing.

I couldn't go through another phone call like that then but, as it happened, Jenny had heard on the grapevine what had happened and came round later, with Susan and Rachel, bringing a steaming hot casserole and some flapjack she had made that day. They stayed and ate with us, mainly, I think, to ensure that we did eat. Granda barely touched the food and sat looking pale and strained, as if he just didn't know how to be now. Carrie had gone into her inner, remote place but it struck me that at least she had her whole future still, even though Marianne would not now be part of that. Granda somehow had nothing, I felt.

I remember longing to go home with Jenny, Susan and Rachel, away from this house of sadness but I strongly felt I should somehow be there for Granda, Carrie and Angela. After they'd left Dad suggested we watch a repeat of David Attenborough's *Life on Earth* . I had never seen it. I loved it and remember finding it intensely comforting. Life and death, birth and renewal, the circle of life. They were showing several David Attenborough programmes as he was still working on *Planet Earth* which took four years to film. Even now I associate his programmes with those deep, dark days of January, February, March 2005.

I snuggled up next to Granda to watch it. I think he found it a comfort as he slipped his arm around my shoulder and pulled me close to him. I noticed Dad kept looking across at Carrie as if to gauge her feelings. Angela went into her studio to paint but as I went up to bed I decided to go and see how she was. She sat staring at her canvas which was a portrait of Marianne looking remote and staring out towards an open window. I asked if she wanted anything like a cup of tea or something.

She looked strangely serene:

'No thank you, Amy love, you go on up and try to get some good sleep. This is a lot for you to cope with. Did you talk to your Mum?'

I told her that I had, said goodnight, and heard the others coming upstairs and saying goodnight to each other. Granda's footsteps sounded slower and wearier than ever.

Chapter 24

I HAD NEVER BEFORE UNDERSTOOD why adults always seemed to get so gloomy about January, but that January, returning to school after Marianne's death, everything seemed dark, dull and intensely sad. It felt as if there would never be anything to look forward to again, nothing to laugh about, nothing even to smile about. And to make matters worse this was when Harry really seemed to turn against me, sometimes quite literally. I would be conscious of him looking at me, almost intently, then quickly turning away. To say this was hurtful just doesn't express the anguish and soul-searching this caused me, the all-consuming racking of my brains to try to work out what on earth I had done to deserve this rejection. I felt physical pain somewhere at my core, my heart hurt, I felt myself to be a lesser, unworthy being. Digging my nails into my palms somehow relieved the hurt but for only the time it took for the trickle of blood to appear.

Rachel was solicitous and understanding about what our household was going through following Marianne's death, but I couldn't talk to her about Harry's behaviour as he was just his same old self with her, relaxed, funny. I avoided them both if I saw them together, they were usually with Finn too. I already felt that I tended to cast a gloomy pall over our encounters, that I carried weighty baggage of sadness. I didn't want this and longed to shake it off. These things combined to make me feel an outcast from our formerly close-knit group.

I found an unexpected form of refuge then by visiting Susan who was renting our house on a short let until she found somewhere to buy. Dad explained to me that this was beneficial for us and for her as it was the time of year when people didn't want to come to Cromer on holiday. I had very little time after school then because of rehearsals and the early dark, cold evenings so these visits were usually at weekends, especially if Dad was training as he always was on a Sunday, or out on a shout or at the Shed, as they called it, with his mates. If he was out on a shout it was comforting and kind of refreshing to be with someone different rather than trying to be cheerful for Granda, though I did my best with that too. He liked to have a long sleep in the afternoons anyway, so I didn't feel as if I was abandoning him. I still encouraged him to tell me stories about his days as a silversmith and setting up home with Gramsda. He always seemed to enjoy that as much as he could enjoy anything then.

Part of me relished going to our old house, another part didn't as it brought back memories of how Mum used to be when she had been so ill there, as I now better understood it. Susan living in the house, though, and stamping her own personality on the house in her unobtrusive way, went some way to laying the ghost of my earlier unhappiness there. This became increasingly the case as time went on, the house itself seeming to expand and somehow relax in the less tense, calmer atmosphere there. Susan seemed intuitively to sense my feeling of rejection from my friendship group and probed ever so gently about how things were at school.

She was very interested in the upcoming drama production, interested as well in how our links with Angela and Marianne and Carrie had come about. She asked so, so sensitively about Mum too; and seemed to take a real interest in me as a person. I found myself growing very close to her, wanting to confide in her my sense of loss and abandonment which I had only just identified as such – mainly through talking to her, I think.

Weirdly, and I remember it really did feel weird to me, I began to see her almost as a mother figure, and actually wanted her to mother me. She was so welcoming to me and provided home comforts in the form of hot drinks and cakes and biscuits and, strangely, despite her physical frailty, more noticeable at some times than at others, I felt I did not have to be strong for her, I could be needy. She told me one day that I reminded her of an egg without a shell.

I was aware though of holding back a bit as I felt that if I once let go and wept long and loud, as I sometimes felt I wanted to, that there would be no stopping the flow. Susan sensed this, it seemed, and in her quiet way made me feel valued as a person as if my life and feelings mattered to her. I helped her with shopping and sometimes offered to hoover through the house if she was feeling particularly tired. Her eyesight troubled her at times, part of the illness she explained to me, so I would select audio books from the library for her, and she would often give me requests, usually of newly published authors whose books she would reserve online and I would then collect. She said she'd love it if I'd read *The Secret Garden* to her as she had not read it for years and she thought it would be fun to hear "Mary Lennox" reading it to her, I had told her that I had auditioned in September and got this lead part in the upcoming April production. And so I read it to her, chapter by chapter, and we loved it. It felt healing to us both just as Mary Lennox, Colin Craven and the garden all find their own form of healing and renewal as the story progresses. This sense of healing was unspoken between us then but we have talked about it more recently, Susan was intensely aware of the healing power of the story at the time, it seems.

Meanwhile our household settled into the familiar, only slightly changed, routines. Granda spent a lot of time with us at Angela's but he seemed to have aged at least ten years, that was depressing in itself. He seemed to me to be vulnerable, frail, diminished somehow. I felt his sadness. The short winter days and long, dark nights dragged on. I asked Granda to teach me some of the Hungarian recipes he had been teaching Marianne. This meant that he planned menus, wrote shopping lists for the ingredients and took an interest in eating again as I had hoped. Dad and Angela were so pleased and congratulated me on this strategy of helping Granda. I found myself, cliché or not, literally basking in the warm glow of their appreciation, there seems no other way to describe it.

We decided to cook a three course, Hungarian meal for Angela's birthday which was at the beginning of February. I found the menu cards I made for everyone the other day, in a big envelope at the bottom of an old suitcase. Taking them out and reading them brought back such vivid memories of that evening. I recall it being the first time I really understood that life did go on after such a devastating death, not only that it did but that it had to really. There was no choice. For Angela's birthday meal we made Hungarian ragout soup with tarragon, chicken paprikash, which was chicken with paprika, onions and garlic, Hungarian-style green beans as a side dish, done with mushrooms and paprika again, and biscuit crust deep-filled apple pie. I remember I found it all a bit too spicy then, but I sometimes enjoy Hungarian food now.

Granda seemed to perk up considerably that evening, having had a bad does of "the 'lergy doing the rounds", as he put it; this was actually 'flu, from which he was starting to recover. Unusually, at first Angela had only wanted family there, this included Dad and me, of course, and Jason, but she later asked me if I would like to invite Rachel and her parents, Susan and perhaps Harry and Finn, Carrie was coming home for the weekend specially. I quickly decided though that it would be better on this occasion if it *was* just us; it also meant there would be a lot fewer people to cook for, I pointed out. I knew, too, that I really didn't want to ask Harry in case he said no, and, at the same time, if he did come, I felt his strange attitude towards me lately would blight the occasion. I felt as well that we sort of needed to regroup as a household, I remember this very clearly.

The meal was a great success and once again Angela's house was filled with warmth and life and love, laughter even. This new beginning, as it seemed, was enhanced by Jason having added some extra touches to the studio with the aim of maximizing all the natural light available. The need for this had only emerged with the changing light of the seasons and it had taken him awhile to come up with a solution. When we later moved the clocks on to British Summer Time at the end of March the studio itself seemed to embrace the longer days with promise of more and more to come by reflecting the soft evening light all around the walls. It was a peaceful, lovely place. Angela was fully occupied with her pupils and commissions then and still seemed to be at least twenty years younger than she was.

Carrie had returned to university after Angela's birthday weekend seemingly focused and determined. Dad drove her again, as she was taking a portable heater for her room and some of her summer clothes, to make use of the car space. He had urged her to keep in close touch and reminded her that he could come and get her anytime at short notice if she wanted to come home for a break. In the event she was home again much sooner than expected.

I went to Cambridge for most of the February half term break. That was fun and it was a relief to be in a house full of liveliness and busyness and laughter. There were some lovely, bright sunny days after a lot of rain – Dad always referred to February as February Filldyke which Rob loved – and the boys and I spent a lot of time outside playing football, hide and seek, and "Covtree", in all weathers. I offered, too, to take them on short shopping missions to the nearby parade of shops. That gave Mum a bit of a break especially when I took Josh in his buggy as well. The children were always very well-behaved as Mum and Rob told them they had to help me take care of the younger ones; we all took this responsibility seriously. The shops were not far away. I sometimes liked to imagine myself as the eldest child in a children's story left to look after several children as the parents were not around. I had never quite worked out why they were not around except I knew it was for innocent, happy reasons, not death or abandonment. I knew I couldn't take any more sadness, even pretend sadness.

But more sadness arrived all too soon on arrival home. Granda had developed a chest infection whilst I was away which he just couldn't seem to shift despite a course of antibiotics. The 'flu in late January had lingered, despite his cheeriness on the evening of Angela's birthday meal, making him very unwell on and off. His characteristic stoicism possibly meant that he delayed seeking medical advice, who knows? He just seemed to become rapidly weaker and weaker. Dad and I went to stay at his flat with him. I remember thinking that that would leave Angela and Jason – "the lovebirds" – I called them sarcastically to myself, to get on with it.

I only discovered the background to his deterioration on my return home. Struggling to get to the bathroom in the early hours of the morning of the day I was returning home from Cambridge and Dad was out on a shout, Granda had fallen and broken his thigh bone, the middle bit, a fractured shaft of femur, and lay, unable to call for help, for several hours. It was the coldest night of the winter so far. Dad only returned just before 8am having been part of the team who successfully rescued an elderly woman who had wandered from her care home and found her way to the beach as the tide was rising. She had dementia but was physically strong and active and had managed to climb some way up the cliff before becoming frightened and stuck.

The irony of this was not lost on any of us. Dad's own and only parent lay freezing cold, injured, in pain, alone in his own home while his only son rescued a stranger who had "escaped" from professional care. Granda was taken to hospital after quite a wait for the ambulance but developed pneumonia and died after three days in hospital, following surgery to fix the fracture, three days during which he faded away before our very eyes it seemed. This was two weeks after his 58th birthday.

And so it was that our household became much diminished, what with Carrie away at university, and Marianne and Granda both dead, long before their time. Dad became an orphan like Carrie, though whether adults are technically orphans, I don't know. I thought then how easily families can be decimated by random acts and I talked to Angela about it, thinking about Rob and his children too, and Jason's of course. She said it made her think of cobwebs after she'd read a description of them in a book which she immediately went off to find and read it to me there and then. She explained that one of the main characters in the book had just found happiness after a difficult time:

he felt this new-found happiness to be suspended on gossamer thread much as a beautifully constructed cobweb, built to entrap nourishment, will catch the dew, the sunlight, withstand summer breezes, yet can be destroyed by a single wanton act.

I often think of this image.

The days after Granda died passed in a blur. A tiny part of me felt relieved that he would suffer no more "arthuritis" pain and that he would no longer be suffering the loss of Marianne or Gramsda but mostly I felt so sad that he would not be seeing the daffodils, *bright, brave beauties*, he used to call them, standing defiant in the brisk March winds, catching the sunlight as they reached out their trumpety heads to bask in its long-forgotten warmth ultimately succumbing to it. This, though, as Granda had explained to me, was only in order to nurture the bulb underground ready for the following spring, the never-ending cycle of decay and rebirth; the difference now was that Granda wouldn't see the next spring, nor any others. He wouldn't see me grow up, take my next steps, be there in the background as I fast-forwarded to all those experiences I craved.

The bright days, warm when the sun shone, with all their promise of growth, of flowering, of burgeoning life, seemed almost to me then to be a denial of death as something unimportant, to be forgotten as quickly as possible as if to linger on it would be to taint such a bursting forth of new life. I wanted Granda to be seeing all this, to hear him saying:

"Let's sit and bask in the sun a bit, Amy love, it'll ease my creaky old joints."

Carrie came home for the funeral; it was a Thursday, so she decided to stay on for the weekend as she only had one lecture on Fridays. Her arrival felt like a breath of fresh air, I remember. Dad went to get her from the station, her train got in at about half past six, and Angela had prepared a special meal for the evening before the funeral. It was a surprisingly merry evening in the circumstances. It had been decided there should be a gathering at Angela's after the funeral and she had also been busy preparing delicious looking one-pot meals to welcome people back to the house. She said it was impossible to know how many people would be at the funeral or come back to the house but that way she could freeze the leftovers, and we could all live on them for a while if necessary.

Carrie was her usual quiet self, but at times she seemed to be subdued and preoccupied too, over and above her sadness and shock at Granda's death following on so soon after her mother's. She confided to me the evening after the funeral that she had started seeing somebody who lived in the flat opposite hers and was doing the same course, Steve. They had met when walking in together for lectures, the halls of residence were about a fifteen minute walk away from campus. This sounded very exciting to me, but she seemed quite conflicted about it.

'He's nice, quite funny, understanding, sort of, after Mum died, good to go out to things with, he's got a good bunch of friends, but he seems very young to me even though we're the same age...' her voice tailed off a bit. 'You must promise not to tell anyone here, Amy, or anyone at school. I just don't want them getting the wrong idea, it's not that serious, he just makes me feel less lonely.' Of course, I promised straightaway not to tell anyone.

Once the funeral was over and Carrie had returned to her university life the increasingly bright, lengthening, late March days seemed to me more and more to be a cruel mockery of Granda's and Marianne's deaths and death in general. I thought of him and Marianne missing all the promise and loveliness of spring, their own futures gone in an instant, Marianne, especially, never knowing how Carrie's university life was going. If I woke up at night and heard rain or wind battering at the window, I would think of Granda and Marianne alone, cold, in the dark, underground and I couldn't bear it. They had both chosen to be buried in the nearby green burial site, their closeness in death underground with everything stopped seemed meaningless to me.

On top of this weight of sadness, hanging like a pall over every aspect of my life, I noticed that ever since Dad had returned from taking Carrie back to the station, he had seemed even more tired, sad, and strained-looking than ever, defeated somehow. The busyness of the funeral arrangements and the sociability of the day itself had appeared to carry him along on a fast-running tide of activity. He and I moved more completely into Granda's flat shortly after the funeral while we thought what was best to do with it. He told Angela we had invaded her life and space for long enough, and that he would be forever grateful. Angela told us that there would be a home for us there anytime and to remember that Carrie would be home for the holidays and the odd weekend and she may like to have some young blood about. Dad explained to me that the flat would be his once probate was settled, as Granda had left it to him in his will. He explained what probate was sounding weary and a bit overwhelmed by it all. I put my hand in his.

I remember telling him that I was sorry he was an orphan now and that I would always be there for him. But to me, and I think Dad too, leaving Angela's felt like another huge loss at that time. I loved her house and garden, the spaciousness, the homeliness. Granda's flat in contrast seemed to hold a depressing aura of sadness and hush. It was as if all the familiar spaces were now filled only with his absence. I missed him terribly. We needed to sort out his things too, that was hard. I missed coming home from school to Angela's welcome. She would often have baked scones or flapjacks, or fruit cake and we would sit with a cuppa, as she called it, telling each other about our days. I loved Angela actually, I realised.

Chapter 25

SCHOOL DRAGGED ON DURING THAT seemingly endless spring term. I had to summon all my reserves of energy to carry on with the school production. The show would be in the second week of April just before the Easter break. In some ways I think the show kept me going. I was playing the lead role after all, Mary Lennox in *The Secret Garden*. The show *must* go on, that well-worn phrase felt apt. I wanted to do the best for my two favourite teachers, Mrs Gordon and Mrs Hebden, and for the show, for the school, for Susan, for Harry working backstage. I realised this last with a jolt of surprise or shock that I should even care what he thought, especially when he continued to be so strange and remote, ignoring me, turning away if he saw me.

At that time, I felt such a sense of loss and longing, not only for Granda and Marianne but for my life at Angela's. I missed the warm embrace of that household in its many forms. The welcoming kitchen, the light-filled studio, the garden, the understanding and love shown to me by Angela and, in a different way, by Marianne. I remembered how she'd closed her hand gently over mine when I dug my thumbnails into my palms as we sat in the back of the car together, so recently it seemed. She had said to me afterwards:

'You cannot cure hurt with more hurt, Amy, trust me on this.' Then she'd taken my smaller hand in hers and stroked it very gently, saying: 'You have beautiful hands, Amy, look after them, don't punish them.' And since she had spoken those words to me, I had stopped hurting myself in any way – until now. Remembering those words as I thought about Marianne when I was lying wakeful and afraid one night, I determined to stop punishing my beautiful hands as she had advised.

I felt, too, a disorienting sense of unbelonging after Granda died, of being adrift with no anchor to hand. More than ever I wanted to fast-forward my life to somewhere I truly belonged. My everyday life had changed beyond recognition since Dad and I had moved to the flat. He got home much later than I did on the days when I didn't have a rehearsal. He was often pretty tired and, of course, there was his ever-present pager. I almost began to understand how Mum must have felt at times but quickly shook that thought from me. Needing to get home to Sheringham meant that even though the days would be getting longer it would still only be possible to see Susan at weekends. She was suffering quite a flare up of her MS at that time and had asked Dad if she could stay put, renting the house, as she simply could not face a move at that time. Of course, that was fine, it was good having her there, the house cared for. More important, we had all grown to like Susan a lot, and I felt particularly close to her.

At that stage Dad and I on our own in the flat decided to try and finish off the food that Granda had in the house. The freezer had been very well stocked by Marianne as he had been finding shopping increasingly difficult. There were plenty of quite useful tins too. So I would think of something for Dad and me to have for tea, or we would plan it together in the morning and he would give me money to stop on the way home from the bus to get some fresh vegetables if necessary. It was busy though with rehearsals three days a week finishing at six, and then we would discuss which bit of Granda's food store we would raid. I remember feeling very tired a lot of the time too, and I still had to fit in homework.

I put all this loss, hurt, sadness, longing, loneliness, and anger too, into playing Mary Lennox. I felt I could enter into the very soul of her character. Rachel told me that her mum cried a bit when she came to see the play and tried to hide it. Apparently, Angela did too, Jason told me. I wished Carrie could come but I completely understood that she had end of term exams and just couldn't. Amazingly, Dad came on the last night, a Saturday, having turned his pager off. He told me he was bowled over by my performance and found it very moving seeing his "little girl", as he put it, up on stage playing the lead role so sensitively. I felt so proud.

I recognised that many of the cast did really well too and show week was a high spot in a very dark time. The end of show party in the school hall was fun with Harry and Finn having devised the playlist. Carrie told me I could choose something of hers to wear. We talked a lot by text at that time, it was a few years yet before Facebook arrived worldwide with its messaging facility and then WhatsApp of course. I still sometimes wonder where all those messages we sent each other are now, whereas I can still read and hold Dad's letters which he continued to handwrite after most shouts as he found it relaxing, cathartic, he explained, his own, personal debrief.

Carrie had made most of her special, "going out" clothes. She had left behind some that she had become too tall for and I chose a V-necked sleeveless dress with a low back made of shimmery, dark navy silk with subtle hints of turquoise throughout which somehow enhanced the sense of fluidity in the iridescent fabric as I moved. I looked forward to dancing in it and thought about what Harry would think of it. I remember wondering why on earth I even thought that. I asked Carrie if Rachel could borrow something too and we had fun choosing something for her: a dark red dress with big black buttons, I remember, and a wide skirt. Angela said we both looked stunning. Jenny said the sight of us growing up brought a lump to her throat though she knew it had to happen.

I remember Harry and Finn just staring at both of us when we had changed and walked into the hall. They had brought smart shirts in to wear with their black school trousers, needing only to swap them for the black T-shirts they had to wear as backstage people. It seemed so simple for them. They were busy with the music mostly. They also ran a slideshow of some of the action from the play on the big screen which they erected in front of the closed stage curtains. It was brilliant but strange to see myself as Mary Lennox so often as it ran.

Rachel and I danced together, the boy who played Colin, James Eliot, danced with us both too. Finn emerged from the music booth to dance with us both, but Harry remained in there managing the music. Sometimes lots of us danced in a group. I felt very sad that it was the last night of the show as we all did. But somehow, my sad despair lifted a little as the Easter holidays arrived with, amazingly, flurries of snow and hail for the first few days, followed by really warm spring sunshine. It was strange, weird.

In retrospect the sadness probably didn't last as long as it felt at the time although sometimes quite unexpectedly, and it happens even now, I am assailed by a sense of the loss of something very precious thinking about Granda's early death. It literally takes my breath away and leaves me with a deep feeling of longing, poleaxed. I want him close by, I want the almost daily contact with him that I used to have, I want him to know what's happening in my life, I want him to be enjoying life with Marianne. It feels as if it's too long since I've seen him and that that void stretches ahead with no end in sight.

Life was busy though and we were all moving on with our lives as we must. Rachel, Hannah and I offered to be flunkies at the school prom which was to take place on the last Saturday in June at the end of exams. We were told to wear black trousers or skirts and white tops. We wanted to see everyone dressed up and be prepared for our own prom in a couple of years' time. Angela took a great interest in it all even though she found it funny that this idea from America had infiltrated British high schools. I remember her saying wonderingly:

'Whatever next, it'll be cheerleading and pom poms and baseball in no time at all, you mark my words!'

It was only the third year our school had had a prom and a lot of effort went into fundraising for it. There was even going to be a chocolate fountain! Hannah told us that Harry would have his first suit and that he and Finn were going into Norwich with her family to choose suits for them both. We all wondered who their prom partners would be. The idea was that they could get waistcoats or cummerbunds or pocket squares to match the girls' dresses. After a lot of discussion their partners were Sarah and Holly who had been backstage helpers. The thought made me feel strange, but I didn't know why and didn't share the thought with anyone, not even with Rachel.

Mum had her baby, a little girl, Jessica, two days before the prom on 23rd June, the day after Joshy's birthday but three years later. I looked forward to meeting baby Jessica and life felt fun and exciting again, full of hope and promise, a feeling helped by the long, warm, June days filled with bright sunshine and cloudless blue skies most days. Cromer was in full holiday season mode with the resort pulling out all the stops for those precious few months of high season. At this stage it was mainly the "old and bold", as Dad always called them, out and about making the most of the lovely weather before the schools broke up for the summer.

The pavements were crowded and the shops crammed full of beach paraphernalia: buckets and spades, windbreaks, inflatables (which always made me shudder a bit knowing so well, and having witnessed so often, what could go wrong, sometimes ending in tragedy). Restaurants and cafés did a brisk trade with brightly covered tables adorning the pavements where space allowed. The one-way system through town seemed to seize up periodically and car parks were full by 10am.

I often thought of all this teeming, busy mass of humanity flocking to our bit of coast for all the fun, fresh air and excitement on offer at the very edge of the world, as I saw it, before it gave out onto the vast emptiness of the North Sea. Sometimes I imagined the holidaymakers tumbling into the sea like lemmings, limbs flailing as they tried to save themselves. This was weird, I knew, and I would physically shake my head to get rid of the image.

And then, just as life seemed to be getting back to some sort of hope-filled track, a terrorist attack, to become universally known as 7/7, happened in London on 7th July 2005. Four coordinated bombings took place during the morning rush hour on public transport, two tubes and two buses packed with people as they went about their busy days. Fifty-two people were killed: six at Edgware Road; seven on a train at Aldgate Station; twenty-six at Kings Cross/Russell Square, thirteen were killed on a Number 30 bus at Tavistock Square. Seven hundred were treated for injuries and hundreds more suffered psychological trauma and ongoing suffering, many still suffering.

As the news broke (somehow we got to hear about it during school – I cannot now remember how exactly) I remember feeling fearful for London, Londoners. I vividly remembered the fun day trip with Granda and Dad, I could imagine the places teeming with people, the London buzz I had so relished that day. I felt relieved that Granda was not here to witness this – he had once talked about the IRA attacks and persistent threats of attack in London in the 1970's, 80's and 90's. I recall Harry's outrage on hearing the news of the 7/7 attacks and watching the events unfold on the rolling news channels – outrage seems the only way to describe his reaction at 16 years old. He became silent, tense, and when he spoke, he was almost incoherent with indignation that this should have occurred.

'Whatever the reason, the "cause",' he emphasised the word derisively, 'you do not kill innocent citizens, you just don't.' He almost shouted something like that I remember. I recall his parents being troubled by his reaction, his mother making futile attempts to soothe him. Unusually, Rachel, Finn and I were all at Harry's and Hannah's after school, it was a Thursday, I remember, because it was Finn's birthday and we planned a pizza and film night at theirs as Harry and Hannah had not been allowed to go to Finn's house party the next evening, despite knowing Jenny and Paul well. We all thought it was ridiculous so this was a compensatory evening celebration, reluctantly agreed to by Harry's and Hannah's parents. This meant we were all at Harry's watching the news whilst the pizzas cooked before our planned binge watch of *Harry Potter* dvd's.

But it all felt very tense with Hannah's mum hovering, Harry's reaction to this news and the general horror of it for all of us. I remember we managed to lose ourselves in a marathon watch of the first two *Harry Potter* films, which we had seen in Cromer when they were first released. We had intended to watch *Prisoner of Azkaban* because the next one, *Goblet of Fire*, was due to be released in November that year so this was "revision" as we explained to Harry's mum, but she was having none of it and put her foot down because it was a school night. I remember feeling almost relieved to be leaving the tense atmosphere even though we called her a "fun sponge" at the time, unkind I know, and it was late by the time the we finished *Chamber of Secrets* to be fair. I was struggling to stay awake at one point even though I loved the film.

Harry's outrage at the attacks made him determined then to pursue a career in counterterrorism and he started making focused enquiries about routes into counterterrorism, subjects to study at university, training for the police even. He told me he had discovered there were numerous different aspects of counterterrorism policing such as detective work, firearms, family liaison and undercover policing. He felt specially drawn to the undercover work, I recall. I cannot now remember when he changed his mind about this, but I do remember he was incandescent with rage that day. And so the summer moved on whilst the victims and their families continued to suffer.

Russell's International Circus was making its annual visit to Cookie's Car Boot site in Sheringham in late July. This was about half a mile from the Beeston Bump, laughingly known to locals as the tallest mountain in the world. They would be there for five days before moving on to the racecourse at Great Yarmouth. Rachel, Hannah and I planned to go and to see if Harry and Finn could come. As it happened, we just couldn't fit in all going together so we had to wait for another opportunity. When we did manage to visit the circus it turned into one of Angela's famous not without incident occasions – but I'll come to that.

The other big event that summer was Angela's and Jason's wedding on the last Saturday in July. Carrie and I were to be bridesmaids, Angela said, because even at her age she wanted our moral support. There had been a bit of a discussion about whether to have Jason's little Tiffany as a bridesmaid and the boys as pageboys, but Angela felt it made it all too complicated and palaver-ish for an oldie like herself. Tiffany was too young to be disappointed and the boys just were not pageboy types, she and Jason decided, and they were pleased that they weren't, they didn't want to dress up in silly clothes, they said.

When Carrie came home for her long university vacation that summer the first thing she did was to design and make the dresses for us. We decided we wanted matching dresses, not too bridesmaidy and ones that we could wear again. Carrie found some beautiful, turquoise, Indian silk decorated with a kind of motif of silver and gold grapes which caught the light as the fabric moved. Angela said it reminded her of the poem by Christina Rosetti, *A Birthday*. She spoke it for us, softly, beautifully, verbatim, then and there. I loved my dress and still do. And that poem holds a special place in my heart to this day.

Angela was keen not to look like "mutton dressed as lamb" as she put it, or to be what she described as a "simpering bride in white", so she asked Carrie to make her a plain turquoise silk dress which showed off her long, elegant neck to perfection. She set the outfit itself off by wearing a large hat swathed in the same material as our dresses but with the addition of a deep red ribbon threaded through. Her shoes were turquoise, satiny with medium high heels. We all carried bunches of deep red roses picked from her garden.

It was lovely to have Angela's house full of life and laughter and celebration after the loss of Marianne and Granda. Angela and Jason's marriage was blest in Holy Trinity Church in West Runton, which was Angela's local parish church, at 2pm. The marriage ceremony itself had taken place at North Walsham Registry Office that morning. This was because Jason was divorced so couldn't get married in church, we were told. This seemed to me to be harsh. Only Carrie and me and Dad attended this ceremony.

Many of Angela's local friends attended the blessing in church as well as some cousins from further afield who stayed locally; some decided to use the time to have a proper Norfolk holiday and stayed for about a week close by. Rachel came with all her family, and Susan. Jason's parents were there of course with the three children who they were looking after at their house in Sussex for the first week of their school holiday. This meant they left with the children during the late afternoon before the evening celebrations. Angela and Jason had asked Harry and Finn to do the music for the wedding reception. They had given them some ideas but basically had allowed them a freehand as they trusted their judgement. They asked them to consider the ages of all the guests carefully. I was excited to think they'd be there and would see me doing my bridesmaid bit, specially Harry, I realised.

Carrie, home for the summer, had asked Angela if her boyfriend, Steve, from uni could come to the wedding and stay for the weekend. This was the only jarring note really. He just didn't fit in somehow and Carrie didn't seem to be relaxed with him. He appeared to me to be quite boring and immature (he was about the same age as Carrie) and, try as Angela and Jason and – to some extent – Dad, might try to talk to him about uni and his family and future plans, that sort of thing, it all felt very sticky and uncomfortable.

The other odd thing about the day was that Dad seemed to be on edge throughout, not relaxed, just distracted and well, unhappy really. This seemed strange to me as he was very fond of Angela and got on well with Jason, I couldn't work it out. But the day went by in a whirlwind of activity, so I didn't stop to think about it much. I loved having such an important role at the wedding. Angela and Jason had decided to use caterers for the wedding feast, or breakfast, as I discovered it was called. They used her kitchen to prepare the delicious three course meal preceded by mouth-watering, delicate canapés.

The newly-weds were going away on honeymoon to the Seychelles early on the Sunday morning and we all stayed in her house on Saturday as Dad and I were taking them to the airport, Heathrow. I remember it being a very short night as the celebrations finished late and we needed to leave at 5am in time for their check-in. I didn't feel tired in any way, quite the opposite. I felt wakeful, strangely buoyed up, trying to work out what I had overheard Jason talking about after most of the guests had left. I wished Rachel had still been there to tell me I hadn't imagined it. Just as I left the bathroom having cleaned my teeth ready for bed, I had heard the end of something Jason was saying to Angela in their bedroom, it used to be just Angela's of course:

'... and as for Harry, well, poor chap, it's obvious he fancies the pants off her and doesn't know what to do about it!' He was laughing as he said it.

Angela pretended to be shocked:

'Is that any way to talk to your wife on her wedding day, wedding night even, about her surrogate granddaughter, I presume it's my little, lovely Amy you're referring to?'

Jason laughed sheepishly:

'Come on, wife, let's sleep. Long day tomorrow. We can honeymoon properly once we're there in our bridal suite.'

I pondered briefly what "surrogate" might mean but, more than that, I suddenly really understood the expression: "ears burning". Mine were on fire, my whole face was on fire, what did all this mean? I remember looking up "surrogate" later and becoming engrossed in the whole concept of surrogate pregnancy, but I was reassured when I understood Angela's meaning to be simply a deputy grandmother in place of a real, blood, one.

On the way to the airport if anything Dad seemed even more distracted and unhappy. We were all talking about the wedding: the details, how well it had all gone, how good Jason's little children had been, how lovely Jason's parents, Alan and Margaret, were and how well they fitted in and chatted to everyone, Angela and Jason's long flight ahead – that kind of thing. But Dad was quiet mostly and I just couldn't stop thinking about what I had overheard.

At Heathrow, which seemed to me to be a very exciting place: buzzing with activity, flights going off everywhere, planes coming into land from all corners of the globe, we found a place to have a lovely breakfast as we were in plenty of time for their check-in and very hungry. As Angela hugged Dad goodbye and thanked him for the lift to the airport just before they went into the departures bit, I heard her say:

'Look after her won't you, Doug. Try to get rid of that oaf as soon as possible.' I knew they were talking about Steve of course and I thought it was funny. Dad replied, 'I'll do my best, don't worry. You two have a lovely time and just relax. I'll make sure she's alright, never fear.'

Chapter 26

I REMEMBER FEELING VERY FLAT as we made our way back to the short-stay car park. It was hot, sultry weather and I wasn't looking forward to the long drive home. Dad seemed preoccupied still and I was worried about him. We chose some music from the cd collection in the car and settled into the journey, both of us lost in our own thoughts, just making the odd comments about crazy traffic, crazy drivers, that kind of thing.

After about an hour Dad seemed to shake off a bit of whatever it was that was getting to him.

'Are you alright, my love?' he asked reaching for my hand. 'Did you enjoy the wedding and being a bridesmaid? You looked lovely by the way.'

'I loved it, Dad, loved the whole day, loved my dress. Carrie's so talented.'

'She is, yes,' replied Dad smiling and looking thoughtful. 'Do you think she's happy, Amy, enjoying uni, I mean? Obviously, it's not long since she lost her mum and she was very fond of Granda. And I know she has mixed feelings about Angela and Jason's relationship, now all legal of course,' he chuckled quietly.

'I know she loves her course, Dad, but she finds all the deadlines for coursework quite stressful, still gets homesick.' Dad remained silent so I continued. 'She was expecting all that, she told me, though she misses home more than she'd anticipated she would, she said,' I paused briefly, then: 'I think Steve's a prat and I think she saw that a bit yesterday. She seemed embarrassed by him at times,' I heard my voice sort of peter out, uncertain what Dad was thinking, feeling as if I was on unsteady ground suddenly.

'Do you think so? I've always thought you were a good reader of people and situations, love.' He seemed to perk up a bit then. 'I noticed that a bit at times too.'

I went on: 'I do think so, yes. I think she just wanted a boyfriend because all her flatmates had coupled up and Steve just happened to be there, you know, and she met him just after Marianne died, so...' Again, I hesitated, uncertain about everything suddenly.

'Hmmm, yes, you could be right. Oh, Amy, the youngest, wisest and most perceptive of us all.' And we drove on in a companionable silence.

We stopped for lunch just before Newmarket and Dad seemed more relaxed. As we sat down to eat he said out of the blue:

'You're a lovely daughter, Amy, I don't think I tell you that enough. Would you be happy if we stayed on at Angela's for a bit, just while they're on honeymoon? It's a bit sad at Granda's sometimes isn't it and I don't like to think of Carrie there on her own, to be honest, or on her own with Steve there come to that,' he grimaced slightly. 'I don't know how long he's planning to stay… do you?'

'No idea, but I know his parents have asked him to dog-sit when they go on holiday, not sure when that is though. Have you remembered I'm going to Mum's on Tuesday by the way? Is that OK still?'

'Of course, it is, love, you'll want to meet your new little half-sister, I'm sure. Work's so busy during August anyway, I've got the first week in September off but no holiday at all in August. I think it'll be my turn next year. I felt quite worried to be honest about you being on your own a lot with Angela and Jason away for three weeks. I knew Carrie would be around of course and I knew you'd be going to your Mum's at some point. It'll be busy at the Shed too no doubt.' Dad seemed quite a lot more relaxed after this conversation, I noticed.

Just as we were starting off again after lunch, I got a text from Rachel:

Hey Amy hope the trip to the airport's ok. Susan had a fall this morning and she's in hospital with a broken wrist. She rang Mum and we went round and took her to A&E, she needs an op...pins or something. We've been with her but we're home now as she's pretty tired.

She added a sad face emoji, a brand new feature on her new phone. I told Dad and asked if we could call into the Norfolk and Norwich hospital en route but he was obviously keen to get back to Angela's and said Susan would probably be sleepy after the operation but we could ring tomorrow to see if she was coming home and go and fetch her. Jenny and Rachel were going to go round later that day to straighten the house up a bit before she came home.

When we got back to Angela's, Carrie and Steve were just carrying out the last of the bin bags, the hoover was in the dining room ready for action but that was the last of the clearing up. Dad was so pleased to see it all looking pretty spick and span. There was an air of tension between Carrie and Steve though which was palpable. I went off to ring Rachel and offer to help at Susan's house, well, our old house, of course. Dad and I did a quick check of what food was left over from the wedding and decided we didn't need to shop for that evening's meal. Carrie told us that Steve was returning home that evening and asked if Dad would be able to give him a lift to the station. The atmosphere seemed to lighten then and I said I'd finish off the dining room hoovering as they had done all the other clearing up then go over to Susan's to help Jenny and Rachel. Dad said he'd do it, so I went off to our old house on my bike.

There wasn't that much tidying and straightening at Susan's as she kept the place very tidy and clean despite her limited mobility. It was really just a question of a little bit of washing up, making her bed and tidying up the bathroom which was where she had fallen. Jenny had brought round some one-pot meals she had made to put in the freezer. It felt strange being in my old house, almost as if I had never lived there, and I suddenly remembered that I wanted to fetch an old suitcase from the loft which Granda had given me ages ago, long before Marianne and Carrie and Angela had entered our lives. It was quite small and contained letters between him and my grandmother, exchanged when they first met, and some he had written to his foster parents after meeting her. I felt like looking at them now maybe to bring Granda at least closer, if not back, to me.

Jenny asked if I wanted to go back to theirs for tea. That sounded good. I wouldn't be seeing Rachel for a while as I would be in Cambridge for about a week and we wanted to chat/gossip about the wedding. I decided to keep what Jason had said about Harry to myself, I was still trying to make some sort of sense of it. She asked if I thought Dad would like to come too and I explained he was taking Steve to the station and that he and Carrie were going to raid the wedding remains for their evening meal. She looked worried for an instant then seemed to shake herself out of it.

'Okay. I'll just go and do a bit of dead-heading and we could bring some flowers in for Susan's return, couldn't we, then we can be getting back.' The house looked lovely and welcoming as we left, and I looked forward to seeing Susan back in it the next day.

I texted Dad, he said it was a good idea to go to Rachel's, reassured me again that he and Carrie would raid the wedding remains for their tea. He said he would come and pick me up at 10. In the event Paul took me home as, almost inevitably on a summer Sunday, Dad's pager had gone off just as they were having their posh soup and sandwiches, as Carrie called it, because it was wedding food leftovers. He had turned his pager back on on our way home from Heathrow just as we crossed the border into Norfolk.

A kite surfer had set off as the sun was setting but somehow failed to launch properly, his kite had become sodden and he was drifting in the sea near Cromer pier as the tide was going out. Somehow his legs had become tangled up in the lines. He had been in the water for about forty-five minutes and was beginning to show signs of hypothermia and exhaustion. He was checked over by paramedics back in the Shed and was then able to contact his parents who came to take him home.

Dad wrote:

3rd August 2005

Home safe and sound now, Amy love. It was a textbook rescue technically. Amazing that we managed to untangle the lines with a bit of calmness and teamwork. Just a young lad, 20, I think, home for the holidays from uni, nice lad but close to panic when we got to him and very, very cold. Parents were sensible. Lovely to think of him home, warm, safe and dry. I love this part of my life.

Sleep well, sweetheart.

Your ever-loving Dad.

I found this the next morning slipped under my door as usual but I had heard him coming home and telling Carrie about the rescue, not the details, but I knew he was safe and fell fast asleep. It was good to get the letter in the morning.

As it happened, I was not to see Susan back in the house for very much longer than expected. Dad and Carrie and I went to the hospital the next day, the day before I was due to go to Cambridge, but we weren't able to take her home as she had a slight fever and they needed to monitor that and investigate why. She stayed in hospital for a week recovering from a chest infection which they thought had probably contributed to her fall and, in the event, I stayed in Cambridge for the rest of the summer holidays – but I'll come to that.

When we got back from the hospital we made a quick lunch of wedding leftovers again then Dad and Carrie wanted to go for a long walk to shake the "hospitalness" out of their heads they said, but I said I wanted to stay home. I had a strong urge to read Granda's letters. I remember taking a hot chocolate and a few more wedding leftovers, "pudding", into my favourite corner of the garden after they'd gone and opening the case to see the stacks of letters.

I found even peering at the addresses and the stamps and the postmark dates fascinating. The letters made me want to fast-forward yet again to taste life in all its richness and variety, to experience things I could only dream about. Truth to tell I didn't even know what these things were that I was wanting so much. I was just aware of a void that needed filling, a sense of waiting and of things leading up to something which I simply couldn't articulate.

6th July 1968
Dear Sue,
Hmmm, never have I ever tasted a Cromer crab and salad sandwich like it! You have the equivalent of green fingers for cooking. Lunchtimes feel different now. You can vary it every day if you like to keep me guessing but I think I'll never forget that very first Cromer crab sandwich you made me, gosh just 2 weeks ago now.
See you at 12.30 again tomorrow arvo. I'll leave this for you in our secret place on my way in in the morning.
Seb.

12th July 1968
Dear Seb,
It's taxing my brain thinking of different sandwiches every day, but it keeps

any sandwich shop boredom at bay at least. I like watching people choose their sandwich too, there's one chap who literally takes about 20 minutes to choose, then says he's in a hurry. I mean how different can cheese and pickle be from cheese and tomato? He always has the same bread, white.

Enough of sandwiches... you mentioned about meeting up after work. I'd like that, yes. We could go and eat fish and chips on the beach then go to the cinema maybe? Two treats in one. Sound of Music's still on... I've seen it twice before, but I love it. Have you seen it? Putting this in a letter which I'll drop into your place so that you can think about it and say no!

Sue.

15th August 1968

Dear Sue,

I wanted to write to tell you how I'll miss you when you're on holiday with your family for 2 weeks. 2 whole weeks, my heart is broken. Only joking... you must have a lovely time away from sandwiches and sore feet.

Think of me in my glittering emporium fashioning trinkets.

How would you fancy going to London for the day when you return? Just hoping you can get a weekday off before you return to Exeter. I'd love to show you some of my favourite places. Did you say you'd only been on a school trip?

Look after yourself in sunny Scotland lovely girl.

Xxxx

24th August 1968

Dear Sue,

Thanks for the postcard. It looks wild up there. Pleased you're having some sunshine.

She's a bit of an old dragon isn't she, your boss? Not exactly smiley. The sandwiches taste like dust in my mouth now. Not sure if it's because I'm missing you or because she actually substitutes sawdust for butter or something... she probably gets it from the butcher's sweepings.

So please come home soon.

I must tell you about this bizarre order I've just had in which is really sweet, I think. An old woman came in because she wants to pass on her ancient white rocking horse to her little great granddaughter who's 3 years old on 1st September. She wants to present her with the white rocking horse on that day but also with 10 rings for her fingers including her thumbs and a set of tiny bells to tie round her toes with white ribbon – she brought me the exact measurement! Sweet. But as the little girl would only be able to wear them for such a short while I suggested I make expanding bangles instead, 5 for each wrist, and 10 tiny bell-shaped pieces of silver that she could peel on and off her little toes with some good, harmless sticky stuff I have. Genius though I say so myself! The old woman was so delighted, and she started singing the nursery rhyme in the shop substituting "bangles on her wrists" for "rings on her toes". Tuneless but lovely. There was a couple in the shop looking for an engagement ring and they lingered to hear her and then chose a really expensive one. It was a good morning!

Would you like rings for your fingers and bells for your toes, darling Sue?

I'm starting to plan our end of September trip to London.

Have a lovely time when you visit Edinburgh. See you soon, now that is a good thought.

Your ever-loving,

Seb

Reading the letters brought Granda so vividly to mind that I half expected him to be calling me in for a cuppa. The sense of loss when I realised that this would never happen again was so acute that I had to stop reading the letters immediately. I closed up the suitcase, placed it carefully in the bottom of the wardrobe in the room I always slept in at Angela's, my room, when all's said and done, and waited for Dad and Carrie to return from their head-clearing walk.

Chapter 27

BABY JESS WAS JUST OVER 6 weeks old when I arrived in Cambridge the next day. Joshy was 3 and the older three children were all still only young: 10, nearly 11, 9 and 6, so it was a busy household. Rob came to meet me from the station in a new people-carrier type of car. I sat in the passenger seat and the other four sat two by two on the two rows of rear seats having argued about who would be going in the very back, their favoured place it seemed.

'Quiet, everyone, now!' roared Rob after this had been going on for about five minutes. 'Amy doesn't want to hear all this fissel fussel.'

Fred seemed to be a lot taller and still quite serious. He appeared to be pleased to see me and asked me to tell them about some lifeboat rescues. It felt like a big change for me to be in a car full of chattering children, quite overwhelming at first, I remember. I thought almost longingly of serene Carrie, gentle Dad, kind Angela, wise Susan and the different type of chatter of my own group of friends: Rachel, Hannah, Harry and Finn, and Jordan. This was just a fleeting thought though as I immediately became caught up in the day to day reality of life with young children.

Rob explained that we needed to call into Sainsbury's to do a big shop and that it would be very helpful if I could take charge of the four little ones.

'I usually set them the task of finding the things we need. Two teams works well. Fred and Joshy in one and Aidan and Jack in the other with you but you must keep those two in sight, they're only little after all. Actually, better idea, let's divide and conquer – I'll give you half the list and you take Fred and Joshy and I'll have the other two. Safer. We'll get it done in half the time – in theory,' he added ruefully, 'and it'll give your mum a bit of p and q for a bit longer, she's pretty exhausted poor love.' He rubbed his hand across his hair. He looked pretty exhausted himself to be honest. 'Oh, Amy, it's lovely to have you here again, I know she can't wait to see you.'

Alarm bells rang faintly then for me, Mum exhausted was never good. I knew having a baby was a big thing and it could be tiring, I remembered that from when she had had Joshy. But it was Rob's air of weariness, his uncharacteristic, albeit brief, sharp tone with the squabbling children in the back of the car and his too-quick reassurance that Mum was looking forward to seeing me that put me on edge a little. Still feeling frayed at the edges from the loss of Granda and Marianne, confused by Harry's unfriendliness towards me, and missing Dad, Carrie, Rachel, Susan and Angela, I quickly realised that I wouldn't be able to seek comfort from Mum, nor be the child that I sometimes longed to be, much as I also yearned to fast-forward to shape my own future untrammelled by the complexities of family life.

Rob and I set ourselves to the shopping task with a sense of undertaking a military operation and in fact it was soon done, and quite fun. He decided we all deserved and needed an ice cream as a reward. This was more like the old Rob and, as we made our way to the cafeteria in the supermarket having locked our loaded trolleys into the spaces provided, I started to relax a little and enjoy the chattering children and hurly burly of busy family life again. I metaphorically squared my shoulders for the busy week ahead determined to be as helpful as possible to Mum and Rob and a fun, big sister to all these children.

Rob had texted Mum to say we had finished the shopping, had an ice cream and were now on our way home. But he had looked worried when he saw her reply which he showed to me once we had got all the children safely into the car again and done our best to mop Joshy up a bit.

'This is what's happening, Amy, just so that you're aware,' and he showed me her response.

OK. Nightmare here. Jess just won't feed, she's crying and fretful. See you soon.

'That means she won't have had any of the planned p and q, oh dear,' he rubbed his hand over his eyes. He really did look tired out, too, I realised.

When we arrived at the house, I helped get all the children out whilst Rob took the bags in. He made a kind of game for us all tiptoeing in and whispering just in case Mum and Baby Jess were asleep. I took my lead from him and continued the game by putting my fingers on my lips, handing out packages from the shopping bags to the children to pass to Rob turning it into a game of sort of pass the parcel by having them form a human chain. Surprisingly, the job was done in no time. Rob went through to see how Mum and Jess were and tiptoed back out, smiling.

'They're both fasters in the living room so the rule is: "let sleeping babies and Mum sleep on"! I'll show you your room, Amy. The others'll all want to come so up we all go,' he said sounding more cheerful, taking Josh by the hand and picking up my bag with the other.

I was in the same bedroom as before, overlooking the garden, newly decorated in pale primrose yellow ready for Jess when she moved into her own room. The boys were already doubling up in the other two bedrooms and the plan was to convert the loft into a spare bedroom, Rob told me, when he and Mum had saved up enough money to do this. This could be used for Fred as he got older, Rob explained, or for a spare room, as necessary, and for me when I came. This gave me a warm feeling of security and belonging. Rob, still whispering, said he was going to make a salad lunch while I unpacked. He looked doubtfully at the three younger children. Fred had gone to his room to get something he wanted to show me, and Rob said to them that I didn't need their help. But I quickly said that they'd actually be really helpful as we could play pass the parcel again especially as I had bought little presents for each of them which were wrapped and concealed amongst my clothes. I explained that they had to stay quiet as mice while we unpacked though.

I passed a couple of folded T-shirts, shorts, jeans, then a sweater which I had used to hide one of the presents, telling the children that when I whispered *Freeze* the person holding the parcel would open it and it would be theirs. I had bought four little sailing boats from North Lodge café in Cromer, each one painted a different colour, all with the RNLI logo on the sails. I deliberately whispered *Freeze* when the parcel reached Joshy. He was so excited and wanted to sail the boat there and then. I promised we'd find somewhere to sail it soon and already planned to ask Rob if they had a paddling pool. And so the game continued and when they all had their boats Fred helped by saying we could put the paddling pool out that afternoon.

Just as we finished unpacking and I was suggesting, still whispering, that they all thought of names for their boats, we heard footsteps and turned to see Mum, standing smiling in the doorway, holding baby Jess on her shoulder.

'Do I have to whisper?' she asked, laughing. Josh rushed over to show her his boat proudly explaining that they were going to sail them on the paddling pool. Mum admired the boats, saying:

'Gosh, what an inspired choice of presents for your brothers, Amy. You *are* a clever girl. Train alright?' She held out her free hand to me and kissed the top of my head as she came further into the room.

'Fine,' I replied. 'Rammed. I bought this for Jess,' I said, holding out a little, pale yellow rabbit, with soft, white paws and ears and face. Mum took it in her free hand and stroked it gently.

'Oh, Amy, that is kind. Another lovely choice, we'll take the rabbit down and try to distract her with it while we have lunch,' she said, 'meet your baby sister,' and she bent down gently so I could see Jess' little face. I stroked her baby hair and whispered softly to her:

'We're in this together, little sis, you and me and four brothers.' Mum thought this was really funny and was still chuckling to herself as we trooped downstairs for lunch. Josh was tasked to think of a name for the yellow rabbit and it immediately became known as Binky. Binky went everywhere with Jess until she was about 4 when he was relegated to be just a bedtime companion.

That first week in Cambridge turned out to be the hottest of the year and that August was the hottest since records began. This meant we all wanted to stay around the house, playing outside with easy access to cold drinks and shady indoors when we wanted it. Mum relaxed and seemed so pleased to have me there. I overheard her and Rob discussing plans for his return to work. I didn't realise then how recently men had been entitled to paternity leave; it had only been allowed since 2003 and has, it seems, gradually become more generous. I couldn't imagine then how Mum would've coped if Rob hadn't been home.

I asked about it one day when it was just the three of us, me, Mum and baby Jess, as Rob had taken the boys to his parents for the day, partly to give her more of a restful day with just me for company and there to help.

'Yes, I can't imagine either to be honest. I've no idea how single mums do it. He would've had to request holiday but, being school holidays time, he may not have got it. But having you here, Amy, is just so fantastically helpful and lovely too. I feel calmer. You're so good with the boys too. Rob and I think you're our lifesaver.' I felt myself literally glowing with pride, warm inside and out.

Mum continued:

'We're just hoping you're having a bit of a holiday yourself though, there's a lot of domestic slog involved with looking after small children and babies.' She smiled wryly as she said this. 'Domestic slog is not my strongest point I know, nor is looking after young children to be honest, as you well know, only too well.' She sighed lightly. 'Sorry, Amy. I'm not really some kind of earth mother, I know that, so does Rob. We wondered how you'd feel about staying on a bit longer, no pressure, but it would mean that Rob would feel happier about returning to work sooner than he thought was possible, and that would mean he could take the rest of his paternity leave at other times. We wondered if you'd like to ask Rachel to come for a visit, either a day trip or for a few days, we can squeeze one more in easy peasy. When there's so many children it's honestly true that one more doesn't make much difference.'

I thought about this over during the next couple of days, still feeling that warm glow of pride that I was so valued and needed. To be honest I loved the fun of being with all the little children, away from some of the strange undercurrents and tensions which I sometimes sensed at home, and away from the sadness and emptiness of Granda's flat. I knew Dad was busy and I worried about Susan coming home and not having me to help her, but I knew Jenny would step in there, and Carrie to be fair, if I asked her. Harry and Finn were down in Cornwall doing their beach lifeguarding course and staying down there with Harry's aunt for the rest of the summer before sixth form started. Rachel was due back from holiday with her family soon, it would be fun to show her my Cambridge family and for her to see Mum being normal. It would be good to see her, definitely.

And so, it was arranged. I phoned Dad and explained the situation. He sounded very relaxed and happy, reassuring me that he and Carrie would make sure between them that Susan was alright. He said that though he was busy with work and shouts, being August, luckily there had been no tragedies so far, and he was enjoying helping Carrie set up her sideline of making beautiful outfits and selling them online. She had moved away from the mermaiding thing and was just concentrating on using interesting fabrics and repurposing old clothes to turn into things of beauty, he said.

'I never knew that you could make clothes out of bamboo, Amy, and bicycles apparently, did you? Amazing!' he chuckled. I did know about bamboo clothes but not bamboo bicycles. That was something different I learnt that day too.

Jenny would bring Rachel over on Tuesday, just two days' time. Iain was going to be spending the day at Sam's with a sleepover as it was Sam's birthday, so they would both spend the night and Jenny would leave the next day with Rachel staying on for a bit longer. Rob would return to work on Monday. He talked to me about it on my own, saying how relieved and grateful he was to have me there and how much better Mum had been since I'd arrived; he had been very worried about her, he confided to me. He also wanted to make sure that I didn't feel pressurised into staying. I was easily able to reassure him on that point. Thinking back, it strikes me that Jenny might have brought Rachel over rather than putting her on the train to Cambridge because she perhaps wanted to make sure all was well with Mum and Rob and me before leaving Rachel to stay with us. I don't know.

Mum was obviously delighted to see Jenny and to introduce her new family and new life to her. As it was so hot, they spent most of the time inside, chatting. Baby Jess seemed to pick up on Mum being more relaxed and fed well and contentedly with just the occasional, loud, indignation protest if somebody didn't immediately see what she was fussing about. I sometimes walked up and down with her to give Mum a chance to do things without having to hold onto her, remembering nursery rhymes, and making up little Jess-related jingles.

Jenny suggested seeing if she would spend time asleep in her pram in the deep shady bit of the garden. She had brought a baby gym for her as a welcome to the world present and we were able to rig up a big parasol, and put Jess on a rug, with the gym in place to she could look at the bright colours and mobiles on it. Sometimes she seemed to like just looking at the leaves moving in the gentle summer breezes or at the tiny white clouds scudding across the azure blue sky.

Rachel's visit was really fun. We would put the paddling pool out first thing in the morning and, when necessary, devise various paddling pool games for the boys often involving their sailing boats. We also rigged up a kind of wigwam with old blankets and a few bamboo stakes which Rob had found for us. Josh, Jack and Aidan liked to fill it with various treasures they garnered either from the garden or from their toy collection including pretend plastic food. Aidan would pretend to be a waiter wearing a tea towel round his waist and proudly using a small notebook to take our orders. Jack was the chef. We feasted endlessly on plastic fried eggs, plastic slices of bacon, plastic slices of bread. Fred was the manager writing out bills and generally overseeing things, quite bossily at times. It was funny.

The garden hose provided lots of fun too, either for topping up or refreshing the water in the pool or for doing proper gardening jobs, that is, watering. Rob told us only to water the plants once they were in the shade and we stuck to this rule which became a kind of test of who noticed a newly shady bit first. When it came time to empty the pool at bedtime it was really good showing the boys how to jump on the sides of the pool and let the water stream out over the lawn. I loved thinking of the dry grass quenching its thirst and greening up overnight in the comparative coolth.

Rachel and I did lots of shopping, always taking the four boys with us, and plenty of cooking too. This felt like fun rather than a chore with the two of us talking to Mum about what to cook for tea. We always made picnic style lunches which we laid out indoors because of ants and other creatures outside but the boys were allowed to help themselves and take the food into the wigwam if they wanted to, the strict rule was that they brought their plates in and washed them up. Even Josh was able to help a bit, standing on a little stool to help dry up.

When Rob came home he always managed to fit in a game of football or French cricket with the boys after tea, as well as helping with Jess jobs, or just holding her and singing to her if she was fretful as she often seemed to be in the evenings. Rachel and I cooked and learnt lots of new recipes taking care to keep things simple for the sake of the boys and conscious of some of Rob and Mum's money worries with lots of children, and Mum on maternity leave. They talked openly about this, not in the tense, worried, hurried, almost shouting match approach that Mum and Dad had towards their money worries, but in a very calm, measured way with complete understanding of the fact that a short-term reduced income was way, way worth it for the joy of all the children. It was lovely to hear. Once again, I felt myself to be a close observer of adult lives with all their complexities, constraints, compromises at times, but in less of a guilty, frightened way than I usually did at home. It was good to have Rachel with me during some of this time.

Mum was still very tired though and, as I remembered only too well, this would cause sudden, quite frightening, mood flips. At these times I glimpsed the fear and fragility in her eyes and felt myself reverting suddenly to the frightened 7-year-old needing to take charge, needing to cope. I hated this, fleeting though it was.

The difference now, though, was that I was not the sole recipient of these moods, nor the only one dealing with them. What I remember most was that Rob, if he was there, or me, would be able to change the mood with humour. A particular occasion stands out in my memory. Unusually, Mum had wanted to cook the evening meal and she decided to make macaroni cheese with grilled tomatoes. We started eating it, the sauce seemed *to* be a bit thin and tasteless, and Mum suddenly remembered she'd forgotten to add the cheese which she'd already grated. She burst into tears, berating herself, saying how useless she was, and yelled at Aidan for *saying* "Yuck" when he took another mouthful. I noticed his terrified little face and Fred's look of fear before he turned away, Josh was crying loudly, Jess, in her bouncy chair, seemed just to stare at us all with that knowing look very young babies have..

Rob took Josh on his lap, putting his hand over Mum's, saying gently:

'It's OK, Magsy, love. You said it was the American version, mac *and* cheese, so Amy, would you serve the cheese, love? We'll have it as a side dish.' Mum laughed, really laughed, not close to tears, almost hysterical laughter but normal, letting go, laughter. The fear left Fred's face, Aidan grinned, I felt myself relax. We all agreed it was delicious that way as we stirred in the cheese into that macaroni and white sauce on our plates though Josh decided to eat his cheese separately.

Mum talked to me later about how she knew her mood flips were only to do with tiredness, nothing more. She said it was horrible to feel sudden intense irritation, or even anger, with those she loved most, knowing it was unreasonable. She said she wished somebody would invent a "night nanny" service but she knew that this sleep-deprived phase of Jess' life would pass one day. With me at that age, she confided, she believed it would go forever.

I remember Rob and Mum asked if Rachel and I would like to go into Cambridge to have a look around, some fun and freedom, they said. It was suddenly tempting to be just us, away briefly from the incessant demands of small children. It was still very hot, and my main memory is of the two of us sitting by the Cam, watching the tourists punting, and Rachel mentioning that it would be fun to come back with Harry and Finn one day. I took the opportunity to ask her why she thought Harry was so unfriendly towards me lately, saying I didn't know what I'd done wrong. Rachel was watching the antics of the people in two punts trying unsuccessfully to keep out of each other's way but turned to me and said:

'Oh, Amy, I can't believe you haven't worked it out, Finn's right about that, he *thought* you had no idea, but I said I thought you had and were playing hard to get. Your best friend, how wrong could I be!'

'Worked what out?' I could hear the puzzlement in my own voice.

'You really don't know do you? Well, here goes then. Harry really likes you but not just as a friend, he fancies you, idiot, you, I mean, for not noticing, not Harry for fancying you.'

Things about Harry's behaviour seemed to fall into place then, it all suddenly made sense and I felt that persistent worry and sadness float away from me into the bright summer day. Again, I felt warm inside and out but excited and bit fearful too.

Something else which stands out for me about that day was catching sight of some of the Cambridge University colleges for the first time. I thought they were really beautiful, awe-inspiring, breathtakingly so, but Rachel found them to be a bit weird, not quite real, too "other", she said. I could see what she meant but I also felt there was something precious about such old beauty, something to be treasured. I loved the contrast of imagining the place in term time, full of students – mostly young – milling about just as generations of young students had in amongst these ancient seats of learning and current home to so much knowledge and progress in so many fields. Such a continuum of knowledge and innovation. Little did I know then that Cambridge University would become significant in my life. I spent another week in Cambridge after Rachel returned home to Norfolk and found myself looking forward to returning home myself with excited anticipation of all that the new school year would bring.

Chapter 28

JUST AFTER SCARY YEAR 10 STARTED Rachel, Hannah and I did manage to fit in a visit to Russell's Circus later that summer. The circus had returned for a late summer visit to Great Yarmouth racecourse timing its visit to coincide with the Maritime Festival there which featured the Tall Ships display. Dad was busy working, Carrie was very involved with helping backstage at the Cromer End of Pier Show, specifically with costuming, before she returned to university. In fact, through a chance encounter with somebody who was also involved with that, she was later invited to be part of the team making costumes for the famous Hippodrome Circus in Great Yarmouth. This had an amazing floor that turned into water for its Water Show of beautiful, skilful, underwater acrobatics and synchronised swimming. She absolutely loved it and was able to earn reasonable money whilst still studying.

Jason knew his boys would enjoy the Maritime Festival: being able to climb aboard the ships, pretend to be pirates, that sort of thing. He decided that taking them to the Hippodrome Circus could be their surprise Christmas outing/treat later in the year. So, Jason and Angela took the three little children, and Jenny and Paul, who also fancied a trip to the Maritime Festival, took the three of us. When we saw the sign for Russell's Circus we begged and pleaded to go to that after the Festival and make our own way home later on the train to Norwich then Cromer. It would be fine, we said, blithely, suddenly craving independence and fun on our own. Jenny and Paul pointed out that that could be a three-hour train trip with having to change at Norwich, but this seemed to us then to be all part of the fun.

Angela was her usual carefree self, saying that it was important to have some fun and freedom and independence when we could. Jason was keen for his children not to realise that we were going off to the circus because he was under strict orders to return them to their mother that evening as they were going to meet her new partner the next day. This meant that he kept well away from the discussion. It felt as if, by going on this jaunt, we were somehow prolonging summer jollity, gleaning every last morsel of summer fun as Year 10 already seemed to be full of GCSE pressure.

And it all started off so well – this too became a bit of a family expression when recounting interesting experiences that went wrong, or even when planning such experiences. The Maritime Festival was really fun, and it certainly showed Great Yarmouth at its best. It was a very warm day full of bright, September sunshine, always so special because of the hard to imagine but all too soon approach of winter. The sea was sparkling blue and the array of ships in the harbour, including the incredible Tall Ships, made a magnificent display.

The place was crowded with people out to enjoy themselves. We stopped at a café with tables outside under bright parasols and, while Jason took his three off to the toilets, Angela chatted to us about the soft spot she had for Great Yarmouth mainly because so many people rubbished it. She had a friend who felt it should be taken out to sea and sunk, she told us. For her, though, it was a proud, far eastern outpost standing sentinel, she said, against the rigours of the North Sea. She was impressed by many of the rejuvenation projects, and the Hippodrome Circus, she pointed out, is the last remaining total circus building in Britain and one of only three in the world that put on water spectaculars.

Angela, Jason and the children set off for home at about 4 o'clock. Jenny and Paul dropped us off at the racecourse at about 5 for the circus, which started at 6, telling us to have fun, be sensible and keep safe, reassured that we all had our phones. The station for our train home was only about half an hour's walk from the circus site and it was good to think that we still had lots of hours of daylight left, what could possibly go wrong…?

The circus was just as good as we expected it to be, packed with people on that sunny festival weekend. We managed to buy the cheapest possible tickets, with slightly restricted view, having pooled our resources to do this. Our main extravagance was buying toffee apples in the interval as we felt suddenly really hungry and couldn't resist the smell of the melted toffee. We joined the queue for these, and it was fun to watch them being made, despite being jostled by a large group of French teenagers, about our age. The second act was a bit shorter than the first with a clever magician and his funny helper, amazing acrobats and trapeze artists, a series of daft, but somehow sad, clowns and a beautiful dressage show. The horses seemed really to enjoy it and looked so well cared for.

As we emerged from the Big Top, somewhat mesmerised by the bright lights and the range of incredible acts we'd just witnessed, we noticed a very sudden drop in temperature as big, fat raindrops began to fall. The sun had disappeared behind an enormous black cloud as it began its descent, it was about 7, I think. Although sunset was not until about 8 o'clock the day became suddenly very dark and strangely threatening. We decided to head for the station then and there. Happily, as we were walking along, the day relented a bit, the sun reappeared, and it suddenly seemed as if we still had hours of fun and freedom ahead of us.

We were really hungry again, all of us, really, really hungry. I remember understanding then and there what *hollow with hunger* felt like and, just as we started moaning to each other about this, the most unbelievably enticing, fragrant smells caught our attention, emanating from a side street on our right. Looking down the street we noticed a Chinese restaurant, subtly lit, with very welcoming neon signs. I remember earlier, whilst still at the circus, we had stopped to check how much money we had, made sure we had enough for our rail tickets home and slipped this ticket money into Hannah's purse for safekeeping to ensure that it didn't get muddled up with the money we could spend at the circus.

So, again we pooled our resources, this time for food. None of us had ever had a proper, sit down, restaurant Chinese meal before, though we had all had the occasional Chinese takeaway, and whether it was the sea air sharpening our appetites, as Granda always said, or what, the smells pervading the evening air from the restaurant were quite simply irresistible. We decided to go in, act sophisticated, and pretend going into restaurants, as three 14- going on 15-year-olds was something we did often. The restaurant was crowded with lots of Chinese families, Hannah whispered that her dad always said that was a good sign because it meant the food was good.

The whole place was decorated vibrantly with paper dragon mobiles hanging from the ceiling, interspersed with hanging Chinese lanterns. The wall lights were protected by red lampshades casting a comforting, low light, the overall effect being to create a warm, welcoming, red glow. There were pictures of scenes from China on the walls, and the tables all had crisp, white, cotton damask tablecloths, and napkins which were folded into dragon shapes and placed inside wine glasses, each table having little individual night lights set in the middle.

The waiter who came to take our order recommended the selection of dishes which they could serve for three to share, that way, he explained, we could sample the best of the chef's cooking. That sounded good. He asked us if we wanted chopsticks and, feeling adventurous, we said yes. The waiter seemed to enjoy our excitement and, on reflection, was probably not deceived by our air of sophistication. He returned with a series of fiery hot metal burners which the dishes would be placed on to be kept hot, then carefully placed the chopsticks beside the usual range of cutlery. He also brought decorative glass finger bowls on which floated different coloured petals. We loved all this.

I can still taste the utter deliciousness of the delicately flavoured dishes to this day when I recall the subsequent *incident*. Succulent sweet and sour pork, fragrant chicken with beansprouts and bamboo shoots, tender beef with ginger, and saffron-flavoured rice are those I mainly remember. It was fun tasting bits of this and that. Knowing we didn't have enough money for any pudding we made the most of this feast. It was only when we came to pay for the meal that we discovered we hadn't thought about a tip. This was embarrassing as the waiter had been so kind. We decided to check the rail fare money to see if we had over-estimated it and it was then that we realised that Hannah's purse, with the carefully separated rail ticket money in it, was missing. This had been in her backpack with all three of our phones as hers was the best backpack for carrying them safely and we hadn't wanted to stuff our phones into our jeans' pockets, as that, ironically, had seemed a bit risky. All three phones were missing too. We ransacked the backpack as unobtrusively as we could, going right to the bottom, into all the pockets but the purse and phones weren't there.

Aghast, feeling subdued, we paid for our meal, apologising, embarrassed, to the waiter that we had no money for a tip. He remained charming and wished us a good evening. We decided the only thing to do was to try to hitch a lift home; at least there were three of us, safety in numbers we thought. We felt stupid above all. We had somehow allowed our money and phones to be stolen as they couldn't possibly have all fallen out along with Hannah's purse; we were idiots we felt. By then it was properly dark and quite cold with a brisk, chilly wind. I remember longing for the welcoming warmth of Angela's especially as it had started to rain heavily, the drops were now cold and stinging on our faces, a sharp reminder of winter rain to come in the months ahead for sure.

But, mindful of the need for us all to remain positive, and to keep any fear at bay, we sang as we walked along, backs to the traffic, thumbs raised every time we heard a vehicle approaching. I remember we started with songs like *Oh, I do love to be beside the seaside* not knowing many of the words, moving on to *Sailing* and then to made up jingles using the word "Cromer" to rhyme with "home" somehow, or with "Loam" which was the name of Hannah's road in Bessingham. We had only been doing this for about fifteen minutes or so when we heard our first lift slowing down, then stopping. This was a large white van; Hannah knew it was a Ford transit van as their neighbour drove one.

The driver, Dan, explained that he was only going as far as Potter Heigham as he was needing to get home to babysit so his wife could go in for her night shift at what was then known as North Walsham Cottage Hospital. But, he said helpfully, she could then take us as far as North Walsham. Why it did not occur to us to ask if we could phone Angela's from their house to see if someone could pick us up, I have no idea other than we still felt really stupid, ashamed and reckless that we had spent all our money on an expensive meal without realising we had had our rail ticket money nicked. I think, too, that we didn't want to waste their time as Dan's wife was already late for her night shift and obviously cross and worried about this. So Dan's wife, her name was Jackie, I remember, took us as far as North Walsham Hospital. She was quite distracted as she was running a bit late and was worried about her 6-month-old baby, Ryan, who was fretful with a cough and a cold. I remember sensing that she blamed us a bit for her husband's delayed return home, though she never said as much, and a bit annoyed that we had delayed her further as we all needed to use their toilet.

By the time Jackie dropped us off at the hospital main entrance which was some distance from the welcoming lights of the hospital buildings, it was about 10pm, I think. Her shift was supposed to have started at 9.15pm. She looked a little doubtfully at us and briefly worried, but she obviously had a lot on her mind, and said:

'You'll be alright, won't you? You look like a sensible trio. Good luck.' And with that she drove at some speed along the internal road in the hospital grounds taking her to the car parking bays nearest to the hospital entrance.

The road past the hospital, which is about nine or ten miles from Cromer, the A149, is notorious for being quite dangerous, with lots of dips and turns and straight bits which Dad always said boy racers used for racing practice. It was really cold now with a chilly wind whipping the stinging drops into our faces as we walked along in the direction of Cromer. The fun-filled, sunny day in Great Yarmouth felt like a distant memory and our Chinese meal by then seemed ages ago as we shared our memories of it. A couple of cars passed us at speed without stopping but only splashing muddy water onto our legs as they zoomed past. Rachel pointed out that both cars seemed to be packed full of "young bloods" as her Dad called them doing just what my dad said those types did.

After about fifteen minutes of this misery a car pulled up. The woman passenger wound down the window and asked in a whisper if we were alright. Wondering why she was whispering I peered into the back of the car and saw three tiny children, one perhaps about 18 months old, fast asleep, and baby twins, probably under 6 months old, all strapped in and, again, fast asleep. Still whispering and putting her finger to her lips to encourage us to do the same she explained:

'It's the only way we can get the twins off to sleep at the moment, and Jake's teething so he wakes up when they cry, they wake each other up, it's mayhem in our house,' she sighed wearily. 'This trip in the car is our sanctuary. We just wanted to check you were okay though.'

'We're fine,' I lied. 'We'll get a lift soon and we're not far from home now. Thank you for stopping.' With that they whispered a cheery good luck and went on their way.

We tramped on fantasising about puddings, sometimes falling silent, then one of us determinedly starting a new activity to keep our spirits up, we even started doing times tables, I remember, sheer desperation, but it kept us going all right. After about twenty minutes or half an hour we heard the sound of an engine but it sounded like a big vehicle, not a car we decided, probably a diesel engine we thought, at least Hannah did, she seemed to know these things. The rain at this point was heavier than ever and showed no signs of letting up. We turned round to see what was coming behind us and saw the most unbelievable sight: a double decker bus, fully lit up, seemingly empty was racketing along, swinging about a bit because of the bends and the wind and it came screeching to a stop when it saw us.

'It's the Knight Bus from *Harry Potter 3*!' gasped Rachel.

The driver barked at us:

'What the hell are you three doing out at this time of night hitching lifts? What in God's name are you thinking of? What in God's name are your parents thinking of? Climb aboard. I'll just have to put up with you making my bus wet and muddy I suppose. Come on, come on, don't hang about. I'm out of service and heading for the depot, this is not a bus route. Where are you going?'

The driver was wearing an old-fashioned peak cap under which it was possible to see he had long ginger hair held back in a ponytail. He had three missing teeth in the front and a livid scar which ran from his left ear, across his cheek, stopping just short of his left nostril, and a gold stud through his lower lip. His eyes were two startlingly different colours, one blue and one green. He was somewhere in his thirties or forties, I think.

'Cromer,' I said, my teeth were chattering by now, cold and fear and tiredness. It was half terrifying, half reassuring, half dream, half nightmare, hard to explain. It felt bliss to be out of the rain and wind to be honest and, though not exactly friendly, he was obviously concerned for our safety. I gave him Angela's address. We all sat together on the back seat realising he wasn't about to make idle chat with us and the bus racketed and swung its way all the way to Angela's. He stopped to see the front door open to us before clattering off. Angela opened the door and said benignly:

'Have you had a lovely time? Oooh, you *are* wet. I'll make hot drinks. I assume you're all staying? Your mum rang a few times, Hannah, probably best to let her know you're here, and you, Rachel, love.'

We found ourselves alternately laughing and crying as we explained haltingly to Angela what had happened, the lost phones, the lost money, Dan and Jackie, the Knight Bus. Dad was on his way home from a successful shout. Carrie appeared then at the top of the stairs towelling her hair dry after a shower and Jason emerged from the living room.

'What the… oh good grief, anything could've happened. Hmmm, one of those *incidents* this household seems to attract,' he said looking somewhat accusingly at blameless, lovely Angela, then smiling fondly at her as he saw that she was calmly making hot chocolate and rounds of toast for us, whilst we took it in turns to have showers, luckily quite quick using the two bathrooms.

Carrie found us plenty of spare things to sleep in and we sorted out who would sleep where. We decided we'd all go in my room feeling we needed to be together for mutual support after our dramatic incident. Dad appeared then, upbeat, buoyant after the rescue also in need of a hot shower and hot chocolate and toast. And actually, regaling him with the tale, the *incident,* was tremendously therapeutic; it felt cathartic especially as we all ended up laughing our heads off and slept like logs that night. It wasn't until the following morning we realised that, although the brightly lit bus had waited at the end of Angela's drive, perfectly visible from several parts of the house, and the driver had waited until the front door opened to us, nobody, not one single person, had mentioned seeing it.

'Course they didn't coz they didn't see it, they're Muggles, suspected it all along, proves it!' I giggled.

A little while later that morning I was pleased to have Hannah and Rachel with me when the penny suddenly dropped with a massive clunk. It was the way Carrie looked at Dad and he at her as he left for work. Carrie went off to do more costume design and sewing. It was obvious that they had "feelings" for each other. My thoughts were in turmoil, I remember, including, pointlessly, why did it have to be so obvious in front of Hannah and Rachel – as if that would matter. As we cleared away our breakfast things Rachel suggested we all went out for our favourite walk from Angela's and down to the beach. I nodded but felt tight-lipped and tense, not wanting to make eye contact.

We reached our favoured spot and it was Rachel who reached out to me, obviously feeling she was treading on eggshells:

'Talk to us, Amy, what is it? Think about that conversation you had with your Granda and Carrie at the beach that time – about age differences, remember? You told me about it, the *yuck factor* one about age differences.' Rachel then quickly summarised the main points for Hannah who nodded slowly.

'So,' Rachel continued, 'given that your Dad and Carrie are both adults what's the issue?'

'It seems, well, strange, wrong, yuck, yes,' then I laughed as I realised, I had fallen straight into the trap of needing to analyse this *yuck factor*. I missed Granda suddenly, massively, the feeling threatened to overwhelm me. I felt Angela might be helpful. Jenny was arriving later to pick Rachel and Hannah up, Carrie would be going to work at the pier, it could be a good time to chat to them we thought as we headed for home after a quick game of skimming stones.

When we got back to Angela's it was about 2 o'clock. She and Jenny were lingering over a delicious looking salady lunch laid out ready for anyone who wanted to help themselves. Carrie had already left for the pier. We helped ourselves and sat down and I decided to launch straight in.

'We wanted to talk to you both about Dad and Carrie because we all noticed the way they looked at each other this morning, it's obvious they have feelings for each other, it's hard to get our, well my, head around it. Granda said once it was important to analyse the *yuck factor*.' I stopped abruptly as I suddenly remembered on that occasion he had actually been talking to Carrie and me about Angela and Jason. Honestly, my household, surrogate family was so complicated!

'Oh, Amy love, I'm so pleased you mentioned it. Yes, let's do it,' said Angela with a delighted grin, 'nothing I enjoy more than analysing yuck factors, challenging assumptions. I've already converted Jason about this,' she said chucking softly. Jason was at work.

'So, Carrie and Doug everyone, Amy's dad, or Mr Appleton to you two as we were once taught to call our friends' parents,' she said turning to Rachel and Hannah, smiling, 'actually, Jenny and I were just talking about this. Now, as you know, Amy, you are the most important person in this, I think,' and she reached over to hold my hand as she spoke. 'I know for certain that your lovely father has always behaved with absolute propriety towards Carrie, I *know* this,' she repeated firmly, 'it's not just an optimistic thought. So this means that, when all the no-smoke-without-fire, mud-sticks stuff was going on after the rescue, I was able to give both him and Carrie my absolute support. We have to remember that Carrie herself turned 16 a mere three months after the rescue, so technically... well, you know what I mean don't you, girls?' Rachel and Hannah glanced at each other, Hannah looked particularly wide-eyed as she listened to Angela, Rachel was more used to her.

Angela continued: 'So if it *is* the case that Doug and Carrie, as consenting adults, are now an "item" as they say, and I for one think they are, can we discuss what might be worrying you girls if anything?' I could almost hear words like *wrong, gross, weird* whizzing around in Rachel's and Hannah's minds and being rapidly suppressed. To be honest it didn't feel to me like any of those things strangely enough. Carrie had always seemed to me to be older than her years, and Dad younger in some ways. I felt very secure in his unconditional love for me, that was the main thing.

I said quietly: 'I feel very happy for them actually. We should let them be.' I felt Angela squeeze my hand gently and Jenny smile at me with that kind of deep understanding she had always shown to me and which, once again, as ever, made me feel secure, safe, and understood at a profound level.

Rachel, Hannah and I more or less simultaneously decided we needed to be away from the adults, partly embarrassment, partly we needed time to process this on our own, I think. So I asked if we could call in on Susan, we would walk there we said, spurred on by this sudden need to be on our own and away from Angela's for a bit. Jenny said that would suit her fine if it was okay with Angela for her to linger for a longer chat.

'You know the answer to that Jenny,' Angela said looking pleased. 'I'll just go and pack up some pro-things for the girls to take to Susan. She's struggling a bit poor love.'

Angela was always talking about "pro-things" when discussing shopping, picnics and suchlike. She told me it came from *Winnie the Pooh* and was short for "provisions" which the animals, or toys, whichever way you saw them, packed up for their "expotition" to the North Pole led by Christopher Robin. I liked it.

Chapter 29

IT WAS QUITE A SHOCK arriving at Susan's, my old house of course, that afternoon to see how much she had deteriorated from the point of view of her MS and her accident. Strangely, on the way there, we didn't talk about the Carrie and Dad thing at all. We talked about school a bit, talked about the fact that Rachel had just started going out with a friend of Harry and Finn's, Marty, who was in the first year of sixth form with them, Year 12, at Paston Sixth Form College in North Walsham. Marty hadn't been at Cromer High School with us. They were all doing similar science subjects.

Susan was very unsteady on her feet, caused mainly by periods of intense vertigo, she explained. She was having a great deal of double vision and her speech sounded slurred at times. She was, though, as upbeat as possible, and offered us all drinks and biscuits which we fetched. The weather was still lovely enough to sit outside so we used the garden furniture and Susan took my arm as we went out onto the small patio area. It was obvious that talking tired her quite a bit, and she seemed breathless at times, but she was very keen to know how the new school year was going, what books we were doing for GCSE English, that kind of thing.

She asked after all our parents and Angela and Carrie and seemed so interested in all we had to say. I enjoyed telling her about my trip to Cambridge and about all the little children and baby Jess. She asked how Harry and Finn were getting on at Paston too and told us to tell them they were welcome here anytime, explaining how much she loved being with people our age, being on the cusp of adulthood, as she put it. I think because Rachel and I had been friends for so long it was easy for Hannah to feel a bit out of it and hold back a bit but Susan, noting this, was able to bring her out of her shell a bit. Of course, we all regaled her with our Great Yarmouth adventures, incredible that it was only yesterday, all of us contributing. It lost nothing in the telling. Susan loved it, every detail, gasping with suspense at the bit when we discovered our money and phones were missing, looking quietly horrified at our decision to hitch hike, exploding into laughter at our description of the Knight Bus.

She asked us whether we had thought about our next steps after GCSE's. We explained that we would go to some of the local sixth form open days the following September but that, at the moment, our preference was for Paston because it had a good reputation, and offered a really good range of subjects at A-level and did not seem too schooly. Susan chuckled when we said this.

'Oh yes, there definitely comes a time for most when school seems too constraining. Actually, I used to find it a bit odd seeing our Year 10 and 11 boys in their PE kit. Not in a weird way,' she added hastily, seeing us glance at each other, 'it was just those great, long hairy legs...' she broke off then seeing us look at each other as if to say, "yep, well, we really, really don't need to know this".

Partly to change the subject I asked Susan how she was managing for shopping and cooking and things like that. I said I could help her as much as time allowed with school as I was the nearest. Rachel said her mum would always help and she knew Harry and Finn would too. Rachel told Susan then about her new boyfriend, Marty.

'Oh, that's kind, all of you. I feel surrounded by kindness and help here actually. I bless the day when I met you all, but we won't go into that,' she smiled. 'I do my shopping online; the delivery drivers are so helpful. The substitute items are a bit strange at times, or *random,* as you youngsters would say. I got some revolting smelling peach-scented shampoo instead of peaches the other day, and a pack of twelve tubes of extra strong mints instead of a pack of beef mince! Oh, yes, another time I got three kilogrammes of courgettes instead of three courgettes!' We all found this very funny.

The three of us cleared away, loaded the dishwasher and asked Susan if there was anything we could do to help before we headed back to Angela's. She asked if we could just unload the washing machine and put it on the dryer as we were there, only because she felt so very tired, she explained.

'It's not a big load,' she said, 'but a job that would take me about forty-five minutes with breaks would probably take you girls ten, if that.' Of course, we were happy to help and I said I'd come round again tomorrow after school.

On the way back to Angela's I told Rachel and Hannah how much I liked being back in my old house even though it brought back some awful memories and felt a bit weird at times. I explained haltingly that although I loved Angela, loved the house, loved being there, I thought that maybe she and Jason would like some "just married together time", putting it in inverted commas deliberately.

I explained that when Dad and I were at Granda's old flat it felt just plain sad, and that Dad was out a lot. I told them I was considering asking Susan if I could move in with her for a bit. This had only just occurred to me actually as we were helping with the washing. I realised that I could be really helpful to her, make sure she was safe, I liked her a lot. It felt as if I was thinking it all through as I talked to my friends.

'If I did move in with Susan,' I continued, 'it would mean that while Carrie was still home from uni she and Dad could have some "together time" at Granda's flat so that Angela and Jason could have some "together time".' Again, I put the phrase in inverted commas and said half laughing, half crying, 'God, all these couples!' I told them Carrie was still a bit uneasy around Jason, and if I moved in with Susan she wouldn't be on her own with "the lovebirds", kind of hating myself for the sarcasm in the words, spoken, again, in air quotes.

'Sounds like a good idea, kiddo,' was Rachel's easy response.

Hannah nodded: 'Your life is really exciting compared to mine, Amy, I feel sort of envious.'

She looked distracted for a bit then:

'Actually there is something I discovered only yesterday, about my family, I'm still kind of in shock to be honest. Harry forced my parents to tell me because I was getting really mad with the way my mum babies me, to be honest. It's so embarrassing and annoying. Anyway, we had a really fraught evening yesterday, Harry just suddenly confronted them, it was awful and good at the same time.' Hannah looked at us both a little warily: 'I haven't been able to stop thinking about it and it explains Mum a bit.'

'Tell us if you want to, Hannah, but no pressure, honestly,' I said, aware of her tormented expression. Rachel nodded in agreement. And now I remember so clearly Hannah telling us her family secret, haltingly, tearfully at times as we walked along the coast path back to Angela's.

Hannah had been an identical twin but her sister, Rachel, died the day after their second birthday during a birthday party for the little girls, postponed by a day so it could take place on a Saturday when all the parents could come. Harry and Hannah's family lived in Mundesley then. Their house had a swimming pool, the twins' birthday was on 12th July and the following day, the 13th, was one of those glorious summer days, cloudless blue sky, about 25 degrees all day long, no wind. It sounded like classic *eye-off-the-ball-stuff* as Dad sometimes called it. I remember having that thought even as Hannah relayed the events of that terrible day to Rachel and me, events she had only just been told about.

It's easy in retrospect to see how it happened. All the parents were milling about, chatting, helping themselves to food which was laid out indoors. The guests brought it outside to eat, either sprawled on garden rugs or at the garden tables and chairs put out, some borrowed from neighbours, some choosing to sit and shelter under a couple of borrowed gazebos, needed for shade on that baking hot day rather than because of rain.

In view of the large number of small children at the party (Hannah didn't know how many there were) the pool was strictly out of bounds and Hannah's dad had rigged up a temporary fence round it. Somehow little Rachel had wriggled her way through a gap in the fence with nobody noticing for some time. She had been used to jumping in off the shallow end steps with one of her parents always there to catch her and start to teach her some swimming strokes. This meant that the pool was familiar, fun territory, it held no fear for her, but she couldn't swim. It was thought that she must have jumped in as usual, it looked very inviting on that hot day, and it was not for some time, nobody knows quite how long, that people wondered where she was. Hannah's parents each thought the other knew where all three children were, Harry was only 4, after all. It was Harry who found Rachel, face down in the pool and ran screaming for his parents.

Rachel and I were lost for words when we heard this. We had stopped at a bench overlooking the sea at this stage. After about five minutes of absolute silence, which was somehow appropriate and comforting, I tentatively asked

Hannah if she ever felt that something or somebody was missing in her life.

'All the time, all the time. I think that's why I'm a bit weird,' Hannah was laughing and crying at the same time now, 'but the worse thing, the worse thing is that nobody ever talks about Rachel, has never talked about her, and they kept her a secret from me all this time, all this time, can you believe it?' I can hear in my mind her anguished repetition of some of the phrases to this day.

'I think that's why me and Limpet get on so well, actually. Oh, I shouldn't call him that.'

Limpet was a boy in our year, Jordan Linmet, who, since the end of year 9, had started to hang round us three, so much so that it was hard to shake him off and I'm sorry to say that that's why we called him Limpet amongst ourselves

'Jordy lost a twin too, did you know?' Hannah continued. 'Identical as well, but he was stillborn. They called him Simon and they talk about him a lot, apparently. His parents explained to Jordy what had happened as soon as he was old enough to understand. I guess for them the difference is that there's was no guilt. But Jordy does say he sometimes feels as if he's a poor substitute son for them, so we all have our hang ups, I guess. And he wonders if his parents just felt too sad to enjoy his new baby and toddler time and whether they always see a gap when they look at him. His parents told him that when he was a baby he was always turning to look at something on his right when he was awake and just sort of gurgling, you know how babies do that thing. And he did it when he was asleep too, they said, turned his head that way, I mean. Jordy told me that he always felt there was something major missing in his life, always, way before he'd been told about Simon. Weird isn't it?'

Rachel then asked her if she remembered the incident at all and I can see Hannah now shaking her head slowly as she said:

'No, no, nothing at all, I had literally just turned 2 don't forget.' She paused then answered the question that was uppermost in my mind without me having to ask it. 'But Harry, poor Harry, he remembers it all vividly, he had nightmares for months apparently. As he got older, he blamed himself and realised that that was why Mum was so over-protective towards me.'

I'm ashamed to say that my first thought was why had Harry never told

Rachel, Finn and me? Why hadn't he told *me,* followed almost immediately by wondering why I should even care about that aspect of it. 'It's all me, me, me with you Amy,' I berated myself inwardly, 'and here are my friends, Harry and Hannah coping with this and Harry has coped with it for most of his life?'

Hannah continued: 'Mum and Dad wanted to move away from the house as quickly as possible so that's why we moved to Bessingham, kind of hidden away from everything, everyone.' I found myself beginning to understand Hannah's parents' slight reserve, a sort of holding back, a keeping of people at arms' length, and their need to work hard, keep focused and protect their children; it all seemed to make a sort of sense to me then. There was none of the easy warmth and affection of Rachel's parents, not between the two of them, not towards us, their children's friends, not towards Harry for sure. Hannah's dad, Fergus, was a lawyer of some sort and her mum, Diane, worked at Norwich Union, later to become Aviva, in some senior role.

'I'm so pleased to have you two as friends,' she continued as we walked up the drive to Angela's. For our part we never referred to Jordy as Limpet ever again and he became one of our close-knit group.

'How's Susan?' Angela asked as we trooped in. 'Are you three alright?' she asked brightly. 'You all look a bit shell-shocked. What's up? Still analysing the *yuck factor*?' That conversation suddenly seemed to have taken place ages ago.

'Oh no, no, that's all fine. I'm happy for them,' I responded quickly and perhaps unconvincingly; once again I could feel Jenny looking into my very soul, or so it felt. 'No, it's Susan,' I said quickly, 'we're a bit shocked by how much worse her MS is. So much so, I was thinking I might move in there for a bit to help her, if she'd like that. Being in Granda's flat makes me miss him so much and Dad's out a lot, either at work or at the station, training, or on a shout, so I was thinking of moving in there at least until Carrie returns to uni, then she could visit Dad at the flat as much as she likes.' I felt the explanation for our mood sort of rushing out, sentences tumbling over each other almost.

Angela looked very thoughtful and then said

'Well, on the face of it, I think it's a very good idea, but you have to remember that school is quite...' she hesitated briefly, *'full on,* I think was the expression you used, Amy,' she grinned: 'you also must understand that you always have a home here, *always*, we love having you, and I know your dad will feel the same about your home at your grandfather's flat. Did Susan or your dad tell you she's decided to go on renting your house, with his absolute blessing of course? Obviously, she just cannot house hunt at the moment nor cope with the hassle of moving. Her rent pays the mortgage on it, and actually, she did tell your dad and me recently that she has no wish to own another house, she can't see the point. She loves it there and that way, as she said, the house is still your dad's after she dies.' Angela paused briefly. 'Actually, after that conversation, completely off his own bat, your dad made his will leaving the house to you,Amy, of course. I think it's important you know that.'

It was only much later, very recently in fact, that I discovered that Mum decided when she left us to give up all financial responsibility for me in exchange for Dad keeping the house and doing what he wanted with it. She wished then to have nothing to do with it, or me, it seemed – this latter thought only comes to me in my bad moments. Certainly neither of them wanted any battles over money. But then, I remember, the thought of Dad making his will made me shudder inwardly, and both Hannah and Rachel looked stricken, but Jenny chipped in:

'It's just a sensible thing to do, nothing to worry about, practical, much more hassle and worry if there's no will,' she said matter of factly but looking at me in her sort of penetrating but kind way.

I talked to Dad later, when we were on our own at Granda's flat, about my thought of moving in with Susan. Again, he considered it carefully and replied:

'I completely understand what you mean about Granda's flat and I know I'm out a lot, love, it's weird for you. I just don't want you to feel pushed out or that you haven't got a home here, you're my best girl and always will be. I can see Susan's difficulties too.' He paused, then, 'Angela told me she explained to you about our house as it seemed the right time to tell you, she said. I would have told you, of course, but, to be fair, Susan only discussed it with me a few days ago and it feels like we've hardly seen each other,' he seemed rueful for a moment, then looked at me very directly and took both my hands in his. 'Talking of the right time,' he said quietly, 'it feels like that's now to explain to you about me and Carrie; Angela mentioned that you'd noticed we'd got closer.' I must have looked a bit uncomfortable or something because Dad said gently:

'No, we need to talk about this, Amy, we really have to. You of all people need to know the truth. You are the most important person here.'

We were sitting next to each other looking out at Granda's sea view as he spoke. I remember the light was fading gradually, and the sunset was one of those muted, subtle ones making the sea ripple with alternating shade and light, as if welcoming the forthcoming darkness into its soft embrace; it was late September.

Dad continued thoughtfully: 'It's true to say that when I rescued Carrie all those years ago, what is it… five, five and a half years ago now, I felt there was something very special about her. By any purely objective, unbiased viewpoint,' he smiled, 'she is very beautiful in her delicate, golden, fairy-like way, totally different from your dark-eyed, clear-skinned, stunning bone structure, beauty, love. You're both beautiful. But, as I know Angela has explained to you, I have always, *always* behaved with absolute propriety, as Angela says, absolute propriety,' he repeated, 'towards her, not only of course when she was technically a child, but even as she has grown up.' He hesitated briefly, 'that was until last month when you were at Mum's. She had ditched that oaf, Steve, and she made the first move as a fully consenting adult.'

He looked at me then and continued: 'And, Amy, this *absolute propriety* business was hard, really hard for me because I knew I had "feelings" for her, I'll spare you the details, love, you're my daughter after all, and that would be tmi!' Dad was looking out to sea now, reflectively, it seemed. I stayed silent.

He went on: 'I sensed she had feelings for me which confused her a bit.' I remember thinking how long the light took to go completely as Dad poured all this out. I didn't want to stop him by interrupting or even moving as I remember.

He spoke softly. 'Fair play to her she was determined to go off to uni and make the most of all aspects of life there, social, academic. As you know the latter was easy for her, she's well on track for a first, pretty good going with her mother's death and everything, but the social bit was hard for her. You can see she's not the clubbing type, but she did all that, entered fully into

Freshers, remember she told us about all the craziness? Well, some of it at least,' he paused again looking troubled for a moment before continuing, 'imagine what knowing this did to me, Amy? Well, no, perhaps not, tmi again, sorry.'

He rushed on as if to purge that thought.

'But believe me, I had many sleepless nights worrying, imagining. She joined things, met people, has had quite nice housemates but she was really homesick for our beautiful part of the world, missed Marianne, missed Angela, missed you and, well, missed me, she's explained all this to me. She was really, really homesick a lot of the time, her saving grace was that she loved the course so was always committed to that, interested, doing well. I see her as being courageous, resilient in so many ways, especially with losing her mum. She looks so delicate but, my god, she has inner strength, Amy, she really does. So, we're good the two of us,' he continued musingly, 'and if the knowledge that we're now a couple upsets any of those mud-stick types, you know what, Amy?' he paused only briefly. 'Neither of us gives a toss because all the important people in our life know the absolute, solid, God's honest, truth.'

I loved Dad more than ever for this conversation and hugged him tightly.

'I love Carrie, Dad, and I'm very happy for you both. Just think – if you get married, she'll be my stepmum, she'd be a very cool stepmum!'

Dad chuckled: 'Very cool, but we're just taking things gently, love. She's planning her future after uni but will most likely do a PhD if she can find a funded one in her field, probably at Southampton, because she knows it, but she's looking at various options, probably a Masters first. Her personal tutor has already tried to recruit her there, but I notice she's been looking into options at UEA lately. She's asked me to help her look!' He sounded quietly excited and went on less guardedly. 'Yay! I'm keeping my fingers crossed but also keeping my opinion to myself, of course. I'm used to holding back now,' he grinned. 'Actually, there's a PhD project at ENV, School of Environmental Sciences at UEA, they're really into all those three letter acronyms there. The project's looking into sea flooding, the title's about a paragraph long but it looks just her cup of tea and it's funded. She's really interested in something called biogeomorphology. I had to ask her what it was,' Dad grinned. I was enjoying the conversation, it transported me into new worlds, opened up for me vistas of the wider horizons that I so craved. It seemed appropriate somehow that we were gazing out at our own sea view as he spoke.

Dad explained that biogeomorpholgy became an academic subject as recently as the late 80's and that it was something to do with interactions between organisms and landforms. 'It does sound interesting to be fair, if a bit of a mouthful,' he said. 'She'd have to do some undergrad. teaching and she'd get a stipend,' he explained to me what that meant, then went on with a kind of boyish excitement: 'I'm so hoping she goes for it, Amy, but it depends if the project's ongoing in a year's time. There could well be a follow on from it, I guess, perhaps the title of the next one would be two paragraphs long!'

This all seemed so exciting to me and yet again made me want to hurry forward to the time when I could be properly mapping out my future, a bit at a time. I remember even at that young age, knowing that whatever I chose to do after school it would need to be something that led to the security of a paid job with a big, safe employer and a guaranteed income. This was almost a subconscious thought. No adult in my life at that time had ever said to me that I needed to be thinking that way, it was simply a thought that was deeply embedded in me and I had never even stopped to think about it until writing this now.

And so it happened that I moved in with Susan, much to her delight and with everyone's blessing, and it was this move which set me on my own future career choice, my own kind of fast-forwarding, just as Carrie, seven years older than me, was taking her next steps.

Chapter 30

SOMEHOW, BETWEEN US ALL, ME, Jenny, Rachel, to a lesser extent Hannah only because she lived in the middle of nowhere as she called it – in Bessingham, Dad, Carrie, Angela and Jason, we set up quite a support system for Susan. She certainly had noticeably deteriorated and really needed our help. Actually, living with Susan in my old home was lovely in many ways, but it also meant I was the one who was mostly involved in helping Susan with her personal care. Somehow, Susan made this easy for us both. I found it a privilege and very humbling to be able to help her in this way. This sounds clichéd but it was the simple truth.

Susan did have some outside support. There was a specialist neurological nurse, Sue, who visited and was able to give knowledgeable advice and information, refer Susan for other support, as well as assess her physical and mental state and sometimes prescribe medication, for example medicines to alleviate Susan's painful muscle spasms. She was a wonderful listening ear for Susan too. Sue also talked to both me and Susan together and separately with great skill and sensitivity about the fact that I, aged 14 (I would turn 15 in March, six months' time) was living with Susan as her primary carer even though Susan was no relation to me. I remember Susan saying thoughtfully looking at me first then turning to Sue:

'Well, we both have our stories to tell, if you have time I'll tell you mine, it won't take long, then Amy can tell you hers if that's okay with everyone?'

How vividly I recall Susan telling Sue how she came to know me and my friends, explaining about the cold darkness both inside and out on that December night, her words, necessarily halting and tortured because of her speech difficulty, serving somehow to reflect the bleak loneliness of those November and December days for her. I remember too they way her speech gradually became easier as she explained how the rescue from her near suicide on the end of the pier and our subsequent welcoming of her into our lives had given her own life meaning. She went on to explain that this house was actually my childhood home and that my father was letting it out to her at a peppercorn rent; this was the first time I had heard that expression but it was easy to work out its meaning.

As I listened, I rehearsed my part in the events. I explained that I had been living in my recently dead grandfather's flat with my dad but how that had been quite lonely because Dad was so busy and that living there made me miss my grandfather even more. I explained that my parents had divorced and that both were now in new relationships, Mum in Cambridge with a whole new family, Dad still at the flat. I was at pains to point out that no one had pushed me out, I had offered to return to my home and look after Susan, that it was much nearer school than my grandfather's flat was, and how helpful Susan was with schoolwork. I remember feeling fearful that somehow I would be taken away from being Susan's primary carer when it was all working so well and I became very insistent, childishly insistent I think, that everything was fine. I remember I really was fearful that "the authorities" would interfere, and I insisted that though I lived with Susan there were lots of adults who helped.

Both Sue and Susan reassured me and calmed me down, I do remember that I needed it, and Sue explained that she needed to let the local authority know that I was Susan's primary carer and a minor and that meant I would be eligible to access their support services for young carers. She explained that this was mostly support groups, online and actual, and that they could be very helpful. Sue also asked if my school knew the situation and, if not, told me that I should tell a trusted teacher. Susan had been urging me to do this so I promised them both that I would. I planned to tell Mrs Hebden, who was my English teacher again this year. I knew this was not an empty promise as they were both being so kind, and I didn't want to deceive them.

As they were talking about this, I remembered suddenly how hard and successfully I had managed to conceal from my primary school teachers and friends, and their parents, apart from Jenny and Paul of course, how much I had cared for Mum. Perhaps it was because she was mentally ill, rather than physically ill, that I felt I had to keep it a secret. I don't know, I only know I longed to be like the other children whose parents always seemed to be around and on top of things. Strangely, I felt ashamed, embarrassed by it, responsible for it and sort of guilty all at the same time.

An occupational therapist, Pat, visited too. This was helpful as he was able to source specialist equipment such as handrails, walking aids and a wheelchair. Most interesting of all to me though was the speech and language therapist (known as an SLT, usually pronounced salt) called Helen, who visited. Susan had already explained to me about her difficulties with speech and sometimes swallowing. At this stage she was suffering from dysarthria and some dysphagia, 'difficulty in swallowing,' she explained, 'not to be confused with the other type of speech difficulty, dysphasia.' These terms had all been explained to her by her lovely SLT, she told me.

Whether it was the teacher in her or just her own insight Susan was somehow able to explain the difference between the two very clearly to me as "dysarthria" being a difficulty in forming words clearly for mechanical reasons, whilst "dysphasia" she explained to me as a disruption between thoughts and language most often caused by strokes or head injuries. I remember so well her musing: 'that must be terrible, thoughts coming out as scribbles and people looking at you pityingly. Much worse than me trying to talk and sounding as if I have mouth full of pickled onions! That's what my dysarthria feels like.'

She explained that in her case the messages were not getting through to the muscles because of the gradual destruction of the myelin sheath throughout her central nervous system, the myelin sheath being the fatty, white substance surrounding nerve cells. This was known as demyelination, she told me, and it caused interruption to, and slowing down of, the electrical impulses passing through the nerve cells 'meaning that these pesky muscles can no longer do what I want them to do and what they need to do, very frustrating,' and she gave an uncharacteristic, despairing shake of her head.

It was this demyelination, in various stages of progression throughout her body, that was the cause of her many debilitating symptoms and signs including her double vision and sort of staggering, swaying gait, 'known as ataxia,' she said, 'and it makes me look as if I've downed a bottle of wine, or several bottles of wine, not a good look.' She grinned as she said it and I grinned with her but I could see a fleeting look that told me more than any explanation could about just how cruel this disease was. Susan explained to me too about her fatigability. 'Different from plain old fatigue, Amy, it's more to do with my muscles getting tired ridiculously quickly. Anyway, that's enough of all that for now, though I must say that the swallowing difficulties are tricky and frightening at times. I'll ask Helen to explain that bit to you.'

And it was when I met Helen, wonderful, inspirational Helen, that my future career path was set out. I found it all so interesting, every aspect. Even the technical bits relating to the brain's anatomy and functioning seemed to me to be easy to understand, much easier than some of the plant and animal biology we were learning for GCSE Biology. The way Helen was able to help Susan, showing her techniques based on her deep knowledge and understanding of the condition was powerfully motivating. Again, that feeling of wanting to fast-forward my life, make choices, ditch compulsory subjects at school that I didn't enjoy much, go into a career where I could help people like Susan, swept over me forcefully.

When Helen was with Susan, they both invited me to be present so that I too, as Susan's primary carer, could help with reminders of the techniques. I found the respect and compassion with which Helen treated Susan very moving. I asked Helen what had drawn her into speech and language therapy as a career and she told me that she had a much younger brother, Dean, who had had a severe stammer from as soon as he was able to talk and how impressed she had been with his speech therapist, what a difference she had made to Dean's life, especially as he had been lucky enough to have been referred very young, aged just 3.

Helen told me that children like Dean needed this input before the age of 7, even younger if possible, for it to be most effective, but that often there were delays to referrals, then ridiculously long waits in some parts of the country.

'It's all to do with money, of course, funding the courses, funding for the jobs, crazy,' she explained. 'Have a look into it and it'll help you make your A-level choices and choose relevant and interesting work experience opportunities to boost your university application when the time comes. I loved my time at UEA,' she said with a hint of nostalgia. 'The course there has a very good name, and it led to registration with the professional regulator after only three years, it was the Council for Professions Supplementary to Medicine then, CPSM. It now comes under the jurisdiction of the HCPC – the Health and Care Professions Council.' She paused, again looking reflective, wistful even, before continuing. 'UEA was great, we had conversation partners during our course, these are "service users", not keen on that phrase to be honest, it's just people needing speech therapy but it's far too generic for me. I mean, after all, we're all service users of one sort or another, bin collections, public transport, lots of stuff.' I loved listening to Helen talk. 'Anyway,' she went on, 'then I never moved away after I qualified because I fell in love with everything Norfolk including my husband.'

She glanced at her wedding ring, and almost subconsciously, it seemed, she started twisting it round on her slim finger. 'We met in our second year, he's a Climate Scientist and now teaches there.' I could see that she was off down memory lane as she spoke, and I listened, rapt as she continued.

'We're both originally from Sussex by pure chance, Chichester, but we didn't meet there. It means we can visit our parents in one prolonged trip, handy. And they sort of share their grandchildren, it all works. And they get on really well, phew!'

It all sounded so exciting; it was great talking to Helen in this way. Both Susan and Helen took a huge interest in my research for A-level choices and universities. Although it seemed far ahead I just wanted to be sure I was set on the right path and there was masses of information about the universities to digest. I also needed to think whether I actually wanted to "go away" to university as that's what people did. I felt very conflicted about this, mindful of Carrie's homesickness, also aware that Norfolk was considered to be the back of beyond by some. So I decided to look very closely at the courses offered, attend open days, and go with my gut instinct. This reflected Susan's advice too.

Meanwhile there were still two more years of high school to go which felt very exam focused and different without Harry and Finn there. I remember it felt as if I'd been left behind. The high spots were the drama productions. That was the year I played Mrs Hartridge in *Goodnight Mister Tom*. It was fun learning my words and practising with Susan's, and sometimes Helen's, help. It was good, too, seeing Harry and Finn back at school in the after-school rehearsals, especially Harry, I admitted to myself. I thought that was because I quite often saw Finn at Rachel's so seeing Harry was more of a novelty.

Life seemed to speed up for me at this stage. Whether it was because I was focused on my A-level and university choices, at last beginning to see my adult future panning out, feeling ready to shake off childhood shackles, I don't know. I remember discussing it with Angela quite recently.

She chuckled. 'Oh, Amy, trust me, as you get older each year feels like a month, each month feels like a week, each week feels like a day… you get the idea, I'm sure. Don't wish your life away, my love, that's my advice, but I do understand, I really do.'

Events or *incidents* stand out of course but I sometimes struggle to remember which year this or that happened and have to search for other identifying landmarks as life sped by. I was discussing the Waxham Beach *incident* only recently with Rachel. I couldn't remember whether it was the summer after GCSE's – *that summer* – or the summer after Year 10. It was Rachel who remembered the obvious landmark, Dad and Carrie's wedding, which was late July, the first Saturday of the summer holidays after Year 10. This *incident* happened exactly a week later, 31st July. Dad and Carrie had, by then, gone to Scotland on honeymoon.

Somebody in our year had sent out a more or less open invitation, open to our year I mean, to an "end-of-exams-for-now" party on Waxham Beach. It was going to start at about 2pm: barbecues, music, that kind of thing. Rachel, Hannah, Jordy, as we now called him, and I all wanted to go together as we didn't know the person organising it very well. Harry and Finn were down in Cornwall doing their beach lifeguarding course. None of us would be able to get there until much later. Rachel and Hannah were both doing some weekend shifts at the ice cream stall at the town end of Cromer pier, finishing at 7, Jordy was playing cricket, his first game in the adult team at his local club near North Walsham, Bradfield Cricket Club, and didn't know when it would be finished, and I had just started a summer holiday job at Roughton Fish and Chip shop, finishing at 9.

So, the carefully laid plan was that Jordy's dad would bring everyone to the fish and shop when the cricket finished, Rachel and Hannah would cycle either there or to the cricket club depending on the state of the game. There was a safe place to leave their bikes either at the back of the fish and chip shop or at the cricket club. As so often though, the weather played its unpredictable part, except that actually on this occasion it *was* predicted, or forecast as they say in weather terminology. There were warnings for exceptionally ferocious thunderstorms and torrential rain. We knew only too well that thunderstorms were often a July thing but these warnings were dire and we were not stupid. We kept an eye on the BBC weather alerts as we all knew a beach party in torrential rain and scary thunder and lightning would not be much fun. And to be fair, the weather warnings had been downgraded considerably by about 2 o'clock that afternoon.

And indeed, the weather, as forecast, relented considerably during the latter part of the day, but Jordy's game had been one of those on/off games with a delayed start and constant stoppages because of the earlier rain. Despite the decision taken at the beginning of the game to reduce the overs from 45 to 30 (it was a second team game) it started at 2, an hour late, and didn't finish until just after 8pm, with the light beginning to go.

They all arrived at the fish and chip shop, Jordy had caught two people out and been praised by the captain for his superb fielding so both he and his dad were on a high. He hadn't batted or bowled but hadn't expected to. They got to the fish and chip shop just as the restaurant was closing at 8.30 but I had already explained the situation to my boss who let us eat there as long as all the customers had left and I had cleared away.

Being used to most parties starting pretty late combined with the relaxed feeling of it being summer holidays, still light until nearly 9pm, Jordy's dad, readily agreed to go along with the original plan of taking us to the Waxham Beach Party. The idea was that Jenny and Paul would pick us up when we were ready to come home. They were having some friends round for dinner to celebrate Paul's friend, Martin, being told he was free of bladder cancer after undergoing surgery and chemotherapy and passing the five year follow up.

Jordy's dad dropped us off with our cans of cider and beer concealed in Jordy's backpack. These were not concealed from Jordy's dad, but we were underage for drinking though of course we had, by then, all been to house parties where alcohol featured. It was at about that stage of the day that the weather decided not to let July go without one last reminder that it was the month for thunderstorms.

Chapter 31

IT WAS ON JORDY'S DAD'S way home that the skies opened again. He stopped and tried to ring Jordy to check we had found the party, but he had no signal. It took him nearly an hour to get home to North Walsham, he told us, the journey would normally be about half an hour at the most. This was because not only could he do no more than about twenty miles an hour, he explained later, because of the lashing rain and low visibility, but also because he kept stopping to try to ring Jordy and finding he still had no signal.

Meanwhile we had been walking down a long, long track towards the sea and started looking up and down the beach which stretched as far as we could see into a vast empty space: no people, no lights, no barbecue, no music. We decided to turn left first to see if we could see any sign of the party as we rounded the first slight curve which had looked much nearer than it actually was. We had only been walking for about ten minutes in this direction when we heard the first low rumble of thunder sounding quite far away. By this time the darkness, previously absolute, was now at least intermittently broken up by the large expanse of sand picking up the occasional bright shaft of moonlight as the clouds scudded along in the wind. The familiar, fairly gentle, rhythmic sound of the sea, with the tide way, way out, was actually quite reassuring, too, at that stage.

I remember that we all simultaneously decided to reset our turnaround point as the slight curve of the beach we had identified seemed to recede ever further from us. There was a large, very dead, tree ahead, obviously uprooted in some storm months previously, and we decided to make our way as far as that, climb onto the trunk, which stretched like a broken limb at an odd angle across the beach, to check if that would give us enough height to see further in both directions. It was just as we all managed to scramble up, apart from Hannah, who couldn't quite manage it, that the next clap of thunder sounded, much louder, much closer, followed quite soon by almost cartoon-like, bright zig zags of lightning.

Rachel thinks that's when the rain started but I can clearly remember it starting just as we got back to our starting point planning to walk in the other direction. Cold, fat, very wet raindrops arrived like warning salvos before another deafening crash of thunder rent the night air (I remember using that very phrase to myself at the time) and the rain started lashing down in earnest. I suggested, instead of walking on into the rain, that we headed back down the track where I had seen a sort of barn that I thought we could at least shelter in.

Rachel and Jordy wanted to continue so we decided to stick together and plough on. But after about five minutes of feeling adventurous and intrepid and certain we would find the party we decided to turn back; at least that way we wouldn't be facing forward into the stinging rain. The thunder and lightning were, by then, coming in frequent, loud, bright bursts. We all knew that the closer together they came the nearer the storm was. The moon had long since disappeared behind heavy rain clouds which were intent on emptying their full load. It was pitchy dark.

Jordy, after consulting us, sent a text to his dad, explaining that we couldn't find the party and asking if he could pick us up. A ping on his phone after a few minutes alerted us to the fact that the text hadn't been sent as there was still no signal. I found myself wishing Harry and Finn were with us, no disrespect to Rachel, Hannah or Jordy, it's just that they were good at having ideas and it was easy to feel safe with them, especially Harry, I suddenly realised.

On arrival home Jordy's dad, also called Martin like Rachel's parents' friend, apparently tried to play down his worries with Jordy's mum, Anna, and eventually managed to get a signal whereupon he received the text from Jordy, sent half an hour earlier, saying we couldn't find our friends and were sheltering in a sort of barn near an adults' only holiday camp. Jordy gave his dad Rachel's dad's phone number and they decided to travel in convoy to find us partly for moral, and possibly physical, help if one of them got stuck in flood water, or skidded or something, and partly to have plenty of room to bring the four of us home in. Jenny and Paul did have a people carrier, but it seemed sensible to have both cars especially as Jordy's dad knew exactly where he'd dropped us off. It was decided that Jordy's and Hannah's mums would stay by their landline phones just in case.

Hannah was mostly worried that her mum would never let her out of her sight again. She seemed uncharacteristically relaxed and almost to be enjoying the adventure. She told Rachel and me afterwards that she felt safe with Jordy, just as a friend, she said quickly, too quickly, Rachel and I thought. We were right of course as by Christmas that year they told us that they were in a relationship.

'Who'd have thought Hannah would be the first of the three of us to have a proper boyfriend?' Rachel voiced the thought for both of us. Marty wasn't a proper boyfriend, it seemed. But I digress, as Granda used to say.

At this stage as we decided to make our way back to the shelter of the barn. I remember we were all really cold and really wet, and a chilling, brisk breeze had appeared. It had been a warm July evening when we'd set out, dressed for a beach party, Jordy having changed at the cricket club, and we three girls in the tiny toilet at the fish and chip shop which was stifling hot.

I remember that as we stumbled along, slipping and sliding in our strappy sandals, we could suddenly see a sort of series of lights over to the left, a bit like floodlights, seeming to stride robot-like in parallel with us. Strangely, they appeared more threatening, a kind of omnipresent evil eye, than the soft darkness of a summer night, even a wild and windy one such as this. I remember clutching hold of Hannah and Rachel in sheer fright when a figure suddenly appeared waving a torch and walking purposefully towards us:

'What the f...' he paused, '...hell are you kids doing here at this time of night? This is an adults' only place, you're not allowed. Can't you read? Scram, the lot of you! Now!' And with that, the man dressed in full waterproof kit strode angrily on his way without so much as a backward glance.

We found ourselves alternately laughing and almost crying with relief as we continued towards the barn. At that point a text pinged into Jordy's phone. It was from his dad and had been sent about ten minutes previously:

We're coming to get you. Can you tell us where you are, any landmarks?

Jordy texted back:

We're heading for a big barn quite a way further down the track you left us on, it'll be on your left as you drive down the track

It was certainly a relief to reach the barn and get out of the ever-strengthening wind and rain. I wanted Dad suddenly, my lovely reassuring dad, so used to plucking people from even direr situations. I thought of him on his honeymoon with Carrie, all lovey-dovey, not a care in the world. *I* wanted him, needed him. This thought felt childish and unfair, but it was hard to suppress it. I vowed to keep it to myself though.

The barn was dry, still cold though, and there were some strange scuffling sounds. We found a place to flop down on the concrete floor, Jordy gave Hannah his backpack to sit on. I felt chilled to the gunwales and told the others how Dad always used that phrase, pronouncing it *gun-wales.* I remember we all checked our phones and none of us had any signal. Rachel was the only one with a different network provider and she had the bright idea of going outside the barn, the rain was still racketing down, to see if she had signal there. We heard about six or seven pings as messages from Jenny arrived, explaining that they too were coming to get us, following Jordy's dad.

The next thing was that we heard heavy footsteps approaching the barn, it sounded like more than one person, and again, the steps were purposeful. We glanced at each other, wide-eyed, it was briefly terrifying. As Rachel slipped back into the barn, hair dripping wet, she was followed by two policemen with torches.

'God in heaven, it's kids,' said one of them.

'What on earth are you lot doing here at this time of night?' the other asked.

'We were supposed to be at a beach party,' I remember answering falteringly, 'but we couldn't find it.' I was conscious of the alcohol in Jordy's bag. We all were, we discovered afterwards.

Rachel chipped in then sounding more confident than she felt, she explained afterwards. 'Our parents are on their way to get us.'

I noticed the policemen looking at each other with relief.

'Lovely weather for a party,' the taller of the two said. They both seemed to find this hilariously funny. 'Well good luck to them finding you out here,' the other said jovially, 'we've got to be on our way – we've been called to investigate something kicking off over there,' and he nodded towards the floodlight, 'we're used to it, Saturday nights.' And with that they left.

That was when we realised that we had all been worried about the alcohol in Jordy's bag which seems a strange and innocent thing to be worrying about, looking back now. We were so, so cold and decided we could either huddle together for warmth or do some PE type warm-ups, choosing the latter as it felt less, well, weird and less as if were dying or something. Also, we were all so wet and cold that we thought we'd make each other even wetter and colder if we just huddled together. It felt a bit too desperate as well.

I remembered singing with Fred clinging onto the buoy in France, but I rapidly put that memory out of my mind, this just wasn't like that. Rescue was on its way in the form of familiar parents. Here, we were simply miserable, very cold and feeling a bit stupid that we had thought the party would still be going on as the weather worsened, despite the earlier downgrading of the weather warning.

The PE jumps and movements were a good idea and also quietened down the ominous scratchings and scrapings and scuffling noises we could here in the barn. We took it in turns to mimic PE teachers we'd known, even the cool ones. Every so often Rachel went to the entrance of the barn and, after what seemed like hours, during one of these sorties, she gave a whoop of joy: 'They've turned in at the gate. I can see headlights, one lot anyway. I think it's your dad, Jordy. Let's start walking towards it, we should see them both soon.'

As we ventured out of the shelter of the barn the wind was even stronger and the rain relentless though the thunder and lightning had by now moved away. We could just hear faint rumblings by now followed some time later by bright flashes of lightning. In no time at all we were as cold as ever and stumbled along full of relief that rescue was in sight.

Jordy's dad took him and Hannah, and Jenny and Paul took me and Rachel. Iain was with them. Paul put the heater on full blast and drove carefully through many areas of quite deep water on the road. Iain regaled us with details of their trip to find us: how Jenny's phone had kept losing signal, how Paul had grabbed two torches on the way out to the car and asked Iain to sit behind him, pausing every so often for either he or his mum to open their car doors and shine a torch out to check exactly where they were on the road as the visibility was virtually nil. When they shone their torches out all they could see were fast-running rivulets of water, it was impossible to see where the edge of the road ended and the ditch at the side of the road began, Jenny added. Paul had said he was driving by the seat of his pants which caused much giggling between the three of us on the back seat safely on our way to familiar warmth and comfort.

On arrival at Rachel's, lovely, warm, comforting, familiar Rachel's, one of my safe havens for many years, I had another moment of suddenly, overwhelmingly just wanting my dad. This took me by surprise. I watched Jenny hugging Rachel and she quickly turned to hug me too, but she had hugged Rachel first, of course she had. This felt so ridiculous, I hated it. Hated myself. Paul suggested hot showers for us two, Jenny suggested we come down for hot chocolate before bed. Hannah texted to ask if it was still alright for her and Jordy to come round to Rachel's tomorrow – that had been the original plan. She wrote at the end:

Mum is being soooooo embarrassing, it's driving me insane, I'm staying at Jordy's, got his dad to say it was much safer than taking me back to Bessingham. Yay! Result!

Rachel and I laughed at this but ridiculously I felt so sad that actually that evening there were no adults in my life who really cared or knew where I was apart from Rachel's and Hannah's and Jordy's parents. To be fair, the plan had always been that Rachel's parents would pick us up from the beach party so Dad, Carrie in brackets, as I put it to myself, Angela, Jason, Susan had no need to worry and in fact they would know where I was because they knew the plan. Well, to be strictly accurate, Dad and Carrie didn't simply because they hadn't known about the party before they went off on honeymoon. The person I wanted to hold me close, though, thankful that I was safe, was Dad, but I could only think of him being lovey dovey with Carrie on honeymoon and felt really alone, unanchored, cast adrift – the dramatic phrases poured into my mind. I felt tearful but cross with myself too. I thought of Harry and Finn down in Cornwall probably at some after course party, lots of girls, suntanned, beautiful, with long blonde hair, all competent, brave lifeguards. What on earth was all *that* about?

Jenny and Rachel both asked me if I was alright.

'Just tired,' I brushed tears away, 'I feel stupid too. Dad would be unimpressed that we'd put ourselves in danger, so would Harry and Finn.' I saw them glance at each other. Jenny came over and gave me one of her lovely hugs. 'Come on, you're both tired out. Everything'll seem better in the morning. Amazing to think this time last week we were all dancing at your dad's wedding. Looking forward to having a good old reminisce about that tomorrow.'

Chapter 32

AND SO WE DID. IT was lovely. Jenny was right, everything seemed washed clean in the morning, all my ridiculous thoughts of being unloved and uncared about gone. The summer holidays stretched ahead. The day was peerless, as Angela would say, bright blue sky, occasional wispy white clouds, warm sun, gentle breeze, the smell of new mown grass, the comforting whirr of the mower as Paul cut the grass. As we were enjoying a leisurely breakfast in Rachel's sunny conservatory at about 11am, Martin arrived with Jordy and Hannah, so they all joined us for breakfast pudding, as Jordy called it. Paul paused in his task and came and joined us with a cup of coffee.

Jenny was commenting what a pretty wedding it had been and all the better for being small. I thought back to the day as the others talked, chipping in every so often. The wedding itself had taken place at Overstrand Church. Carrie had two bridesmaids: me and her closest friend from university, Janey. The two of us had stayed with Carrie at her childhood home in Overstrand the night before, whilst Dad stayed at Angela's. The plan was that Dad and Carrie would live in Overstrand in that very childhood home, which now belonged to her and was mortgage free as Marianne had finished paying it off just before she died, and Dad assumed I would join them there. He would let Granda's flat.

This had all been discussed before the wedding but living there with Dad and Carrie would feel awkward. As it always felt nice seeing my old house, Susan needed help and we liked each other a lot it seemed the sensible thing to do would be for me to continue to live with her. Angela and Jason constantly emphasized that I was always welcome in East Runton, that I had a bedroom there even. Yet again these sorts of conversations just made me want to fast-forward to being independent, earning money, having a job, somewhere to live, not to be a child, no longer a burden, as I believed myself to be.

Back to the wedding: Carrie looked, as she often did, ethereally beautiful, as if she had fairy-light bones, her insubstantial frame reflective somehow of the tremulous excitement she felt at the start of this part of her journey through life, a kind of excitement which she had talked about to Janey and me far into the previous night. She explained a little of her feelings for Dad. 'Sorry, Amy, but it's good if you understand.'

As we sat looking out through the large, floor-to-ceiling window (planned by her parents and installed by her dad just before he died) towards the never-ending expanse of the sea, watching the orange streaks of the sunset gradually giving way to the moonlit darkness, Carrie told us that she'd always felt safe with Dad.

'This was from the very moment that he reached out to pull me to safety all those years ago,' she explained, and emphasized looking from me to Janey and then to me again, that there was never anything *inappropriate* between them. 'I know I sound like Angela,' she laughed, she always called her grandmother Angela, 'but he made me feel sort of as if I'd come home,' she explained. 'Sounds cheesy but it's how it is.' She was looking out to sea unknowingly mirroring Dad's halting explanation to me of his feelings for Carrie, as he too had looked out to sea just round the coast from Granda's flat not so very long ago, a view that seemed to me then to have shaped all our lives in its subtle and various ways. *For better for worse*, I found myself, thinking. And remembering how Granda would sometimes murmur Hamlet's words to his faithful friend, Horatio, as he told me stories of his own journey through life:

> *There's a divinity that shapes our ends* [Amy]
> *Rough-hew them how we will...*

Carrie continued. 'When I went off to uni I wanted to escape that almost-too-safe feeling, to explore, meet people, that sort of thing, but I realised very soon that the only person I ever wanted to be with was Doug. I knew he already felt the same way about me and now I feel so excited for the next stage; it's a kind of excitement I've never felt before, sort of like standing, shivery, shaky, on the edge of a beautiful ocean before diving in. That makes it sounds as if I'm uncertain but it's not that at all, oh, it's difficult to explain,' she shrugged lightly and reached for a little pancake flavoured with dill and delicate shreds of smoked salmon.

Angela and Jason had ordered in for us an incredible, gourmet selection of substantial nibbles which we were making our way through as we chatted. She was cooking a proper meal for Dad and Jason, but she knew that it would be this sort of meal that we three girls would enjoy most, and it was her pre-wedding day treat to us. It was lovely, like a kind of heavenly banquet without any huge, unmanageable portions of things and all the better for having been delivered as a complete surprise by the same local catering firm who would be doing the rest of the food and drink for the wedding.

Carrie's dress, which of course she made herself, was a simple, sleeveless dress in fine, ivory silk, completely plain. I remember Carrie had been so clear about what she wanted. When she had shown me her sketches she had been adamant that she didn't want the top to look as if it was a sort of bra worn on the outside, just a plain round neck and a simple A line style, long but no train, no lace, *no bits*, I remember her saying emphatically. Our dresses were a similar style, also long, and we had chosen a sort of burnished, coppery gold colour originally suggested by Carrie. The three of us had had fun, on a freezing cold, windy, rainy, early April day, choosing summery gold sandals to go with the dresses. Janey had come to stay, and we had shown her the sights of Norwich. She loved the city, I remember, despite the mean weather.

Carrie had always hated cut flowers. I recall Angela telling me how Carrie, as a young child, would cry her eyes out if anyone started picking flowers or if she saw flower arrangements or bouquets. One day, Angela told me, she had been trying to console her when she became upset at seeing a vase of flowers in a friend's house. Carrie had sobbed in really great distress, aged about 5 apparently, insisting that 'it really hurts them, it really does and they go on hurting and they have to watch each other die, one by one, stuck in a stupid vase.'

So of course, for her wedding reception, and for the church, and for us all to carry, Carrie made beautiful flower arrangements out of paper and silk. The very understanding vicar, who completely understood and actually confessed secretly to us that he totally agreed with Carrie about cut flowers, had the very difficult job of explaining this to the church wardens and flower-arranging people at Overstrand Church who always loved that aspect of a wedding.

These flower arrangements were a sumptuous mix of ivory and burnished gold and green "foliage". I vowed there and then to ask Carrie to do similar for my wedding whenever that might be.

Angela had asked the same person who made the wedding cake for her wedding to make one for Carrie's and my dad's, just as she had asked the same small catering business to do the wedding breakfast. The reception was to be at the house in Overstrand. Dad and Carrie had thought about this carefully. The house was much smaller than Angela's but it was going to be a small wedding in terms of the number of guests and they both felt strongly that they wanted to bring this happy occasion to the house which her parents had loved so much but had never lived to enjoy together. They believed that filling the house with people close to them would make it feel like theirs and would set a seal on the beginning of their life together.

The three of us had spent the previous two days cleaning the house within an inch of its life, which was surprisingly enjoyable, and Dad and Jason had worked wonderful magic in the garden. We only stopped cleaning when our gourmet feast from Angela arrived. It was lovely. We could feel completely relaxed following all the honest toil and admire the pristine house as we feasted and drank wine. The wedding was to be at 12 midday, and the marquee was arriving at 9.30 the next morning. Carrie and Dad would travel up to Scotland the day after the wedding. Janey and I would go back to Susan's that night. Susan always loved having young people about as we all knew.

As far as I know there were only about fifty or sixty guests. Some former and current colleagues of Dad's, some lifeboat crew, Mrs Mack and her daughter, Lynette, two of Marianne's close friends, Angela, who was Dad's best "woman", and Jason and his children who were staying for the first two weeks of the summer holidays, plus a few of Carrie's university and school friends, some of whom had already coupled up. Jordy and Hannah, who were very much together at the wedding, came, their parents and Harry, Rachel, Finn, Iain and their parents and Susan. This was the first time Susan had used a wheelchair in such a big gathering but there were plenty of people to help and she looked more relaxed, less precarious, than when she struggled to walk or stand. Rachel sidled up to me when we were waiting around for the photographer to finish his bit outside the church and said:

'Oh wow, Amy, you look just stunning and I know a certain person thinks so too… he couldn't take his eyes off your back view in church,' she grinned cheekily and skipped away as the photographer gave out more instructions.

The speeches came in-between courses at the wedding breakfast. Both Dad's and Angela's brought tears to my eyes and to Jenny's, I noticed, and to Carrie's actually. It was the bit when Dad paid tribute to both sets of their parents none of whom were there to see this happy day. He talked about his mother a bit, how she would have taken Carrie to her heart, just as Granda had, and how much Granda had loved Marianne and how they had been cheated of their own happy life together. He spoke about me too; it was embarrassing but lovely. He talked of me as his loving and lovely, strong, courageous, resilient only daughter. And he paid eloquent tribute to his bride, his wife, her grace and skill and beauty. Angela paid equally eloquent tribute to her granddaughter and her new husband, my dad, also remarking how proud and happy Carrie had always made her mum and that she knew she was with them in spirit today, just as Dad's father was. Indeed I strongly felt Granda's and Marianne's presence all day.

It was all lovely and it was fun dancing in a sixsome: me, Harry, Finn, Jordy, Rachel and Hannah and seeing groups of Carrie's university friends doing similar once we'd started it, feeling confident and at ease on our home turf, surrounded by people we mostly knew well. Angela and Jason and Carrie and Dad did some lovey-dovey dancing which was okay actually. Jenny and Paul were really good dancers. At one point, Finn grabbed Susan's wheelchair and did some gentle whirly turns to the music, she and everyone laughing their heads off. Hannah and Harry's parents danced rather uneasily together, and Jordy's parents danced with abandon, too much abandon, weird moves, but it was funny.

The only jarring note was the story the local paper ran on the wedding:

Lifeboatman, 36, weds rescued girl, 20, he kept hidden as a child

Sacked teacher, Doug Appleton, wed
Carrie Longwater on Saturday at Overstrand Church.
Some will see this as a fairy-tale ending despite
the age gap, others might be thinking Stockholm syndrome.

Gratifyingly, the newspaper published several letters complaining about this report and the online comments were mostly scathing about this angle. As for the family, we ignored it, following Angela's advice not to "stoop to their level." I remember asking Angela what "Stockholm syndrome" was and how sensitively she explained it to me, followed by a robust, very Angela-like: 'all total stuff and nonsense of course.' And even, worried, suspicious, bewildered me, could see that it absolutely was just that – stuff and nonsense.

It was lovely that morning thinking back to it all and chatting about it. The chat moved on to some vague plans for Rachel and her family to visit Harry and Finn down in Newquay at the end of their lifeguarding update. The boys had travelled down to Cornwall the day after the wedding. It was good to feel part of the planning at this early stage rather than as a kind of tag on: *we'd better see what Amy's doing* – sort of thing.

I was feeling much happier on that Sunday morning but I felt permanently rootless, I realised, well, not exactly rootless, as obviously I was firmly rooted in this part of North Norfolk, but more as if I were a young plant which could be set down in various temporary places, just about able to hold its own, but not yet strong enough to take root in its own spot. Anchorless still.

Harry and Finn were staying down in Cornwall for the whole summer holiday earning money and gaining experience at the end of their course by actually working as beach lifeguards down there. This was shortly before we all got Facebook accounts but what happened was that I had accidentally seen some photos which Finn had sent to Rachel by email showing groups of boys and girls their age sitting on rocks, gazing out to sea at sunset.

This was accidental because she got the email when I was with her and opened up the attachments excitedly after telling me that Finn had sent some photos which obviously, we looked at together. Some were of just the two boys, but there were a few taken outside a pub with Finn and Harry sitting at a table with two girls who looked like twin sisters, long, blonde hair, suntanned, slim, languid, confident, beautiful. These pictures caused me actual pain, real physical pain and I hated myself for being me and not being them. I tried unsuccessfully to hide my hurt from Rachel, and she closed the attachments quickly.

Jenny and Paul had both managed to get the last fortnight in August off and it was decided that they would head to Abercastle for the first week and to Newquay for the second. Very luckily, they managed to book a holiday cottage overlooking the beach in Newquay only because another family had had to cancel due to the dad being suddenly unwell. I worried about Susan if I were to join them there but Jenny said that she had run the idea past Dad before asking me and he had immediately said that he and Carrie and Angela and Jason would support Susan and I knew Hannah and Jordy would pop in too. They wanted to stay in Norfolk during the summer both wanting to earn as much money as possible for uni and travelling they said, and Jordy didn't want to miss any cricket.

I was going to Mum and Rob's only for a couple of long weekends as I didn't want to leave Susan for too long. In fact, I remember at this stage Susan was the best I'd seen her for a while mobility-wise, but the disease fluctuated a lot. I decided I would join Rachel and co in Cornwall for just the last week of August, not go to Abercastle too, because of wanting to be with Susan and also needing to earn money for my uni future which was taking on a clearer shape with every day that passed. I remember at this stage feeling so pleased that I was completely set on my future plans about studying Speech and Language Therapy and I remember feeling sorry for those who had no idea what they wanted to do, not smug, just sorry for them because being focused on an end goal simply felt so good.

Rachel was one of those who had no idea what she wanted to do, and I remember both Jenny and Susan reassuring her that it was not unusual to feel like that. I already knew which subjects I wanted to study at A-level and AS level though: English, Human Biology, French and German, probably dropping German after AS. Harry, likewise, had known for a while what he wanted to do, architecture, having taken up Jason's suggestion of offering him a placement at his office for his required Year 10 work experience after he had shown real interest in the design of the studio. Harry had abandoned any thoughts of a career in counterterrorism by then, none of us could quite remember why or when. He still took a keen interest in following the news though, national and international, and was always clued up about what was going on in the world, I liked that about him.

I travelled as far as London with Angela and Jason on my way down to Cornwall as they were spending the weekend there and going to some sort of design exhibition. It was good to travel with them but I also loved the trip on my own from Paddington down to Newquay, gazing out at the ever-changing landscape, again relishing the sense of freedom and adventure, dreaming of the future as the late summer countryside sped past.

I was talking to Angela recently about this time of my life because some of the memories fuse into one, making details hard to recall. She chuckled and replied: 'Just wait til you get to my age, Amy love. You'll start remembering Christmases when you were 3 or 4 years old but not what you went out to the shops for today or what you had for lunch half an hour ago. Memory, it's a funny thing.'

Chapter 33

MEMORY. MEMORIES. TIME SPEEDING UP. Time slowing down. Such a confusion, a mish mash of feelings, scrambled, intense, impossible to unravel. .That holiday in Cornwall, the coastline so very different from North Norfolk's, both beautiful, wild in their different ways, Harry and Finn so at home there, seeming different, older, looking older, being older, suntanned, both had grown beards, the crowds of people their age, laughing, confident, knowing each other, being kind to us younger ones when they had to, feeling out of it, *out of sorts,* one of Angela's expressions, intensity of feeling, realising I thought about Harry at least ninety-nine per cent of the time, wondering what he would think if he knew that, what he would think of what I was wearing, what he would think of what I said, wondering whether I should say anything, the sanctuary and comfort of the holiday home, Jenny so kind, so understanding, highs, lows.

The highs were when the four of us went off exploring on our own, Harry and Finn more like themselves, showing us places, funny, interesting, laughing and shared jokes, talking about school things, teachers, schoolfriends, annoying classmates, Harry and Finn talking about Paston College, Harry taking my hand when climbing over a rocky outcrop on the beach, looking at me properly when I spoke. I remember a crazy, wonderful time when we had been talking about our German teacher who was passionate about her subject and used to love teaching us all the very long, composite German words that were used in English too.

We started trying to make up sentences using mostly those words, like a game, a competition. One of mine won! It went something like: *Full of*

Weltsmerz, angst also both Fernweh and Wanderlust and in keeping with the zeitgeist I packed a rucksack and set off on my travels, my parents had warned me to take walking boots but I didn't want Öffnungsdiskussionsorgien about what to pack, having decided already to travel mit wenig but I later suffered trauma and heimweh when I sprained my ankle and hoped they did not feel Schadenfreude.

We knew it was a rubbish sentence, knew it could be seen as showing off, pretentious even, if it were not just us four but it was fun.

Then the lows: meeting Harry and Finn's friends in the pub, amongst them the two girls, Claudia and Tallulah, who I had spotted in the Facebook posts, monopolising Harry and Finn, all of them hardly looking at us, making in-jokes, Harry not looking at us, not himself, being clever but not in a good way, not noticing or saying goodbye when we decided to leave, no plans to meet up. Intensity of feeling the whole time, unhappy, tense apart from those few moments which stand out like oases, shimmering, illusory, in an otherwise arid waste of a landscape of hurt feelings and a sense of worthlessness.

How to make sense of it all? Strange that it was only recently that I came across the word: *Bildungsroman,* I might have woven it into my sentence describing teenage wanderlust and seeking if I'd heard of it then.

Rachel and I christened Claudia and Tallulah, "Claws" and "Talons". They both had unbelievably long nails which they painted brightly. When we confessed this to Harry and Finn about a year later whilst reminiscing about the holiday, they nearly fell of their chairs laughing and told us their nicknames for them had been "Clutch" and "Tally".

I laughed with Rachel then stopped and said:

'Why?' This caused them all, including Hannah and Jordy who were with us at Rachel's, even more mirth. They laughed and laughed, tears streaming down their cheeks. It was the timing they said, the pause before my innocent "why?". I guess you had to have been there. It was Harry who reached across then, took hold of the fingers of my right hand and started lifting them up as if to count them, then stopped, saying:

'You don't want to know, Amy, you really don't and if you really, really do want to know, ask Rach later.'

By this time, end of year 11 for me, year 13 for Harry, *that summer* for both of us, a long summer of freedom after A-levels for Harry and GCSE's for me, we had become an item. This seemed to happen by a sort of osmosis following an end of exams party for all of us, suggested by Angela, dreaded by Jason, but one which this time went off with no more than minor *incidents* but during which the main event was Harry and me spending the entire evening together and deciding to be boyfriend and girlfriend, properly. Intensity of feeling. Elation. Ecstatic happiness. Whoosh.

This was the first of several end of exams parties that summer and on each occasion Harry and I went as a couple having spent most of the day together, either at his, or at Angela's, or at Susan's. I noticed then how different both Harry and Hannah were when they were in their own home. With their parents there was always a sense of constraint, of things unsaid. There was very little easy-going flow of conversation between the family. Their parents were polite and kind to me in a slightly suspicious, guarded way. It made me want to take Harry away and sort of thaw him out ready to be remoulded to the Harry I knew when he was with me or even when we were in our close-knit group of friends. It was good to see Hannah thawing out, relaxing, when she was with Jordy, both in his own family setting and when they were together as a twosome in our group. Rachel and Marty meanwhile had agreed to split after only a few months with no great distress on either side.

It was good hearing Harry and Finn talking about their university plans which were now almost a reality depending on results. That summer they were both working as beach lifeguards locally and the rest of us returned to our summer jobs, me in the Roughton Fish and Chip shop, Rachel and Hannah at the Cromer pier ice cream booth. Harry and Finn had both passed their driving tests and were insured to drive their parents' cars but then Finn was given a car by his grandparents as they had just given up driving and they covered all the costs, apart from fuel, as an eighteenth birthday present for him. This spelt out freedom for us all and was very helpful for ferrying us around.

I was working evenings only at the fish and chip shop, unless they needed lunchtime cover in an emergency, so that gave me plenty of time to spend in and around Cromer beach, either at the lifeboat station, or nearer the pier with Hannah and Rachel trying not to distract them from their customer service.

Once Susan was safely up and about in the mornings she was very happy to be on her own, either pottering around slowly, holding onto various rails sorted out for her by Pat, the occupational therapist, or wheeling herself around the house which had become much easier for her since it had been made wheelchair-friendly with ramps and the widening of one door. The weather was mostly lovely that summer.

Sometimes it would just be nice to spend time with Susan. At this stage when I was living there, I could wheel her to a close-by, useful parade of shops where we could get everything we needed. It was a slow process but good to see Susan chatting to acquaintances. I felt it was a pity that her health was too uncertain for her to be able to participate fully in any local clubs or groups and meet people in that way. She had toyed briefly with the idea of setting up as a tutor of English for all ages of children but felt that her health was too unpredictable as it fluctuated so much, and she would not want to let people down. She had plenty of company with all of us in and out and, as she often said, she actually preferred the company of younger people to that of people her own age.

During the very last week of the summer holidays, end of August into early September, we decided, the four of us, Harry, me, Rachel and Finn, to head down to Cornwall, just us, for a few days' camping. This was the first time we had all been away together just on holiday with no parents or, in Harry and Finn's case, to do beach lifeguarding courses. We decided to go to Newquay close to where they had done their lifeguarding as they knew it well, knew the campsite, knew the beach. We decided to take a tent for four people, borrowed from one of their friends who had one he had taken to the Reading Festival the week before. We decided it would be better than taking two two-people tents as Rachel and I certainly felt we'd be better with the boys protecting us. We said this to them laughingly, pretending it was tongue-in-cheek, but it wasn't actually. We secretly really meant it. And of course it saved us having to buy one more two people tent as only Rachel and Finn had one.

On the third day of our trip Rachel was really ill after we'd eaten seafood paella in a nearby pub garden the previous evening. I felt very sorry for her especially because it was a bit of a trek to the nearest toilets. I offered to stay with her if the boys wanted to go off, but Finn quickly stepped in.

'No, I'll stay,' he offered quickly, 'you and Harry could do that trip to The Lost Gardens of Heligan that you wanted to do, Rachel and I have been a few times already. It's a good opportunity, we're not here for that long, don't forget. It's only about a forty-minute drive.'

I remember it feeling so good just making our own plans, not being reliant on parents for lifts, not having to use public transport, freedom was ours. That was great too because we decided to get a combined ticket to the Lost Gardens and to the Eden Project and see them both as they were only ten miles apart, about twenty minutes' drive. It worked out cheaper that way than trying to do two separate trips so a lovely long day of just being with Harry stretched ahead.

Both places were completely magical and beautiful in their different ways. We joined guided tours for each and discovered some interesting facts, but it was good, too, when we broke off and started strolling around on our own. In the Mediterranean olive grove on our saunter round the Eden Project we sat on an ancient bench, almost as old as the gnarled, ancient olive trees and talked and talked, this time mostly about our hopes and ambitions.

We had bought ice creams. At this stage of our relationship, young as we were, we knew we would be together, there was no playing games. We both wanted lots of children, we said, about five we thought, a sort of gaggle, who would always be there for each other. Harry said he favoured a sort of rough and tumble childhood for them, a kind of benign neglect, he said. It would be a refreshing contrast to the constraint and tension in his own childhood, he murmured. He told me that he had overheard his parents using the phrase "benign neglect" about me when I was much younger, before Mum left. I was horrified, hurt and obviously looked it.

Harry was contrite. 'Honestly, Amy, I didn't mean to upset you. Obviously Mum and Dad knew nothing of what your mum was going through and what you were dealing with.'

'I know, I know, it just sounds so awful,' I said wanting to return to the excited discussion of our future together. 'Yes, I mean I kind of agree with that but…well, not benign neglect as such for our children, just no constraint and tension and holding back. We'll be the perfect parents, kind and loving 24/7, never a cross word.' I spoke light-heartedly then more sombrely, 'mainly we'll just be there.'

Looking round with care, to check there was nobody about, Harry got up, slipped quickly over to the most ancient specimen of all the olive trees and illegally snapped off a tiny branch which he held out to me for forgiveness. It made me laugh. I still have it, dried out, kept in one of my boxes of keepsakes. I remember, too, that in The Lost Gardens of Heligan, again when there was nobody about, we were just heading towards the tearooms when we saw a gardener, bent double; he looked to be old and was raking a raised bed.

'Ben Weatherstaff,' we said simultaneously remembering the gardener in *The Secret Garden.*

'Come on, Mary Lennox,' Harry said laughing and grabbing my hand, 'I'm starving, let's head for beer and a pizza at Misselthwaite.'

Carrie, to Dad's delight, had been accepted on to a Masters course at UEA. Carrie told me that it felt so good to think that when she started in late September she would be settled and have a proper home and homelife to return to after the days when she needed to be at uni, and not be going back to shared student accommodation with all its frustrations and pettiness.

At this stage, when I was living at Susan's, Dad would let me know he was home safe from rescues, either by text if it was daytime, or with a note slipped under Susan's front door on his way home if it was late. He knew we'd hear the maroons of course. He didn't text at night as he thought I'd be asleep. What he didn't know was that I always kept my phone on for three reasons. First, it was useful for Susan to be able to ring me in an emergency day or night. She hardly ever did even though she sometimes struggled with being able to get up to go to the toilet because of painful muscle spasms and cramps. I could at least help with some vigorous massaging of the painful bits to help her get going then make sure she got safely back into bed.

Another reason was that Harry and I texted each other a lot at this stage, and I became quite addicted to my phone. We would just exchange everyday bits of news, this and that, all day and far into the night. It was very reassuring and lovely. We'd even text things like:

Just poured too much milk on my cereal, how to get it to the table...

And the third reason was that of course I kept my phone on for contact with Dad, brave Dad, out in all weathers. The texts would just be brief, along the lines of:

Home safely darling Amy. Letter to follow

Then, when he got home, he would do that cathartic thing of writing it in a letter for me and slip it through the door the next day.

And it was because of having my phone on, logged into Facebook, that I knew instantly about the terrible tragedy unfolding fairly close to the beach at West Runton, just down the coast from Cromer. A girl at my school, Holly, lived in West Runton. I didn't actually know her that well but I was friends with her on Facebook. That's what people did, it was important at that time to have lots and lots of Facebook friends, that seems strange, looking back. Holly had posted something at about 10.30pm, after hearing from one of her friends, who also lived at West Runton, that something was "kicking off" (her words – annoying) just a little way off from where she and her family had spent the afternoon on the beach there. This was shortly after the maroons had stopped sounding for good. I wondered if my dad had gone out there. I could hear the wind rattling round the house. It was coming from the north-east and was gusting at 7 to 8 knots. I knew this because the wind speed had even been mentioned in the weather report at the end of the news that evening. It was about two weeks before Carrie was due to start her Masters at UEA.

A sailing boat, a *Norfolk Oyster*, had got stuck on the notorious "high ground" at West Runton between Sheringham and Cromer, an area where many boats had come to grief over the years in the shallow water there. So, help was not far off, but the sea was big, a huge swell, and the waves were fifteen to twenty feet high. Dad explained what had happened in a letter under the door which I heard arrive at about 1am, still lying in bed wakeful and anxious, although talking to Harry by text helped a bit. When I heard the letterbox flap, I ran down to pick it up, relief flooding through me that Dad would be safe.

13th September 2007

Darling Amy,

Safely on my way home. It was a strange one and very sad. No failure on our part thank goodness and a successful rescue from our point of view.

My pager went off at about 10pm, one of the worst times, I was already heading for bed, Carrie had just gone ahead while I turned off the lights, locked up etc. I hated to see the fear on her face when she heard it and of course I knew she wouldn't sleep. When I got to the station the pier was being drenched by waves, relentless, they must've been 15 to 20 feet high. Angry waves from a big sea. Out for vengeance for some unknown wrong, I don't know. It felt as if there was a sense of mockery at the stupidity of the boat's skipper setting out to all intents and purposes alone, there was a feeling the sea was mocking us all somehow, I've never felt that before.

But the sea doesn't know everything, Amy. Apparently, he was a very keen and very experienced yachtsman and had simply wanted to introduce his new wife, of only two weeks, to the joys of his hobby. Her plan was to learn to sail, something she'd always wanted to do but had never had the opportunity. She's much younger and had just come through treatment for breast cancer. She's two months pregnant too. I think she's probably about my age. He would be in his mid-fifties, I reckon.

They had planned a short trip setting out from Blakeney where they were staying as part of their honeymoon, just more or less round the harbour and back, and had set off in good time to catch the sunset. The skipper was going to show his wife the ropes – literally. He had a friend who lives locally who was willing to lend them his sailing boat, a Norfolk Oyster, *for the short trip. The boat's called* Olivia, *we nearly called you that, Amy.*

Well, it was spotted by lots of people, some hardy types still on the beach at West Runton, just packing up to leave. Most people had left the beach at that stage as the wind was getting up, it was getting chilly and the tide was coming in rapidly. The vessel was apparently drifting at some speed with the sails flapping. We hailed the boat and shouted instructions to get the sails down. We could glimpse one person sitting rigidly on the deck, seeming not to take any notice of us. There were 4 of us aboard the D-class and we planned to get close enough to get a rope secured and tow her back to the ALB which had come to help after we let them know the situation. Jim and I boarded the boat to find the woman, Ann, she was only able to tell us her name once we were back at the station, sitting sort of stunned, in total shock, totally unaware of the danger she was in.

We quickly understood that she had no knowledge of sailing whatsoever and was just pointing at the tiller, which was moving from side to side uselessly – obviously. It was then that I saw a man collapsed sort of lying underneath it. It was obvious that he was dead even before I reached him and checked for a pulse. His name was Alan we discovered later. I got the sails down, while Jim secured the tow line.

Jim stayed with Ann, luckily, she had a lifejacket on, while our helmsman, Jack, you know him, held the D-class alongside the sailing boat. The waves were high, and we worried about damage to both boats as well as trying to work out how we could get Ann off safely. The wind was biting, vicious, more like January than September.

Jim and I were able to help shift the boat a bit using an oar and huge strength. Luckily, she wasn't taking on much water and didn't appear to be damaged. There was no outboard motor fitted although we later discovered one stowed in the chocks in the forward locker. I remember that even so close to the shore the waves still seemed huge.

The other two somehow managed to get Ann off and aboard the lifeboat through a mixture of cajoling and encouragement, but mostly by physically lifting her once she had been brave enough to get to the very edge of the sailing boat in between giant wave surges.

Phew, glad to be home. We think the man, Alan, probably had a heart attack. Apparently, he was awaiting surgery for some heart problem. Obviously, we had paperwork to fill in.

Sleep well, sweetheart.

Your ever-loving but tired out and hating the sea Dad.

When I read Dad signing off like that, I wondered for the first time if and when he might give up volunteer lifeboating. I wondered if he ever thought how it was for me and now for Carrie, how it had been for Mum. I was not criticising him in anyway, he was incredibly brave and hard-working and committed, I literally just wondered.

I remember clearly asking myself these questions again at Christmas that year. We were all at Angela's and Jason's as we now called it, well, Carrie and Dad, me and Susan were there. Carrie had started her Masters at UEA in late September and was really enjoying it. She had passed her driving test during the summer and was using Marianne's car, loving the freedom, the drive home at the end of the days when she was actually on campus, but she looked exhausted, pale and unwell. She seemed to have hardly any appetite for the usual Christmas delights.

Dad was called out late on Christmas afternoon because a dog had gone over the cliff at Mundesley and both dog and owner were trapped by the incoming tide, though neither was injured. It was a textbook rescue but took ages because of the tricky locality and was made more complicated by darkness arriving so early. Luckily it was fairly benign December weather. By the time he arrived home, it was close to 9pm and Carrie had gone to bed explaining that she wasn't being a fun-sponge but just felt really tired.

She continued to feel unwell during the Christmas break and it was actually her grandmother, lovely perceptive Angela, who tentatively suggested doing a pregnancy test. And so it was that early in the New Year Carrie discovered she was pregnant. The baby was due at the end of July. Carrie's course would have just finished by then – *by great good fortune and the grace of God,* one of Angela's expressions, learnt from her Catholic grandmother, often followed by: *and the favour of the Apostolic See* (which we sometimes chanted before she did). Carrie and I caught each other's eye and muttered 'serendipity' in unison; it was funny. I thought about planned and unplanned babies again. Even if Carrie wanted to continue studying straightaway, the following late September, she probably would be able to she felt.

My third half sibling, little Clarissa, was born on the 20th July, a real summer baby, as fair and fairy-like as her mother, as brave and fearless as her father. I loved her with a depth of feeling of which I didn't know I was capable and took any opportunity I could, and there were plenty, to look after her. At the back of my mind I worried about being so much closer to her than I was to my other half siblings, but it was just the way it was, geography, circumstance, or happenstance, another of Angela's wonderful words.

Chapter 34

THIS ECLIPSING OF TIME, THIS speeding up of life, which Angela tells me repeatedly, will increase exponentially, confuses me. Harry explained the actual mathematical meaning of "exponential" to me the other day, which left me admiring the way his brain worked, admiring the way he could try to explain it, but, if I'm honest, it was just too mathematical for me and added to my confusion about the eclipsing of time.

I enjoyed my time at Sixth Form College, but I find it difficult to recall the details. Perhaps they'll come back to me suddenly in later life! I know it felt so different from school. I was doing my chosen subjects and really felt I was beginning at last to fast-forward to a future which beckoned with increasing insistence as its shape became clearer, like a ship emerging from fog.

I loved hearing Harry's news from uni. He had taken a strategic approach to his choices. He wanted to stay in England, but not London, he liked the idea of a campus or collegiate university and wanted a course which was recognised by the professional registration body for architects. He decided to look only at those which were ranked at eight or higher in the various university league tables. In the end he decided on Cambridge as his first choice and Newcastle as his reserve.

I developed a similarly strategic attitude when my turn came two years later, settling on UEA as my first choice and Essex as my reserve whilst knowing I would do all in my power to get the grades needed for UEA which wanted BBB or ABC, wheras Essex then were asking for BBB or BBC. Everywhere required you to get through the interview for my subject, Speech and Language Therapy. By then I knew I wanted to be as near home as possible. The arrival of little Clarissa, Clarry, as we called her, made this a no-brainer now. Cambridge was never an option for me, they did not run the degree course I wanted. This suited me fine because I really didn't want to follow Harry there. We both felt that being at different universities would be good for our relationship and I liked the fact that our university time would overlap by a few years because of the length of Harry's course. We could be university students together, I liked that, hard to explain why.

I was really interested in the open days for Harry's choices and went to two of them with him: Cambridge and Bath. It was fun; the days were action-packed and full-on. He liked the university at Bath but found the city to be too "other" as he put it, just as Rachel had found Cambridge to be "other". He was a bit put off by the fact that Bath had a noticeable emphasis on science subjects. He liked both Cambridge and Newcastle in their different ways. After the Cambridge open day, we stayed the night at Mum and Rob's and spent Sunday with them. Again, I remember a delicious sense of freedom and excitement especially as Susan was going through a good phase in her illness. I enjoyed introducing Harry to all my other step and half-brothers and sisters. The boys gave him no peace at all, and he was brilliant with them, playing football and tag until even they were worn out. Jess was toddling around, into everything, and little Josh was just one of the boys now, hero worshipping Harry, following him around like a little shadow.

Cambridge required A*AA at A-level whereas Newcastle required three A's, so it was a tough call for Harry. He had studied Maths, Physics and History at A-level plus Art and Design at AS level. Though Harry had mixed feelings about the whole ethos of Cambridge it was the course itself mainly, and its worldwide recognition, that caused him to forget any preconceived notions (which he described to me as "inverted snobbery") and aim for that experience. I had never heard of "inverted snobbery"; it was an interesting concept and I have often been aware of it in various settings since then. Harry confided to me one day that he was surprised how pleased he was that his parents were so delighted with this choice and he felt that it might make them forgive him for his younger sister's Rachel's death. Oh, Harry.

I remember so clearly that we were sitting in the garden at his house, we were the only two at home, and Harry was always more relaxed when his parents weren't around. It was the summer before he went away to uni. To be honest, because his parents were always quite tense and on edge, they made me feel that way too. I remember Harry leant his head on my shoulder as he spoke and was tracing some sort of doodle on my bare arm. He seemed close to tears, as if all the bottled-up feelings of guilt and rejection which he'd held in for his entire childhood, were beginning to be let go. I remember just listening, letting him talk; even I noticed how he would thaw out with me. I longed to be with him in some far-off future, our own place, our own lives with our own responsibility for forging our own ways. It was a fierce longing.

It was good seeing Finn's future taking shape too. He was going off to study physiotherapy in Nottingham. He had the idea that he would like to specialise in Sports Physio, but he knew it was very popular. When the two of them were talking to each other about their choices I cherished the fact that Harry commented that it would be good to be fairly near home so that he could come and see me and vice versa; it was Rachel actually who told me this, Finn had told her. I held the thought in my heart, and it warmed me through.

My chosen subjects at A-level and AS level were English, French, Biology and Psychology, lots of essays. I planned to wait and see which one I would drop after AS level, probably French, I thought. I loved the language, the subject, but I thought the others would be better preparation for Speech and Language Therapy at uni.

I was always fascinated by noticing how when French people spoke their mouths seemed to form into different shapes from ours. I was also fascinated when I discovered that all over the world accents reflected the landscape, in other words: the wider the horizons, the emptier the landscapes, the broader and longer drawn out the vowels. I toyed briefly with the idea of studying linguistics at university, or even French, but I quickly came back to Speech and Language Therapy as I wanted to train for a profession, be able to earn money, always. I sought safety and security in this way, I knew that, but luckily I had also developed a genuine and deep interest in the subject since talking to Helen, witnessing Susan's problems and seeing how much Helen could help her. I wanted to be out there, knowledgeable, skilled, helping people. I had already abandoned the idea of doing A level German as I thought Psychology would be more useful for Speech and Language Therapy.

Rachel and Hannah were both doing English and Psychology, Rachel was doing History and Sociology as well, Hannah Geography and Art, neither at that stage absolutely sure what they wanted to do after sixth form. Jordy was going to go for Law and was doing Law, History, Sociology and Geography. This meant we still saw each other a lot and remained a close group but it was at this time that our friendship group expanded quite a bit with people doing different subjects and coming from different schools.

It seems to be now that these are mere factual memories of that time. What of what else was happening? So, although I missed Harry (he had got the grades necessary for Cambridge), life was busy and the weekends I went to Cambridge and stayed with him rather than with Mum and Rob, were very, very special. Harry fitted into life at Cambridge, St John's College, just like that. Again, that took him by surprise.

Two years on and I am halfway through my first year at UEA and loving the course and my chosen profession, no regrets. I had thought carefully about whether to apply to live on campus. I knew preference was given to applicants living further away but technically I lived slightly further than the sixteen miles away rule. I was aware of Carrie's homesickness at Southampton, and I remembered suddenly that she said she felt cold the whole time she was there. I was also aware of Susan's needs though she was adamant that I mustn't worry about that, she would employ carers if necessary she said. And I was aware that if I didn't live on campus I could be missing out on student life. I was conscious, too, of the expense.

And of course, there was Clarry. In the end the matter was taken out of my hands as I was told I would not be allocated a place on campus, when I enquired, unless they had vacancies by the time term started. The relief I felt made me realise that this was the right decision for me.

I was relishing my cusp of adulthood freedom too. Dad and Carrie had given me driving lessons for my 17th birthday. I passed my test in August that year. Angela passed her car onto me as she had decided to give up driving for good, aged 85, though in fact she had pretty much given it up about two years previously. The car was just sitting in the drive she said. She paid for tax, insurance and all other running costs, apart from fuel, for my entire time as a student.

As it turned out my fear of missing out because of not living on campus was unfounded. I very quickly became friendly with, unbelievably, another

Rachel Willis. She was my best friend at university. What are the chances of my two besties having the same name? Amazing. Uni Rachel always liked to be known as Rach which helped any confusion a bit.

I would often go back to Rach's flat on campus in between lectures, before parties, before going out and often stayed there after nights out. Dad and Carrie would always nip round to check that Susan was alright on these occasions. I got to know Rach's flatmates too. Her home was in Durham so she would frequently come and spend time at Susan's with me at weekends to get away from campus for a bit. She met my whole expanded family and loved everything about Norfolk and UEA, even though, like most students, we often moaned about the rigours of the course, unreasonable deadlines, silly rules, that kind of thing.

People, including both Rachels, have often asked me whether I would ever become a lifeboat volunteer. Harry has been asked this too. We both know that we *never* would, for me there was absolutely no question about this. Harry and I were adamant about it possibly for slightly different reasons in each case. I knew I was simply not brave enough, and I felt I didn't have the physical strength either. Add to that, I had seen the upset it had caused to my mum, possibly it led to the breakdown of my parents' marriage, who knows? Both of us felt that we couldn't commit to the role at this busy stage of our lives, though we knew many did.

There was our relationship, too, to consider. The journey from Norwich to Cambridge, either by train or driving, back and forth, back and forth, became something we could do with our eyes closed, well, metaphorically speaking of course when driving. As far as lifeboat volunteering was concerned, I knew I could *never* do it, simple. Harry was not so sure about never but certainly not now.

Carrie decided to take a full year off after Clarry was born with a view to returning to UEA, a place she loved, to pursue her PhD ambitions. It was good that they had the rental income from Granda's flat, that the mortgage on our old house, where Susan was living, was covered by her rent, and that the house in Overstrand where they lived was mortgage free. It was lovely going there now and seeing it full of Clarry's paraphernalia.

Carrie confided to me that she found motherhood overwhelming, mostly in a good way, and completely discombobulating at first.

'I'm just telling you, Amy, so you know for the future, and also that all the overwhelmingness and discombobulation is one thousand percent worth it.' She paused, smiling slightly with a sort of inner knowledge. 'It's the 24/7 responsibility,' she explained, 'this little thing arrives, naked and squealing, and she is totally dependent on you, totally. As a new-born, if she wants to move, it's up to you, all nourishment, all protection comes from you. You make decisions for her for a long, long time. So vulnerable, so needy. So trusting. And she loves me, Amy, she loves me unconditionally – for now,' she grinned, looking more down to earth suddenly and got up to make a cup of tea.

As I see all the people I love best continuing their journeys through life, and in Clarry's case, just starting out, I sometimes think of the notion of seamanship as my dad explained it to me once. He said it was an essential ingredient in any rescue and encompasses skill, resourcefulness, good, quick decision-making based on sound knowledge and understanding of all the variables. 'Fishermen and merchant sea captains often comment on the incredible seamanship shown in lifeboat rescues of various types especially considering the crews are drawn from all walks of life,' he told me. 'The way a rescue is carried out is based on analysis, experience and the sheer bravery of the crew,' Dad said, 'plus, I realise now that rigorous and regular training, every week, every, single week, rain or shine means that you are always prepared.'

From my own experience of listening to lifeboatmen, including my dad, and from my reading I notice that accounts of lifeboat rescues by lifeboatmen or women, whether verbal or written, simply report the facts. The emotional toll is rarely mentioned but I felt that it was beginning to get to Dad at times. I sensed he felt very conflicted about when, or whether, to give it up.

Dad explained the many variables in more detail one day when both Harry and me were round at Dad and Carrie's, variables presented by the sea and weather conditions. I can still hear his voice describing to me the three dimensions: the surface of the water combined with tides running underneath and the winds above. He explained the added factor of there being three basic motions for boats underway: rolling, the side to side – or port-starboard – motion of the whole length of the ship about its transverse axis; pitching, the up and down motion of the bow and stern about its longitudinal axis; and yawing, this being the side to side movement of the bow and stern about its vertical axis. He explained that any deviation from normal on this axis is referred to as being out of trim. I remember feeling a bit seasick as he explained it all to me, especially when he went on to talk about heaving. He said there were three other motions to think about so six motions in total: heaving, being the up and down movement; swaying, the side to side or port-starboard motion caused either by weather or wind currents against the hull or by the ship's own propulsion; and surging, which, he explained to me, was simply the bow and stern motion on the water. This seemed to be a good, if rather dramatic metaphor for any journey through life. I felt content simply to be underway.

As my memories became more amorphous, one day stands out clearly in my mind like a kind of mixture between a tableau and a vignette. Harry and I were walking back to Angela's after a walk along the beach from Cromer to East Runton. It was the end of March, the 30th , the evening before my twentieth birthday, a Saturday, and Angela was hosting an evening meal to celebrate this momentous event with my close, extended family. Even Jason conceded that there couldn't possibly be any *incidents* on this occasion. Harry would be returning to Cambridge on the evening of my actual birthday so it was decided a Saturday evening do would be better.

Harry and I had arrived back shortly before sunset to delicious smells and were told to make ourselves scarce for half an hour or so. There was a sense of slightly feverish activity coming from the kitchen and dining room. It felt exciting and I felt special. We walked round to the back of the studio – it was quite warm for a March evening – and decided to watch the sunset from there. It was shortly after 7pm, about a week after we'd put the clocks on. I always loved that: longer, lighter evenings for lots of months to come.

As we approached the big window we were both captivated by the red glow of the sun going down, incidentally heralding a beautiful day for my actual birthday, and now striking the window and the back wall of the studio where Angela had hung a painting she'd recently finished of a flock of pink-footed geese in their characteristic v-shaped formations, flying off on their annual return north in early spring. It was the first time I had seen the painting hung, though I knew she'd been doing it, and Harry and I turned to each other incredulously. 'Wow, it's as if you can actually hear them,' he said, 'it's incredible.'

I remember I felt completely mesmerised by the sound and sight of the birds in the painting. I was captivated by them, felt drawn upwards towards them a bit like the children at the beginning of C. S. Lewis' *The Voyage of the Dawn Treader* when they magically become engulfed in the waves of the painting of the *Dawn Treader,* the ship tossed upon stormy seas which would take them on a perilous journey ending ultimately, once again, in Narnia.

I knew that the geese travelled in their same family groups each migration, always using the same route chosen by the geese families for their own, individual journeys each year and that route being taught to subsequent generations. It was while I was still gazing at the painting that I was aware of Harry whispering in my ear, caressing my hair with his lips as he did so: 'Turn round, Amy, look.'

And there they were, actual v-shaped flocks of the very same pink-footed geese, making their way north, their distinctive, determined, other-worldly cries filling the warm glow of the sky, some of the last to leave this late in the spring, having been feasting throughout the autumn and winter on their high energy diet of sugar beet tops, oilseed rape, potatoes and other winter crops easily available after the harvest.

Then, just after this magical moment, we both turned back towards the studio to see Angela, Jason, his three children, Dad, Carrie, Clarry, Susan, and, as a complete surprise, Mum, Rob, and all their children coming through the door carrying presents galore. Angela placed her fingers on her lips as they all trooped towards the studio window to watch the magnificent sight with us. Some of the words of the Rosetti poem came to my mind:

> *My heart is gladder than all of these,*
> *Because my love is come to me.*
>
> ...
>
> *Because the birthday of my life*
> *Is come, my love is come to me.*

Bibliography

Alston C (1996) *Strong to Save – a tale of the 1953 floods in Norfolk*, Morrow & Co, Bungay, Suffolk, UK.

Kipling R and S (1995) *Strong to Save – dramatic first-hand accounts of RNLI lifeboat rescues around the British Isles*, Patrick Stephens Ltd, Yeovil, Somerset, UK

Kipling R and S (2006) *Never Turn Back: The RNLI since the Second World War*, The History Press, UK.

Kipling R (2015) *Call the Lifeboat*, Endeavour Press, UK

Wake-Walker E (2007) *The Lifeboats Story*, Sutton Publishing, UK.

Good Men Remembered: The Disaster of the Wells Lifeboat the *Eliza Adams*. (Booklet to commemorate 125 years since the disaster on Friday 29th October 1880, produced for Saturday 29th October 2005 as part of the commemoration events).

Glossary

Weltsmerz – *world-weariness*
Zeitgeist – *spirit of the time*
Fernweh – *longing to see far off places*
Heimweh – *homesickness*
Schadenfreude – *taking pleasure from somebody else's misfortune*
Öffnungsdiskussionsorgien – *orgies of discussion*
Mit Wenig – *literally 'with little', here: 'travel light'*
Bildungsroman – *coming-of-age novel*

About the author and her other books

ELISABETH (GILLY) HEWETSON, USING THE pseudonym, Elisabeth Clare, has written two books: *The Stealing*, (published in June 2017) and *A Story for Christmas* (published in November 2017, 2nd edition 2018). She lives in Norfolk and teaches Health Care Law and Ethics at the University of East Anglia, latterly just as an Associate Tutor having taught there full time since moving to Norfolk in 1992.